Winifred Holtby

Winifred Holtby (1⌷ ⌷⌷⌷⌷⌷⌷ ⌷⌷ Rudston, Yorkshire. In the First World War she was a member of the Women's Auxiliary Army Corps; she then resumed her education at Somerville College, Oxford, where she met Vera Brittain. After graduating, these two friends shared a flat in London where both embarked upon their respective literary careers. Winifred Holtby was a prolific journalist and novelist. Her fifth novel, *South Riding* (1936) was published posthumously after her tragic death from kidney disease at the age of thirty-seven. She was awarded the James Tait Black Memorial Prize for this, her most famous novel. Her remarkable and courageous life is movingly recorded in Vera Brittain's biography, *Testament of Friendship*, also published by Virago.

Paul Berry

Paul Berry is the joint editor of *Testament of a Generation: The Journalism of Vera Brittain and Winifred Holtby* and the author, with Mark Bostridge, of *Vera Brittain: A Life* (1995). A distant relative of Winifred Holtby, he was also the close friend of Vera Brittain for twenty-eight years, and is the literary executor of both writers. Formerly a Senior Lecturer at Kingsway-Princeton College, London, he is now retired and lives in Sussex.

Marion Shaw

Marion Shaw is the author of *The Clear Stream: A Life of Winifred Holtby* (1999). She is also the editor of *An Introduction to Women's Writing from the Middle Ages to the Present Day* (1997). She is currently Professor of English at Loughborough University, and prior to that she taught at the University of Hull. With Paul Berry she is the literary executor of the Holtby estate.

Also by Winifred Holtby

Remember, Remember!

The Selected Stories of Winifred Holtby

edited by Paul Berry and Marion Shaw

A *Virago* Book

Published by Virago Press Limited 1999

Copyright © Winifred Holtby 1927, 1934 and 1937
This selection copyright © Paul Berry and Marion Shaw 1999

The moral right of the author has been asserted

A CIP catalogue record for this book is available
from the British Library

ISBN 0 86049 164 2

Typeset by Palimpsest Book Production Limited,
Polmont, Stirlingshire
Printed and bound in Great Britain by
Clays Ltd, St Ives plc

Virago
A Division of
Little, Brown and Company (UK)
Brettenham House
Lancaster Place
London WC2E 7EN

Contents

Introduction

Winifred Holtby's first book was a volume of poems published by her mother when Winifred was twelve. Although she continued to write poems all her life, it is really through her fiction, and particularly the posthumously published *South Riding*, that she is remembered as a writer today. Yet she was a prolific story writer and before *South Riding* it was probably as a story writer and a journalist that she was best known.

She seems to have written stories easily and in all kinds of circumstances. Jean McWilliam, with whom she worked in a W.A.A.C. unit in Huchenneville in France during 1918, recalled how 'Winifred used to write stories by candlelight sitting at the kitchen table completely absorbed while cooks and general domestics and Australians and other W.A.A.C. moved in and out and about.'[1] These stories became a sequence, *The Forest Unit*, and told of life in a rural army camp during the war: 'Poor darlings, they were bad, weren't they?' she wrote four years later; 'I am overwhelmingly thankful now that nobody would publish them, though at the time it seemed quite devastating.'[2] As this remark suggests, she had some difficulty in getting her stories accepted during the early years: 'My stories still come home to roost,' she reported to Jean McWilliam in April 1923. But within two years she could write to Jean that 'I have two short stories coming out this week, and a leading article – and five more articles and two short stories accepted for September.'[3] By this time, although she received a small annual income from her father, she was earning a reasonable income from writing and lecturing, sharing a flat with Vera Brittain in London, living a life of independence, usefulness and achievement, according to the feminist ideals she and Vera shared.

Most of Winifred Holtby's short stories appeared first in newspapers and magazines, and complemented her journalism. The papers she wrote for most frequently were *Time and Tide*, *Radio Times*, *Manchester Guardian*, *New Statesman*, *News Chronicle*, *New Leader* and *Woman's Journal*. Both her fiction and her journalism were often autobiographically based, and reflect the Yorkshire farming community in which she was brought up. In her early days as a freelance writer, she mentions 'writing little sketches of life on the Yorkshire Wolds for the Country Page of the *Morning Post*' and several of these sketches developed into stories. 'I am sending this week to you a short story that may amuse you – it is one of a series of Yorkshire things that are appearing in the *New Leader* and the *Manchester Guardian*, and that later I hope to make into a book of Anderby Tales.'[4] Although Winifred did not personally make a book of Anderby Tales, she must have talked about the idea with Vera Brittain to the extent that Vera felt able to publish *Pavements at Anderby* posthumously. A note to Vera with Winifred's will, written in 1933 when she knew how serious and probably fatal her kidney disease was proving to be, mentions the stories as unfinished business:

> I suppose there is one chance in a thousand that I might die quite suddenly if any accident unexpectedly sent up my blood pressure . . . My short stories (in file marked Short Stories & scattered through Time and Tide, & cuttings among press cuttings marked Stories) might make a volume. But I doubt it. Everything else Curtis Brown [her agent] has.[5]

The stories in *Pavements at Anderby* cover a twelve-year span from 1923 to 1935 and therefore, as their original Foreword points out, represent the early Yorkshire phase when she was writing *Anderby Wold*, a novel set in the

Rudston farming community of her childhood, as well as the last phase of her life, when she turned again to Yorkshire, although a slightly different area, for her last novel, *South Riding*. Although there is a contrast in tone between the early and the late stories, the concerns are the same. 'A Windy Day', written in 1923, is a sentimental account of a lonely, self-absorbed individual but so, too, is 'Little Man Lost' of twelve years later, even though its tone is harsh and bleak. Similarly, 'The Legend of Rudston', a late story, is not very different in its deflationary rural humour from 'Wealms', an early story, and perhaps one of the 'Yorkshire sketches' Winifred mentioned in 1922. *Pavements at Anderby* also included a rejected chapter from *Mandoa, Mandoa!*, Winifred's penultimate novel, written when she was coming to terms with her illness. We have included it here because it speaks so tellingly of the courage and idealism and also the fears and disappointments of Winifred's own life.

Truth Is Not Sober was Winifred's own compilation, its stories drawn mostly from the years 1927 to 1933. It has a higher proportion of satiric stories than *Pavements at Anderby*, and it is the product of Winifred's prime as a journalist. Its dedication to Margaret Rhondda is an appropriate acknowledgement of that side of Winifred's life, as well as of their friendship: 'For Viscountess Rhondda / To The Leader, With Homage / To The Editor, With Gratitude / To The Friend, With Love'. Margaret Rhondda was the founder in 1920 of *Time and Tide*, the weekly newspaper edited and directed by women for the new female electorate. Its purpose was to 'treat men and women as equally part of the great human family, working side by side ... by ways equally valuable, equally interesting'.[6] Closely linked with this newspaper, and also the creation of Margaret Rhondda, was the Six Point Group, the feminist organisation founded in 1921 as a pressure group to campaign for women's rights. Both Winifred Holtby and Vera Brittain were members of the Six Point Group and both wrote for *Time and Tide*, Winifred with such success that in

1926 Margaret Rhondda asked her to become a Director of the paper. Vera Brittain tells of Winifred's delight in this position, so much so that she had cards printed with 'Miss Winifred Holtby, Director, *Time and Tide*.'[7] Many of the stories in *Truth Is Not Sober* were first published in *Time and Tide*, along with the numerous articles Winifred wrote for the paper.

The balance between journalism and fiction was one she did not find easy to maintain. What she called 'the reformer-sort-of-person' who found expression in journalism at times overwhelmed the 'writer-sort-of-person' whom Winifred often thought she really wanted to be. Journalism and stories were two aspects of her strong commitment to communicate directly, accessibly and often humorously, about issues dear to her: the value of work, the interdependency of people, the role of women, the need for international cooperation and the dangers of tyrannical and obsessive personalities. Her stories are didactic and opinionated, although not oppressively so; they point out a moral, make wry observations on human nature, are gently ironic about pretension and self-delusion, and have a definite though submerged social agenda. The much anthologised 'Why Herbert Killed His Mother', for instance, is a fictionalised version of Winifred's belief, expressed frequently in her journalism, in the need for women to have interests other than domesticity, and 'The Voorloper Group' briefly dramatises her passionate commitment to the improvement of the lives of black South Africans. One or two of the stories in this present collection, 'Capital of the Canaries' and 'Machiavelli in the Sick Room', for instance, are very much on the borderline between journalism and fiction. Yet both have a sense of scenic invention, of imagined characters, and of the small and humorous dramas of life which just qualify them as fiction and distance them from their autobiographical bases.

Winifred Holtby's lifetime (1898–1935) spanned a period of increased output and interest in the short story. Late nineteenth-century artistic and philosophical concerns with moments of intense insight and states of consciousness provided an aesthetic context in which the short story flourished. The stories of writers such as Anton Chekov and Henry James show a high level of literary self-consciousness, and this was built on by twentieth-century writers, particularly the Modernist writers. When Holtby began to publish her stories in the early 1920s, James Joyce had already published *Dubliners* (1914), Virginia Woolf had begun to publish her stories, and D.H.Lawrence had published *The Prussian Officer and Other Stories* (1914). The short-story writer with whom Winifred Holtby most tellingly compared herself was Katherine Mansfield. Writing to Jean McWilliam in 1922 on Mansfield's newly published volume of stories, *The Garden Party*, she describes them as 'new ... and strong and modern, and much talked about'.[8] Winifred's stories are quite different from Mansfield's; none is as long, say, as Mansfield's 'Prelude' or 'At the Bay'; all are written matter-of-factly, and are not impressionistic or symbolic. Though they sometimes take the form of a dramatic monologue, they do not use the kind of interior monologue the Modernist writers used. In fact, none is what Holtby herself would have understood by 'modern'; none is self-consciously experimental, nor aspired to the high-art status of the work of writers such as Mansfield, Joyce and Woolf. Winifred's workaday and irreverent attitude to short stories is revealed in the 1922 letter to Jean McWilliam; they are, she says, 'nice for chance guests – easy to pick up and less tantalising for one's bedside than a novel that can never be finished unless we put undue strain on our host's fund of hospitality'. Twelve years later, in a letter to Sarah Gertrude Millin, she wrote:

I have no illusions about my work. I am primarily a useful, versatile, sensible and fairly careful artisan. I have trained myself to write quickly, punctually and readably to order over a wide range of subjects ... At odd moments I write works of the imagination – stories, satires, poems and plays. They

are very uneven in quality. They have moments of
virtue.[9]

Nevertheless, in spite of her modest and businesslike attitude, she took pains and pride in her stories. 'I can't feel
sad when my stories come back – I am only sad when I
write them, because they are so unlike the ones I meant to
write.'[10] What she 'meant to write' we can never know,
except perhaps from an admittedly humorous piece of
advice to writing women which includes the following
remarks:

... a bright, intimate, confidential style. Not too
gossipy, and emphatically not My dear-ish ... Your
personality should be brought out in your writing so
that your readers may be interested in you. You are
writing for entertainment, but a certain amount of
instruction must be there. You must have something
worth while to say, always.[11]

Winifred's stories certainly contain instruction and do have
something worthwhile to say. They are brightly written,
even when their topic is a serious one, and they are
entertaining. As for her personality, it is perhaps veiled;
even though she wrote about the events and places of her
life, what comes across from the stories is her way of life
– the busy journalist and activist – rather than an intimate
expression of what she was as a person. As a writer she
was a competent and widely read professional, turning
outwards to the world of other people and of social affairs
and not inwards to her own inner world.

This selection of Winifred Holtby's short stories is drawn
from her two published volumes, *Truth Is Not Sober*, 1934,
and *Pavements at Anderby*, published by her two friends,
Hilda Reid and Vera Brittain, in 1937, two years after
her death. We have also included 'Capital of the
Canaries' which was published in *Time and Tide* in 1927.
'They Call Them the Duchesses', which was published

posthumously in the *Woman's Journal* in October 1937; and three stories, 'The Picket', 'Brenda Came Home', and 'Unto the Hills', which have not been published before. *Truth Is Not Sober* was divided into groupings: 'Satiric', 'Exotic', 'Bucolic', and 'Domestic'. Although we have not used all of her headings, we have followed Winifred's idea and divided this collection into groupings, six of them, each with a brief introduction.

Paul Berry and Marion Shaw
London 1999

[1] *Letters to a Friend*, ed. Alice Holtby and Jean McWilliam, London. 1937, p. 7
[2] ibid. p. 155
[3] ibid. p. 363
[4] ibid. p. 364
[5] MS note reproduced by permission from the William Ready Division of Archives and Research Collections, McMaster University Library, Hamilton, Canada.
[6] Editorial, *Time and Tide*, 14 May 1920, quoted by Dale Spender, *Time and Tide Wait For No Man*, London. 1984, p. 7
[7] Vera Brittain, *Testament of Friendship*, London. 1980, p. 266
[8] *Letters to a Friend*, p. 119
[9] *Testament of Friendship*, p. 139
[10] *Letters to a Friend*, p. 220
[11] The Winifred Holtby Collection, Hull Central Library, Hull.

Autobiographical

Winifred Holtby was born in 1898 in Rudston in the East Riding of Yorkshire, the second daughter of a prosperous farmer and his strong-minded, socially conscious wife, Alice Holtby, who, untypically for someone of her class and time, persuaded Winifred to go to Somerville College, Oxford, in 1917. Winifred stayed for one year, then joined the W.A.A.C., returning to Somerville in 1919. After graduating, she and Vera Brittain settled in London, and remained together, with some absences and in spite of Vera's marriage in 1925, until Winifred's death in 1935. During the last nine years of her life, of her many reformist activities and writing commitments, Winifred Holtby probably considered the most important to be her work to help black South African workers achieve better employment pay and conditions.

The stories in this section relate to the beginnings of Winifred's life in the beloved farming community of Rudston, with its gently rolling hills, rich sheep pasturage and wheat fields, and to the last years of her life when she contended with the incessant headaches and nausea of Bright's disease. Of Rudston she writes with wry affection, and of illness with cheerfulness or with sardonic humour.

The Legend of Rudston

SEXTON (in singsong Yorkshire voice conducting bus party round churchyard). 'This, ladies an' gentlemen, is the square Norman tower of All Saints Church. Built in time of Norman Conquest, 1066 or a bit later. Note battlements an' fortress-like proportions used for defence purposes when churches were the centres of royal influence against the rebellious Britons. And here is this ancient Monolith, the stone of Rudston, note its proportions, shaped, to a point each end, above twenty feet high, and as deep into the ground as it is out, one massive piece of stone, not of local chalk, nothing like it found nearer than Sledmere and perhaps not there. Geologists say it was floated down here as a giant glacier in the ice age but romantic local legend has it that when the angels was building the church the devil threw the stone at 'em to stop it, missed the chancel by half a dozen yards and there it stands up-ended in the ground.' (In a different, more confidential tone, having obviously received a tip.) 'Thank you, sir. Thank you, ma'am. Aye, missus, they *say* so, but I don't believe 'em.

'What's that? What's that? What do I think *really* happened? Well, now you're asking. Do I know? Of course I know. Haven't I lived in Rudston man an' boy longer than any living memory, and I got it from my granny who got it from her dad who heard tell how it happened from an old body who was living between Thorpe and Church Hill back end o' William Rufus' reign – him as was son to the Conqueror an' died of an ill-aimed arrow down south in the New Forest. Aye, if he'd stuck to Yorkshire he'd be alive now, may be. We're better shots up here, as King Edward knew, God bless 'im. Always liked coming to shoot

3

up here, King Edward did. No William Rufus business of arrows behind trees on the Yorkshire wolds.

'Well, I won't say I wasn't thirsty. Maybe down at the Bosville Arms we might have a sup together. Or there's the Blue Ball at the bottom of Church Hill, not so classey may be, but handy-like. Well, seeing as how I can see you're a gentleman and a scholar, I don't mind telling you. The trippers can look after theirselves. Many's the time I've told that about the devil to charabang parties and they find no fault with it, though since we ploughed up yon Roman pavement on Robson's farm they're getting a bit above theirselves, charabang parties is, all curiosity an' asking questions about other folks' business – archeology they call it. Danged impertinence, *we* say! Now in the old days, a bit of talk about angels and devils was good enough for any one. These days they must have dates and Romans and civilisations and all that – thank you, sir, thank you, I don't mind if I do.

'Well, as I was saying, that bit about the Church being Norman is true enough though whether it was Conqueror or Rufus don't make much difference here. We weren't fashing ourselves much with Kings and such like in the East Riding. The local baron was good enough for us and he found it hard going to keep order.

'Thorpe? Well, maybe he did live at Thorpe then, though I've heard tell it was more this way like, near where chalkpit stands now, because from there you caught a good view of country right round by North Burton and up hill to Thwing and south again towards Woldgate – aye, that had been Roman road like, an' they still used it though all Romans was dead. Married Yorkshire lasses, they did, poor chaps, and went extinct like as their betters have done many a time since then.

'Well, as I was saying, the king, whoever it was, sent word for all his barons to build towers what they could climb up to spy on the village-folk like and see what they was doing and tell 'em not to. And if they could call 'em church towers and get the local people to build 'em under false pretences, so much the better. Mean, I call it. But them Normans is sly. Always was. It's the foreign blood, you know. Never trust a Norman, my old dad used to say. And I never have.

'Well, that old Baron gives orders to village he wants a church building and they're to help him. And so far as a church goes they're quite willing, being decent Christian-living folk though not enough to spoil their fun like.

'Now in village there was a chap living, name of Rudd. Yes, sir, you're quite right. We're coming to stone now. Rudd. Ruddstone. Rudston. Well, this here Rudd was a handy chap and good for anything – a game of fisticuffs, or a hod and trowel, or a bit o' poaching. Grand lad, he was. They bred fine chaps in them days.

'Well, Rudd he talks to Baron, and Baron talks to Rudd, and Rudd goes down to village an' stands on bridge over Gypsy Race – yon beck you see there, and the villagers come round, and some was for building church and some for not building and some for taking Baron down a peg or two an' chucking him into beck an' forgetting to pull him out again.

'But Rudd knows a thing worth two o' that, he says. If we build church, he says, we'll be doing a good deed and making summat. An' if we don't build it, Baron'll send for some o' them Normans to put us to fire an' sword and burn our village an' carry off our women – not that that wouldn't get rid of a parcel of trouble for some of us, he says – but they might carry off our pigs an' cattle too, and that's serious. Aye, they said, that's serious, for they thought a lot of their pigs in yon days. So the villagers say O.K. by us, big boy. (Aye, sir, I've been to talkies at Burlington. Aye, I like them well enough. What do I think o' the modern girl? You wait a minute. I'm telling you a story.)

'Well, Rudd gets chaps together from village an' he goes to the Baron on a deputation-like an' he says, I hear tell you want a church building? An' Baron says, Aye, lad. And Rudd he says, With a tower, like? An' Baron says, That's right, lad. An' Rudd says, Well, I've got some of the lads outside and we'll build you yon church. But if you start monkeying about an' using it as a fortress against us or any o' that we'll larn you a bit of old Yorkshire, so watch out. And the wicked Baron he chuckles in his Norman whiskers and says, Carry on, boys. Thinking he'll get church built first an' use spy tower afterwards.

'Well, he didn't know Yorkshire.

'Rudd he calls his boys together and they ups an' builds the church and tower. And Baron he sends for architect chap to come from London – all lar-di-da and eye-glass (aye, sir, London chaps always has been like that. Can't say why – never been to London to find out. Burlington's good enough for me when I wants a bit o' night life, or Kilham on a Feast Day. You'd be surprised.) Well, as I was saying, architect chap comes to teach 'em how to make Norman arches an' all, an' try to put a bit o' Doomsday Book across 'em, but Rudd has his lads well in hand. Big chaps they was then – fists like sledge-hammers, shoulders like bullocks – fell an ox with a blow then. Seen 'em do it with my own eyes – Thank you, thank *you*, sir, another bitter then, don't mind if I do.

'Well, as I was saying, church gets itsel' built. You've only got to look at tower to see it was Rudd's work, standing to this day. No. Church behind it's quite different. Any scholar'd tell you. Oh, aye, Rudd built a church there. Haven't I been telling you? But that's not the one what stands there now. You wait a bit.

'The church was built and the Baron sends for the bishops to come and dedicate it, and the bishop arrives and a great strapping soldier of a chap he is too, with chain-mail under his cassock and a crozier like a ramming post and the King's orders in his pocket to suppress the local Britons. Aye, he had an' all, but a Yorkshire lad takes a bit o' suppressing *I* can tell you.

'Well, the Baron an' the Bishop an' their bowmen an' their squires they ride through village an' come to the grand new church, and there's Rudd an' his chaps with their picks an' hammers drawn up outside porch asking for their money.

'Ho, no! says the Baron. You've built a church to the glory of God and virtue should be its own reward.

'Glory of God, asks Rudd. What about glory of you old Normans? We're good Christians and we were before you came here. And we don't like the look of yon bishop. He's too much like a robber baron for our taste. You get church dedicated and us paid and send him back where he came from an' *we'll* attend to the glory of God, says Rudd.

'Oh will you, says Baron. We'll see to that.

'So Baron and Bishop fix the day, go into committee there in the church porch and do a bit of argy-bargaining, and a nice plot it is they hatch together. What Bishop says is, well, they can't start firing and slaughtering there on consecrated ground or that's sacrilege, but what they will do is to dedicate church and leave tower out of it, for the ignorant and superstitious peasantry won't ever know the difference an' then the Baron can use the tower for spying an' imprisoning the very men who built it. And the Baron thinks that's a grand plan an' he'll be able to make a report to King that'll get him promotion and no one the worse but the brutal and superstitious peasantry.

'So into church they go, Bishop an' Baron an' bowmen and all, an' close the doors to shut out the villagers, so that they shan't know what tricks they're up to inside. And they think theirselves safe as safe, for the villagers will never attack 'em in the tower thinking it sacred, while all the time the Normans would know it wasn't an' could do what they like there.

'A mean trick? Didn't I say, never trust a Norman?

'Well, Rudd he wasn't born yesterday an' he didn't like egg nor shell of that Bishop so he goes up to church and pops his ear against a window where he knows because he built it that there's a bit o' glass missing, and as soon as all the Normans is in church he shouts through window, What about our wages?

'And the Bishop says, Go away now. This is a sacred edifice.

'An' Rudd shouts, Not yet, it isn't. But we are Yorkshire lads an' labourer is worthy of his hire, an' we want our bit o' brass.

'An' Baron says, Go away or I'll have your lands ravaged with fire an' slaughter.

'An' Rudd says, You'll be fired first then. For I've got my lads round church, and we've got petrol and gunpowder an' *we* ought to know if church'll burn well. You hand us our wages or not a man jack of you leaves spot alive. We'll burn you out like wasps from a nest, says Rudd, poking his big head through the window.

'And the Baron says, Boys, they're too much for us.

'And the Bishop says, Let's make a run for it.

'And Rudd, he shouts, First Norman that comes through porch, I'll hit him over the head with my little hammer.

'And the Baron says, Ho! I've got my armour on. I'm a Norman. Who cares? And makes for the door, and as he runs out, Rudd's ready for him and plants his legs square and lifts his hammer and brings it full down smack on that wicked Baron's head and right through into the ground the other end of him. And the villagers set light to the church and burn it down, all except the tower, which stands there to this day as you've seen; but the nave and chancel, they had to rebuild and dedicate 'em properly for the uses of peace an' quiet an' a godly Christian congregation an' no spying on any one, nor has there ever been, sir, after that.

'Why, what's that? You don't see how the stone gets into it? Why, they were big chaps in those days, sir. Could use a tidy tool then. That's the head of Rudd's little hammer just as it stuck into the ground. They left it there as a lesson to Normans an' other strangers not to interfere with us and to pay up wages promptly. Yes sir, Rudd's stone – that's right. Thank you, sir, thank you kindly. Aye, missus, they say so, and the gentlemen like it. But *I* don't believe 'em.'

1935

Harking Back to Long Ago

IN the dark nursery at the back of the long grey brick farmhouse, my sister and I lay awake on Christmas Eve. I was four and she was six-and-a-half, and the hour seemed to us prodigiously, daringly, joyously late. It was a quarter to ten on a bright frosty night, and through the square, uncurtained window the stars glistened, mapped out into unastronomical constellations by the woodwork between the small square panes, just as on our nursery map the continents were marked off into squares by the lines of latitude and longitude. The maids who had been clattering in the pantry below us were silent; in the horse-pasture beyond the garden an iron-shod hoof once clanked heavily on the frozen field road; the night was very still. We lay – not speaking – listening.

Then it came. We sat up in bed, all ears, and heard it; the crunch of feet on the gravel of the drive, the shuffling as men took their places round the light of a single lantern, the schoolmaster's muffled, 'One – two – three'—

Hark, the herald angels sing
Glory to the new-born King.

We were out of bed. We were scampering barefoot along the nursery passage, up two steps into the bad bit of unlighted corridor, past the silver cupboard that harboured ghosts and tigers, on to the front landing and through a door into the best spare room. And peering between the slits of the Venetian blind, there we saw them. The grown-ups had not gone to bed; they had drawn back the curtains from the drawing-room windows, and the

9

lamplight streamed out on to the gravel drive. In moonlight, and starlight, and lamplight, and lantern-light stood the singers. Their faces were pale and their long coats black dark, but here and there a scarlet muffler or a pair of fine, glowing cheeks caught the lamplight. There were twenty men and boys from the choir standing round the schoolmaster's lantern, singing:

> 'Peace on earth and mercy mi-ild
> God and sinners reconciled.'

The draught blew in through the cold bedroom; the chill air was sharp as eau de Cologne, as icy water, on our bodies; we gathered our nightdresses around us and huddled together for warmth.

> 'Mild he lays His glory by
> Born that man no more may die.'

I can close my eyes and see them; I can shut my ears and hear them; in the warmth of my lighted room I can feel the wind on my bare arms, and the chill boards under my naked feet. I can even smell the queer cold, smoky, frosty smell of the unused bedroom. It is all there.

But it is mine. Nobody else can ever hear it as I heard and hear it. No other living memory now carries the echo of those particular singers in that particular garden, though a million children have stolen from bed and scampered like mice through a dark house to hear the carollers on Christmas Eve. When I die, nobody will ever again know that particular sweet fierce exaltation which stirred the rapturous, unblurred imagination of a child.

Or will they? Suppose it comes true. Suppose that men do one day invent a machine which will listen to the past, pick up the sound waves as they slide off the air waves on to the ether, and reproduce for us all sounds that have ever been. Then, perhaps, turning a dial carelessly, a dry-goods salesman in Chicago, or a herdsman in Kenya, or a silk merchant in Rangoon, may suddenly hear the crunch of feet on gravel outside a Yorkshire farmhouse, and the schoolmaster's breathly 'One, two, three,' and the burst of singing that summoned two children from their beds.

But I do not think that that particular little private ecstasy will be recaptured. The world has heard too many Christmas sounds of more imposing significance. If I had my own way, my instrument that listened to the past, my table of dates and latitudes and longitudes, and if I could eavesdrop when and where I would among the centuries, what Christmas Festival would I summon? My own Christmases live in my own memory. I do not need the delicate, terrifying omniscience of an instrument to tune in for me on to the sound of W.A.A.C.s and English Tommies in a hut under French orchard trees toasting the First Christmas after the Armistice in claret cup. I need no help to hear again the village choir, with the squire's son playing the cornet, braying out into 'O come, all ye faithful,' at the vestry door, nor to hear the sound of crackers exploding round the table, nor the gasping scurry at the front door as small children broke in upon us with 'I-wish-you merry-Christmas-n'a'ppy-New-Year-'n-please-will-yer-give's-a-Christmas-box?' nor to hear the shouting of the maids and their young men and my nieces and the rest of us dancing round the Christmas tree, blowing out candles to the tune of:

> *'Sally went round the sun,*
> *Sally went round the moon,*
> *Sally went round the chimney pots*
> *On a Christmas afternoon. Pouff!*
> *Sally went round the sun.'*

And so on, till the last candle was extinguished with a triumphant 'Pouff!'

All that is done. All that is mine. But there are others whose Christmas memories I would most joyously purloin. I think I would turn my dial to Rome, and to the year A.D.

800, the year before Pope Leo III. had been maltreated in the streets, and had appealed for protection to the Frankish king, the great Charles, Charlemagne, the conqueror of Pavia, the conqueror of the Saxons, the patron of the Church, the Hammer of Christendom. Big and robust in frame he was, measuring about seven of his feet in height, great hunter, and ruler, and father; like Solomon, the lover of many concubines, like Judah, a brave begetter of sons. The Church was beset by enemies; the Lombards in the north of Italy, the pagans in Germany, the heathen round the Mediterranean. The Empire had shifted its head-quarters to Byzantium. The Pope was left, guardian not only of the spirit but of the body of Christendom, and times were hard. In the year 800, Charlemagne marched to Rome 'to restore order,' and on Christmas Day he knelt in the church of Saint Peter, the most powerful worshipper in the Western world. And behold, as he rose up from prayer, the Pope set on his head the imperial crown, and proclaimed him Holy Roman Emperor in the name of the Father and of the Son and of the Holy Ghost, and all the people applauded and the warriors in the streets outside clashed their weapons, and it was as though the voice of the people spoke with the voice of God, hailing the birth of a new epoch. It was the birth of a new epoch. From that cry arose the Holy Roman Empire, and the Middle Ages, and Dante's dream of a unified Christendom. And I envy the New Zealanders and Latvians and Brazilians of the future who will one day tune in to hear that epoch-making tumult.

But while my hand was on the dial I would turn back. The Venerable Bede once told us 'that the ancient people of the Angli began the year on the 25th of December, when we now celebrate the birthday of Our Lord; and the very night which is now so holy to us, they called in their tongue 'modranecht' (modra niht) – that is, the mother's night – by reason, we suspect, of the ceremonies which in that night-long vigil they performed.' I should not understand a word of the rough tongue spoken by my forefathers in their pagan Christmas; I should only hear shouts and the rattle of oaken spears, perhaps, and the grinding of stones, and perhaps the shriek of a victim sacrificed. Or would there be a gentler ritual on modranecht, mother's night? I should like to hear.

I should like to listen to the first English Christmas after Charles II., the Merry Monarch, came back to his kingdom, and banished the gloom of the Puritan festival with laughter, and feasts, and dancing. I should like to tune in to the court of Saint James, where the jokes might be a trifle coarse, and where the noblest princes would belch and spit like coal heavers; but my loud-speaker would only give me sound, not scent nor sight. The flickering candlelight, the heat from the great fires, the stew of sweat and paint, and stuffiness and cooking, and perfume and humanity, and wine and cosmetics would be lost to me. But I might hear the King's deep, witty voice, and Lady Castlemaine's mad, musical laughter. There are conveniences about a medium which appeals to one sense only.

And while I was in London, and Westminster, and the seventeenth century, should I tune in to the year 1662, and go with Mr Pepys to the chapel in Whitehall, coming 'too late to receive communion with the family,' but in time enough to hear Bishop Morley preach upon the song of the Angels, 'Glory to God on high, on earth peace, and good will towards men'? No. Here I think eyes are better than ears, for I would rather read Pepys' ever-unspoken comment, 'A poor sermon, but long'. How excellent that 'but,' as though length compensated for poverty in preaching! I would rather listen on another year to the Pepys household. '1668. Christmas Day. – To dine alone with my wife, who, poor wretch! sat undressed all day till ten at night, altering and lacing of a noble petticoat; while I by her making the boy read to me the *Life of Julius Caesar* and *Des Cartes' Book of Musick*.' I should hear the boy's voice, and the rustle of Mrs Pepys' noble silk and her husband's yawn as he turned from Julius Caesar.

Slowly, slowly the dial would turn, and the years fall away, and I think that one place I would linger would be on no land, but 'in the chops of the Channel, with the Scilly Isles on a vague bearing within thirty miles of us, and not a breath of wind anywhere.' And there I should find the young Korzeniowski, encountering his captain on a foggy morning, with the ship 'wrapped up in a damp blanket and as motionless as a post,' and I should hear the Polish sailor politely greet his superior in English with 'Merry Christmas, sir,' and the grimly-scathing reply, 'Looks like it, doesn't it?' Or is it better to restrain the dial and read instead the account of it all in Joseph Conrad's own essay, *Christmas Day at Sea*?

The world would then be mine, and all the sounds thereof. I might swing round the globe to New Zealand, to listen to a picnic party in the sweltering sun, eating plum pudding in the bush – a grim achievement which yet might sound the same as any Christmas dinner in an English country house, with snow and mistletoe and robins. I might go south to a lonely hut in the vast wilderness of the Antarctic, and listen to a small company of gentlemen making merry with their leader, one Captain Scott. Or, while I was visiting adventures, I might find the year of grace 1497; the place, a green-wooded bay dipping down to the Indian Ocean; the scene, a wooden ship sailing through mild summer weather; the day, Christmas Day, and the excited cries – unhappily for me, in Portuguese – as Terra Natalis, the land of Christmas, Natal first was named. Anything less like a Christmas land than that fair province, half upland, half semi-tropical coast, I hardly can imagine. But there would be a sound of water, and the bells of the ship, and the rattle of ropes, and the noise of wind in the sails, and the voices of the sailors. I could hear well enough to distinguish the boat, poor linguist though I am, if I listened. And, using my privilege, I might steal inland, and hear other cries, the amazement of black watchers on the shore as, in the words of an old carol, they 'saw a ship come sailing by, on Christmas Day in the morning.'

I could have tropical Christmases and Arctic Christmases, Christmases pagan and Christian, ancient and modern, a grim Christmas with John Knox, a lofty Christmas with Sir Walter Raleigh on the high seas, a jovial Christmas with a bourgeois German family in the last century. And I know that some will ask me, and I should ask myself, why, since I have the power, should I not go back two thousand years, to Palestine, to a village inn, and an inn stable? For there, though I could not understand the language, and though the noises from the streets would all be strange to me, I might hear the cattle moving in their stalls as I have heard them in the dark shed near our farmhouse; I might hear voices, and a hurrying to and from the crowded inn, and the questioning of shepherds, and the cry of a child.

I might. But then, I might not. Sounds are confusing. One night is strangely like another night. I have heard a small child crying, and his mother's voice comforting him. I have heard the humble, homely rustlings, and munchings, and stirrings of cattle among the straw; I have heard shepherds striding down from the hills to a village inn. And among so many sounds, how should we know the sound that changed a world? What was one mother's voice among the village women? Or one child's cry in that crowded town?

The shout of the Frankish warriors when Charles the Great was crowned, the thundering of Bishop Morley rating the Court, the laugh of Lady Castlemaine – these would be easier to distinguish than those quiet sounds.

> *He cam al so stylle*
> > *Where his moder was*
> *As dewe in Aprylle*
> > *That fallyt on the gras.*
>
> *He cam al so stylle*
> > *To his moder's bowr*
> *As dewe in Aprylle*
> > *That fallyt on the flour.*

I would rather turn to a much later Christmas and hear in

a Kent village a girl's voice singing that ballad. Its fresh sweetness tells us more than we might learn from our most ingenious instrument, our most erudite expert in Semitic languages.

I am glad that we have more than one sense through which to perceive the world. I am glad that when all the five senses are stilled memory takes up the tale. I am content to leave some sounds to memory and imagination.

1929

Facilis Descensus Averni

'Racing, gambling, drinking,' said Uncle, 'they're the curse of the nation. You begin with a little flutter at a Point-to-Point, and you end in the bankruptcy court, or worse. The fatal facility of crime. Too easy in this sport-loving country, alas!' And he shook his head over fatal facilities.

I, who had been disillusioned about facility before, reflected sadly upon those feats which others found so easy and I so difficult, such as turning the heel of a sock, playing a no-trump hand, and tuning-in to Daventry on the crystal set. What if racing also were a mystery to be learned only after laborious apprenticeship?

Auntie had no such doubts. She rocked up and down in her chair, her knitting-needles clicking, as she shook her head and repeated softly, 'Only too easy. Only too easy.'

But after Uncle had left the room she looked up with that bright twinkle which preceded many of her most unexpected remarks, and observed, 'All the same, my dear, I should like to sample a little vice before I die.'

With Auntie, one never knows. Meek and gentle as she seems, she is too wide-awake for perfect virtue.

'The Devonshire Point-to-Point meets on Friday,' she continued. 'Uncle will be in London.' She paused. 'It's not as if a Point-to-Point were an *ordinary* race, dear. Besides, the Prince is going to ride there. We might go just to see the Prince.'

Not all the water in the rough rude sea can wash the balm from an anointed head. When Uncle returned, Auntie told him that we should like to see the Prince go by on Friday.

'I've never seen the Prince; it's a sort of patriotic duty, I feel. He does not often come to Devonshire.'

'Then you must take care and wrap up,' said Uncle, whose own tendency to chills makes him suspicious of the weather for every one else. 'This awful traffic. A lot of hooligans from the Town. Take care to stand well away from the main road. You might ask the vicar to let you watch from his windows as they ride from the station.'

Royalty on its way to a race is still royalty; but the races were not mentioned.

Uncle went to town. Friday came, cold and bright. At half-past eleven we were ready, with a rug, a thermos flask, sandwiches, mackintoshes, umbrellas, jerseys, and Auntie's little brown purse bag clutched very tight because of pickpockets.

'The charabanc starts from the Town Hall, dear. And I've changed five shillings into two half-crowns, one each for us – for – you know what, dear.' I knew. We were launched upon our way of infamy. Never had two sinners entered upon their career so full of hope.

But the way of the transgressor is hard. The hand of judgment was indicated first by the fact that the charabanc was full up, and to save the extra shilling we had not booked places. We had to squeeze into the 'bus and change half-way.

The roads were full of traffic. As we approached the racecourse, crowds appeared from lanes and fields. Crowds arose like a flood and blotted out the Devonshire land-scape. When we descended from the 'bus, we asked, 'Which way to the races?' 'Follow the crowd,' they said. But a crowd, to be followed, must have front, rear and direction; and this crowd was without form and void, like chaos. It talked incomprehensibly; it wore breeches; it smelt of beer and straw. It thrust us into a road, through the gate; into the field, one of those bright red Devonshire ploughed fields, so picturesque on post-cards, so burdensome upon the boots. We were faced by an eight-foot bank, as steep as a wall.

'Where is the gate?' gasped auntie, grasping her umbrella, the thermos, the rug and a mackintosh.

'Hup, ma!' shouted a voice, and auntie was seized behind and translated like Enoch while yet alive on to the top of the bank.

Below us, before us, behind us roared the crowd. The whole fair world was drowned in people. Above the steady clamour of voices, the shrill squeal of a Punch and Judy, and the shattering clangour of bells, we heard a hoarse but pious voice admonishing, 'Praise God! Praise God!'

'It must be the Salvation Army,' said auntie.

Some men in check breeches were writing lists of names and figures on blackboards. One shouted, 'Any more for the field?' Another, 'Two-to-one, bar one! Two-to-one, bar one!'

The man roaring 'Praise God!' passed us, and then we saw that he was selling little booklets. We bought one each for sixpence, hoping for holy comfort in this turmoil of Mammon.

'Race card,' ran the heading of our little books, and we realised that once again had enunciation deceived us. But the race card conveyed little to us.

1. Fairfield. Mr G. R. Bristowe. Dartmoor. B. G. Owner.
2. Pretty One. Mrs L. Granger. The Quorn. Bl. M.

It was an unknown language to us; but we had moved right up to the Punch and Judy show.

'I haven't seen one for years!' cried Auntie, and we stood entranced.

The voices round us rose and fell. We heard more bells, more cheers. The crowds round the blackboards rocked and swayed. A stall at which a fat old woman sold winkles in saucers reminded us that we were hungry, and we ate our sandwiches under a hedge. They were crumbly and we had lost the thermos.

'But I always said Jane could make nice potted meat,' said Auntie. 'And how very fortunate that it's a fine day. Now I wonder which is the Prince? I'm going to put half a crown on him, even if it is a mortal sin. The dear, bonny boy! If it were not for telling your uncle afterwards, I'd put five shillings.'

The half-crown was there. But the knowledge of the art and craft of gambling was not. How does one put on half a crown? Where does one put it?

'I wonder if I could ask that gentleman over there? He's so like your Uncle George, dear, he has such a nice, kind face.'

But when we approached the gentleman he was using a language unintelligible to either of us, and auntie decided that he was not as much like Uncle George as all that. We moved away.

'Try your luck, lady. All odd numbers on the black squares and you get your money back! Even numbers and you double it! Bad luck, sonny. Try again, sir!' Two shabby men were inviting us to throw pennies on to squares of linoleum.

'Just like the lino in the kitchen, dear,' said auntie. 'Now, there's a horse!'

It was the first horse we had seen, and the man who rode it pushed away the crowd with such an authoritative manner that we thought he must be the Prince, or at least an outrider of His Royal Highness. But when we asked, some one said that he was only a clearer of the course. And the crowd closed in on us, and for a terrible moment I lost Auntie, and she lost her umbrella, and people shouted louder than ever, and somebody began fighting behind us, and when we met again we were both much out of breath, but the crowds were scattering.

'Now, dear, we shall be able to get nearer the course,' said auntie. 'I wonder which way—?'

'Please can you tell us the best place to see the races?' we asked a fat, good-natured-looking man.

'Races, races? A bit late in the day, aren't you? Last race over ten minutes ago. Prince came in second.'

'Well,' said Auntie, as we climbed into the bus, 'Providence must have saved us from sin. I always say that our guardian angels watch over us. And we had a very enjoyable day, I'm sure.'

It may have been providence. I don't quite know. But what I am sure about is that it is much harder to be a rake than people make out. We wanted to gamble; we intended to gamble. I still have the half-crown that Auntie gave me. And now the Prince has sold his hunters and will ride in the Point-to-Point no more. But there must be something about racing that we don't understand, and I always knew that when uncle muttered, 'Facilis descensus averni,' he didn't know what he was talking about, never having tried it himself.

1929

'Wealms'

I WILL say this for Augusta, she meant well. Though the trouble the Lord must have dissecting all our good intentions sometimes passes my understanding. Of course, the real moral of the whole business is, 'Don't have visitors'; but I can't help thinking that would make life a little dull. And, anyway, father never knew. Augusta was romantic, and intense, and wrote things for the papers. She came to stay on our farm in the East Riding. It is a mixed farm, about four hundred acres on the wolds, and Augusta was charmed. She wanted to know everything, why we didn't graze our sheep on grass, and why our paddocks were all round the buildings, and whether there was a ghost in the barn, and when we were going to milk by electricity. My father bore with her for a week, then turned her over to me, with the command that whatever else she wanted to ask, I must answer. He was busy.

So I told her how many hens we had, and why we salted the butter, and who planted the rose tree among the red-currant bushes and all that sort of thing. I let her talk to Watts, our groom-gardener; I showed her the young hedgehogs under the rhubarb bed. Nobody could have done better. But suddenly after tea on the Friday she came up to me and asked, 'What are Wealms?'

'Oh,' I said, 'the Wellums?'

'Wealms,' said she. She has one of those refined voices that make me feel Yorkshire.

Of course I know the Wellums. It is a grass field, about twenty-four acres on the wold, intersected with ditches, and decorated by several mossy mounds. We use it for young horses. Wellums, as I explained, is just a name. It has always been called that. But Augusta was not satisfied. She began to ask questions. Why had that field and no other a name? Why was it left grass when I had told her that we always ploughed the wold fields? Why was it covered with dykes and mounds and earthworks? Wasn't there some sort of history about it?

These people who want to know reasons for everything are intolerable on a farm. I nearly told her so. But after I had confessed that in the War father had been forced to turn nearly all his pasture into arable land, but still the Wellums remained unploughed, she almost lost her head. She began to hold forth about the blindness of the stolid Yorkshire folk. Here at our very door lay Mystery and Romance, a field with a queer name that no one understood, that no one would plough, that possibly held ghosts, or bones, or buried treasure, and we never showed the slightest interest in it.

I must confess that I began to be impressed. Augusta was clever, and perhaps we had been taking things too much for granted. When, three weeks after she had left us, a letter came from London, I very nearly showed it to my father. Nearly, not quite. We don't show things to father unless we feel pretty certain. The letter told us that Augusta had seen in the British Museum Roman coins and pottery and whatnot, dug up from a farm close to ours. She vowed that this explained the secret of the Wealms. Might it not be a Roman burial ground, lying, as it did, not two miles from the Roman Road that once had led from York to the sea coast? She could see endless possibilities. But the name still was puzzling her, and she determined to find out the origin of Wealms.

People like Augusta do things properly. Ten days later I had a wire, 'Discovered derivation of Wealms, confirms theory amazing developments.' Augusta always writes like the headlines of the *Daily Mail*.

The discovery that she made had been through a philologist, an expert in North Country dialects. He had told her that Wealms, in Lancashire speech, meant 'fairies.' In

23

Yorkshire, very probably, hundreds of years ago, it would mean 'ghosts.'

'So here,' she wrote, 'we have the key to the mystery. And what a key! Of course the place was a burial ground after a fierce battle between the Britons and the Romans; of course it is haunted by ghosts, which have preserved the graves and kept them sacred. I talked to Croxton the archaeologist and he says that almost certainly we should find coins and weapons and armour of immense importance. For seventeen hundred years or more, though long ago forgotten by man's memory, the slaughtered Englishmen have kept their guard above the hidden treasure of the wold. Can you not see the Roman legionaries marching along the great road from Eboricum? The furious resistance? The desperate defeat? The captive women wailing o'er their lovers? The mounds of dead? The rapid burial . . .' There was a great deal more that Augusta could see, and that I could not, but the practical outcome was that Augusta would arrange among her clever friends for an immediate expedition for excavations. Local labour might be employed for the digging, but she would have Merkin, the eminent archaeologist, to direct operations. And whatever profits might accrue should be divided between my father, who owned the ground, and Augusta, who had made the discovery. 'The name, you see, the name preserved the Treasure. Just "Ghosts," and there's the clue to the whole story. My dear, How wonderful. Just think of all this out of a chance question! You Yorkshire people are amazing in your power of taking things for granted.'

So Augusta was right, and after all our scoffing it seemed that she was going to make our fortune.

Tentatively I went to my father and asked him if he had ever wondered why the Wellums was never brought under the plough.

'I don't wonder,' he said, 'I know. There used to be a brick-yard there in my grandfather's time, and they dug it about and messed up the surface until it's more trouble

24

to plough now than it's worth. Chap name of William Robinson. They still call it Willums, or some say Wellums, after him.'

Sentence of Life

ONCE upon a time there lived a man who did not know that he was mortal.

He was not ignorant. He knew that men were born and that they die. In his childhood he had accompanied his parents to church, and sung hymns affirming that

> Brief life is here our portion

or

> Days and moments quickly flying
> Blend the living with the dead.
> Soon will you and I be lying
> Each within our narrow bed.

But the words had no personal application for him. Life did not seem brief to him, nor did the days and moments fly quickly, especially during the periods of Public Worship, or of school preparation, or during the tea-parties when his aunts came and he had to sit like a good boy in the drawing-room.

Indeed, as he grew older, it was not the brevity of life, but its interminable length that most impressed him. He was all too conscious that there are sixty seconds in a minute and sixty minutes in an hour, and twenty-four hours in every day. And it was too much.

He did not lack the common benefits of mortality. His Aunt Emily died, leaving him a legacy of ten thousand pounds. His father died, leaving him the commodious house in which he had been born. His mother died,

26

relieving him of the sense of obligation which had disturbed him during her widowhood, for he was a tender-hearted son. The death of his immediate superior in the merchant's office where he worked provided him with his first opportunity of promotion.

He took it. He prospered. He eventually became himself a city merchant.

He built a new wing and added conservatories to his house; he married a pretty girl who believed every word he uttered; he joined an expensive golf club and took his handicap seriously; he begot two daughters and one son, and cultivated begonias and the county families. His bank manager respected, and his gardener resented, his habit of planning for tomorrow rather than today. He frequently boasted that his hand-made boots would wear for thirty years.

As he grew older he became more successful; but he did not grow more happy. He was distressed by the manners of his children who, in spite of their expensive education, did not show him the deference that he considered suitable. He was distressed by politicians, who did not carry out the policies he thought desirable, by servants whose deficiency varied in inverse ratio to their wages, by his wife, who compensated herself for her loss of looks by increasing irritation of temper, and by his own digestive apparatus which, in spite of golf, morning exercises, and patent medicines, constantly aroused in him acute discomfort.

He was not happy and he was not interested. Time seemed to him very long and very tedious. Though he could make money he could not buy with it satisfaction. He said one day to a golfing acquaintance that he did not know what the world was coming to, and sometimes he thought he would be better dead. The friend said that they all felt like that occasionally, advised consultation with a doctor, and repeated the old joke about 'it depends on the liver'.

The joke displeased the merchant; but he took the advice and made an appointment with his family doctor, who

examined and questioned him, and sent him to a distinguished specialist, who sent him to a radiologist, who sent
him to a bio-chemist, who sent back a report, which the
family doctor spread on the desk before him when he told
the merchant, 'You know, old man, it's no use blinking
at the truth. You are the head of a family. You have
responsibility. I think that you ought to know that we
consider you to be in a very grave condition. The trouble
is long standing.'

'D'you want to cut me up?' asked the merchant, for he
was terrified of surgery.

'I am afraid that an operation would hardly be advisable
in the circumstances. It *might* prolong life for a few extra
weeks, but—'

'Prolong life?' cried the merchant. 'Do you mean that I
am going to die?'

'These things are not in our hands,' said the doctor, who
was a pious man.

'Then they damn well ought to be!' swore the merchant,
appalled by the thought of all the money he had spent
unavailingly.

But after he had left the doctor's house, and reflected
upon what he had just learned there, his thoughts moved
in another direction.

'I am going to die,' he told himself. 'I am going to
die.' He looked down at his corpulent body and tried
to imagine it enclosed in an oak coffin. He looked at the
pleasant suburban road in which his house was situated,
at the geraniums and lobelia bordering the garden beds, at
the chestnut trees which had blossomed before his father's
birth, at the cars passing, and the boys on bicycles, and the
freshness and gaiety of the summer day. He tried to imagine
its existence when he was not there to see it. He thought of
his wife, of her uncertain temper, her angular elegance and
frigid rectitude. He tried to imagine her, in widow's weeds
weeping above the grave. He tried to imagine his daughters,
demure in fashionable black dresses, luxuriating in their
new-found freedom. He thought of the office, and tried

to imagine his son carrying on the business without his controlling will.

'The young fool will mess it all up,' he told himself, exasperated by the memory of an important deal timed to yield its full profit only five years ahead. 'But I shan't be there,' thought the merchant. 'I shan't be there.'

He returned the salute of a passing neighbour, and asked himself what that fellow would think if he knew that he was greeting a man under sentence of death.

The drama of the situation exhilarated him. He was a doomed man. He had been condemned by the doctors. To-day, to-morrow, the final dissolution might begin. He felt as though every other man must live for ever. He alone was destined for imminent death. He opened his gate and entered his garden. He saw the new apple-trees impaled and spread against the sheltering wall. Would he never see their blossom?

It occurred to him that the sight of apple blossom was one of the most exquisite of human pleasures.

He might live until the trees shed their leaves, but he would certainly never see another spring. He had hitherto considered the beauties of the year's renewal, the daffodils in his orchard, the eggs in the thrushes' nest, the showers scattering through the silver birches, as amenities provided by Nature for his comfort. He knew now that they would continue when he no longer could enjoy them.

His daughters came out of the house, slim and graceful in gay summer dresses. They were his girls, his children; he had made them, educated them and clothed them; they were his possessions moulded by his taste. But he saw now that they had also independent existences which would continue long after he had ceased to fret over their manners, or to take pleasure in their youthful grace.

He entered the cool quietness of his house, and saw the damask, the mahogany, and the roses in the big silver bowl. His possessions were solid, invulnerable, constructed for endurance. Regarding them he became conscious of his fragile body, constructed for decay.

The grandfather's clock in the hall-way ticked implacably, 'Tick, tock! Tick, tock!' squandering its rare treasure of time, and flinging to left and right the days and moments that now fled all too quickly.

Life was brief, brief, brief. Each second marked the passing of a unique, an irrevocable period.

'I am going to die. I am going to die,' cried the merchant in his heart.

And he knew that life was sweet.

He sat down to the table with his family and tasted the good food, sipped the rare wine, and saw that his daughters were fair and his boy stalwart, and that his wife was graceful and dignified and a true lady. All lovely things became lovelier, because he might be looking upon them for the last time. All tedious things became more tolerable, because he might never have to suffer them again.

And thus he continued.

Each morning the merchant awoke, thinking, 'Perhaps this is my last awakening,' and he gazed at his familiar room with eager recognition. He observed his children with an intensity hitherto unknown to him, and discovered new and interesting qualities in their characters. He exerted all his powers over his business and, in spite of fatigue and physical discomfort, found the work infinitely fascinating. His friends told him that he looked younger every day. He complained no longer that life was not worth living. He was in love with life and counted every hour a miracle that he wrested from the oblivion of death.

On an appointed day he returned for examination by his doctor, and inquired after the progress of his disease.

'You are a marvel,' replied the doctor. 'With the symptoms I found in you when you last visited me, nine men out of ten would be by this time on their death-bed. I believe that you are going to prove the exception. You may live to a good old age yet.'

'I may live?' gasped the merchant.

'As long as I,' replied the doctor. 'Of course' – he laughed jovially – 'we all have to die one day!'

'Why, yes,' said the merchant. For the thought was novel to him.

He knew now that though the sentence had been postponed, it had not been repealed. He was alive, but some day he must die. The sun still shone; his garden still was sweet; his daughters still were beautiful; his work still lured him by its promise of conflict and of triumph, its satisfaction of achievement. But now he knew that it is the brevity of life which makes it tolerable; its experiences have value because they have an end. Earth's imperfections could charm him for a season, but they would be tedious throughout eternity. He was glad to live because he understood now that all men must die.

He thanked the doctor for his trouble and went down into the street, musing upon the crowning mercy which gives life its rarity value and intensifies experience. Thus dreaming, he never noticed the vehicle which, swinging rapidly round a corner, killed him instantly.

The kind doctor grieved, blaming himself for having passed mistakenly on his patient a sentence of death to overshadow all his final days. He did not know that it was the sentence of life which he had spoken.

1933

The Second Alibi

At Anderby, where the slightest domestic irregularity is censured, we still measure a girl's success in life by her ability to evoke temptation. Millie Dawson tempted nobody. She was a great, broad-chested, loose-limbed creature with a sallow skin, who had lived for nearly forty years without having derived any other distinction from her sex than the duty of keeping house for an invalid father, instead of keeping sheep for an outlying farmer.

She did not mind so much being plain, and having no sweetheart. It was the isolation of her irreproachable virginity that daunted her, the whispered confidences checked at her approach, the laughing quartettes which she never joined. Her complete respectability afforded her neighbours neither interest nor scandal, and her inefficiency deprived her of their respect.

She stood, slightly withdrawn from the crowd, her clumsy shoes shuffling on the rank, trampled grass. Feast Day, the annual festivity of Anderby, was drawing to its twilit close. Beyond the field, in a glare of orange naphtha light and glittering booths, the swing-boats tossed between black, seething earth and colourless sky, maddening the close-locked lovers with their breathless rhythm.

Here, too, in the sports field, the girls leaned beside the barrier, chaffing their sweethearts. Millie, standing alone, unnoticed, heard their jesting cries. Alone, she watched the athletes in silence, especially Joe West, the wagoner at Ridley's, he who had done time for poaching five years ago, and round whose brown head circled the halo of malefaction and of penitence. He leapt the hurdles; his fine body, slender and strong as a flying fawn, flashed past her

32

in the dim green light, and she, who had not meant to cry on Anderby's gayest day, felt the hot tears flow over from her eyes and drip on to her purple cotton blouse.

As she turned from the field, the thought of her neglected solitude, noticed, and perhaps pitied by more fortunate girls, utterly defeated her. She trudged, now sobbing unashamedly, up the two miles that led from the village to her father's cottage, when suddenly she saw a figure, familiar in its careless grace, vault lightly over a gate in the hedge, and vanish silently into the mist-grey field.

Her misery dulled her wonder, but when she found the ochre yellow squares of lamplit blind blocking the cottage window, she dared not face her father's restless questioning, nor his rough compassion for her tear-stained cheeks. She crouched among the gooseberry bushes, and wept until damp and cold and the pale dawning sky drove her to bed. In the cottage her father called her to bring him a drink; but she did not hear him. Next morning he looked at her swollen eyes with new curiosity, but did not ask what had delayed her.

Her rare brief holiday ended, she was confined as usual to the cottage, but still news came to her, surprising news, most welcome to her father who, having lived a virtuous life till crippled by rheumatism, now found his sole consolation in learning of the lapses from virtue of his neighbours.

First, the butcher's boy, calling on his mid-week round, told them that Bob Emmott, the under-keeper, had been shot by a poacher in Edenthorpe Woods on Feast Day night. On Thursday came the gossip concerning Joe West's guilt.

'What ah say is, once a poacher, allus a poacher. An' why did 'e leave sports before obstacle race when every one knew 'e put naame down for it, unless 'e'd gone on business of 'is own, like? Not but what 'e's bin a decent lad sin' Ridley took 'im on, ah will say. A bad job, all on it.'

Then Millie, rolling pastry heavily with red clumsy hands on the wooden pin, remembered how her tears had suddenly been checked by the light grace of a man who vaulted over the low gate to the woods. Her mind worked slowly, feeding over and over on a single thought. When she arranged the crumpled blankets of her father's bed, instead of their hot, human smell, she felt the cool night wind upon her face. When she shifted his knotted body, she saw instead the line of slender hip and thigh against the low-lying fields. Her imagination had been nurtured solely upon the more scurrilous Sunday newspapers and village gossip, and with the certainty of the ignorant she knew that when a young man steals from the sports field before his race, his objective is either love of a woman or hatred of a man, or simply sport, and its attendant danger. Accepting the third explanation, it occurred to her that the world might possibly accept the first. When news was brought her of the man's arrest, she said with stolid certainty, ''E never did it.'

But Joe was taken to Hardrascliffe police court.

On the day of the trial, Millie rode down early in the carrier's cart, and sat among the spectators in the court. Nobody was much surprised to see her, for all Anderby would have gone had it been able. They said that the evidence went hard against poor Joe, and he would surely be sent to York Assizes. Millie said nothing, but stared with wide, expressionless eyes at the prisoner, while sometimes her mind pictured that brown head bowed in gratitude. Half of the evidence she did not hear, the other half she could not understand, but when the presiding magistrate began to speak, she shuffled to her feet, and stood there breathing heavily, an uncouth, unexpected figure.

She heard a voice that was not like her own say, 'But 'e didn't do it.'

They called her to order. Somebody clutched her skirt, trying to tug her down. She only repeated woodenly, ''E didn't. Ah know 'e didn't. 'E war wi' me, you see.'

They heard her after that. They led her to a box of polished wood like a chapel pew, and told her to say incomprehensible sentences. Meek as an animal, she followed and obeyed them. One thought burned like a light through all this dimness.

They questioned her.

'Where were you when, as you say, he was with you?'

'Along back end of our lane.'

'When did you go there?'

'At end o' sports.'

'When they were quite over?'

'No. At end o' sack race.'

Somebody could answer for that. She had been seen to leave.

Had she left the field with the prisoner?

No, he joined her in a minute or two.

Where had they met?

'I' th' lane, by Ridley's gate.'

And here it was the prisoner's turn to gasp suddenly, like a man emerging from deep waters.

'By arrangement?'

She did not follow.

'Answer me, please. Had the prisoner asked you to meet him?'

'Yes,' she said, and this time the gasp came from the crowd.

'How long did you stay there together?'

'Ah dunno. Mabbe till morning.'

'Had it begun to grow light?'

'You live with your father?'

'Yes.'

'Did he notice your absence?'

'Aye.'

'You know that we could get his evidence?'

She nodded. Again came that gasp from the crowd, and now the spectators could see that Jennie Ridley, the farmer's pretty daughter, was crying brokenly. The magistrate was whispering to another man. Millie stood, mute and obstinate.

Suddenly the prisoner spoke unprompted.

''Tisn't true,' he cried. 'It's all a lie. Ah never . . .'

His solicitor silenced him, and some of the spectators thought that he was shamed, not by her nobility which saved his life, but by her ugliness which shamed his manhood. To kill a keeper on a poaching raid might be heroic, but to go with Millie Dawson was simply ludicrous.

But the magistrate, and the majority of the spectators, agreed that this young man refused to take his liberty at the price of a woman's dishonour, and honoured him for his denial.

The case was finally dismissed, and Millie found herself surrounded by incredulous, admiring neighbours.

She refused to respond to their romantic interest.

'Mind yor own business, and ah'll mind mine,' she said.

That night Joe West came to her. He found her in her muslin blouse, the kitchen newly swept, awaiting him as a bride awaits her lord.

'What d'you want me to do?' he asked her angrily, for he was all unnerved and shamed to the heart.

She held out her hands with an awkward, trembling gesture.

'Ah doan't mind, for sure, Joe,' she said. 'You did it in fair fight, ah reckon. Ah saw you lep ower Ridley's gate. Ah swear ah'll never tell.'

He swore suddenly and explosively. 'You thought I did it?'

Her wide eyes opened. 'What, didn't you, then?'

'Shot Emmott? By God, ah wish ah had. Ah was off to Jennie Ridley. 'Er father wouldn't let 'er come t' sports, because 'e thowt what I were after her, and she sent me a message to come if ah could, but ah never got there, for ah slipped by ditch back to Edenthorpe Woods an' hurt my leg an' forearm, like they found, but they wouldn't believe me when ah said ah done nowt all night, but sit and yelp i' hedge bottom because me leg hurt. And now . . .' With concentrated bitterness he looked at her broad face, her staring eyes and lank brown hair. 'Now, Jennie thinks that I were out wi' you.'

Her face never moved. She stared and stared at him, but her whole body burnt with shame at his rejection.

Then he said, realising perhaps that he had been at fault in his ingratitude, 'Ah can't tell why you said what you said, but ah'm in your hands.' Slowly she looked at her hands, coarse and red and swollen, grimed at the nails, and scarred with inefficient work. Then she looked up at him where his tall figure seemed to fill her small, cluttered kitchen. And he was in her hands. She drew a deep breath of gratification. Then she said, 'Ah'll go an' tell her, Joe. Ah'll put it right. Ah'll go to Ridley's an' ah'll tell her.' But suddenly she saw her way clearly both to his happiness and hers. 'You mun never tell. Never let on t' the others.'

He thought her mad; but all the world was mad, and Jennie crying for him in the red farmhouse. He promised her that it should be as she said.

He turned and left her, walking along the road to Ridley's farm. She stood at the cottage door, watching his eager stride as he went to his Jennie, and though the easy tears crept to her eyes, she smiled.

Down in the village a score of tongues were wagging. 'Joe and Millie, Joe and Millie.' But no one told her father of this latest gossip.

On the wedding day of Joe West and his master's daughter, Millie walked down the village street, marked by all eyes as the heroine of a queer romance. And she was happy.

1924

Machiavelli in the Sick-Room

A FORTNIGHT after I had left my sheltered and disciplined Girls' Boarding School, I found myself in the starched apron, collars, cuffs, belt, cap, and other preposterous impedimenta of a probationer nurse in a London nursing home. For a year I polished sterilisers, made beds, cleaned wash-stands, helped to bed-bath patients, handed swabs in the operating theatre, and endeavoured in sundry other less orthodox ways to earn the £18 a year 'uniform money' which was my due. For another year in the W.A.A.C. as a hostel forewoman I nursed influenza, administered number nines, rubbed sore throats, bandaged scalds and cuts, and took suspected temperatures. Since then I have performed the usual feats of home nursing demanded from any woman who has learnt to know an ear-syringe from a thermometer. And for the last nine months I have been more or less of an invalid myself.

I mention these qualifications just in case any one should think that I do not know what I am talking about when I say that the phrase 'to enjoy bad health' is not an ironic paradox; it is a practical human experience. There is no reason why one should be less happy when one is ill than when one is well. It is all a question of the right technique. And having studied that technique from both sides of the draw-sheet, so to speak, I am infinitely distressed when I see people painfully enduring nice neat little illnesses, perfectly adapted by circumstances for enjoyment, without the slightest idea of how to make the best of them. It is such waste! And, life being what it is, it seems a pity to waste any chances of enjoyment.

Of course there are certain conditions that should be

observed. It is the neglect of these which has given illness its bad name.

First of all, the disease must have good honest physical symptoms. I am sorry to blight your hopes, ladies and gentlemen; but neurasthenia won't do. Hypochondria won't do. A nervous breakdown, or whatever you choose to call it, is of no use to any one. Its disadvantages are multiple. They are both positive and negative. Positively, neurasthenia by its own nature makes its victim miserable. I never yet heard of a breakdown into happiness. It is part of the disease that one should feel as ill as possible – in fact, more so. There is sometimes a queer masochistic pleasure in an acute accountable physical pain; there is absolutely none in a pain that is not really there. And it hurts just as much. Break your legs, strain your hearts; inflame your appendixes as much as you like. But, whatever you do, if you want to enjoy your illness, keep your nerves clear.

As for the negative disadvantages of neurasthenia, they are equally distressing. Owing to the poverty of human imagination, sympathy for its sufferers is far more difficult to secure; and there is nothing in the world more disheartening than to be told, as you drag your aching limbs from a bed to which the household refuses to carry any more invalid trays, 'Why, come along, old thing. Pull yourself together. You can't expect any sympathy from *me*, you know. There's nothing really wrong with you. Remember what the doctor said. It's all nerves.' Quite. But, nerves or no nerves, it is enough, and a little too much.

For the same reason, I advise avoidance of all kindred illnesses – neuritis, shingles, sick-headaches and the like. They are usually accompanied by a nervous condition that leaves one little able to bear them; they are painful; and they are not dangerous.

Now it is an interesting, if perhaps not wholly creditable, phenomenon of psychology that the more precarious life seems, the sweeter it becomes both to ourselves and to other people. That is why the wisest principle for those choosing an illness is 'the maximum of danger with the minimum of discomfort.'

During my childhood a fashion flourished among middle-class households, encouraged doubtless by venerable associates of the Royal Academy, for a species of mural decoration known as the 'Problem Picture.' The chief problem suggested by most of these to the domestic mind, was 'Will it cover the stain on the spare bedroom wallpaper?' And indeed, many a time, after arrival at a strange house, have I glanced up from washing my hands in a monstrously heavy china basin decorated with gilt roses and magenta swans, and found myself staring at dolefully dramatic representations of 'The Fallen Idol,' 'Faithful Unto Death,' or 'The Sentence of Death.' Particularly 'The Sentence of Death.' . . . It was a favourite guest-room splasher among my relatives; and when, during my nursing home period, I heard that a distinguished Gynaecologist had served – somewhat unsuitably perhaps – as the model for the specialist passing sentence of death upon a middle-aged gentleman (surely it should have been on his wife?), I became so excited that, when pouring out water in which he was to wash his egregious fingers, I nearly scalded them to the bone out of sheer reverence.

Still, it was a pretty dismal picture, not because the incident itself was tragic so much as because it was conceived tragically. Actually, for a number of people, the experience which the middle-aged gentleman found so devastating, may be far more like a sentence of life than a sentence of death. For very few men and women over thirty have learned how to preserve their sense of ecstasy. They hardly know that life is good until they are specifically warned that it is fleeting. They hardly see the sun unless they fear to look upon it for the last time. That perhaps is why nearly all our literature of joy in physical life has been written by invalids such as Keats and D. H. Lawrence. In any case there is something intensely dramatic and stimulating in the moment when the unfamiliar specialist, in his frock-coat, hums and haws at the solemn mahogany desk, and says,

'Well, perhaps it's not so much a question of getting better, as of adjusting. If we can help you to adjust . . . Of course, I don't say it isn't possible . . . ahem, ahem . . .'

One young woman of my acquaintance was so highly stimulated by an interview in which a specialist told her – erroneously – that she was unlikely to recover from the disease afflicting her, that she went straight from his consulting-rooms to telephone to an unknown hero of her youth, inviting herself to tea. She was a shy creature, and nothing but the prospect of her imminent demise could have stirred her to such audacity. Afterwards she explained that she would have considered it a definite stain upon her courage had she let herself die without having met him. It happened that he was in; he came to the telephone; he knew her name slightly. Surprised but benevolent, he invited her to tea. They sat and talked tête-à-tête for two hours. He lived up completely to her notion of him, and she had never enjoyed herself more in her life. After that, it was a mere anti-climax to be told a week later that the first diagnosis was wrong and that she might live to a good old age. 'But the point is that if I hadn't thought I might fall dead to-morrow,' she said, 'I should never have had my tea-party.'

The hymns that warn us of 'days and moments swiftly flying' or tell us that 'brief life is here our portion,' do their best; but they can never match the authentic thrill of the specialist's voice when it singles out, not the whole human race as doomed to mortality, but the small exclusive intimate unit who is you or me. Then, and then alone, all lovely things become lovelier, since we may lose them, and all intolerable things more tolerable since we may do them for the last time.

So select, if possible, an illness severe enough to heighten the tension of existence, and to lend dignity to your tentative efforts to keep alive, remembering also that a spice of danger increases your importance in the eyes of the healthy. You cannot possibly be ill without being a nuisance to somebody, and friends and relatives are more likely to bear

41

that nuisance with generosity if moved by the prospect of losing you altogether. They will cut the toast thinner and take the skin off the hot milk more readily if feeling that next year, perhaps, you will not be there to worry them.

But with the maximum of danger must go the minimum of pain. Occasional pain is not completely undesirable. There is something almost satisfactory about a strenuous animal anguish which is short as well as sharp, and the peace which comes when it has passed is notably inimitable. But long, nagging, haunting pain, that wakes you up in the darkness night after night, pain that alienates you from the normal world of the healthy – has inadequate compensations and is to be avoided.

Now, having chosen your illness, the next thing is to accept it. Do not be resigned. That is a poor, weak, whining attitude beside the sturdy vigour of acceptance. And to worry is futile. 'I'm ill,' you say to yourself. 'I'm going to be ill for several months. That means I shan't be able to earn any money. I shan't be able to pay the instalments on the dining-room furniture. I shan't be able to meet the doctor's bill. I shan't be able to look after the children. Oh! Oh! Oh!' And if these reflections lead you to fight your illness, to chafe against it, and refuse the beef tea the doctor ordered, there's going to be trouble. You won't enjoy yourself, and your husband, father, wife, mother, friends and family won't enjoy themselves. And ten to one you'll get worse rather than better, and all the catastrophes that you foresee will come to pass.

No. The thing to tell yourself is, 'If I'm ill, I'm ill. And either I shall die or I shall get better, or I shall remain an invalid for life. If I can't earn money we must live on our capital; and if we have no capital, we must live on our relatives or the State. The dining-room furniture must go – in a plain or fancy van, as the case may be – and good riddance. What are kitchen tables for, anyway? The doctor will have to sing for his supper, and, as for the children, well, where's Aunt Lottie? Where's Cousin Mary? What are aunts and cousins for anyway? If I were dead, they'd have to manage without me.' And they would too. It is tiresome and a little humiliating to find how dispensable we all are.

So there you are – ill, and resigned to it. Wherever possible I should suggest that the next wise step is to get away from home. Go and be nursed where people are paid to look after you, and have proper off-duty times, so that you will not constantly be torn between your desires and your conscience. At home, where all attendance is gratis and amateur, you may, if you are that kind of person, lie for hours with a cold hot-water bottle like a dead fish rather than ask some one to boil a kettle. The kinder you are by nature, the more inclined to 'put up with things' and 'make do' rather than 'give trouble,' the more important it is to go away.

But if you cannot, if circumstances are such that neither hospital, nursing home nor infirmary can hold you, you must be very clever. Be grateful. Stifle the invalid's natural irritation, and forget that the arrowroot was too thick, and the mattress badly turned. Remember that at the best you are a nuisance, that every one has to pay for service somehow, and that, for all that has been said in their dispraise, fair words are current coin in a sick-room. Tell your sister that she looks pretty as well as capable in her white apron – even if she doesn't. Tell your mother that the milk-tea was delicious – even if you loathed it. The Lord loveth a cheerful lier, and gratitude is the surest bait for further favours.

Next, cultivate the vanities. Illnesses which spoil the looks are to be avoided. When they have, by negligence on your part, come upon you, by all means forget yourself and your appearance. But in most cases, a little titivation is a pleasantly painless indoor sport for invalids. One friend of mine, recovering from childbirth, too worn and exhausted to read, to knit, to talk much, filled in the intervals between sleeping, eating and feeding her baby by learning the art of manicure and making up her face. During her busy life she had never before had time to do this. She emerged from her sick-room with vivid cherry-coloured nails, bright lips to match, and the most amazing eyebrows. Opinions varied about the aesthetic effect of her experiments, but the process had amused her; it cost very little; and her husband disliked it far less than he pretended.

This vanity business not merely provides an agreeable occupation for invalids. It enhances self-respect. I do not know why one should feel more like approaching the tedium of convalescence if one's finger-nails have been enamelled coral – but so it is. The occupational side, however, is important. 'Bed is so boring,' many people say. I protest.

In many illnesses the invalid literally has not a minute to himself. There are bed-baths; there are dressings, feedings, massage, injections, wash-outs, little naps, doctors, visitors – and the day is done again. In others, there are quite long periods to be filled in somehow. Now the important thing about leisure is to remember that it is not an ordeal, but a luxury. How many hours in ordinary days dare you lie dreaming? Dreaming of what? Tastes differ, of course. Some compose laws for ideal republics; some trim non-existent hats; some create perfect lovers; others design petrol-engines. The point is, that there, open and exquisite, lies the whole world of fantasy before you, easy, accessible, and entrance free. For some invalids, reading is possible. For some, knitting. For some, woolwork, and for some conversation. Personally, I am addicted to patience (the card kind, I mean). But the important rule is to ration the day's pleasures, to save them up – always to withhold something as a special treat, to establish a kind of gambling discipline – that you won't play another game of Miss Milligan until the doctor has been, or eat another grape until after the last dose of medicine. This is not childish. It is a rule based upon long experience – on the old, hedonistic motive for asceticism.

Then there are visitors. The important rule for dealing with visitors is to impress them sufficiently with the security of your illness without appearing to complain.

What you want from them, presumably, are sympathy, flowers, grapes, magnums of champagne and magazines. What they want from you are feelings of gratified and pleasurable sociability. It has always been considered a work of mercy to visit the sick – however charming and conveniently situated the sick may be. Invalids therefore should play the game. Even if their visitors drink tea at their expense, eat the grapes Uncle Arthur sent them, pour out their troubles in too vulnerable ears, and otherwise enjoy themselves very much, the invalids must show becoming gratitude for one act of noble charity.

For, after all, illnesses would be very dull without visitors; and the nice ones give us pleasure, while the troublesome ones make us feel superior, so we have it both ways.

As for convalescence – the proper technique is delicate and difficult, but well worth while the trouble of achievement. You must steer between the Scylla of making too many demands upon your friends and the Charybdis of making too few. Remember that convalescence brings certain disadvantages. You may not bathe, nor play tennis, nor ride a motor-cycle. You will be unwise to visit Aldershot Tattoo or fly to India. You should not – though Winston Churchill once did it – stand for Parliament with an unhealed appendix wound. (He didn't get in, anyway.) But on the other hand, you can claim privileges. You can go to bed early. You can breakfast in your room. You need not travel to the seaside with the children, but can go in lordly isolation, first-class if possible, leaving some one else to cope with Bobby when he is sick – as usual – in the carriage. The sound rule here is to see that the privileges outweigh the deprivations. For every joy forbidden by the doctor, invent a harmless legitimate indulgence, even if it is only sucking bull's-eyes. Offer to perform duties which you know that your friends and relatives would never dream of allowing you to do. You will acquire a reputation for generosity with only the smallest risk of inconvenience to yourself. Do not discuss your symptoms with your family; who will by this time be bored by them; but find a nice plump landlady, a greengrocer's wife, or some other sympathetic soul to whom symptoms are a hobby, and pour out the whole tale to her enraptured ears, being prepared in return to receive even more intimate confidences about bad legs and wind. Many a tray has been carried up to the third floor back without a murmur in exchange for a good gossip about kidneys.

As for diagnoses, treatment, and the more scientific side of illness, the safest line is to choose your illness and stick to it – firmly. This is harder than the unsophisticated might imagine. Symptoms are easy. One can feel one's own pains. Temperatures can be taken. Blood pressures measured, hearts cardiographed, insides X-rayed. But diagnoses are different. Do not think that absence of all medical knowledge debars acquaintances from diagnoses or from prescription. I began to keep a list once of the illnesses from which my friends told me I was suffering, but when I had covered one foolscap page and half the side of another, I grew tired and gave it up. Friends can be divided into the pro-doctor and anti-doctor types. The former are the more numerous, the latter the more vociferous. Friends who would have you live upon one orange a day; friends who would send you to one German spa and one alone; friends who would have you given a water cure – among them all, it is not hard to lose your head. But be firm. Be polite. And above all, be calm. Remember that this is your own illness and that you have got a right to your own treatment of it. In this world, probably no régime is perfect. But better an erroneous pill than thirty different plasters. Fortunately, we can only die once.

Of course, I could suggest detailed courses of technique for special cases: how to be the most popular patient in a nursing home; how to be happy in hospital; how to convalesce calmly, and so on. But these may be worked out by intelligent invalids along the broad lines that I have already suggested. The great general rule is to choose your illness wisely, to accept it enthusiastically, and to enjoy it as heartily as your nature will permit.

1932

Domestic

This group of stories expresses Winifred Holtby's preoccupation with the role of women, particularly married women, in the transitional interwar period when domesticity was no longer the only life option open to middle-class women and when the vote had for the first time given them the responsibility of citizenship. Although she can be sympathetic in 'The Casualty List' towards the at-home wife whose heroism lies in domestic service, she is critical, in 'The Maternal Instinct', of the woman for whom motherhood has become an excuse for political indifference, and she is equally critical of the wronged woman, in the story of that name, who traps a man into marriage. For Winifred, neither motherhood nor marriage should absolve a woman from honourable behaviour or social responsibility. This is one of the beliefs that underlies the debate in the longest story in the collection, 'Episode in West Kensington', described by Vera Brittain as 'a complete incident omitted from Mandoa, Mandoa!'. It is perhaps the most interesting of the stories in what it reveals about the tensions in Winifred's life as an unmarried, exhausted, and even at times embittered reformer.

Anthropologists' May

In May, 1933, Mrs Brown, of Tooting, having completed her spring cleaning and replaced the open hearth of her drawing-room by an elegant electric radiator, rolled up her brass fire-irons in some old newspapers, put them in the lead-lined antique chest in the hall, and subsequently forgot all about their existence.

In May, 3149, Professor Ignatius Labariu, the distinguished anthropologist, was examining the relics dug up by an excavation party on the site of the vanished suburb of Tooting, in order to gather material for his monumental treatise on 'Modes and Social Codes of the British Islanders,' when he came upon the fire-irons of Mrs Brown. The newspapers were crumbling to dust, but before they completely disappeared he contrived to capture a few fragmentary lines of print by instantaneous ray photography, together with one almost uninjured portrait. These exceedingly valuable and unique remains of a byegone civilisation excited him intensely, and since the ways of anthropologists had not altered much within 2000 years, he proceeded, after careful examination, to build up from them a theory of the May customs of the British Islanders about as accurate as most anthropological reconstructions can hope to be.

MEMORANDUM ON TOOTING RELICS

1. *The Instruments*. – One pair tongs. One ladle? (Scoop? Shovel?) One brass rod with ball handle. Shapes clearly indicative of sexual significance. Probably instruments used in fertility cult during mating season – tongs suggest female,

rod male. Shovel – obscure meaning – possibly associated with food preparation in Love Feast. For Love Feast compare Eskimo ceremonial feasts – Phalgun festival in Northern India. Possible uses: (*a*) Symbols of fertility buried by unmarried women? Parents with unmarried daughters? At mating season to ensure happy union. (*b*) Instruments of domestic torture to penalise unsuccessful quest of husband.

(*Secretary's Note.* – So far as I can gather, torture was discontinued in British Isles after Seventeenth Century.)

2. *The Papers.* – Fragmentary condition, but date of all clearly May. Month of May obviously the mating season. Supports theory of instruments. These papers probably part of the curious system whereby the islanders printed daily the story of those events, real or imagined, which they thought to be of most importance in their folk life – interesting example of the deliberate myth.

3. *The Season.* – The importance of the month of May in English life shown by allusions to The Season – 'Opening of the Season,' etc. The Season obviously indicates the spring mating season – apparently celebrated by pilgrimage to London. Some confusion of evidence here. One paper says, 'Now of course every one is back in London,' but on same date gives account of 'Liberal Women's Conference at Scarborough.' If there were still sufficient inhabitants to form a big meeting left in Scarborough, how could every one be in London?

(*Secretary's Note.* – Scarborough may refer to part of London as well as to town on north-east coast.

Cf. – Lincoln and Lincoln Inn, Scarborough may mean Scarborough Inn abbreviated.)

Interesting that the countryside should be denuded in the corn-sowing season.

4. *Liberal Women.* – Interesting that these should hold a conference at this time. Liberal = generous. Possible reference to sexual characteristics. Compare with debutante. Most probable that those women who are completely

satisfied in sex-life hold separate meeting as part of fertility-cult ritual.

5. *May Day*. – Opening of the season celebrated by processions to Hyde Park. Young men and children in carts waving red flags accompanied by girls with scarlet handkerchiefs on head. Very full account in one paper – procession accompanied by singing. Significant line of ceremonial hymn preserved 'The people's flag is painted red.' (Red a colour of profound sexual significance. *Cf.* Contemporary proverb, 'A Red Rag to a Bull.' 'Bull,' obvious allusion to John Bull, islanders' masculine tribal deity.) Processions apt to become disorderly. *Cf.* – Greek Dionysiac ceremonies.

Demonstrations against 'Black Shirts' or 'Nazis.'

'Nazi' – derivation from Niger = Black?

6. *Black Shirts*. – Obvious antipathy expressed by crowds to men wearing black shirts. Especially noticeable among those wearing red. Black clearly the symbol for the opposite of red. Therefore, probably indicates coldness or perversity. Photograph of undersized youth in black shirt confirms this thesis.

7. *Debutantes*. – Another class of young women, possibly those who failed to secure husbands in the last mating season – or the sickly ones? Evidence of this strengthened by one photograph of a young woman with a strained and suffering expression – a band across her forehead, a veil and long robe hiding her figure – feathers on head-dress. She is clearly suffering from some disease of the head, skin and eyesight – photograph called 'One of the most interesting debutantes.' Also some reference to her marriage after Presentation.

8. *Presentation*. – Early in the month the Debutantes were apparently Presented to the King and Queen – possible survival of 'Touching for the King's Evil' – superstition that royalty had healing powers – probably believed by the mothers of these girls that the touch of a royal hand would bring them success in love. Elaborate clothing – long train – probably to cover the diseased or unattractive body.

9. *Feathers*. – All debutantes wore feathers on their heads. Possible explanation: (*a*) If cock – symbol of masculine power – relates to mating ceremony. (*b*) Hygienic explanation? To prevent the King or Queen from having to touch possibly infectious invalids? (*c*) Obscure totem reference. *Cf*. Phrase mentioned 'Getting the bird.'

10. *Premier*. – Continual allusions to Premier proves conclusively that the Premier was, as we believed before, a politico-religious figure – priest – ruler – who led the ailing debutantes to the King and Queen in the Presentation Ceremony. Symbol of male superiority. Leader of fertility cult? Account of 'Attack on Premier in Lords' suggests that the young males resent his domination. Lords = a famous cricketing ground frequented by young male aristocrats.

11. *Race-meetings*. – Continual references to these. See also 'summer racing' – 'flat racing.' Considering the biological importance of the race, and the islanders' concern for racial development, these would appear to be large open-air meetings for procreative purposes. Possibly concerned with the breeding of the proletariat. (See reference to 'The Derby' as 'The People's Race.') Compared with aristocratic mating of Debutantes.

12. *Crazy Night at the Palladium*. – It is difficult from the fragmentary references to this to gather what exactly happens in this ceremony. But apparently royalty was present. Obviously culmination of season's effort. Probably survival of Teutonic 'Walpurgis Night' – an organised orgy.

13. June naturally follows as 'The Month of Marriages.'

1930

Why Herbert Killed His Mother

ONCE upon a time there was a Model Mother who had a Prize Baby. Nobody had ever had such a Baby before. He was a Son, of course. All prize babies are masculine, for should there be a flaw in their gender this might deprive them of at least twenty-five per cent. of the marks merited by their prize-worthiness.

The Mother's name was Mrs Wilkins, and she had a husband called Mr Wilkins; but he did not count much. It is true that he was the Baby's father, and on the night after the child was born he stood Drinks All Round at the Club; though he was careful to see that there were only two other members in the Bar at the time he suggested it, because although one must be a Good Father and celebrate properly, family responsibilities make a man remember his bank balance. Mr Wilkins remembered his very often, particularly when Mrs Wilkins bought a copy of *Vogue*, or remarked that the Simpsons, who lived next door but one, had changed their Austin Seven for a Bentley. The Wilkinses had not even an old Ford; but then the buses passed the end of their road, and before the Prize Baby arrived, Mrs Wilkins went to the Stores and ordered a very fine pram.

Mrs Wilkins had determined to be a Real Old-Fashioned Mother. She had no use for these Modern Women who Drink Cocktails, Smoke Cigarettes, and dash about in cars at all hours with men who are not their husbands. She believed in the true ideal of Real Womanliness, Feminine Charm, and the Maternal Instinct. She won a ten-shilling prize once from a daily paper, with a circulation of nearly two million, for saying so, very prettily, on a postcard.

Before the Baby came she sat with her feet up every afternoon sewing little garments. She made long clothes with twenty tucks round the hem of each robe, and embroidered flannels, fifty inches from hem to shoulder tape, and fluffy bonnets, and teeny-weeny little net veils; she draped a bassinet with white muslin and blue ribbons, and she thought a great deal about violets, forget-me-nots and summer seas in order that her baby might have blue eyes. When Mrs Burton from 'The Acacias' told her that long clothes were unhygienic, and that drapery on the bassinet held the dust, and that heredity had far more to do with blue eyes than thoughts about forget-me-nots, she shook her head charmingly, and said: 'Ah, well. You *clever* women know so much. I can only go by what my darling mother told me.' Mrs Burton said: 'On the contrary. You have a lot of other authorities to go by nowadays,' and she produced three pamphlets, a book on Infant Psychology, and a programme of lectures on 'Health, Happiness and Hygiene in the Nursery.' But Mrs Wilkins sighed, and said: 'My poor little brain won't take in all that stuff. I have only my Mother Love to guide me.' And she dropped a pearly tear on to a flannel binder.

Mrs Burton went home and told Mr Burton that Mrs Wilkins was hopeless, and that her baby would undoubtedly suffer from adenoids, curvature of the spine, flat feet, halitosis, bow legs, indigestion and the Oedipus Complex. Mr Burton said, 'Quite, quite.' And every one was pleased.

The only dissentient was the Wilkins baby, who was born without any defect whatsoever. He was a splendid boy, and his more-than-proud parents had him christened Herbert James Rodney Stephen Christopher, which names they both agreed went very well with Wilkins. He wore for the ceremony two binders, four flannels, an embroidered robe with seventeen hand-made tucks, a woolly coat, two shawls, and all other necessary and unnecessary garments, and when he stared into the Rector's face, and screamed lustily, his aunts said: 'That means he'll be musical, bless him.' But his mother thought: 'What a strong will he has! And what sympathy there is between us! Perhaps he knows already what I think about the Rector.'

As long as the monthly nurse was there, Mrs Wilkins and Herbert got along very nicely on Mother Love; but directly she left trouble began.

'My baby,' Mrs Wilkins had said, 'shall never be allowed to lie awake and cry like Mrs Burton's poor little wretch. Babies need cuddling.' So whenever Herbert cried at first, she cuddled him. She cuddled him in the early morning when he woke up Mr Wilkins and wanted his six o'clock bottle at four. She cuddled him at half-past six and half-past seven and eight. She cuddled him half-hourly for three days and then she smacked him. It was a terrible thing to do, but she did it. She fed him when he seemed hungry, and showed him to all the neighbours who called, and kept him indoors when it rained, which it did every day, and nursed him while she had her own meals, and when she didn't gave him Nestlés. And still he flourished.

But what with the crying and the washing that hung in the garden, the neighbours began to complain, and Mrs Burton said: 'Of course, you're killing that child.'

Mrs Wilkins knew that the Maternal Instinct was the safest guide in the world; but when her husband showed her an advertisement in the evening paper which began: 'Mother, does your child cry?' she read it. She learned there that babies cry because their food does not agree with them. 'What-not's Natural Digestive Infants' Milk solves the Mother's problem.' Mrs Wilkins thought that no stone should be left unturned and bought a specimen tin of What-not's Natural Digestive Infants' Milk, and gave it to Herbert. Herbert flourished. He grew larger and rounder and pinker, and more dimpled than ever. But still he cried.

So Mrs Wilkins read another advertisement in the evening paper. And there she learned that when Babies cry it is because they are not warm enough, and that all good mothers should buy Flopsy's Fleecy Pram Covers.

So, being a good mother, she bought a Flopsy's Fleecy Pram Cover and wrapped Herbert in it. And still Herbert flourished. And still he cried.

So she continued to read the evening papers, for by this time both she and Mr Wilkins were nearly distracted, and one of the neighbours threatened to complain to the landlord, and Mrs Simpson kept her loud speaker going all night and day to drown the noise, she said. And now Mrs Wilkins learned that the reason her baby cried was because his Elimination was inadequate so she bought him a bottle of Hebe's Nectar for the Difficult Child, and gave him a teaspoonful every morning. But still he cried.

Then the spring came, and the sun shone, and the bulbs in the garden of Number Seven were finer than they had ever been before, and Mrs Wilkins put Herbert out in the garden in his pram, and he stopped crying.

She was such a nice woman and such a proud mother that she wrote at once to the proprietors of What-not's Natural Digestive Infants' Milk, and Flopsy's Fleecy Pram Covers, and Hebe's Nectar for the Difficult Child, and told them that she had bought their things for Herbert and that he had stopped crying.

Two days later a sweet young woman came to the Wilkins' house, and said that What-not's Limited had sent her to see Herbert, and what a fine Baby he was, and how healthy, and could she take a photograph? And Mrs Wilkins was very pleased, and thought: 'Well, Herbert is the most beautiful Baby in the world, and won't this be a sell for Mrs Burton,' and was only too delighted. So the young woman photographed Herbert in his best embroidered robe drinking Natural Digestive Infants' Milk from a bottle, and went away.

The next day a kind old man came from Flopsy's Fleecy Pram Covers Limited, and photographed Herbert lying under a Fleecy Pram Cover. It was a hot afternoon and a butterfly came and settled on the pram; but the kind old man said that this was charming.

The next day a scientific-looking young man with horn-rimmed spectacles came from Hebe's Nectar Limited and photographed Herbert lying on a fur rug wearing nothing at all. And when Mr Wilkins read his Sunday paper, there he saw his very own baby, with large black capitals printed above him, saying: 'My Child is now no longer Difficult, declares Mrs Wilkins, of Number 9, The Grove, S.W.10.'

Mrs Burton saw it too, and said to Mr Burton: 'No wonder, when at last they've taken a few stones of wool off the poor little wretch.'

But Mr and Mrs Wilkins saw it differently. They took Herbert to a Court Photographer and had him taken dressed and undressed, with one parent, with both parents, standing up and sitting down; and always he was the most beautiful baby that the Wilkinses had ever seen.

One day they saw an announcement in a great Sunday paper of a £10,000 prize for the loveliest baby in the world. 'Well, dear, this will be nice,' said Mrs Wilkins. 'We shall be able to buy a saloon car now.' Because, of course, she knew that Herbert would win the prize.

And so he did. He was photographed in eighteen different poses for the first heat; then he was taken for a personal inspection in private for the second heat; then he was publicly exhibited at the Crystal Palace for the semi-finals, and for the Final Judgment he was set in a pale-blue bassinet and examined by three doctors, two nurses, a Child Psychologist, a film star, and Mr Cecil Beaton. After that he was declared the Most Beautiful Baby in Britain.

That was only the beginning. Baby Britain had still to face Baby France, Baby Spain, Baby Italy, and Baby America. Signor Mussolini sent a special message to Baby Italy, which the other national competitors thought unfair. The Free State insisted upon sending twins, which were disqualified. The French President cabled inviting the entire contest to be removed to Paris, and the Germans declared that the girl known as Baby Poland, having been born in the Polish Corridor, was really an East Prussian and should be registered as such.

But it did not matter. These international complications made no difference to Herbert. Triumphantly he overcame all his competitors, and was crowned as World Baby on the eve of his first birthday.

Then, indeed, began a spectacular period for Mr and Mrs Wilkins. Mrs Wilkins gave interviews to the Press on 'The Power of Mother Love,' 'The Sweetest Thing in the World,' and 'How I Run My Nursery.' Mr Wilkins wrote some fine manly articles on 'Fatherhood Faces Facts,' and 'A Man's Son' – or, rather, they were written for him by a bright young woman until Mrs Wilkins decided that she should be present at the collaborations.

Then a firm of publishers suggested to Mr Wilkins that he should write a Christmas book called *Herbert's Father*, all about what tender feelings fathers had, and what white, pure thoughts ran through their heads when they looked upon the sleeping faces of their sons, and about how strange and wonderful it was to watch little images of themselves growing daily in beauty, and how gloriously unspotted and magical were the fairy-like actions of little children. Mr Wilkins thought that this was a good idea if some one would write the book for him, and if the advance royalties were not less than £3000 on the date of publication; but he would have to ask Mrs Wilkins. Mrs Wilkins was a trifle hurt. Why *Herbert's Father*? What right had Paternity to override Maternity? The publisher pointed out the success of Mr A. A. Milne's *Christopher Robin*, and Mr Lewis Hind's *Julius Caesar*, and of Mr A. S. M. Hutchinson's *Son Simon*, to say nothing of Sir James Barrie's *Little White Bird*. 'But none of these children was my Herbert,' declared Mrs Wilkins – which, indeed, was undeniable. So the contract was finally signed for *The Book of Herbert*, by His Parents.

It was a success. Success? It was a Triumph, a Wow, a Scream, an Explosion. There was nothing like it. It was The Christmas Gift. It went into the third hundredth thousand before December 3. It was serialised simultaneously in the *Evening Standard*, *Home Chat*, and *The Nursery World*.

Mr Baldwin referred to it at a Guildhall Banquet. The Prince used a joke from it in a Broadcast Speech on England and the Empire. The Book Society failed to recommend it, but every bookstall in the United Kingdom organised a display stand in its honour, with photographs of Herbert and copies signed with a blot 'Herbert, His Mark' exquisitely arranged.

The Herbert Boom continued. Small soap Herberts (undressed for the bath) were manufactured and sold for use in delighted nurseries. Royalty graciously accepted an ivory Herbert, designed as a paper-weight, from the loyal sculptor. A Herbert Day was instituted in order to raise money for the Children's Hospitals of England, and thirty-seven different types of Herbert Calendars, Christmas Cards, and Penwipers were offered for sale – and sold.

Mrs Wilkins felt herself justified in her faith. This, she said, was what mother love could do. Mr Wilkins demanded 10 per cent. royalties on every Herbert article sold. And they all bought a country house near Brighton, a Bentley car, six new frocks for Mrs Wilkins, and an electric refrigerator, and lived happily ever after until Herbert grew up.

But Herbert grew up.

When he was four he wore curls and a Lord Fauntleroy suit and posed for photographers. When he was fourteen he wore jerseys and black finger-nails and collected beetles. When he left one of England's Great Public Schools he wore plus-fours and pimples and rode a motor-bicycle and changed his tie three times in half an hour before he called on the young lady at the tobacconist's round the corner. He knew what a Fella does, by jove, and he knew what a Fella doesn't. His main interests in life were etiquette, Edgar Wallace, and the desire to live down his past. For on going to a preparatory school he had carefully insisted that his name was James. His father, who knew that boys will be boys, supported him, and as he grew to maturity, few guessed that young James Wilkins, whose beauty was certainly not discernible to the naked eye, was Herbert, the Loveliest Baby in the World. Only Mrs Wilkins, in a locked spare bedroom, cherished a museum of the Herbert photographs, trophies, first editions, soap images, ivory statuettes, silver cups, and Christmas cards. The Herbert vogue had faded, as almost all vogues do, until not even a gag about Herbert on the music hall stage raised a feeble smile.

But Mrs Wilkins found the position hard to bear. It is true that the fortunes of the family were soundly laid, that Mr Wilkins had invested the profits of his son's juvenile triumphs in Trustee Stock, and that no household in South Kensington was more respected. But Mrs Wilkins had tasted the sweet nectar of publicity and she thirsted for another drink.

It happened that one day, when (Herbert) James was twenty-three, he brought home the exciting news that he had become engaged to Selena Courtney, the daughter of Old Man Courtney, whose office in the city Herbert adorned for about six hours daily.

Nothing could have been more fortunate. Mr Wilkins was delighted, for Courtney, of Courtney, Gilbert and Co., was worth nearly half a million. Herbert was delighted, for he was enjoying the full flavour of Young Love and Satisfied Snobbery combined, which is, as every one knows, the perfect fulfilment of a True Man's dreams. The Courtneys were delighted, because they thought young Wilkins a very decent young man, with none of this damned nonsense about him. And Mrs Wilkins – well, her feelings were mixed. It was she, after all, who had produced this marvel, and nobody seemed to remember her part in the production, nor to consider the product specially marvellous. Besides, she was a little jealous, as model mothers are allowed to be, of her prospective daughter-in-law.

The engagement was announced in *The Times* – the reporters came, rather bored, to the Kensington home of Mrs Wilkins. She was asked to supply any details about her son's career. 'Any adventures? Any accidents? Has he ever won any prizes?' asked a reporter.

This was too much. 'Come here!' said Mrs Wilkins; and she led the reporters up to the locked spare bedroom.

What happened there was soon known to the public. When (Herbert) James, two evenings later, left the office on his way to his future father-in-law's house in Belgrave Square, hoping to take his fiancée after dinner to a dance given by Lady Soxlet, he was confronted by placards announcing 'The Perfect Baby to Wed.' Taking no notice he went on to the Tube Station; but there he saw yet further placards. 'The World's Loveliest Baby now a Man,' and 'Little Herbert Engaged.'

Still hardly conscious of the doom awaiting him, he bought an evening paper, and there he saw in black letters across the front page: 'Herbert's Identity at last Discovered,' and underneath the fatal words: 'The young City man, Mr James Wilkins, whose engagement to Miss Selena Courtney, of 299 Belgrave Square, was announced two days ago, has been revealed by his mother, Mrs Wilkins, to be Herbert, the Wonder Baby.' There followed descriptions of the Perfect Childhood, stories taken from the Herbert Legend; rapid advertisements rushed out by What-Not's Natural Digestive Infants' Milk, Flopsy's Fleecy Pram Covers, and Hebe's Nectar for the Difficult Child, illustrated by photographs of the Infant Herbert. The publishers of the *Book of Herbert* announced a new edition, and a famous Daily Paper, whose circulation was guaranteed to be over 2,000,000, declared its intention of publishing a series of articles called 'My Herbert is a Man, by Herbert's Mother.'

Herbert did not proceed to Belgrave Square. He went to Kensington. With his own latch-key he opened the door and went up to his mother's boudoir. He found her laughing and crying with joy over the evening paper. She looked up and saw her son.

'Oh, darling,' she said. 'I thought you were taking Selena to a dance.'

'There is no Selena,' declared Herbert grimly. 'There is no dance. There is only you and me.'

He should, doubtless, have said: 'You and I,' but among the things a Fella does, correct grammar is not necessarily included.

'Oh, Herbert,' cried Mrs Wilkins, with ecstatic joy. 'My mother instinct was right. Mother always knows, darling. You have come back to me.'

'I have,' said Herbert.

And he strangled her with a rope of twisted newspapers.

The judge declared it justifiable homicide, and Herbert changed his name to William Brown and went to plant tea or rubber or something in the Malay States, where Selena joined him two years later – and Mr Wilkins lived to a ripe old age at the Brighton house and looked after his dividends, and every one was really very happy after all.

1931

The Maternal Instinct

'BUT, of course, he's lovely, Cynthia,' Fanny said.

Cynthia looked across her son's drowsy head at her old school friend and smiled.

Perhaps it was the smile that infuriated Fanny; but Cynthia had not meant to be superior. She was only thinking of the firelit nursery and the shadows darkening the green garden beyond the windows; of Robin's sweet confident weight upon her knee, and her husband's income, and the security, the comfort, the steadying sense of responsibility, and of life fulfilling itself.

And here was Fanny, come after ten years, to witness her apotheosis. Dear, odd Fanny, who had always admired her so absurdly. In the days when Cynthia too was poor and irresponsible they used to go about together, to cinemas and galleries, and parties in draughty studios, whenever Cynthia had a free night from the Art School, and Fanny actually had no political meeting which she felt she ought to attend. And now here they were together again, and Cynthia was grown up and a wife and mother, while Fanny was still the same rootless, excitable, immature young woman. All women, Cynthia decided, really were children until they had children of their own.

So she looked across at Fanny and she smiled.

'Anthony must have done pretty well,' Fanny remarked clumsily.

'Oh, yes. I suppose he has. Though, of course, what with taxes and things, it doesn't come to much. And there's his old father to keep. He's always a marvellously good son.' Four thousand a year really was not such a tremendous lot. Not with super-tax.

Cynthia was rightly proud of her husband. When he had been demobilised his sole assets were a small gratuity, two decorations, a scar across his face, a dependent invalid father, a young wife, and a knowledge of flying. From these he had made all this. His courage and enterprise gave Cynthia a poor opinion of those ex-soldiers who were always complaining that they had never found a proper job since the war – like that young man who was to have married Fanny. Anthony had never found a job; he had invented one.

'You went to South America, didn't you?' Fanny asked.

'Yes,' said Cynthia, bored. She had told the story so often. 'After the war Anthony hadn't a bean, but he took an old plane out to Buenos Ayres as agent for the manufacturers and flew it all over the continent, booking orders. He used to visit little tin-pot states, and put the wind up them saying how many planes their rivals had bought, and how awkward it would be for them if they started bombing. They fell for it like anything. It was fun at first, but a bit boring afterwards, and we were awfully glad to come home and settle down. Weren't we, my blessing?' She buried her face in the baby's lovely neck, that smelled of buns and talcum powder, and warm flannel.

'Do you mean military aircraft?' asked Fanny harshly.

'Any old craft we could sell. Fanny, as nurse is out, will you help me to bath him? Every woman ought to know about babies, says I.'

'I suppose you know about this Chaco business?'

'This what?'

'This fighting between Bolivia and Paraguay.'

'Not I. I don't read the papers. I've got something better to do, haven't I, my precious? I leave all that to Tony – except a glance at the gossip paragraphs. Really, when you have a child—'

'This ought to interest you.' Fanny had flushed bright red and was licking her dry lips. Funny, unmarried women were, Cynthia thought. Was she trying to change the conversation because she was shy at seeing Robin undressed? Full of inhibitions, probably, poor thing.

'Bolivia and Paraguay – I expect you know them – have been fighting intermittently in the Chaco district for about four years now. There's no real reason why they should go on. They accepted arbitration once. They're both wildly in debt. But they go on buying armaments. The other day in parliament some one asked the President of the Board of Trade about our own exports, and it seems that we've sent out in the past twelve months over five million cartridges to Paraguay, and over a hundred machine guns, some tanks, and ammunition of all sorts to Bolivia. It's paying somebody to keep them at it.'

'I dare say. Do you mind passing me that basket? Now, look at him, Fanny!'

'Cynthia, the statement didn't mention aeroplanes, but then it only went back a year. They have got aeroplanes.'

'Now for the hot water. Just a second, Fanny. Somebody ought to invent a self-filling bath for babies. I think babies are really shamefully neglected by inventors.'

As Fanny made no gesture of help, Cynthia thrust Robin into her arms and fetched the water herself.

'Last August,' persisted Fanny, 'the Paraguayan Minister in Paris protested that Bolivian planes were bombarding not just forts in the Chaco but Mennonite colonies. Villages, you know, with defenceless civilians – old people and babies.'

'Really?' Cynthia was inspecting a tiny rough patch behind Robin's ear.

'Do you remember that air-raid during the war, Cynthia? When we saw the house just after the roof had fallen in on three children and that wretched mother, who'd just run down the path to bring the dog in, had to be held back by neighbours because she struggled to go in to them, while the walls were still crumbling in?'

'Don't be so ghoulish. It's horried to gloat over horrors in front of Robin.'

'I suppose that these women in the Chaco love their children. And the Minister said that hospitals had been raided too, five times. Cynthia, how can you bear it? Those aeroplanes may be the very ones your husband induced them to buy by rousing suspicions against their neighbours. Those people are only peasants . . . They wouldn't want to organise air-raids unless some one taught them to do it . . . How can you bear it for your lovely Robin to be nursed on blood? That's what it is. All this' – she waved her hand round the nursery with a wild gesture – 'paid for by that.'

'Well, really, Fanny. I do think you might try to control yourself a little. What morbid, disgusting nonsense. "Nursed on blood" indeed! If you knew these villages you'd see they were only savages. Anthony's one of the few people who really have done well for the world. He's encouraged trade and given employment and done pioneer service. Robin will grow up to be very proud of him.'

But Cynthia did not lose her temper. She made allowances. Some frustrated spinsters really were not fit, she knew, for civilised society. She must find Fanny a nice husband. She drew the bath nearer towards her and took Robin from Fanny's arms and sat for a moment, her son upon her knee, wrapped in the comforting consciousness of love and virtue, a serene and noble figure of maternal dignity.

1933

The Wronged Woman

OH, no. I don't hate her. I'm not vindictive. No one could say that about me. Though when I think of the wrong she did me and how easily I could get my own back, I'm sometimes amazed at my own generosity. It's all a matter of breeding, I suppose. Noblesse oblige. And then I've always said that a woman should stand by a woman, though of course when it comes to a matter of life and death – or love, though for us that's pretty much the same thing, isn't it? – you can't get away from the fact that each of us has to fight for our own hand.

It was seeing her picture in the *Tatler* that brought it all back to me. You see, since I pointed out to Dick how much more money he could make in private practice, and he gave up his hospital job and we came to settle down in Harrogate like an old married couple, I'd hardly given a thought to Rachel Tyson. Of course, she always wanted Dick to go on specialising and so on; but a wife has the right to expect her husband to keep her decently, hasn't she? And I like Harrogate, although it's cold. There's good bridge and golf and generally a few nice people stopping in the hotels.

'Dr Rachel Tyson,' the paper said, 'the brilliant young medical woman whose work in India has succeeded in almost halving the infant mortality rate.' Young, they call her. She must be well over forty. Of course that's an old photograph, I expect, though with permanent waving and make-up you never can tell really in these days, can you? As for infant mortality, well, I could say something about that. Of course I never actually knew what happened. But I do wonder what all these people who think her so wonderful to-day would say if they knew as much as I know.

The *Tatler*, too. Almost as if she were a débutante or an actress. I suppose she knew some one on the paper who put it in for her. Now, that's the sort of thing I never could do. It may be old-fashioned of me, but I hate women who advertise themselves all over the Press, and what is more, I know that men don't really like it either. These women explorers and M.P.s and so on may think a great deal of themselves, and some of them may even find a man to marry them, but that doesn't alter the fact that no man who is a man likes a woman to look at him as Rachel Tyson used to look – as though he were a medical student she was examining, and she hadn't quite decided whether she'd let him scrape through.

Of course, we were always very carefully brought up. That's another difference, I suppose. Father was in the Indian Army, and Phil and I lived with an aunt until we were old enough to go to a school at Bournemouth because of the sea air. Mother died while we were there and I don't remember much about her, except that once when she was going back East she said, 'Now don't forget that Father's a soldier, darlings, and I want you always to remember to behave like English gentlewomen, and be worthy of him.'

Of course, Rachel's people were hopelessly lower-middle-class, from the North country somewhere. Why, she even had a sort of accent when I first met her. Well, more a sort of roughness than an accent – a blur on her vowels. But you can always tell an uncultured voice, can't you?

By the time Phil and I came home and came out, father had retired, and married again a woman much younger than himself. We all lived together in a jolly little house near Ascot, but she never got on with us. I suppose she was jealous. I've never been able to escape for long from the jealousy of women. We're not really sisters under our skins, you know; we're rivals.

I've always had bad luck, because just when it was my turn to come out, father lost most of his savings in a

Mexican mine or something. I've never really understood business, of course. I don't think women can, do you? Although once when I told Dick that all that sort of thing made my brain reel, and that you oughtn't to expect a woman to understand stocks and shares and things, he gave me such a look, as though he was remembering how good at business the Tyson girl was supposed to be. But, of course, I meant normal women.

It wasn't much fun after that. We had to move into a smaller house, and although we played a lot of golf, and sometimes went up to town for a matinée, it's miserable being short of money, isn't it? I used sometimes to think I'd rather not go to dances at all than go in gloves cleaned with benzine and my last season's frock dyed blue. You don't have the same chance either, if you're poor. Of course, Phil married Chris Wiggisthorne, who was something in the City and quite well off, but he's years older than she is, and even then was a bit bald, without much figure. Still, beggars can't be choosers. And our stepmother obviously wanted us out of the way.

It wasn't that I didn't get on with men. I did. I've always been what you might call a man's woman. I'm a good dancer, and I've never been bad-looking, and I'm sure I know how to wear my clothes as well as any one. I never was at a loss for admiration. But somehow, if you're known to be poor, and you've been out more than a year or two, men are nice to you, but they just don't propose. They always seemed to be on the edge of it, and then just didn't. It went on and on.

Sometimes when I look back on that ten years, I wonder how I stood it. Of course, Phil's marriage helped a lot because she always was quite decent to me, and sometimes gave me clothes, and she could chaperon me to dances and all that. I was with her when I met Dick.

It was at Reggie Dawson's coming-of-age dance in June, 1914. I hadn't wanted to go, because I hadn't a frock – only my old bridesmaid's dress done up with tulle. But when I showed it to Phil, and how stupid it looked with a loose skirt when every one else was wearing them tight and draped, she lent me a new black one of hers – oldish-looking, but very chic and sophisticated. It suited me frightfully well.

It was a glorious night, though coolish, as June nights in England often are, and the Dawsons' garden was heavenly, sloping down to the river, all moonlight and roses. I couldn't help thinking of Myrtil Dawson, with that lovely house and all that money behind her. Life's so easy for some girls, isn't it? And so hard for others.

The Dawsons' dance seemed at first as if it was going to be like dozens of other dances. I knew a fair number of people, and there were always two or three men who asked me to dance, but each year somehow they seemed to get older and more married and ineligible, while I felt as young as ever. They didn't crowd round waiting for my programme in the way they used to do, and the really wretched thing at the Dawsons' was that no one asked me for the supper dance. Of course it seems silly in these days, but it mattered frightfully then. You could manage to camouflage somehow if you hadn't a partner for other dances, but the supper dance – no. It wasn't any use to slink away into the cloakroom either, pretending to mend a torn frill, because some one always asked questions. It was the questions that were so awful in those days, and the way the other girls looked at you, bright and patronising.

I wanted to run right away and cry and cry and cry, because I was twenty-eight and had been out ten years, and everything was so hopeless. But it wasn't any good, and I had the first two or three dances booked, so there I was, waltzing and two-stepping and trying to seem gay, so that my partners would ask me for another dance.

I'd just been waltzing with old Colonel Salter, who looks like a trout and gets as moist as one after a dance or two, when Mrs Dawson came up to me, all smiles and syrup, though cattish to the bone inside, and said, 'Oh, Daisy, I do want you to be sweet and take pity on poor Dr Forsyth. He was delayed at a case and has only just got here. I know you're always so much in demand, but could you spare him *one* dance?' And I looked at my programme and pretended to be considering it, though of course I was really almost fainting with relief, and said, 'Well, perhaps I might spare him an extra,' and she said, 'Oh, how very good of you,' with that sort of spiteful look that seems to say, 'I know you're a liar, but I'm too well bred to say so.' And off she went to find her Dr Forsyth.

I was standing by the wall when she came back with him, and I can remember to this day just how he looked. Threading his way among the dancers who were scattering to their seats, taller, almost, than any of them, with that dreamy, absent, yet concentrated look, as though he were composing poetry, though probably he was thinking about bones and appendixes and all sorts of unpleasant things.

I don't remember quite what happened about the introduction, but I do remember that I didn't want him to get hold of my programme, as I had meant to say I might be able to spare him one dance or – perhaps two. But he had a way of just taking what he wanted, and before I knew what had happened he had got it, and was writing his name against all the dances that weren't already booked. I hadn't had such a thing happen to me for years. It quite took my breath away. It was only when we began to fox-trot together that I realised what a rotten dancer he was. I was quite relieved when he broke off suddenly and said, 'Let's get out of here,' and almost dragged me into the garden.

I thought he was the queerest boy I'd ever met – rude, you know, and yet you couldn't take offence at it. A pukkah sahib, but with something wrong. I don't mind confessing now that I had a queer sort of feeling that he might have fallen head over heels in love with me at first sight, as boys sometimes do. That black frock, after all, was very becoming, and what with the moonlight and the roses, it wouldn't have been difficult to lose one's head.

He plunged straight down the lawn and through the rhododendron walk, saying, 'Oh, let's get away from them all,' and we found a seat at last right down by the river, and sat down. He said, 'Do you mind if I smoke?' And of course I didn't, though what I did mind was being there without a wrap, because it was really very cold, and Phil's dress was awfully airy.

Then suddenly he said, 'You know, I just couldn't bear it. You don't mind, do you?'

And I said stupidly, 'Don't mind what?'

'All those girls dancing. I had to get away.'

And while I was still staring at him, he added, 'You see, I lost my first patient to-day – a girl of eighteen with peritonitis. We operated too late. I never ought to have come here, only I'd promised, and the Dawsons have been so decent to me.'

After that it all came out – all about this being his first job as locum, and his keenness to get back to hospital, and his work and everything. Of course, I didn't know a thing about doctoring, and medical details bore me still, really. Only he was so sweet and keen somehow, and I do like to see a man keen on his job.

But it was cold. If it had been any other man on earth, I'd have sent him in for my cloak, but something told me that Dick had to get this talk out of himself – intuition, I suppose. So I sat and sat, trying not to shiver, and wondering how soon I could decently make a move, when his voice faded and faded, and there he was, fast asleep, with his head fallen across my shoulder.

Of course, it was comical in one way, but in another way it wasn't. It was somehow exciting. It got later and later but no one seemed to notice us. I suppose my black dress didn't show much against the bushes. And he was very sweet somehow, lying there. I just couldn't resist it. I dropped a kiss on to his nice black head.

Well, whether that woke him or not, I can't say, but he did wake up, and was frightfully apologetic, especially when he found that I was half frozen. I used to tease him afterwards and say he wouldn't have been half so interested if he hadn't thought that I was going to get pneumonia. But as it was he took me in and got me hot soup and whisky, and came round next day to Phil's home with arms full of flowers to ask how I was.

I had caught a cold too – but luckily on my chest, not in my head, which is always so unbecoming, and he was frightfully penitent and insisted on making me up prescriptions and all sorts of things. And after that, somehow, I saw a good deal of him. He used to come and play golf on Saturday afternoons, and I persuaded Phil to let me stay on with her, because I felt somehow that I didn't want him to go home and see in what a stuffy sort of way we had to live. But I got Father to come one afternoon and give him tea at the club-house just to show him that my people were really pukkah.

And then, right on top of that tea-party, the War came.

At first it didn't seem to make much difference, though Dick looked worried and talked about the R.A.M.C. I used to chaff him a good deal and tell him it would all be over before he had time to get fitted for his uniform. He was very careless about clothes in those days – didn't care what he wore. Of course, I've smartened him up a good deal nowadays, though it's a pity he's losing his figure. I think a doctor's appearance matters so much, don't you? Mind you, all this time he'd never spoken definitely about love, but he was one of those boys wrapped up in his work, who somehow wouldn't come very quickly to the point. He was having to help his people, too, with money. I knew that and made allowances. He sometimes mentioned a girl called Rachel who used to be a student junior to him, but only as if she was most awfully clever, not as if she meant anything personal to him.

I did hate the idea of his going to the War. But pretty soon I felt that it had to come. And then I began to grow scared. For I knew somehow that while I was seeing him almost every day like that, I could hold him. But if he went away without speaking, that might be the end of it all. And I couldn't, I couldn't face the thought of another ten years like the last, shut up in that little house with no money and a stepmother who didn't want me. Dick seemed to be my only chance. I used to lie at night wondering what would happen if he went off and got killed without a word.

Of course, if we were married, there would be the pension, and I should be Mrs Forsyth, and everything would be different. I used to try and think what I should do to make him propose.

Well, of course, the crisis came just when I didn't expect it, as crises so often do. I had gone back home and was washing-up the supper things one evening. The maid had gone out and Father and my stepmother were spending the week-end in town. Poor Father thought he could get a job at the War Office or something, though of course he never did.

I heard a ring at the bell and I thought it was a girl about the parish magazines, and didn't bother to pull down my sleeves or anything. But it wasn't the girl. It was Dick.

To this day the smell of cold stuffiness reminds me of the drawing-room, where I took him. Being alone, I hadn't lit the fire; but I did remember to draw down the blinds, and then I turned round to look at him properly. He was in uniform.

We just stood holding each other's hands, and I kept on saying, 'Oh, Dick. Oh, Dick.'

Of course, he was all wrought up too. All these war books and things that they publish now never seem quite to show what a frightful wrench it really was to the men who'd just got started in on their work and had to throw it up. And then I do really think, still, in spite of everything, that he was sorry to leave me.

Of course, if he'd told me about Rachel . . .

But he didn't. He cheated. And how was I to know, when I let myself fall into his arms, that he was really engaged all the time to another girl? I tell you, men aren't fair to women, never have been, and I was justified in anything, anything that happened afterwards, because of the way he didn't tell me.

I dare say I did lead him on. But then it wasn't as if he

was a child, and I just couldn't face the thought of his going away and leaving everything unchanged.

So when he went away, he had changed everything for me. And still we were not actually engaged.

After that, I went through a really frightful time. Father came back from London more difficult than ever because the War Office hadn't given him a job, and my stepmother was hateful, and I waited day after day for a letter from Dick, but nothing came except an occasional card. He was up in a field dressing-station then, and I wrote and I wrote, but he didn't always get my letters. It was the spring of 1915 and posts were sometimes a bit disorganised. But he did get one letter I wrote – the most important.

You see, I'd begun to get into a panic. I couldn't help thinking how utterly ghastly it would be if I were to have a baby. All through that first month – it was a kind of nightmare. And then I suppose, what with nerves and one thing and another, it seemed as though I were right.

I went up to Phil's, although they didn't want me to go, because the maid had left to do war work or something, and my stepmother wanted to turn me into a general help. But I was feeling simply frightful, and when I told Phil all about it she said there couldn't be much doubt, and that I simply must make him marry me. She was perfectly furious, and yet awfully interested. I believe she was really rather jealous in some kind of way, because she'd never gone off the deep end over anything in her life, and it seemed somehow a little romantic to be a wronged woman.

Well, I wrote to Dick and told him, but it was a little while before I got his reply. So far as what he said went, it was all right. If he'd wronged me, he was prepared to marry me as soon as he could get leave – the sooner the better for the sake of the child. But the way he said it wasn't so nice. It was awfully cold somehow, not a bit a lover's letter. Still, it would do, and Phil said that it would be perfectly conclusive in a court of law, if it ever came to that. I wasn't quite so cynical as Phil, but knew that I was pretty desperate and would be prepared to do almost anything. But it never came to that, thank heaven.

Of course, it wasn't the sort of wedding I had hoped for. No wreath or veil or reception, though Dick's father came down from Cumberland and Phil gave a luncheon party, and of course we said it was quiet on account of the War and everything.

But the honeymoon was pure farce. Dick had changed a good deal. He seemed much older, somehow, and jumpy, and not nearly so sweet to me as he had been, though always perfectly polite. But the really comic thing was about the baby.

Dick insisted on having separate rooms, and I must wear low-heeled shoes, and not smoke, and drink only water – which was all very well, but no one wants a hygienic honeymoon, and I was pretty sure by that time that the baby was a false alarm. We hardly ever talked about ourselves, though Dick told me of the separation allowance, and lots and lots of things about babies and how to have them. That's the worst of marrying a doctor.

When he went back I'd had no more satisfaction out of my marriage than if I'd been staying in Brighton with the family practitioner. But at least I was Mrs Forsyth, and had a ring and an allowance. It was the first money really of my own that I had ever handled. They were nicer to me at home too, and the other women treated me quite differently. I was inside the circle somehow – a married woman with a husband at the front.

But of course I had to do something about that baby, so I went off to stay with Phil, who was in it all, and wrote from there to say I'd had a fall and been frightfully ill, and though I was better now, there wouldn't be a child this time, and of course I was terribly upset. The funny thing was that Dick sounded upset too, when he wrote again. I really believe that he was quite keen about that baby.

If it hadn't been for Rachel, it would all have been perfectly all right. It was the most rotten luck in the world that she should see me just then. Roddie Parsons, one of my old flames who hadn't come up to the scratch, was on leave and asked me to lunch with him in Soho, and do a matinée. The men who used to shy off a bit before I was married began to be frightfully sweet to me again. I suppose they thought I was safe. Anyway, I didn't see any harm in having a little fun. And of course when we found that the Barclays, some people Roddie knew, were lunching at the same place with a girl in V.A.D. uniform, I never thought anything of it. I noticed she stared at me rather queerly when we were introduced, but I never even noticed her name. She was a plain little thing, and even Gladys Cooper wouldn't have looked a charmer in those round V.A.D. straw hats.

Well, of course, I never thought anything more about it. I was having a pretty good time, what with one thing and another, stopping with Phil at Ascot and going up to town almost every day for dancing or a show. After all, it was part of our job to be nice to the boys who were on leave, and I always had been a good dancer. I don't mean that there was anything wrong in it. I've always been a faithful wife to Dick. It has been he who wronged me over and over again.

Dick didn't get leave again. He sent me cards and very short letters from time to time, and the separation allowance came through all right, but when I asked him why he didn't get leave like other people, he never answered. If I hadn't been doing my best to amuse the other boys and keep my end up, I should have missed him dreadfully.

It was in 1916 that I had a letter signed Rachel Tyson from some one who wanted to see me. The signature meant nothing to me and I hadn't the least idea what she wanted, but I supposed she might be organising a Red Cross bazaar or something. One was always getting asked to do queer things in those days, and she wrote asking me to lunch with her at the College Women's Club in Piccadilly, which seemed respectable enough. I wanted a day for shopping in town, and I never minded a free lunch because, for all my separation allowance, and although Dick was a

major now in the R.A.M.C., I always seemed to be short
of money.

I didn't recognise her at all when we met at the Club.
She wasn't in uniform now, though her hat was no prettier,
and her hair hadn't been waved or anything. I remember
how coarse and red her hands were – with scrubbing, I
suppose – and there was a button off her coat, with the
threads hanging out. I do hate a woman to look untidy.

She said right away that she'd just come back from
France, where she'd been nursing, and was going to finish
her medical course in London.

'I've been working with Dick Forsyth, you know,' she
said, and looked straight at me across the table. 'Dick,' I
thought. Well, of all the cheek! But I was quite sweet to
her, and said, 'Oh, how lovely of you to come and tell
me. *How* is he? *Is* he overworking? Are they quite safe at
Étaples? How lovely to get first-hand news of him!'

'You don't remember me at all then?' she asked. And I
began to feel uncomfortable somehow, but said no. And
then she said, 'Do you remember lunching at Cappaccio's
on June 14th last year?' And I said 'June? June?' I'd lunched
at so many places. Only it was in June that I'd written to
Dick about the accident. I began to think that there was
something behind all this, but I wouldn't look frightened. I
noticed she wasn't touching her food at all. It was a rotten
lunch, anyway.

She said, 'You know, I think I've got to tell you all about
it. It's only right that you should know what happened.
You don't seem to remember my name, though Dick is
sure he sometimes mentioned it to you. We were medical students together in London, and though we weren't
actually engaged, there was an understanding between us
that after we both had qualified, we were to be married and go on working together. We were both interested in gynaecology, and I'd always had the idea that
men and women ought to work in partnership on a job
like that.'

Her voice was quite colourless, and she looked frightfully

ill. Pale, you know, and lifeless, though there was a kind of fire in her too.

'He was my senior by two years as far as the work goes, though actually I am the same age. But I'd had a rather difficult time scraping the money together, to take my course. He qualified two years before me, and went to take a locum near Ascot in 1914.'

'Oh,' I said, still quite sweet and kind to her.

'Are you trying to tell me that my husband was engaged to you before he met me?'

'Well, as I said, I wouldn't let him say we were engaged, because at the time I didn't think it fair to tie him down. Of course, I see now that it was a mistake. It wasn't fair to him – or to you – or to me either, for that matter.'

I remember that the waitress came up then and asked if we'd have prunes or jelly, and Rachel said, 'Prunes, please, and coffee,' without even consulting me, though I loathe prunes. After the prunes came, she went on:

'Of course, Dick told me he'd met you, and how decent you'd been to him that night after his first patient died. He was always like that, frightfully sensitive and rather dependent really. He needs looking after.'

And I nodded, and said, 'Men are such children, aren't they?' Because I was determined to be nice to her, even though I thought it was awful cheek of her to come and try to tell me what my husband was like.

'After he went to the front,' she said, 'I couldn't bear just being a medical student any longer. I knew how frightfully a sensitive person like him loathed the War. I couldn't bear for him to have to face all those horrors, and me safe in England.'

'I know,' I said.

She gave me another of her queer, rude looks. 'Do you?' she asked. 'I'm glad. Well, they were needing V.A.D.s, with some medical knowledge, and I got taken on at once. And just after I'd gone into hospital Dick wrote to tell me he was coming home on special leave to marry you.'

'I see,' I said. 'I'm afraid it must have been a shock.'

'Yes,' she said. 'It was. Of course, he didn't say why.'

That seemed an odd thing for her to say, but I just nodded again, and smiled at her.

'Just before I went out to France I met you at Cappaccio's, and that friend of the Barclays introduced us. I wasn't sure at first that it could be you, but afterwards the Barclays said, "Why, surely you knew Dick Forsyth, didn't you?" And I remembered all you said about dining the night before, and such a hectic week and so on. You looked very well and pretty.'

'Thank you,' I said, laughing, but I was beginning to feel awful, because I saw that there was something behind all this, and knew what there could be behind it.

'I didn't mean to give you away,' she said. 'You may not believe me now, but I do assure you it was quite accidental that I got sent out to Dick's unit. I'd been wangling for that ever since I'd joined the V.A.D., and though I knew he was married I knew too that I would keep a hold on myself. I wanted to tell him that it was all right, and that we could go on being friends, and that nothing mattered except his being happy.'

'Very noble, I'm sure,' I said. I couldn't resist that, because I had realised then that we were enemies and that it was war to the death between us.

'It was a little while before I actually met him,' she went on. 'I was in Étaples, but not in the same hospital, but of course after a time we did meet, and went off to have tea together, and it was then I said, "Oh, Dick, I've seen your wife and I think she's awfully pretty." And naturally he asked when and where I'd met you. But I didn't expect him to look as he did look when I told him. You do see how it happened, don't you? It really was all unintentional. But it just came out.'

'I don't see what you mean,' I said.

Then she looked straight at me again, and said, 'Oh, yes, you do.'

'I don't in the least.' I was very indignant and felt I had a right to be. 'You ask me here to lunch and then insult me at your own table. And you call yourself a lady.'

'I don't,' she said. 'That's a luxury I've had to leave to other people. I'm a woman and I've loved Dick ever since I was a child, and we stole a boat together on a holiday in Cumberland and went rowing in Derwentwater.'

'Don't you think,' I said, 'that even if it is not ill-bred, it is rather unwise of you to come and tell me that you are in love with my husband?'

'It may be unwise,' she said. 'But it's necessary. Do you want me to tell you exactly how you persuaded him to marry you?'

'I think,' I said, very dignified and calm, 'that you must excuse me. I am not accustomed to this sort of behaviour.'

'To tell the truth,' she said, and she actually had the face to smile a little, 'brawling over other people's husbands has never been exactly a hobby of mine. But in fairness to you as well as me, we've got to get this matter settled.'

'May I ask,' I said, 'what you would like me to do?'

'Yes,' she said, very white and her lips trembling at last. If ever a woman looked guilty, she did. 'I want you to divorce Dick.'

'Well, really,' I said. 'Is that all? So that you can marry him, I suppose. Are you sure you wouldn't prefer that he should divorce me?'

'Well,' she had the impertinence to say, 'I dare say that is another possibility. And as far as Dick's reputation is concerned, it would be better. Fortunately in War-time these things don't matter so much, however. I don't think a divorce will ruin his reputation now.'

'I see. That's very generous and thoughtful of you. And I suppose you want me to hunt for evidence against him?'

'Oh, no. You needn't do that,' she said, quite cool again, and even a little amused. 'I can give you ample evidence and I promise you that the suit won't be defended.'

'I think,' I said, 'that I've never heard anything quite so

barefaced in my life. Are you trying to tell me that you're my husband's mistress?'

'Yes.' she said.

'You dare to sit there and tell me that though you knew he was married, you deliberately followed him out to France, pursued him, got yourself transferred to the same place where he was, and – and – well, really – I simply don't understand you.'

'No,' she said. 'I don't suppose you do. But in fairness to Dick I want you to know one thing. He had no thought of being unfaithful to you until he realised your trick about the baby.'

'You've got no proof,' I said. 'What you are suggesting is libellous and blackmail. You've dared to libel me to my husband, to make the most wicked insinuations one woman can make against another, with a motive for making them so obvious that it couldn't deceive a child, and then you come to me and calmly suggest that I should quietly clear out and make room for you. If any one had just told me that a woman was capable of behaving like that, I shouldn't have believed it. Have you anything more to say?'

'Only that I'm going to have a child,' she said.

'Indeed, how interesting. I should have thought a clever young woman like you could have managed to avoid that little complication.'

'I did mean to,' she said. 'I didn't want Dick to be worried again and I haven't told him. I only said that I felt I ought to go back and finish my training because doctors were so badly needed. I shan't tell him unless you agree to divorce him. He's got enough to trouble him already.'

'You're suddenly very careful about him,' I said. 'You ought to have thought of all this before. I don't know what sort of a person you think I am. But if you imagine that I am quietly going to hand over my husband to the first young fool who comes along saying she wants him, you are mistaken.'

'I'm not suggesting that there won't be compensations,'

she said. 'Naturally you, as the wronged party, would get alimony. And if Dick and I were both working we could pay a pretty high one.'

'The wronged party,' I said. 'Much you have thought of the wrong you've done me!' And I began to think of all the things they'd say about me if I had to divorce Dick.

For people can say what they like about divorce. There is this thing that's such awfully bad luck about it. I do really believe that it hurts the wronged woman more than the usurper. A few of the strait-laced or stodgy may turn their backs on a woman who has been divorced, but it's the really jolly people, the men who would otherwise be nice to one, and all that, who get suspicious of a woman who's divorced her husband. They feel that there must be something hard and intolerant about her, and stupid too, because she couldn't hold her man. It's the innocent woman who pays, every time. If I'd been younger I might have considered it, because, sweet boy as Dick was, he never had been entirely my sort, and I knew that after a bit all his medical talk would bore me. But I was perfectly well aware that if I divorced him I should be back where I was in 1914 again, with nothing to do but go home and live with my people, and the men sheering off in case I wanted to marry them.

So, of course, I didn't do anything of the kind.

I never even mentioned to Dick about that woman's visit, and I don't believe she did either, for she said that until I could make up my mind to free Dick she would clear out so as not to worry him.

I didn't see her again for nearly a year. Then I was selling flags in Regent Street and she came and bought one before she recognised who it was. She looked awfully shabby, and she only bought a twopenny flag, and her gloves had a hole in them.

I had Dick at home then. He'd been wounded. I had him to stay at Phil's and we made a great fuss of him, and everything was all right again, so I could afford to be generous.

I said, 'Oh, how do you do, Miss Tyson. Or are you Dr Tyson yet?'

And she said, 'I'm very well, thank you. And I'm taking my finals next year.'

I longed to ask, and how's the baby?

But I felt it was too risky, and besides, there are some things a lady doesn't do.

I didn't tell Dick I met her, and indeed we've never spoken of her all this time, though when she started to do that work after the War I know he used sometimes to hear of her from other doctors. I'm sure I was wise to make him come up North, because he hasn't forgotten her even yet. It's dreadful sometimes, feeling that there's always this memory standing between us, though of course we are perfectly happy, and Dick has a comfortable practice, and we have a lot of friends and rub along together as well as most married couples, I suppose. It's a pity in one way we haven't had any children, as Dick thinks he's so fond of them, but I always say he gets enough of them in his practice, and what with the trouble of getting nurses, and the cost of everything nowadays, it certainly does simplify things to have no family. Naturally in other circumstances I should like to have had children. Every normal woman would, but I always say you can't have everything in life, can you?

And suffering undoubtedly does bring experience and deepens the character, I always think. Only when I saw that picture in the *Tatler* and thought of all the hideous wrong that woman has done me, I wondered for a moment whether I wasn't rather silly to go on being so generous and keeping her secret. After all, I suppose she realises that I hold her reputation in the hollow of my hand, and that's something to make her think, anyway.

Well, I shan't let Dick get hold of that picture, all the same.

1930

The Casualty List

Mrs Lancing came into her drawing-room and added another silk poppy to the bunch growing annually in the cloisonné vase. Another Armistice Day's duty done; another Two Minutes' Silence observed at the Memorial Service in the Parish Church which the dear Rector always held. He had lost one of his own boys in 1917. It was very sad.

It was all very sad. The war had been terrible, terrible. Going to see *Journey's End* with Margaret last month had brought it all back to her. She had been thinking about that play all through the service; about poor young Stanhope, drinking like that, and the funny servant; but most of all about that queer, tense, terrifying yet exciting call, 'Stretcher-bearer! Stretcher-bearer!' in the last act. It had a curious effect upon her, as though it almost, but not quite, released the secret of a hidden fear.

Well, she was tired now. Those new patent-leather shoes were not really comfortable. It had been a relief to get into slippers again. Thank goodness there was still half an hour before lunch time in which she could rest and look at *The Times*. Arthur had left it on the sofa as usual. He had not looked very well that morning; but then, who could look well every morning? When you were eighty-two. Why, she hadn't felt any too well herself, and she was nearly nine years younger. She sat down in the big arm-chair and stretched out her feet towards the dancing fire.

Of course, it wasn't as if she had had boys herself. With Arthur too old really, even to be a special constable, and the girls doing a little light secretarial and orderly work at the local hospital, she had never been able to feel that she was really in the war. She had done her bit, rolled bandages, and knitted socks, and served on the Refugees Committee, and rationed her own household so sternly that two of her best maids left; but that had not been quite the same thing. And she had always hated to feel out of anything – of the best set in the town, or the Hospital Ball, or the craze for roller-skating – or even the war. She had read the Casualty List every morning carefully, and written sympathetic, admiring notes to those other women whose husbands and sons were among the wounded or the fallen; but she could not sometimes help wishing that her own situation was a little more heroic. Those Wonderful Mothers who Gave their Sons held an immense moral advantage over the ordinary women who only coped with a sugar shortage and the servant problem, and the regulations about darkening windows. When Nellie Goodson's only son was killed, she had felt almost envious, of the boy for his Glorious End, of the mother for her honourable grief. Her sin had always been to covet honour.

During the ten years following the war, she had nearly forgotten this strange feeling of envy, just as she had forgotten the taste of lentil cutlets and the fuss about meat cards. There had been so much to think about, Margaret's wedding to her smart young Deryck, and Celia's wedding to Dr Studdley. Funny she could never think of him as Eric – always as Dr Studdley – and the grand-children, and the new bathroom, and Arthur's operation, and putting in Central Heating and her own neuritis. Life had been very full and complicated and busy, for Arthur's business had not done so badly during the war, and though of course he had retired, he still drew dividends.

It was a pity that she had never been able to persuade him to settle anything on the girls. That night she stayed with Margaret to go to *Journey's End* she remembered the girl, already in her becoming blue theatre frock, setting the grapefruit glasses on the polished table – for she was always up to date although she kept only a day-woman – and sighing, 'If only we had a little capital.' If Deryck had

had a little capital, perhaps they would have felt that they could afford a baby. These modern ways were all wrong, thought Mrs Lancing. And yet, when she remembered Celia and her four, and another coming, and the untidiness of the Studdleys' little house, with one meal always on top of the next, she could not reproach Margaret. It seemed a pity, perhaps, that young people needed the money, while old people always had it.

Of course she had paid for the theatre seats and taxis and everything. She had not really wanted to see *Journey's End*, but every one had been talking about it, and she felt so silly when she said she had only listened in on Arthur's wireless. She really liked a nice, amusing play, something you could laugh over, with a little love story and pretty frocks. Still, Margaret had seemed quite glad to take her, and it had been a change from hurrying back after visiting poor Nancy.

Once a month since Nancy's second stroke, Mrs Lancing had gone up to town to see her sister. She was astonished at the difference that Nancy's illness made to her. The sisters had never been deeply devoted to each other, and for many years their relationship had been one of mutual tolerance and irritation. Yet ever since Mrs Lancing had seen Nancy lying in bed, between the chintz curtains covered with hollyhocks, her poor mouth twisted and her speech all thick and blurred, she had been afraid. The weeks passed, and a sudden ringing of the telephone had only meant that the butcher could not send the kidneys in time for dinner, or that the Burketts wanted a fourth for bridge; but still Mrs Lancing was afraid. They said that the third stroke was always fatal, and Mrs Lancing did not want her sister to die. For when she had gone there would be no one left to share those memories of her childhood which grew more vivid with each passing year. There was no one else who remembered the hollow at the roots of the weeping ash-tree, that had made a beautiful kitchen range whenever they had played at Keeping House. No one else remembered poor Miss Wardle, the governess, who had lost the third finger of her left hand and spoke with a lisp. And no one else remembered that exciting night when the wheel came off the brougham driving home from the Hilaries, and they had to walk in their party slippers through the snow.

Even Rita Washburn, naughty little Rita who came over from the Rectory to do lessons with them, was dead now. Only two months ago Mrs Lancing had covered the blue front of her black dress with a scarf, before she set off to Golders Green Cemetery for Rita's funeral.

Perhaps it would be as well to ask Madame Challette to make her next dress with two detachable fronts, one black, and one coloured. For in these days one never knew. Every time Mrs Lancing picked up *The Times* she looked down the Deaths' Column with apprehension. She never knew who might go next. Why, there were hardly any of the old Bromley people left. That was the worst of being the baby of a set. Every one else seemed to grow old so soon. Mrs Lancing did not feel old at all, only sometimes she got a little tired, and always nowadays she was conscious of that lurking fear.

She picked up *The Times* and held it between her and the fire. Well, there was one comfort, she would never see Nancy's death there, as she had seen their father's, because she was on holiday in Scotland with Arthur and they had not known where to find her. She had made arrangements with Nancy's household now to telephone to her at once if anything happened, because she knew so well how, in the confusion of death, important things were neglected.

She knew so well. She had become quite expert recently in the technicalities of sudden illness, death and funerals. There had been her mother, her elder brother Henry, cousin Jane, and her great friend, Millie Waynwright. Millie's children had both been abroad when it happened, and she had had to arrange everything. Somehow it was just like Millie to give every one as much trouble as possible. Dear, wayward, lovely, petulant Millie, a spoiled pretty woman to the end, her white hair waved and shingled, her neck tied up with pale mauve tulle, and fresh flowers brought by her husband every day. But she had never really got over Roddie's death. He had been killed accidentally by a bomb exploding in England, and somehow that was really worse than if it had happened in France.

Mrs Lancing picked up *The Times* and looked at the Deaths' Column in the front page. 'Adair, Bayley, Blaynes, Brintock, Carless.' Frederick Carless – now, would that be Daisy's husband? Seventy-five – why, not so much older than she was. Mrs Lancing had begun to count her friends' ages eagerly, finding comfort in her own comparative youth. 'Davies, Dean, Dikes.' It was a heavy list to-day. There must have been an offensive.

How absurd. She was thinking of it as though it were a casualty list; but this was peace time. The war had been over for more than ten years. It was Armistice Day, the day on which the nation thought proudly of its glorious dead.

> They shall not grow old, as we that are left grow old,
> Age shall not weary them nor the years condemn;
> At the going down of the sun and in the morning,
> We will remember them.

We who are left grow old, thought Mrs Lancing. The years condemn us. We fall in a war with Time which knows no armistice. This column in *The Times* is the Casualty List.

She looked up at the scarlet silk poppies in the vase. In Flanders fields the poppies grow, because the young men died, so the Rector had said only an hour ago, in order that the world might be a better place for those who stayed behind. But the old who died because the years condemned them, was there no honour in their going? Of course, they had to pass on some time, and leave the world to the young. Mrs Lancing thought of Margaret, and her sigh, 'If only we had a little capital!' breathed without malice and without intention. She did not mean to hint anything to her mother, but of course she knew that when her parents went, there would be £12,000 each for her and Celia. The old must pass on. The young must inherit.

The shadow of death darkened the world when one was over seventy; yet save for one fear it was not unfriendly; it was not dishonourable. It was just part of life. Only she had not liked the look of Arthur's face that morning and she did wish that his heart was stronger.

The sudden opening of the drawing-room door roused her. She sat up, and saw the scared, white face of the young parlourmaid.

'Oh, please, 'm, will you come? The master's had a fainting attack or something in the smoking-room.'

Arthur's heart. Of course. It had to come.

As though with her bodily ears, Mrs Lancing heard ringing through the house the queer, exciting, alarming, sinister cry of 'Stretcher-bearer! Stretcher-bearer!'

She knew that this was the fear she had not dared to face, that this was the hour she had awaited with unspoken terror. Yet now that it had come, she was unshaken.

She rose quietly from her chair, placed *The Times* again upon the sofa, said to Ethel, 'Very well. I will come at once. Please telephone to Dr Burleigh.' And with a steady step walked to the door.

She was not out of it this time. This was her war, and she had learned how to behave.

1932

Episode in West Kensington

(Omitted from *Mandoa, Mandoa!*)

ON a cool May evening Jean Durrant tentatively steered the car that she had learned to drive in Scotland through the obscurer districts of West Kensington. She was good with a car, and quite fearless, but when she had reached her destination and climbed out, she stood, panting a little as though from strong exertion, her hand on the door of the coupé.

This was such a street as she had lived in before going to Mandoa, such a street as one finds in all great modern cities. The large houses had once been known to agents as 'this desirable family residence,' but were now let off in flats and single rooms. The massive pillars beside the doors were cracked, their basements black and cavernous, their curtains motley. At this hour of the evening, a few children still darted on scooters, rattling along the broad, untidy pavements. Young couples sauntered towards the tube stations and cinemas. Girl typists, hurrying home to boil their supper eggs over gas-rings, gazed wistfully at the young mothers pushing prams back from the park; and the young mothers, tired and depressed, gazed wistfully at the smart unburdened typists.

Each little room, flatlet or maisonette, Jean reflected, contained as in a sealed casket an isolated unit of private life. Mr and Mrs Brown played their gramophone with the *insouciance* of the newly-wed, into the ears of an unknown Mrs Jones worn out by three fretful children on the floor below, and of Miss Robinson, wretched and lonely because not wed at all, on the floor above. Respectability had replaced sociability; neighbourliness and swift, spontaneous friendships were unknown. Mr Smith in number 149c had been dead with a gas-pipe in his mouth for five days before the accumulating milk bottles outside his door suggested to the girl in number 149d that something might be wrong. That was the sort of street it was, with the shops and buses running at right-angles across the top, and the shabbier road above the Underground at the bottom.

Jean tapped her newly-manicured nails on the shining door and whistled softly. She recalled another street, eight times as broad, with squat red huts, dilapidated and casual, huddled along it. At this hour in the evening the children, their black round bellies tight with food, rolled and scuffled in the doorways; young couples strolled off together; slave girls hurrying past towards the market place gazed wistfully at the young mothers with babies strapped to their heavy breasts, kneading dough-cakes for their husbands' supper; and the heavily burdened mothers gazed wistfully at the slender, hurrying slave girls.

That street was shrill with continuous conversation. Every one talked to every one. Young men shouted obscenely humorous comments to each other, watching the slave-girls pass. Unmarried freedmen's daughters called back quick retorts. Not a wart on a month-old baby, not a bruise on a young wife's arm, but was debated with vigorous animation by twenty neighbours.

Jean and Maurice had been entertaining to lunch that day Lord and Lady Lufton, Fanshawe the anthropologist, a philanthropic Conservative lady Member of Parliament, and Frau von Schelden and her little husband.

Fanshawe had been deploring the discovery of Mandoa, and comparing its sociable savagery with the respectable sadism of West Kensington. 'You'll turn Lolagoba into a kind of African Margate,' he cried, 'with artificial "pleasure" instead of natural happiness. You'll gain security, comfort, hygiene, a longer expectation of life, in return for – what? Isolation instead of community understanding, the perverted decorum of artificial standards of behaviour instead of spontaneous enjoyment. You will be faced by the frustration of normal human appetites.' Frau von Schelden had enlarged upon the horrors of cruelty and oppression and ignorance in Lolagoba; but Fanshawe would have none of this. He had cursed the Nordic superiority complex which could feel pity for the victims only of other types of culture, but none for the victims of its own.

It was Doctor von Schelden who sounded a note of apprehension. 'What is the use of all this planning, philanthropy, reform, eh? To-morrow – Crash! Down comes the world. The next war within six months, and you talk of freeing slaves! It is not a question of "Can civilisation save Mandoa?" – but of "Can civilisation survive, no?"'

Lord Lufton had been fussy and sympathetic, always hoping for the best in the best of all possible worlds, calming his conscience by the reflection that things were never so bad as ardent reformers thought them.

Maurice had been happy enough, enjoying his vantage point as host, and, as man of the world, discounting wild prophecies and dreaming of virgin markets, spheres of influence, order, travel, big business and world trade, of power which he would wield with justice, of profit which he would gain with equity, and of responsibility which was his privilege.

Jean had been silent, not feeling well, swung between two memories, apprehensive, still stirred by vague yet passionate visions.

Lord Lufton was wrong, she thought. Sometimes the worst did happen. She thought of the war which had destroyed her brothers, and of the insecurity of the world into which she must bear her child. Fanshawe was wrong. Mandoa was not only sociable and friendly; it was fierce and terrible. Maurice was wrong. The gifts that Prince's carried to the world were not all good. And Frau von Schelden's practical philanthropy was all very well as far as it went; but what was the use of propagating ideas which the modern world had used only for self-destruction?

She wished that they would all stop talking and sit silent

for a moment, enjoying the frail, precarious present, the good food served with such precise and decorative ritual, with cut glass and old silver and cream-coloured lace, the formal beauty of Maurice's dining-room, the May sunlight, and the bees humming warmly among the wallflowers in the window boxes.

But they would not stop. Nothing would stop. The traffic flowed like a river along Brompton Road; the politicians discussed, lunched, quarrelled, rushed across continents and back again; ships reached their ports, poured out their destined cargo and sailed again, reladen; letters were written, speeches made, aeroplanes piloted and orders given, hurrying the world along to whatever future awaited the child now growing inevitably, implacably, within her womb. Nothing would stop, even for a moment. And to-night she must dine with Evelyn Raye.

Standing beside her car, she wished for the hundredth time since her return to England that her marriage had been unaccompanied by its material advantages. She thought of Greta James and her tragi-comic husband-hunt. She thought of Evelyn Raye and her dead lover. And she thought of herself, reappearing after months of absence, like the heroine of a *Home Chat* serial, armed with wedding ring, fur coat and sports coupé, a rich, indulgent husband, and the ominous nausea before meal-times which attends the early months of pregnancy.

She felt ashamed and embarrassed like a *nouveau riche* visiting poor relations. She was conscious of something vulgar in her appearance, as she dragged herself up the eighty-two steps to Evelyn's top-floor flat. The smell of unwashed prams, tom-cats and dead dinners assailed her nostrils. She was panting dizzily when her hostess opened the door.

'Oh, here you are!' Evelyn greeted her. 'That's good. Nice coat you've got on. I expect these steps seem a bit steep after Knightsbridge, don't they?'

It was not due to Knightsbridge that the steps seemed steep, but Jean felt an explanation premature, so said vaguely, 'Not at all,' and slipped out of the too-luxurious coat which she flung carelessly on to Evelyn's narrow divan bed.

'I ought to have worn my tweeds,' thought Jean. But that would have been silly, for though one should not gloat over prosperity before one's spinster friends, one would be mistaken to play up to their complexes. She was almost inclined to feel irritated by Evelyn. Evelyn was swift and arrogant in her movements; she was handsome and dominant. But she was not, like Jean, trained to domestic ease. The dinner she had provided was unappetising. Jean's queasy stomach revolted against tinned salmon splashed carelessly among pink watery juices on to an ill-washed dish, and bullet-hard dried peas, inadequately cooked. Fanshawe had been raving against the iniquity of the Tinned Food Habit. Well, here it was.

'Sorry I hadn't time to do chops or something. If I fry chops, the room stinks to Heaven for hours afterwards,' Evelyn said brusquely. 'But after Mandoa, I expect you can eat anything.'

Jean thought of the chicken and sweetmeats, and the strange rich vegetables served at the Commissioners' camp on their first night's journey. But she replied valiantly, 'This is nectar and ambrosia compared with exceedingly high game fried in bad butter.' She fought against her growing nausea, pursuing peas with a fork to which remnants of egg still clung.

No, no; it was not necessary to feed squalidly even if one lived alone. She had lived alone, and her Chelsea cottage had been spotlessly clean.

She felt Evelyn's critical eyes upon her.

'I'm behaving like a bride,' thought Jean. 'Oh, Lord, don't let me behave like a bride. Evelyn's a better woman than I am, any day, but it's not a crime to marry. It's not a crime to be fortunate. And, after all, is it fortunate to feel as sick as I do?'

Desperately she battled against the salmon, talking very quickly about Mandoa, about insects and American visitors, and the Fire, and the hurried exodus from the city afterwards, when every one feared typhus or cholera from unburied corpses and polluted water. She minimised pleasures and exaggerated discomforts, that Evelyn might not think she was boasting her own advantages.

'So you found it all very frightful, and have returned flaming with crusading zeal?' asked Evelyn.

'I don't know about crusading zeal. But we've got to do something. Going close to a place that you've always heard of at a distance has a curious effect,' Jean answered. 'When I thought of Mandoa in England, I thought of a perfectly simple problem. There was a wicked and corrupt native state where half-bred Portuguese-Abyssinian nobles oppressed Negro slaves. So one sailed in, denounced the nobles and freed the Negroes. The oppressors were worthless; the oppressed innocent. Compensation was undesirable as well as unnecessary. We courageously determined to expose the corruption and the isolation which made it possible, to substitute order for chaos, civilisation for barbarism, and justice for oppression.'

'Yes, yes. I have typed many leaflets full of such aspirations. There's nothing you can't tell me about maternal mortality and slave-prostitutes in Lolagoba. Have a piece of bread?'

'Thanks, I will. What I was going to say was that it's so much more complicated when you get there. We expected opposition from the slave-owners. We found, on the whole, that they welcomed us. They're so keen to have what they think is civilisation – spats and brilliantine and motor-cars, and diplomatic representation – and, of course, no one expects emancipation to happen all at once. They don't mind leaving that problem to their sons, if they can have the bicycles and gold tooth-fillings at once.'

'I understand that everything's going on well, as you might say,' said Evelyn in a hard voice, 'with your husband's firm as the chief agents of civilising influence.'

'Oh, Maurice is full of schemes. At present, the idea is that he's to manage the material side – trade and transport and tourists and so on – and I'm to keep an eye on the ideals. I know that sounds stupid. But, as a matter of fact, there *is* a lot of work that we must do. There *is* a terrible lot of disease and suffering; they chain up imbeciles, for instance, and starve them to death. Children die like flies. Lepers are isolated in hideous dens among the hills. As for the slaves – that business is terrible.'

'Pleasure and profit hand in hand,' Evelyn observed dryly. 'You and your big business man working together to turn Lolagoba into something like Welwyn Garden Suburb. Well, good luck to you, I say. I only hope that the Mandoans will be duly grateful.'

'Do you think it's not worth while? I mean, honestly?' asked Jean.

'Honestly, I don't know, and don't care. Why should I?'

'You work for the International Humanitarian Association.'

'My *dear* Jean. Have you so soon forgotten? I suppose you have. You young married women with your rich husbands and plump allowances can afford the luxury of disinterested enthusiasms. But we poor devils, employed by philanthropic missionary institutions, we work because we must. We can't afford to give up our three or four pounds a week – whatever it is. What do I care for slavery? I who am, from nine till five-thirty – and often to six or seven – every working day, a slave? What do I care for famine victims? I, who am hungry myself for a thousand things I can never have. I clothe the naked, while I'm depressed and dowdy, wearing last year's coat-frock dyed out of all reasonable shape, and three-and-elevenpenny gloves I loathe. There are hundreds of us, and you know there are, or you used to know when you were one of us. We fly to the shelter of safe unadventurous secretarial jobs, and then we're caught for life, clinging to them, growling over our particular bone, terrified of losing it. We give our bodies to be burned all right; we give our pride to be humbled, our strength to be impaired, our eyes to be strained, for Chinese and Hottentots and Armenians and God knows whom – not having charity. So is our sacrifice worth nothing except four pounds a week and a two-roomed flatlet in West Kensington.'

Jean sighed. It was all very difficult. She wanted to help Evelyn. She wanted to make her feel that the secretarial work she did in London was important, that somehow, tame though it seemed, it was laying the foundation of a new and orderly world.

But the messages of comfort died on her lips. Her idealism seemed like the cheap sentimentality of the compensation myth. Her only urgent concern at the moment was her rising nausea. Involuntarily, she pushed her plate away.

'You feel like that about it, do you? Well, I don't blame you,' said Evelyn. 'Let's leave this filthy food and come and sit in more comfortable chairs, and I'll make coffee. I *can* make coffee, you know. It's my one useful legacy from an abortive love affair.'

Gladly Jean accepted the suggestion, but her white sick face as she crossed the room provoked her friend to a sharp question. 'Are you going to have a child?'

'Yes,' Jean confessed, thankful to get it over.

Evelyn gave her harsh, barking laugh. 'Congratulations. How splendid it all is! Husband, car, furs, fortune, baby. And by exchange you'll leave us the office and the work for future generations, eh? Thank you.'

'But I'm not leaving them. I'm going on. I'm coming back to do publicity work after the child's born.'

'I see. *How* noble of you. You'll leave the office for a few months, and then return a voluntary worker, enthusiastic and superior, only the least little bit in the world contemptuous of us, the poor, lethargic, paid employees. You'll be *ever* so popular with the Executive. 'Dear Mrs Durrant, *so* charming, and *so* efficient, goes everywhere, knows every one. Gives *such* nice little dinners. Has *such* a good social manner. Her husband's just contributed £5,000 to the central fund. Ah, she's exactly the kind of helper we need.' Can't you hear old Beaton? You'll return from interesting holidays in Russia and China and Tibet delightfully dressed, glowing with health and vitality, full of bright suggestions which mean more work for us, when all *we* want is a quiet life. Oh, no, my dear. We shan't be able to compete with you at all. You'll have it all ways. Blessed are the rich, for to him that hath shall be given. Blessed are the rich, for it is more blessed to give than to receive, and only the rich can give – the poor are too hard up, thinking of next week's rent. Blessed are the rich, for they can buy the Kingdom of Heaven.'

'This is even worse than I thought it would be,' Jean told herself. 'I meant to make things better for her, and I'm only making them worse.' She was suffering acutely, for it was her instinct to give people what they wanted, and there was nothing that she could do for Evelyn. She made another effort.

'That's not true, you know. I've been poor and lonely and defeated myself,' she cried. 'When you got me my job on the I.H.A. I was down to my last pound – and my last ounce of courage. I'm nearly forty, remember, and I tell you, out of my experience of both worlds, that it is not the rich who give; it's the poor. Sorrow and frustration have their power. The world is moved by people with great discontents. Happiness is a drug. It can make men blind and deaf and insensible to reality. There are times when only sorrow can give to sorrow.'

'Pretty,' said Evelyn, pouring out the coffee. 'But it just happens not to be true. Look at us now – who's behaving the better? You, the sympathetic young matron who can afford to be generous, or I, the embittered, jealous spinster? Oh, I know I am a cad! Scatting at you, in your delicate condition and all. But why should I let you off? I think the thing that maddens me, Jean, is that you were always so superior. Oh, no. *You* didn't want a husband. *You* didn't want children. All you wanted was to work for the I.H.A., and to go on working. A little travel, a little fame, and that was enough for you, you said. You allowed us all to give ourselves away to you, and then you went off quietly to

Mandoa on your own and got what we all wanted. Here's your coffee. I haven't put arsenic in it.'

Jean took the coffee, and sat stirring it. She had for the moment forgotten Mandoa, that other country which lay as the background of all her conscious thoughts. She was thinking wholly of how to help her friend.

'I suppose,' she said tentatively, 'it would seem a little like that. But to tell the truth, just before coming to see you, I wasn't at all inclined to think of my great luck. It's you who've made me count my blessings. The proof of good behaviour's in its effect. What you call my sympathetic generosity seems to have made things worse for you. Your envy's made me realise my good fortune. Who's given most to the other, you or I?'

'You're very clever, but quite unconvincing. You – who are so fortunate. How could *you* be depressed?'

'Oh,' cried Jean eagerly and seriously. 'I was full of distresses. I've been feeling so ill lately, and I'm not accustomed to physical disabilities. This baby that you think so much of – I'm glad in a way, of course, that I'm going to have it – but at present it appears to me mostly as a nuisance. It means that I can't travel with the East Indies Commission. It means that I feel sick every morning. It means that I have to face years of small domestic responsibilities which I loathe. Oh, I had too many babies to deal with in my childhood, Evelyn! When other expectant mothers dream soft sweet dreams of curly heads and toddling feet and all the rest of it, I am only too well aware of nappies and teething and contentions between nurse and housemaid about who should brush the creature's crumbs off the carpet. I know all about measles and colic and whooping cough. I know that just when I want to dash off to a conference in Geneva I shall have to arrange for isolating chicken-pox! No woman who's going to be a mother ever ought to have been an elder sister in a large family. Then there's the money question. I'm not earning anything. For the first time since I left Highgate I'm dependent. And I don't like it. Kind and generous as Maurice is, I *don't* like it. There's more pleasure in spending sixpence that you've earned, than six hundred pounds handed with a complacent kiss from a rich husband. Then there's Mrs Durrant – a nice enough little woman, and one might have worse mothers-in-law. But, for some inconceivable reason, she will persist in harping upon her old idea that I should have married Bill, not Maurice.'

'And you hate that, eh?'

'Yes, it's rather painful.'

'Because it's true.'

'Oh, it's not true! Bill never wanted me. He never wanted any one. He's not quite human.'

'Human?'

'No, no. No, no. Sometimes you think he's odd and subtle, with strange, latent powers, a poet, half a mystic – going off by himself to remote places, doing difficult, unexpected things, and you attribute to him elevated motives when all the time he's probably only lazy – sitting and drinking sispri with the natives.'

'Jean, you *are* in love with him.'

'Am I?' Jean frowned, wrestling with her confusions, determined upon candour. 'Perhaps I was, a little.'

'You *are*,' ruthlessly persisted Evelyn.

'Perhaps I am.' Oh, she must hold back nothing! She must open her imperfect heart, lest it contain even one grain of comfort for this hungry daw to peck at.

'Perhaps I am. Only, in the end, love like that – which is only glamour – a quickening of the pulses – a deluding vision – doesn't count really, Evelyn, does it? What counts is need. You go where you're most needed.'

'Need?' asked Evelyn. 'You chose the rich, successful brother instead of the poor prodigal, because the rich one needs you?'

'Yes. Oddly enough, that's true.'

'That's very interesting. Need is the last quality I should have imputed to that highly successful, complacent, self-confident young man.'

'Oh, but he's not!' cried Jean. 'He's not complacent,

he's not self-confident, and until recently he'd never even thought himself successful.'

'The more fool he. If that isn't success, I'm damned if I know what is. And he looks as though he knew it too.'

'Ah. Don't you realise that these self-confident and superior manners are almost always built across a gulf of loneliness? They're defences that the insecure and unhappy set between themselves and an unsympathetic world. The really unfrightened, sociable people can afford to be easy and unassuming. They're so sure of themselves that they don't have to pretend anything. But Maurice – he has always had to fight for everything – for self-possession, for his mother's respect, for a place in business, in Parliament, anywhere. He had to fight for self-confidence to carry things through at all. He's never for a second felt secure. I think that's precisely why he has fought so hard and done so well. Maurice came second – always. Maurice didn't go to the War. Maurice wasn't popular at school.' As she spoke, Jean saw him in a pinafore, running confidently to young Mrs Durrant to be received by fretful injunctions not to crease her dress. She saw him on the school playground, a thin, nervous little boy with chilblains, bullied by stolid, brainless games captains. Poor little boy. Poor lonely little boy! She saw him, as she had seen her younger brothers, his gallant stiff little spine, lightly furred with brown hair, his taut rounded buttocks, his childish ribs heaving in and out, standing on the high diving-board of the school baths, dreading the jump, hating it, loathing it, forcing himself to become one of the school's crack divers.

She understood what his Mandoan adventure had meant to Maurice. Sir Joseph had needed him; that was the first reassurance. Bill had arrived in Khartoum and threatened his position; that was the recurrent danger. Bill had offered the gesture of flight to Lolagoba, and, with that, terror had leapt upon him. Oh, Maurice knew what it meant if Bill flew away and left him to face his mother's anguish. He knew the shame and horror of immunity. He had chosen almost certain death rather than face that again. His choice had freed him. Jean knew that from the hour he entered the monoplane, Maurice had been a free man. He had dared everything – the flight, the rescue, the control of a highly perilous and complex situation. His daring fed his courage; his courage gave him power to satisfy his need.

'Well, it's all highly romantic,' Evelyn said. 'Is gossip right when it declares that he carried you off like a fairy prince from the place where you were all imprisoned, and proposed to you in the aeroplane?'

Jean laughed. 'Not quite. But it was fairly precipitate. Actually, when he carried me off, I was too tired to know or care who he was, or what he did. It was after the fire and the exodus that he asked me to marry him. You see, we were in quarantine, but he was allowed to see us because he had been with us already in the aeroplane – and I helped to nurse Mr Beaton and Frau von Schelden while the hospital staff dealt with the fire victims. I saw a good deal of him.'

And all the time he was gaining self-confidence. The royal wedding, the fire, the frightful quarrel in the High Council, the defeat of Talal, the ascendency of Ma'buta, might have been designed by Providence to give Maurice an opportunity to prove his courage. The month of March had meant a retreat of Prince's Limited from Mandoa. But it had been a retreat in good order. And out of the confusion, Maurice had risen pre-eminent. The hour had made the man. This was his story that all the world might know.

But the fear and frustration of his twisted youth, his bitter rivalry, the sense of his own inferiority to his brother, these were buried now between him and his wife. Jean's husband, whom all the world might know, was the resourceful organiser, the imaginative and audacious business man, the junior statesman. But her secret lover was the lonely, miserable little boy, the fierce, vulnerable young man, storming the world, armed with an academic technique of success. For a moment, because Evelyn's need was great, because Evelyn was a victim of this civilisation upon which Maurice battened, Jean had lifted the curtain.

Evelyn should not be deceived by the brave show of appearances. She should be admitted a little further into the hidden truth, to draw some comfort from reality.

But now Jean dropped the curtain. That raw and aching need was her husband's secret. Not even to Evelyn could she expose his weakness, nor confess that the richest gift he had brought to her was just that naked hunger.

There was silence for a little between the two women. Then Evelyn rose from her seat on the floor, stretching her long limbs and saying flippantly, 'You know, my charlady's an embittered spinster like myself, Jean. And the other day she came to me with a long story about her younger sister who has married a commercial traveller, and lives in a nice little semi-detached villa in Purley, and has a maid, and a pretty baby – and won't even ask my charlady to stay there for her holidays. "It isn't as if I cared," she kept on saying, and "It isn't as if I was jealous." Well *I* do, and I am. I do care. I am jealous. And I'm not going to pretend that it's nice for me that you've got all the things I always wanted. Why should I spare your feelings?'

'No reason why,' said Jean, sadly. She saw no reason. She felt worthless and impotent, without justification. In misfortune, she had never looked to life for justice, and she did not find it now that good fortune had belatedly fallen to her lot. She had little hope for the stability of her own happiness, having always seen mortal life as very brittle – a crust of paper-thin ice above the black fathomless waters of death. Any false step, and through one went, down, down, beyond all reach of love or hatred.

She had little hope of personal consolation for her friend, nor did she see herself as one having the right to offer favours.

What right, indeed, had any individual to the fine privilege of generosity? Wealth and poverty, suffering and ease, were accidents. There had been, she reckoned, about seven thousand people killed and injured in the Mandoan fire. She had seen children crippled for life, and young men blinded. She had seen slaves grown old in misery, their wrists hard as horn from old scars where irons had chafed them. She had seen girls newly snatched from burning villages, with heaving flanks and eyes like startled antelopes', defying their captors.

Did these sin, or their fathers, that such things came upon them?

'No reason,' she repeated. 'All the same, I came here partly to ask you to do something for me.'

'I – for you?' mocked Evelyn.

'We've taken a house at Frinton,' Jean blurted out clumsily. 'For the summer. Sea-air's supposed to be good for expectant mothers. Maurice, of course, can't come except for week-ends, but Mrs Durrant will doubtless keep me company, and lament Bill's bad luck in being alone in Lolagoba instead of rejoicing with a pregnant wife at Frinton. It's a nice house, though, with a lovely garden, and a bathing hut on the beach and everything. If you aren't fixed up for all your summer holidays I'd be so frightfully grateful if you'd come for a week or two. I know I shall be aching for female conversation and office gossip. And – in fact, it would be very, very good if you could occasionally come over for week-ends as well. I – you – you'd come, of course – as my guest – I mean – railway fares and things. Oh, Evelyn – don't *please* turn me down without considering.'

Evelyn began to walk restlessly round the room. She picked up Jean's coat and stood with the fragrant fur against her face. 'Lovely!' she said. 'I just adore touching such things – no, Jean, for heaven's sake don't offer to give me one. I should be tempted to accept. And I haven't got to that yet. But I'll come to Frinton. I'll travel at your expense. I'll come abroad with you later. I'll take your presents. Your company and your kindness will probably be the brightest things in my life. I'll warm myself at your fires. But I warn you, I shall resent that always. I shall cadge from you, and grumble at you and be jealous of you till I die. Only there's one thing I promise I won't do.' She smiled again at Jean, her sudden, enchanting smile. 'I won't be meek. I won't be a useful "aunty" to your children. I won't give them presents and be their godmother, and drop in to help you bath them on their nurse's half day out.'

'All right. I won't ask you.'

'No,' said Evelyn, wandering to the window and looking out above the chimney pots at the rising moon. 'No, Jean. I won't give way to you. When you're tied to your children, I'll flaunt my freedom at you. When you're sick and ill, I'll take advantage of my health. When you're bound by domesticities, bearing your double burden, I'll get myself sent to Mandoa.' She turned back to the room, her arms stretched against the window behind her. To Jean, sitting beside the fire, her thin figure seemed crucified in moonlight. 'Oh, I can see our future,' Evelyn cried. 'Look, I'll prophesy to you! I shall grow queerer and queerer, and more and more self-centred. I shall eat my heart and poison myself with it, and become a nuisance to my friends and a discredit to society. When you give parties, I shall be hurt if you don't ask me, and if you do ask me, I shall come wearing your cast-off dresses and my second-hand memories, and be a bore to your guests and a misery to your tender heart. I shall cling to my job and write pamphlets urging charity, with my mind full of black hatred. I shall work for Mandoan slaves, longing for half a chance to oppress any one but myself. I shall speak on platforms denouncing greed when my own soul is eaten away by hunger. And I shall invent a lying dogma that only by such as myself is the future served. For I'm not generous. I can't remember that humanity's more important than myself. Impersonal devotion is not an act of will; it's a gift of genius – as much a gift of the gods as music or poetry. Very few people have it. You know, I've often thought that Arthur Rollett was one. At the office, of course, it was not quite done to approve of him, But he always impressed me a little. You were there, Jean, weren't you, when he died?'

'Yes – I was.'

'What did you really think of him?'

Jean covered her face with her hands and sat, looking

into darkness set with fiery rings, feeling again the rage and fear and horror of captivity, the sickening hope, the lethargy of despair. But most of all she thought of Arthur Rollet, whose anguish had been the living core of the terror. He had been fastidious and resolute; he had been sensitive and tenacious. He had told her, in the orchard at Stoney Ridge, that she had beautiful hands; but that they were less important than her scale of values. He had faced without malice but without compromise the strength of his detractors. And he had died in unspeakable squalor and humiliation. He had been conscious, at the last, not only of his own suffering, but of the horror that it inflicted upon his opponents – the commissioners whose policy he had sought to forestall, but to whose persons he wished no evil. He had been aware that he was not only defeated, but confounded, and that even his death could achieve nothing.

Again the anarchy of injustice overwhelmed her.

'What is so terrible, so terrible about the dead,' she cried, 'is that you can't even tell them they weren't defeated. To be so helpless. It's intolerable! Intolerable.' The tears ran down her cheeks, but it was not alone for Arthur Rollett that she wept. She beat her knee with her clenched fist; but it was not against impotence only before the dead that she protested. 'You can't reach them. You can't get at them. You'd give your right hand to touch them – to do something – but you're helpless. There's nothing to be done – nothing to say.'

Then Evelyn came forward and knelt down beside her.

'My dear, don't I know? Don't I know?' she asked softly, taking Jean's beating, twisting hands in hers.

'Yes. Of course you know. That's why one can explain to you,' sobbed Jean. 'It was so terrible. All that nobility. All that effort. All that vision of good – wasted, wasted. He knew; he saw; he cared – and he had to die – like that – so, so *dreadfully*. While we, the half-hearted, the careerists, we, so easily diverted by personal interests – we were left, to betray his cause. Oh, it's so unfair. It's so unfair.'

'Why should you betray his cause?' asked Evelyn, but gently, not with her sharp arrogance.

'Don't you see, his was a faith in absolute justice? He believed in sacrifice and single-hearted service. He saw the obligation of the privileged, to go forward, righting wrongs, teaching the ignorant, building a new, fine, unconfused and ordered world.'

'But you are going forward. You are going on with his work. Isn't that just what you've been telling me?'

'Ah, but it's all so muddled. We work so slowly, through reports and committees, and rows with rival bodies. We play for our own hands. We advertise our own efforts. We push for publicity. Our work for a new world is all bound up with our careers and our self-interest. Maurice will grow rich on reform.'

'And you'll grow famous.'

'Yes. That's just it. We stake our reputations and our fortune – and then we no longer are disinterested. It all becomes part of the success game. We're not detached.'

'But if you are detached, my dear, you lose interest as I've done and so don't care a damn. That's the devil of it. But it's life, Jean. There's no escaping it. Profit and power – and progress – all confused, except for a very few, very rare, very fortunate men like Rollett.'

'Fortunate? But he failed – he died in anguish.'

'Failed? Died? Oh, you sentimentalist! Why do you only look at the end of life? Rollet lived splendidly, in complete integrity. He was an artist, who never once corrupted his vision. What is one week against a lifetime of valiant effort?'

'But the effort was wasted.'

'Was it? Weren't you just now grumbling most unreasonably against this child that's coming because it's going to interrupt your attempt to answer Rollett's challenge? Jean, Jean, don't you think I know you – after all these years? I know you're one of the enrichers of life. I was unfair. Don't tempt me by believing all that my jealousy says. Don't you realise that I understand what's happened to you, and that Rollett's death has been as important to you as your marriage? Oh, you won't betray Rollett. I know you. He's given you something I'd give my right hand to possess. You'll go on from strength to strength. You'll take up his battle. You'll free your slaves. You'll send your maternity nurses. You'll build your leper colonies and your schools. You'll make Mandoa a land fit for tourists to play in. No! That's unfair. I can't stop myself being unfair. Can't you *see*, Jean?'

She clutched Jean's hands as though she felt the danger of being dragged away from the rock of that friendship and understanding, out on to a sea of jealousy and misrepresentation.

'Listen. Listen quickly! Before I forget the truth and fashion a philosophy to meet my own dilemma – before I lose my humanity and hate you. To work for the good life – for that long age before us, to rebuild Mandoa, to be deterred neither by fortune nor misfortune, never to accept happiness as a substitute for effort, nor to excuse yourself from responsibility because you see no justice – that's your business, Jean. That's what you've got to do. Remember that. And when I tell you that the whole thing's not worth doing – don't believe me. Don't believe me when I say you can't eat your cake and have it. Don't listen to my jealousy and my cowardice when I tell you that no woman can bear the double burden.' Evelyn laughed a swift broken laugh. 'How does the hymn go? – "Lay hold on life" – ah, I have it—

> Lay hold on life, and it shall be
> Thy joy and crown eternally.

That's it – that's what you've got to do. Shrink from no experience – live in this world and work for your better one.'

'But will it be better? How do I know we shan't turn Mandoa into – into – West Kensington?' cried Jean.

'You won't know. You'll have to do the best you can

with the knowledge and the material you hold already. Personally, I think West Kensington is only the confused and wretched prelude to a very long story. I believe we are so little, so ignorant, so feeble an infant race crawling on a planet between immensities we haven't even begun to understand, that really we have no grounds for either congratulation or despair. It's beaten me, this world. I acknowledge it. Don't expect me to come with you on your gallant expedition to find the future. I shan't hinder you. I may even, if you pay me well and treat me nicely, help you a little. But it would be asking too much of human nature to expect me to care as you care. I wasn't in the hut when Rollett died. I only sat in a hospital waiting-room with a frigid, patronising family who resented the intrusion of my grief. I'm no good. I'm done for. All I want is a little fun – a little comfort. I don't believe in the impersonal-service . . . compensation myth. But you'll go forward. Even if you accomplish nothing, you'll have that satisfaction.'

Jean was still crying, but quietly.

Evelyn sat back on the hearthrug and grinned with a touch of her old sardonic malice.

'So, in the end, I have to dry your tears,' she said.

'Yes. Isn't it queer?

'You must go home now. I've upset you enough. Can you drive that opulent-looking machine all right, do you think? Or shall I get a taxi?'

'I shall be all right.'

Evelyn held her coat for her. Evelyn led her down the dark ill-smelling stairs. They stood for a moment in the twilit street.

'Don't forget what I said,' smiled Evelyn. 'I shall probably never say it again.'

'I shan't forget – ever,' Jean answered, and climbed into the car.

'And I'm coming to Frinton first-class, not third,' Evelyn told her.

'All right. Anything within reason. But don't forget the slump,' Jean contrived to answer.

Evelyn suddenly put out her hand and took Jean's fiercely.

'Good-bye, my fortunate friend,' she said, and turned, and ran back into the darkened house.

But Jean, driving home, saw a belated paper-seller outside the tube-station, and read on his poster the words, 'America says No.'

She did not know what it meant, but, seeing it thus, it revived the sense of apprehension that she had felt at lunch-time, She thought of the huge confused stream of life hurrying forward towards its unknown goal. She might make brave resolutions of service that seemed to her so important and considerable; she might listen to Evelyn's gallant challenge to action and reform; but what could she do? What was her strength? What was the life within her? What was Mandoa, when a world could end?

She thought of human frailty and the accidents of birth and death. Nothing was fixed, nothing secure. Perhaps even now events were rushing forward to the disaster which would wreck all dreams.

But something indomitable about her, something limited and practical, made her repress her apprehensions. The seed of life within her body, the resolution within her mind, impelled her. Cautiously, competently, she drove forward.

1932

Fantasies

These futuristic or fantastic imaginings, which Winifred Holtby used for satiric or moralistic purposes, are worldly stories in which her knowledge of political and social behaviour is given in the exaggerated and simplified outlines of unrealistic writing. They are homilies on the frailty of wealth and power, the contrariness of personality, the trivialisation of women's achievements, the unreliability of authority, and the ambition of those who are society's benefactors. Vera Brittain commented that Winifred had a 'capacity for swift exasperation' and that towards the end of her life she displayed 'critical, satirical and ruthless characteristics'. Most of the stories in this group were written late in her life, and do indeed display the satiric element Vera described. But her satiric tendency was an aspect of her progressive attitudes, an impatience at humanity's failure to realise its potential for rationality and good will.

The Truth About Portia

An Extract from an Interview in Olympus
By our own Correspondent – Mr W. H.
(whose identity has no connection with the Mr W. H.
to whom Shakespeare dedicated his Sonnets)

W. H.: . . . So, Mr Shakespeare, in spite of its popularity with academic examiners and amateur dramatic associations, you think *The Merchant of Venice* an unsuitable comedy for young people?

Mr Shakespeare: Unless, as I say, you believe in giving the natural cruelty of childhood something to bite on. I did. Bull-baiting of one kind or another being a favourite sport of the quick-witted and ruthless Londoners of my day, I provided them with *Twelfth Night* – which, you may remember, I subtitled 'What You Will' – to give them the pleasure of seeing a Puritan bullied, humiliated and spiritually tortured; I gave them *The Taming of the Shrew* to gratify the common impulses of masculine sadism and feminine masochism in seeing a woman's spirit broken; and in *The Merchant of Venice* I let loose a little contemporary anti-Semitism together with some profound observations on the nature and origins of cruelty.

W. H.: Anti-Semitism? But nowadays so many of our best Jewish actors play Shylock and make him a dignified figure putting to shame the Christians.

Mr Shakespeare: I have observed the fashion with some amusement. It proves my theory that one character in his time is played as many parts even upon the stage. But obviously I wrote Shylock as the perfect rôle for a full-blooded, melodramatic player of villains. Remember

his first snarling entrance – 'Three thousand ducats – well
. . . For three months, well. Antonio shall become bound,
well.' Then the quick change to the snapping staccato
of 'But ships are but boards, sailors but men; there be
land-rats and water-rats,' and so on. Remember how his
servant called him a 'kind of devil' and left him for a poor
man; his daughter described his house as hell and thought
nothing of cheating him. Cheated, he thought more of his
ducats than his daughter . . . 'I would my daughter were
dead at my foot and the jewels in her ear.' He was never
even an imaginative patriot. 'The curse never fell upon our
nation till now; I never felt it till now.' I filled the text
with references to his bearded grisling misanthropic age
and ugliness. But no. On the strength of two passages,
the 'Hath not a Jew eyes? hath not a Jew hands, organs,
dimensions, senses, affections, passions?' – a good piece of
stock oratory, superbly written, I grant you – and the final
exit, 'I pray you give me leave to go from hence. I am not
well' – actors have played him as though he were a King
of Jews . . . No, the real excuse for Shylock was Antonio.
    W. H.: Antonio – the 'royal merchant'?
    MR SHAKESPEARE: The royal bore – bore royal, bore
insufferable.

> In sooth, I know not why I am so sad.
> It wearies me: you say it wearies you.

It does, my friend, it does. He had what you would call
to-day the superiority complex. He would say to a friend
who was leaving him,

> I take it your own business calls on you,
> And you embrace the occasion to depart—

expecting passionate protests.

> I hold the world but as the world, Gratiano,
> A stage where every man must play a part,
> And mine a sad one;

when everything was going splendidly with him. Then 'I am the tainted wether of the flock,' and that final touch of mock-humble malice in sending for Bassanio to see him die. The only thing to be said for that was that Bassanio, being an insensitive, fortune-hunting, unimaginative, unscrupulous young prodigal, probably would have endured the ordeal better than most.

W. H.: Then I gather you do not think much of Bassanio, though you gave him a handsome speech in the casket scene, and Portia, surely, loved him very well – or was not Portia really a golden lass? Did you mean her, too, to be malicious or a fool?

Mr Shakespeare: Not a fool. I never made a heroine with a better-ordered mind. Beatrice had quicker wits, Rosalind prettier fancies. But Portia was an educated woman of great intelligence, high quality, charm and courage. Malicious? Of course she was malicious. She enjoyed baiting Shylock as she enjoyed tempting Bassanio to betray her ring – as she enjoyed mocking and deceiving her unattractive suitors. But she was the victim of an impossible situation. The real butt of *The Merchant* – my private butt, not the butt of the groundlings – was the law and its vagaries. Portia was writhing under the harrow of the law. That was why she knew so much about it.

W. H.: Ah! she was really learned then? She didn't just borrow her arguments from Bellario?

Mr Shakespeare: No. Bellario may have been her tutor. But she had learned her business before Shylock claimed his forfeit. Remember that she was a great lady, an heiress; she administered her own estates. It was the 'great' world of which her 'little body' was weary. But she was bound by her father's will under the intolerable settlement of the caskets. She had to marry the suitor chosen under that hazard. She respected the law, but she found its burden horrible. Naturally she had taken an interest in what oppressed her, as an ailing man will pore over tomes on medicine. She had sought loopholes of escape and found none. So her mind was constantly playing on legal terms and parables. She could not tell Nerissa of her linguistic difficulties with her suitors without saying, 'and you will come into the court and swear that I have a poor pennyworth in the English.' She could play with words more glibly than a barrister, telling the Moor,

> Yourself, renowned prince, then stood as fair
> As any comer I have look'd on yet
> For my affection,

which might be – according to the letter of the law – true enough, considering how ill she thought of them all; but she was ready enough when he had chosen wrong, to remark nonchalantly:

> A gentle riddance. Draw the curtains; go.
> Let all of his complexion choose me so.

She was colour-conscious as well as anti-Semitic. She was apt with legal maxims:

> To offend, and judge, are distinct offices
> And of opposed natures.

At Bologna, in my time, lived a young doctor of law, Bellissima, the most popular lecturer of her age, they said. Perhaps her career was in my mind a little.

W. H.: If she was so wise, why then did she love Bassanio whom you call an insensitive prodigal?

MR SHAKESPEARE: Have you seen so little of the world that you can fail to understand that? He was handsome, he was a gentleman, he came to visit her in good company while her father was alive and life seemed simple and happy. He was reputed a scholar and a soldier. And he was forbidden to her – unless of course by some improbable chance he happened on the right casket. She was attracted by him at that first encounter; she fell in love with his memory when surrounded by drunken

Germans, coltish Neapolitans, affected Frenchmen, inarticulate Englishmen, proud Spaniards, austerely valiant Moors. She knew nothing of his spirit, but he seemed a man of her own kind. Being quick, vital and generous, she longed to love. Loving, she longed to humble herself.

> . . . the full sum of me
> Is sum of something; which, to term in gross
> Is an unlessoned girl, unschool'd, unpractis'd:
> Happy in this, she is not yet so old
> But she may learn; happier than this,
> She is not bred so dull but she can learn;
> Happiest of all is, that her gentle spirit
> Commits itself to yours to be directed
> As from her lord, her governor, her king.

That is the common reaction of the first glow of love.

> One half of me is yours, the other half yours,
> Mine own, I would say.

Quick as her wits are, passion is quicker and tumbles her into a sweet confusion. Just because she knows her worth she yearns to abase it.

> But now I was the lord
> Of this fair mansion, master of my servants,
> Queen o'er myself.

She was a proud woman. That was partly why her father's will was so cruel and so bad for her.

W.H.: You said she was malicious.

MR. SHAKESPEARE: Of course. Malice is for some the natural reaction of strained nerves and high spirits. She avenged herself on her suitors for endangering her liberty, by mocking them. She avenged herself on the law by using it in court to break a Jew who was – in general – a social outcast, and in particular, the enemy of her husband's friend and of her happiness. More than that – do you imagine that from the first moment Bassanio confessed

> O sweet Portia!
> Here are a few of the unpleasant'st words
> That ever blotted paper,

and explained his debt to Antonio, that she ever felt quite the same again towards him? She had fallen in love with the imagined counterpart of her own nature; she had asked only that her gentle spirit should be committed to him for tutelage. And within five minutes she found him something less than his appearance and herself bound to pay his debts to save his honour. Of course she took it out of Shylock. Of course she took it out of Bassanio, inventing that cruel trick with the ring. There is more than light-hearted fooling in her

> If you had known the virtue of the ring
> Or half her worthiness that gave the ring,
> Or your own honour to contain the ring,
> You would not then have parted with the ring.

In her swift flight to Venice and her risky venture to save the honour of which her husband had been so careless, she had learned something about virtue, worthiness and honour, and, among other things, that there was little of any of those qualities in Bassanio. The fairy story of *The Merchant* ends with Bassanio's choice of the right casket; after that follows the disillusioning reality. No. I don't think I should call it a good piece for schoolrooms. It is too near to the raw marrow of the nerves.

W. H.: Thank you, Mr Shakespeare. And now, would you be good enough to give me your opinion on the influence of the Talkies?

date unknown

The Queen's Justice

A FAIRY STORY ABOUT COMPLEXES

ONCE upon a time in the same country there were born two children; and to the christening of the first went all the good fairies, but to the christening of the second went bad fairies only.

The good fairies bestowed upon their godchild health enough to keep him cheerful, without that insensitiveness which makes men brutal; good looks enough to give him confidence, without that beauty which makes men self-conscious; and talent enough to excite his own ambition, without that genius which would render him ridiculous to others. To these natural gifts they added two advantages of circumstance. They gave him a family loving enough to teach him the arts of friendship, yet indifferent enough to let him go comfortably when he wished to travel; and money enough to save him from insecurity, without great wealth to delude him into thinking idleness an obligation.

The bad fairies bestowed upon their godchild ill-health enough to depress his spirits, without disease sufficient to free him from responsibility. They gave him looks plain enough to rob him of self-confidence, without ugliness sufficient to render him distinguished, and they gave him genius enough to make him miserable, without talent sufficient to exercise it profitably. To these natural infirmities they added two disadvantages of circumstance. They gave him a family so loving that it surrounded his youth with apprehensions, yet isolated his adolescence from all other friendships, and they gave him wealth enough to accustom him to elegance and comforts, without security to ensure him against the chance of losing them.

When the Fairy Queen heard of this partial distribution of favours she was angry, declaring that she would not suffer injustice in her kingdom. So she called the good fairies and bad fairies together, and bade them hand over to her each one more gift. The good fairies gave her a tender heart, and the bad fairies gave her a grievance, and she looked at them both for a minute, then said, 'These will do,' and tossed them down on to the cradles of the children.

'Ha, ha!' cried the bad fairies. 'You've muddled it, after all. Don't you see that you've given the lucky child the tender heart and the unlucky one the grievance? Do you call it justice to give more good gifts to those who have them already?'

'As it happens,' said the Queen severely, 'that is justice. You will see for yourselves if you have a little patience. Now run away and play.'

So the fairies went away, and the two children grew up into manhood. The fortunate boy, being healthy, handsome and talented, was also charming. Having experienced no cause for terror, he was courageous; having no reason to fear rivalry, he was generous; necessity never having driven him to deceit, he was candid and honourable; having no pain to stifle and no apprehensions to overcome, he was never tempted to excesses; having found pleasure and success in work, he was industrious; accustomed to kindness, he treated others with consideration, and, expecting like treatment in return, was rarely disappointed. Thus when he went out to seek his fortune in the world, its foundations were already laid within himself.

The unhappy boy, lacking health, looks and confidence, was driven to drown his timidity in dissipation; conscious of genius, he yet lacked efficiency, and, thwarting his own power of achievement, grudged all his rivals their success. Learning from his own envy to expect no generosity from others, he became incapable of friendship, and living in fear, suspicion, jealousy and disappointment, was daily driven to cloak his misery in deceit. Thus when he also went out to seek his fortune, its ruin was already pre-doomed within himself.

'There's not much chance of justice here,' laughed the bad fairies.

'You really are rather stupid,' said the Queen. 'Remember my gifts.'

Now it happened one day that both young men applied for the same appointment in a great public institution, and sat together in the same room, awaiting interviews.

The godchild of the good fairies drove up in a taxi. His eye was bright, his smile steady, his costume irreproachable and his manner charming, for, having an independent income, he sought the post through desire for the work rather than through fear of penury. His attitude towards his prospective employer was, therefore, that of a free man towards a possible colleague rather than that of a slave towards an inevitable tyrant. No one, indeed, could have been more prepossessing.

The godchild of the bad fairies was quite different. He had thrown over less remunerative work to seek this post, and regarded it now as a final barrier between himself and beggary. Assured of his continual misfortune, he had spent his last guinea on whisky, acquired from the whisky a loud voice and an uncertain eye, fallen from the bus step into the gutter, splashing his coat, cutting his hand and destroying the remnant of his nerve, and had arrived at the institution in a condition of irritability and confusion bordering on hysteria.

Both young men were interviewed by their prospective employer, who said that he would tell them his decision later, and as they left the building the godchild of the good fairies, with his habitual hospitality and friendliness, suggested that his rival should now lunch with him. The unfortunate young man, convinced that the other had robbed him of his chance, decided to take at least one good meal in exchange, and accepted the invitation.

During lunch, prompted by his grievance, he began to narrate the story of his misfortunes, his ill-health, his poverty, his loneliness, his genius which separated him from society, and his ill-luck which hindered him from success.

His companion listened with attention, his tender heart increasingly afflicted. He could not exchange confidences, for the recital of his own felicity appeared tactless; but he expressed his admiration for one who had borne such blows of fate with fortitude. The fortitude, perhaps, was not conspicuous, but it is a habit with tender-hearted persons to assume the presence of those virtues in others which they have not yet had opportunity to discern.

'Ah, well,' sighed the godchild of the bad fairies. 'I shall need courage. For certainly I shall not get that job, and if I don't get it, I am ruined.'

'Oh, don't say that,' cried his tender-hearted host, suddenly aware that it would be intolerable to inflict yet another burden on one so terribly beset already. And directly lunch was over, he returned to the institution and withdrew his candidature in favour of his rival.

'But that is impossible,' said the employer. 'I had already decided to offer you the post, and if you will not take it, I shall certainly not offer it to that young fellow. For you are strong, capable, friendly, eager and intelligent, and I perceive also that you have a tender heart, which is a great advantage in employees. But your friend is twisted, clumsy, egoistic and a drunkard, and I perceive also that he has a grievance, which would make life difficult for his employer. So the best thing you can do is to begin your work here on Monday morning and make full use of your advantages.'

'But is that fair,' asked the young man, 'when I have already so much and he so little?'

'You know the rule of Fairyland,' said the employer. 'Unto him that hath shall be given, and from him that hath not shall be taken away even that which he hath. It is so sensible. You will start with a salary of twelve hundred pounds per annum.'

The young man went away sorrowful; for he had great possessions, and he saw that it was a far more difficult matter than he had supposed to hand over even a fraction of them to the poor. But he did his best, finding his new friend a minor post in the same institution, offering him lavish hospitality, and inviting all the most distinguished celebrities of the day to meet him.

The godchild of the bad fairies, however, was invincibly fortified against these benevolences by his grievance. 'It's all very well for you,' he declared bitterly. 'You have the authority, the wealth, the friends and the successes. You can afford to let crumbs fall to me from your table. Do not the laws of Fairyland assure us that it is more blessed to give than to receive? Your ability to give is one of your chief privileges. Practice it on me if you like – by all means. We failures exist in order to provide the pleasures of patronage for the successful.'

And, indeed, it seemed as though he spoke the truth, for the more his friend sought his advantage, the greater the profits he acquired for himself. If the fortunate young man suggested that his friend deserved promotion, he prompted the employer merely to raise his own salary. When he attempted to find his friend a wife, the lady fell in love with him instead. When he praised the other's genius, he merely reaped credit for his own unselfishness. The greater his success, the more painful became his relations with his colleague, the deeper the suffering of his tender heart.

At length he could endure it no longer, so he persuaded his friend to go with him to the fairies, and ask them to take back their gifts, or at the worst, exchange them. 'For life without justice is intolerable,' declared both young men.

'Well,' said the fairy godmothers, 'we can't take back our gifts, but we can exchange them, if you both desire it. A very odd request certainly, but that's not our business. There is one thing, however, that we cannot do – anything that the Fairy Queen herself gave, we cannot alter.'

The young men agreed to risk this, and returned to their employment. The exchange of gifts soon became apparent. The godchild of the good fairies lost his fortune. His health failed him, and with his health, his looks and his efficiency. His employer found his work no longer satisfactory, so degraded him from his position and gave him one of the minor clerkships in the basement office. Being now sickly, poor and unsuccessful, the young man could not afford his former hospitality, and his friends, embarrassed by the need to condole where they had once congratulated, stayed away.

The godchild of the bad fairies, however, was promoted to the post and salary vacated by his friend. Having become wealthy, he was able to buy remedies for his ill-health; good health brought him good looks; good looks, self-confidence; self-confidence at once improved his manners; his better manners brought him popularity; popularity stimulated his genius, and he was able to show the world his hidden merits.

But because the gifts of the Fairy Queen were not transferable, the first young man still kept his tender heart, and the second his grievance. So when one day they met again, and the godchild of the good fairies asked, 'How are you?' the other young man cried out, 'How am I? I'm utterly exhausted, and no wonder. Life becomes simply unendurable. The cares of office! The complications of friendship! The fatigue of responsibility! The burden of wealth! The wearisome treadmill of success! Ah, now I see how wise you were to choose obscurity, peace, the gentle liberties of slender means, and the exquisite irresponsibilities of ill-health!'

'Really!' said the first young man. 'You must be right. I hadn't quite thought of it like that, but now you describe your life, it does sound most exhausting.'

'It is indeed. It's all very well for you to look sympathetic. You've got out of it all very prettily. A nice trick you played me. And now I suppose I shall have to go on bearing your burdens till the end of the chapter.'

'Oh, don't say that,' cried the tender-hearted young man. 'I can't bear to see you so unhappy, and still less can I bear to think it all my fault. Come, let us go together to the Queen and ask for justice. She is honour itself, and she will not deny us.'

So together they went to the Fairy Queen, where she sat in the Courts of Fairyland with the good fairies and bad fairies before her; and they told her all about it.

When they had finished she looked down at the fairy godmothers and began laughing very softly.

'Well,' said she, 'have I not done justice? Here are these two young men. To the first you gave health, beauty, talents, friendship; to the second you gave poverty, ugliness, failure and disease, and all I gave to set the balance even was a tender heart to one and a grievance to the other, and now see what has happened. Armed with his grievance, the second man was able to rob his friend of health, wealth, fortune, success and popularity. For a grievance, which some call an Inferiority Complex, is the most powerful weapon of attack in Fairyland. No tender heart can stand against it, and with it a man can get everything but happiness. As for the first, he has lost everything but his tender heart, yet still thinks himself more fortunate than his robber. For a tender heart, which some call a Superiority Complex, is the most powerful weapon of defence in Fairyland. Armed with it a man can lose everything but the privilege of pity. So you see, in giving these two gifts, I acted with perfect justice and made things remarkably even between your two godchildren.'

'Oh, no,' cried the man with a grievance. 'You can't get out of it like that, your majesty. I may be successful, but you yourself admitted that I could not be happy. This Inferiority Complex you gave me is not a happy thing.'

'And I,' protested the young man with the tender heart. 'I am not happy. How could I be, when I am still the cause of suffering to my poor friend here? This Superiority Complex you gave me is not a happy thing.'

'Who said it was?' retorted the Fairy Queen. 'I never promised anything about happiness. You came to me for justice, and you've got it. You'll have to go back and make happiness for yourselves if you want it. It has nothing to do with justice, and no fairy godmothers can give it. Now, run away and play. I'm tired of you. It's twelve o'clock already. Next case, forward!'

And the courts of Fairyland resumed their daily task.

1932

127

The D.O.I.: An Interview of the Future

August 17, 1951. *London*

SILENTLY, swiftly, the aspiring lift bore me upward through the towering tunnel that pierces the most mysterious building in London. I was there. I was I. It was It. I was in the third New Building of the British Broadcasting Corporation, on my way to interview the Director of Inventions. It was incredible.

Hunky, the most famous lift-boy in the world, the cherub-cheeked Mercury known to a thousand broadcasters, shifted his gum from one cheek to the other.

'Hunky,' I said, 'is it true that your parents on both sides were in the police force?'

But already the lift was still. 'Forty-eighth floor,' read the dial.

'Third to the right, fourth to the left, and mind the step, please,' said Hunky. There was no step. I recognised his old-fashioned courtesy.

The Director of Inventions is guarded by three secretaries, four porters, and an armed detective. A mental specialist is always in attendance to deal with those lunatics whose appearance has deceived the porters. Seventy-five attempts on his life have been made by disappointed inventors; he has been involved in eight breach of promise cases, five libel actions, and three cases of attempted murder. 'Inventors are savage fellows,' his secretary told me. Only my credentials from *The Radio Times* opened those guarded doors to me. I have interviewed Mussolini, Kemal Pasha, Greta Garbo, Mr Hoover, and the late Chief of the Ritz at Baden-Baden; but I have never felt the same thrill that I felt when approaching the Magician of the B.B.C., whose genius has transformed England.

I found the Director sitting at his desk, with a photograph of his little son beside him, and a bowl of dewy roses fresh from his grounds in that most exclusive residential district, Shoreditch Garden City.

'Is it true,' I asked him, 'that you never take a holiday?'

'Quite true,' he said. 'Holidays are unnecessary to the well-regulated system. I take four hours sleep, rise and ride in Victoria Park for three hours before breakfast. I breakfast on grape-fruit and a cup of black coffee with a dash of milk in it, motor to my office here, attend to my correspondence till noon, lunch lightly on another grape-fruit or a cup of orange-juice, work again until five o'clock, when I have a board meeting with my colleagues. After which I dine simply on half a cutlet, work at inspecting inventions until ten-thirty, when I listen to music from Vladivostock until midnight, when I retire.'

'Yes, I see,' I said. 'And – your hobbies?'

'I am passionately devoted to my garden, my children, and my wife. Home life,' said the great man, 'has made England what it is. I always make a point of playing with my son from five-fifteen to five-twenty every Sunday. A deck-chair, a pipe, and a good book. Family love. Roses. Poetry. Shakespeare, Epstein. Tennyson. Hugh Walpole. The laughter of little children. Hygiene. Truth. These things endure.'

I bowed my head. 'You are a philosopher?' I suggested humbly.

'I am a scientist.' The brave words rang through the great apartment. 'I believe in knowledge. I believe in action. I believe in virtue, courage, work, work, work. I believe in simple human contacts, in the Great Simplicities.'

Silence fell in the room. The Director took up his pen and signed seven more documents.

At length I asked: 'There is one thing. Our readers are specially anxious to know if there is any truth in the rumour that the B.B.C. once turned down an invention which might have staggered the world.'

He rose. An expression of intense emotion passed like a cloud across his handsome, ascetic, immobile features. He went to the window and stood looking across the city whose life he had so notably affected. Then he turned to me with a gesture of manly acquiescence.

'It is true,' he said. 'For years I have kept silence. But I believe that sooner or later I owe the truth to England. Yesterday I was shot at again by a lady whose invention of special earphone attachments for parrots, to teach them the use of foreign languages by wireless, I had turned down on the grounds of disapproval by my psychological advisers, who believe that too great an intellectual strain on parrots causes neurosis. Any day my lips may be sealed for ever. I will speak.'

He returned to the desk. His fine, sensitive fingers played with a pen-wiper. My heart beat so violently that it almost drowned the words of his gentle voice.

'Tell my country this,' he said at length. 'Ten years ago a young woman, a student from Chelsea Polytechnic, invented a receiver by which she could listen to any day after to-morrow.'

'Only she?' I asked. 'Or any one?'

His brows contracted very slightly. I was silent, accepting his reproof.

'She brought it to us,' he continued. 'We tested it. Her claim was true. We had come upon the most wonderful discovery of modern times. The future was no longer veiled in mystery. The secrets of the Stock Exchange were ours. Manufacturers could anticipate a rise in trade, a change in fashion. Picnickers could know for certain whether it would be fine. Doctors could foretell epidemics. Statesmen could see the result of a division.'

'Then why, why in Heaven's name,' I cried, 'did the world never hear of this marvel?'

'The first thing I listened to on the instrument was my own voice telling the Director-in-Chief that we must turn it down – for the sake of England. I should say' – he gave a little deprecating smile – 'I should say, remembering our Scottish listeners, of Great Britain.'

'But I should have thought that the nation—' I began. 'Surely it would be a good thing. To know the future? To be able to anticipate—? What possible disadvantage—?'

'Have you never thought,' said he, 'of the great, the appalling disaster which knowing the future would involve? No. Nor, I will confess, had we. I admit here that the British Broadcasting Corporation almost failed in prescience. We called a meeting. The Directors spoke. Art, learning, statesmanship, humour, pedagogy approved. Nothing more momentous had ever been offered to one of our momentous meetings. We were all jubilant. Then the Sports Director spoke. "I propose that the invention be bought immediately, the inventor handsomely rewarded, sworn to secrecy, and the model, plans, designs, and all clues of the instrument destroyed for ever." Our consternation was as you may imagine it. We asked, as you are asking now, why, why? He told us: "You must destroy the instrument or you will destroy the soul of Britain"; and when we implored him to explain, he said: "You will destroy Sportsmanship."'

The Director of Inventions leant across his desk and emphasised his words by tapping on my fingers with a marble paper-weight.

'Do you realise that sportsmanship depends absolutely on uncertainty?' he said, with slow, impressive emphasis. 'Do you realise that if we knew what was going to happen the day after tomorrow, the whole of our national life would be disorganised? The result of the Derby, the result of the Cup Tie Final, the result of the Oxford and Cambridge Boat Race would be known beforehand. Speculation on the Stock Exchange would be unnecessary, indeed impossible. No one would want to play tennis, knowing already who would win. All future Waterloos would be lost because the playing fields of Eton would be deserted. If we could listen beforehand to the future, general elections would be rendered superfluous because

we should know already what party would be in power.
Who would ever want to ask a question if they could tune
in and know the answer? Who would enter a competition
if they knew already to whom the prize would be awarded?
Have you ever pictured to yourself what would happen if
the vast insurance system of this country broke down?
What would be the effect on our financial stability, on
regular readers, on the *Daily Mail*? But if we all knew
beforehand just when we should break our legs; if the
insurance companies knew beforehand who would be the
victims of fatal railway accidents – how would you like
never to be able to register as a regular reader because
the Insurance Manager of a paper knew that you would
be drowned in Wales? Think of what would happen to
our political system if every one knew beforehand what
would be in next year's Budget! And as for morality: How
many brides would go to the altar if they knew that their
husbands would go bankrupt within three years – or take
to drink? How many bridegrooms – But no, no. Whenever
I think of the appalling consequences of a moment's fore-
sight I am horrified.' Another cloud of intense emotion
passed across his handsome, commanding features. 'When
I look into the abyss – But there. We learned in time. We
were saved. England was saved – I mean, Great Britain.'

The clock above his desk, synchronised with Big Ben by
wireless control, warned me that only two minutes more
of my precious interview remained. I remembered my duty
to my readers.

'I am so interested,' I said. 'Now there is one other little
matter – if you *would* be so kind. Will you just tell me in
three words your opinion of the Modern Girl?'

1931

The Comforter

ONE day an angel walking through the Heavenly Mansions came upon a newly-arrived soul weeping bitterly.

'Who are you? What is the matter?' asked the angel.

'I am a sinner,' he was answered.

'Is that so?' said the angel. 'Show me your record.'

The sinner produced his record, and the angel read that he had been a great patriot, noble and courageous, the saviour of his country and the champion of his political principles. With wholehearted devotion he had subdued rebellion, maintained order, inspired loyalty and led his conquering people to their hard-won triumph. When others had faltered he had known no weakness; seeing his duty he had dared to do it, and when he died his name had become his people's glory, a song on their lips, a light in their eyes, a banner on their ramparts. And now he had come to enjoy eternal bliss.

'Well?' asked the angel, returning the record to its owner.

'Lies, all lies,' wept the sinner. 'Of course I once believed them or I shouldn't have come here. I didn't know that Heaven was the place where you learn the truth about yourself.'

'Truth is one of the properties of Heaven,' said the angel.

'But I cannot bear it! I cannot bear it!' moaned the sinner. 'Who shall deliver me from the burden of the truth?'

Then he heard a voice through Heaven, saying:

'Come unto me all ye that labour and are heavy laden and I will give you rest.'

'Let us go,' said the angel, and led the sinner through the Heavenly Pastures up to the Throne of God.

But as the sinner walked it seemed to him that the starry flowers in the meadows shrivelled, the crystal sea splintered like glass and the songs of triumph roared intolerably in his ears, so that when he came to the throne he flung himself down and cried out in extremity of desolation.

The angels and archangels gathered round him, but he turned on them fiercely.

'Go away! Go away!' he cried. 'You all are sinless creatures, spirits and flames of fire. What do you know of earth and man and the complexities of trying to live in a world where souls are imprisoned in bodies, bodies in societies, and all men tangled in the trap of time? Your crowns, your songs, your triumphs only torture me.'

The angels round the throne chanted in answer:

'Surely he hath borne our griefs and carried our sorrows. He was despised and rejected of men, a man of sorrows and acquainted with grief. He was wounded for our transgressions, he was bruised for our iniquities; the chastisement of our peace was upon him, and with his stripes we are healed.'

'But I am not healed,' said the sinner. 'And if I were, what does it matter whether I am healed or not, when I have seen what I have done to others? I could not bear to be healed knowing now as I do their torment. What does the Son of God know of my sorrow? You were wounded by men, but I have wounded them. You were punished for the sins of others; but I inflicted punishment. What do you know of treachery, who only were betrayed? But I despised gentleness. I rejected mercy. I laid my chastisements on others and told myself that my rage was fine and noble, that hatred was sacred when it was impersonal, that vengeance and malice were righteous indignation, that indulgence of cruelty was a purging fire. I have set the fine spirit of man in prison, till endurance failed and valour was destroyed, and what was once strength and beauty became vile idiocy and cringing ugliness. Who are you, oh, conqueror of the Cross, who now can reign eternally in Heaven, to speak of my sorrow?'

Then the King beckoned to a woman who stood beside the throne, and she came down to the sinner, and tried to comfort him, saying: 'I know. I know. I had to see Him suffer. I had to turn over and over in my mind this thing or that thing I might have done to stop it. I had to recall each day of His growth, each hour of my watching, to learn where I had failed that it had come to this. He knew in His own body the measure of His anguish; but ever afterwards, that sword pierced my heart also, and there was no limit to my pain.'

The sinner raised his head and spoke humbly to her.

'I know, woman,' he said, 'that you have suffered. But you stood by the Cross. You faced the executioners. You saw the resurrection. But I gave orders and never saw their consequence. I signed letters and read numbers and confirmed decisions. I sat in an office where everything was polite and easy, and never in my life uttered an angry word, nor made an uncouth gesture. Every woman I met remarked my courtesy. But now that I am in Heaven I can see everything. I have learned how slow is the growth of life in the mother's womb, how gradually it takes possession of her body, how inexorable is the law of its development until it is born in pain and helplessness. I have learned to count the hours of that nine months' servitude to creation, when the will can no longer say, "This will I do," "This will I leave undone." I have experienced the hope, the fear, the agony, the exaltation. And I know now that birth is only the beginning of the mother's travail. I have felt the strong tug of heart and nerve back to the playing child, the sleeping child. I know what dread there is in storm or famine that may harm it, what joy in a blossom, an orange, a sunlit day, because these things may please it. And I have seen what happens when a town where children are living is bombarded, when the shrapnel splinters the safe, familiar windows, and instead of security there is terror, and instead of kindness, there is pain. The happy confident play is checked; the laughter on the child's face turns to resentment. "What has done this? I don't like this? What are you doing to me?" the child cries, and no one answers it. I commanded the stern suppression of insurrection, the enforcement of orders – for the sake of discipline. I did not see how the child would drop its orange and scream at the blood flowing from its shoulder. What do you know of sorrow, Mother of God, who only saw what others had done to your Son in His manhood?'

Then the woman turned away and beckoned to a man who came slowly and sat beside the sinner.

'I think, perhaps, that I understand you,' said this other. 'My name is Peter. I had sworn that though I should die with my Lord, yet I would not deny Him. And before the cock crew, I denied Him thrice. It is not a thing to be forgotten.' And again in the court of Heaven, with bliss encircling him like the blue sharp light from the crystal sea, Peter bowed his head and wept bitterly.

The sinner looked at him with bitter envy.

'What is denial?' he asked. 'You could not save Him. You hurt no one but yourself by your own cowardice. You repented immediately, and lived a noble life and died a gallant and very painful death, and upon the rock of your faith His Church was founded. But I have betrayed faith. I have denied decency. I taught men to hate and called it loyalty. I taught them to spy upon each other and called it citizenship. I taught them to condemn one another and called it preserving a high standard of morality. I murdered happiness and peace and friendliness, and accepted complacently the praise I won for it. Who are you, first of the Apostles, who can enjoy the friendship of your Master, to speak to me about denial?'

Then the King beckoned again, and from the outer courts of Heaven came one who approached the throne with some timidity, as though he could not be quite sure of his right there. But at a word from the King he spoke to the sinner.

'I also,' he said, 'know how a man can choose evil instead of goodness. In life I was a thief, hugging my vileness. I stole, not from need, but from love of going one better on a fellow creature. I enjoyed turning confidence into fear, and a fine handsome lad, a bit gay with wine, into a bloody, mangled bundle by the road-side. I betrayed women; I sold innocence to lust; I defiled children. I gloried in my vanity, my filth, my ugliness. Of course in the end I made the mistake we all make and got caught for it, and then I whined and whimpered, until when actually upon the cross I saw, for the first time in my life, what goodness was. Then I derided it. Though in my soul I recognised the truth, I spat upon it, and died calling the light darkness.'

The sinner laughed. 'You served your own dirty little sins and took your punishment,' he said. 'Your evil proclaimed itself upon your twisted body, your foul mouth and leering eye. You were a warning as well as a menace to society. People remembered you and your wicked life and hideous death, and were more careful. But I made sin seem splendid. My statue stands at the street corner; my picture hangs in all the country's schoolrooms. Children are taught to follow my example, because I was a good man and a great patriot and a staunch upholder of the righteous cause. Who are you, little felon, who can creep forgiven into the back-ways of Heaven, to talk to me of sorrow?'

Then the King said: 'I will not leave you comfortless,' and took the sinner and led him out of Heaven across a great gulf into another place. And again he beckoned, and a man came running from a far distance, and the King left the two of them together.

'Who are you? What is the matter?' asked the stranger.

The sinner told him everything that had happened.

'Then perhaps you can help me,' said the stranger. 'For I need comfort, and the two of us are brothers. We should understand each other.'

'What have you done to need comfort?' asked the sinner.

'I sold my Lord for thirty pieces of silver. I did not need the money. Like you, I thought that I was doing something clever – precipitating a crisis when His Father would give him more than twelve legions of angels to prove his power.'

'You betrayed only one innocent man,' said the sinner.

'Insomuch as I did it unto Him,' answered Iscariot, 'I did it unto the least of these, His brethren.'

'You repented,' said the sinner. 'You went out and hanged yourself.'

'Yes,' said Iscariot. 'And found myself in Heaven. But how do you imagine that I could bear that place? Heaven is only tolerable for those who have learned how to forgive themselves. So I came here, where, if we are in torment, we may at least share the pain we have inflicted. We are not called upon to suffer the horror of immunity. And, perhaps, in the fire we may learn to cleanse ourselves. At least, perhaps, we may learn to help each other. For God in His infinite mercy will not suffer even one sinner to be tortured by the incongruity of eternal bliss.'

Then the sinner, turning to comfort Iscariot, entered gladly, as into his natural element, the flame.

1934

'There Was a Sound . . .'

I BELIEVE that the sight which I have seen will become historic. When another Byron leads another Childe Harold round the Europe of 1931, and shows him Germany in travail, Austria fainting, Hungary capitulating, Great Britain in crisis, a sense of apprehension everywhere, the bankers conferring, statesmen flying at three miles a minute from town to town, the mark staggering, the pound trembling, the people buying paper after paper to learn what may be the latest blow of fortune, he will, like Byron, begin one of his cantoes:

There was a sound of revelry by night.

The scene will not be Belgium's capital. It will be the capital of no national state, for the actual territory on which the building stands is geographically French, politically Monacan, and spiritually cosmopolitan. The place is the new Casino at Monte Carlo. The time was the hour of European crisis.

The building itself is astonishing enough. Coming upon it as I did by night, driving down the famous slope past shops and a terrific new luxury hotel, where, two years ago, when I was last there, I saw bare rocky cliff, it blazed out of the darkness at me, an incredible Babylonish palace. Every possible ingenuity of lighting has been used to conceal and reveal the sharp angles of 'modern' wall and balcony. Along the terrace overhanging the sea burn great metal flowers of white and silver, electric lights under their vast curving petals. A gigantic Negro in a white uniform stands at the doorway. Inside, the immense vestibule is crowded. There are women in navy-blue woollen trousers and jerseys, women in chiffon pyjamas, women in light washing summer frocks, women in evening dresses more voluminous of skirt and exiguous of bodice than any I have ever seen. The men who escort them gleam in the black and white of full-dress suits, or glow in the gorgeous blues and oranges of sleeveless shirts, worn with shorts and coloured handkerchiefs; or they wear flannels; or mess-jackets; or the tweed suits of travellers; or indeed, anything by nothing, and almost that.

Here, indeed, all the ends of the earth are gathered, Jew, Greek, Russian Armenian, French and Italian, Russian and Pole, hundred per cent. American and almond-eyed Japanese. A Russian Grand Duke, reputed to be one of the assasins of Rasputin, sits on a high stool beside the cocktail bar, next door to a famous American blonde who has broken all matrimonial records by wedding five million-aires in succession. A celebrated English novelist turns from the tables as a Chinese lady, smoking a cigarette in a long holder, hurries past. The gathering is as international as a dream of world order. Beauty and chivalry, gathered here, are drawn from every continent and climate. The lion lies down with the lamb. All racial prejudice is lost in a common interest.

A girl, immaculate, scented, slender, the exquisite product of immensely skilled and elaborated processes, walks slowly down the steps. 'Lost?' asks her companion. 'My shirt,' says she, coolly. 'Eighteen milles. Shall we dance?' They dance. In a corner two men, middle-aged and indubitably distinguished, argue tenaciously that after the trente-deux the seize does, or does not, come every second time. In every corner, at every table, with pencil and paper, mathematicians from every nation sit with the magnificent concentration peculiar to Homo Sapiens, indefatigably attempting to calculate the incalculable.

There is a sound of revelry. For the new Casino is not like the old Casino. The old Casino was grim, a solemn temple of unreality, its air poisoned by the bitterness of frustrated hopes. Only the rioting goddesses and loves and garlands of its mural decorations spoke of a careless world of love and happiness. The mural decoration of the new gaming rooms is austere; but the goddesses and garlands have come down from the walls and ceiling and move about the lighted terrace, the huge dance-room, the restaurant along the balcony. The noise of the Negro Band rises jubilantly above the babel of tongues. The musicians hurl themselves on their percussion instruments, shake long brown arms into the air, and rock in an ecstasy, a torment of rhythm, braying 'Sweet-heart! Sweet-heart!' The dancers walk, turn, sway, along the polished terrace, between the dining-tables. The white and black flowers pour forth their steady radiance. Skilfully through the traffic the waiters guide their little wagons, bearing pockets of ice for the champagne, and rose-coloured lobsters, and the vivid jade of salad. Ice puddings rise from foam and melt in the torrid air. 'Sweet-hea-a-a-a-art! Sweet-hea-a-a-a-rt!' There is no tenderness in the long, vibrating cry.

I leant over the terrace, above the flower-decked marble balustrade, watching them. Suddenly from the darkness, a frail white ray felt its way across, tentatively, clutching, till it found and seized a tall, thin silver ladder rearing up, up into the night. The band crashed out a steady roar and then a tremolo of drums. Up the ladder a girl in a scarlet bathing dress began to climb, the ray following her up, up, up. When she stood a hundred feet above the crowd she stopped. She turned and stood, small as the doll on a Christmas tree and rather less real, looking down at the people eating lobsters. 'She is going to dive,' they said. I saw then a quite small barrel below the ladder. 'Not into there?' I gasped. 'She does it every night when there is no wind,' they said. Had she seemed a real flesh and blood woman I could not have borne it. But she seemed so far away, so small, that even the possibility of her falling hardly moved me. A man moved across the terrace and began to spray the water in the tub. He was covering it with petrol. To people accustomed to losing eighteen thousand francs on one turn of a wheel, the mere spectacle of a girl diving a hundred feet in the darkness is not sensational enough. The man set light to the petrol and the whole tub rose in flame. The girl waited a minute, timing her fall. Then her body curved forward and she dropped down through the flame. The splash she made helped to extinguish it. She came up unhurt, tore off her cap, waved her hand. The diners had hardly time to applaud. The waiters were running along the terrace with the chicken in aspic. The band struck up another tune.

But in that enchanted palace nothing is real. The very sea is tamed. At the proper moment it throws up coloured fountains. Rows of them. It sustains two captive floats, and on certain nights the seeking ray picks out the brown bodies of acrobats, writhing in perfect precision, in absolutely trained and controlled movement. Every muscle has been disciplined to order. Every turn of the wrist is calculated.

'Mesdames, messieurs,' drone the croupiers, 'faites vos jeux.' They say that no one has ever bribed a croupier, that the rigidity of honour among English judges is no stricter than the honour among croupiers. No gambler breaks the ritual. The terrific, irrational, imperturbable doom of the wheel rolls on. The rakes sweep in discs for a louis, discs for ten louis. The severe, earnest faces of men and women bent in harmonious community of purpose, without distinction of sex or race or creed, presents a picture of startling falsity. For a moment I thought that I was looking on a gathering of those men and women of intelligence and goodwill who might, one sometimes hopes, if drawn together from all the world and bent only on that one purpose, straighten our financial and economic tangle. So they seemed.

'Falling in love again, never wanted to,
        what am I to do?
                Can't help it!'

The musicians were all on their feet, instruments laid

aside, singing the tune, clapping thin, pink-palmed hands, shouting, rocking, howling.

At this moment, I thought, farmers are reckoning their harvest at so much loss per acre; in America they are restricting the output of oil; they are talking of destroying a third of the cotton crop. There is a famine in China, and farmers in Yorkshire are ruined because there is no market for their wheat. Every one who knows anything about currencies has a different theory of how they ought to be controlled. 'Faites vos jeux. Rien ne va plus.' Perhaps this is all there is to it. Perhaps the whole business is as irrational as roulette. It is all impossible.

'Do you know,' asked my companion, 'they say Monte Carlo never was as smart as it is this year? Nor as gay? Isn't it all marvellous?' And, marvelling indeed, I replied, 'It is.'

1931

The Celebrity Who Failed

ONCE upon a time in a slightly-too-much-inhabited island lived a young woman called Amelia who learned how to walk on water. The feat was not unprecedented. Two or three young men had already performed it, and a clergyman's wife picnicking with her husband at the seaside had scrambled for nearly half a mile over quite choppy water in order to retrieve a lost picnic basket. But her husband attributed that effort to the power of prayer, and as the newspapers did not know what to say about it, nobody took much notice.

The attitude of the Islanders towards the achievement of young women was remarkable. Cherishing an old tradition that it was more difficult for men than for women to perform anything except child-bearing and teaching kindergarten, they supported their belief by making other accomplishments almost impossible. When Amelia announced her intention of learning how to walk on water, nobody definitely forbade her. Her mother said, 'Well, of course young people in these days do as they like, and I can hardly expect you to pay any attention to my feelings.' Her pastor said, 'Unhappily all this athleticism and publicity is lowering our High Standard of Ideal Womanhood, and diverting the attention of our island women from their true function of motherhood.' The president of the local Athletic, Aquatic and Sea-Walking Association said that he could not possibly admit Amelia to membership, entitling her to the use of pacing boats, stop-watches, dressing-rooms, and so forth, but that she might possibly be allowed to join as an associate member, a privilege hitherto reserved exclusively for the wives of members.

Amelia, however, being an obstinate young woman, and seeing that nobody would help her, determined to help herself. She got up at six every morning before she went to teach in her kindergarten, and practised walking on water. First she walked across the open-air swimming baths; then she walked across the river; then she ventured out on to the sea. When she had practised for some time without attracting any particular attention to herself or otherwise damaging the Islanders' ideal of perfect womanhood, she announced that she was going to walk to the mainland.

Now the island was separated from the mainland by thirty miles of rough and difficult channel. Upon two occasions previously young men had managed to walk across this, after several months of careful preparation. The National Athletic, Aquatic and Sea-Walking Association had sent out launches and trainers and floating kitchens for their assistance, the rubber firms had competed to supply them with free waders, and the Cinema News Service had arranged for a special film of their performance. But when Amelia announced that she was going to make the same attempt, these two young men laughed at her, saying, 'Since we, with all the undoubted superiority of our sex and the assistance of our fellow-countrymen, only just managed to achieve this heroic feat, how can a girl succeed?' The leading press syndicate arranged a symposium by a novelist, a film star, a retired judge and a bishop, on the subject, 'Why Girls Can't Walk on Water,' and Amelia's mother said, 'Now don't be silly, dear. Sit down quietly and finish your needlework.'

But even this did not deter Amelia. She bought a second-hand compass, a pair of bargain-basement waders, a tin of meat jujubes and a sixpenny walking stick, and wrote a note to the kindergarten saying that she might be absent for one or two days. Then, very early one morning, she set out on her adventure.

For the first mile nothing happened. The sea looked very large and empty, and Amelia remembered all the tales she had been told of young women who set off on wild-goose chases and came to a bad end. But as she entered her second mile a retired sea captain, looking through a telescope from his bedroom window as was his custom every morning before shaving, saw her small figure bobbing along over the faint ground-swell. He immediately rang up the police station, which rang up the coastguard's office, which rang up the lifeboat, which dropped a hint to the local reporter, who rang up his city news editor, who rushed out a late morning edition of the paper, with the headlines, 'Amelia Sets Out.'

The lunch-hour edition carried a couple of photographs of Amelia at home, and a leading article on 'Our Island Spirit.' The evening papers carried an interview with Amelia's father, a picture of her out at sea taken from an aeroplane, a descriptive paragraph of the kindergarten where she had been teaching, and a chat with the president of the Athletic, Aquatic and Sea-Walking Association, who said, 'Our girls are wonderful. We are proud to have Miss Amelia as a member of our association.'

By the time that Amelia had reached her tenth mile, the channel was strewn with launches, motor-boats, yachts and pleasure steamers, and the announcement was made that she had beaten the sea-walking record for the first seven miles. The two young men champions, when interviewed, declared that for a girl Amelia had done wonders, and the leading press syndicate changed its symposium from 'Why Girls Can't Walk on Water' to 'Do Sea-Walkers Make Good Mothers?'

But the wind was rising, the waves grew steeper, and many of the spectators were overcome by sea-sickness. Night was falling, and Amelia, already weary, had to scramble up huge breakers, high as houses, and slither down again on the other side. She lost her compasses, the meat jujubes began to make her feel sea-sick, her waders were full of water and her sense of direction failed. In the dark and the storm she lost touch with her many followers, and the morning papers were able to go into three editions carrying the headlines, 'Amelia Missing.'

But in the morning, wet, footsore, hungry, chilled to the bone and green with sea-sickness, Amelia was seen again, struggling on gallantly towards the mainland coast. When she saw that she was nearly there, she cried a little from pure relief and had to borrow a handkerchief from a young reporter who rushed up to her from a speed boat, and then sent back by wireless to his paper a snappy paragraph on 'Our Wonder Walker's Girlish Tears.'

Two hours later, she dragged herself out of the water on to the mainland shore, to find a crowd of twenty-five thousand people, the representatives of thirty newspapers, twelve cinematograph operators, the president of the Mainland Aquatic Association and the Mayor and Corporation, all awaiting her. She was received with splendid ceremony; school children dressed in waders presented her with fifty-nine bouquets and the mainland king sent her a silver walking-stick. 'Thank you very much indeed,' said Amelia, 'and now, if you don't mind, I should like a hot cup of tea, and to go to bed.'

'Oh, but I am afraid that is impossible,' said the Mayor. 'We have arranged a reception for you in the town hall, which has already cost us several hundred pounds. Now that you are a celebrity, you must not disappoint your public.'

'But I really am very tired,' said Amelia.

'Celebrities are never tired,' said the Mayor.

So Amelia was taken in an open carriage through streets lined with cheering people, to a reception where five city councillors, two cabinet ministers, a professional footballer and the chairman of the Association of the Promotion of Better Relations between the Island and the Mainland, all made speeches to her. She did not hear much of the speeches because she felt so cold and tired that she nearly fell asleep, only she was too hungry; but when they were finished, she was told that she must make a suitable and gracious reply. 'But I can't speak,' said Amelia. 'On the island girls are not allowed to make speeches.'

'Girls who are celebrities must always make speeches,'

147

they told her. 'If you disappoint your public you may undo the good work which you have already done in cementing the loyal friendship of our two nations.' So Amelia got up and made a speech, but it was not a very good speech, and only the people just under the platform could hear her, and the rest said, 'Well, we do think that she might have spoken better. When one takes all this trouble over a celebrity, she ought to show a little more *savior faire.*'

'And now, please,' said Amelia, 'might I have just a cup of soup and go to bed?'

But they told her that a very grand luncheon party had been organised in her honour at the Mayor's house, and they set before her lobsters and caviare, and *tournedos à la Belle Amelia*, and ice pudding, which she could not eat very well, because she still felt rather sea-sick. But after luncheon there were more speeches, and then she was taken to open the new wing of a children's hospital, and asked to say a few words about Preventive Medicine.

'But I don't know anything about preventive medicine,' said Amelia.

'Of course you do,' they replied. 'All celebrities know something about everything. If you cannot say a few simple words, you will be letting down your sex, your country and your generation.'

So Amelia said a few words and then was taken to a football match and asked to kick off for the opposing teams. 'But where shall I kick?' asked Amelia.

'How very foolish you are,' they told her, beginning to lose patience. 'You don't have to kick anywhere. You just kick off. All celebrities kick off.'

So Amelia kicked off, and then she was taken to the broadcasting station and asked to broadcast for half an hour a bright informal talk on 'Sea-Walking as a Career for Girls.' 'But I can't broadcast,' said Amelia, 'and I don't know anything about sea-walking as a career for girls, except that to judge from my experience it's pretty awful.'

'Oh, you can't possibly say anything like that,' they told

her. 'Do you realise that eight million people are hanging upon your every word, and that we have arranged for the United States to relay a coast to coast hook up, and that you cannot disappoint your public?'

Amelia said that she would hate to disappoint any one, but that really, she would prefer to go to bed. However, when she saw that there was no help for it, she consented to broadcast. She did not broadcast very well, because she had nothing to say and her throat had begun to be sore, and she stopped in the middle, and all the newspapers had large headings, 'Amelia Disappoints on Wireless. Heroine of Water-Waves Fails on Sound Waves.'

She was very sorry to have been a disappointment, but she had little time to repine, as she was taken to a beauty competition, to judge the most perfect figure among mainland girls, and to give a brief talk upon 'Is Sea-Walking Good for the Complexion?' She was hoarser than ever by this time, but she was only half-way through her talk when a man appeared, saying that he must speak to her, because his paper was very angry, as it had bought the exclusive rights of her publicity for twenty thousand pounds, and her broadcast talk had contravened their contract. 'But I don't understand anything about contracts,' said Amelia. 'In the island young women are not allowed to learn anything about business.'

'Then you have no right to be a celebrity,' said the man. 'Celebrities always have to do a great deal of business, and we have lost a hundred thousand pounds over this affair.'

'I'm terribly sorry,' said Amelia. But then her throat, which had been growing sorer and sorer, gave out altogether, and she lost her voice and began to cry. The Mayor sent for a doctor, and he ordered her to bed with hot water-bottles and red-currant tea, and said that she had a bad cold. All the newspapers in the world then rushed out articles saying that a girl's strength was not really equal to walking on water, and that the island had been quite wise to discourage athleticism among members of the weaker sex; the young water-walking champions stated in exclusive interviews that they had realised from the beginning that Amelia's exploit was doomed to failure, and that girls lacked the stamina necessary for great feats. The bishop wound up the syndicate's symposium with an earnest and soul-stirring article in which he said that water-walkers obviously could not make good mothers, since Amelia had displayed her lamentable ignorance of preventive medicine. And Amelia went home to her mother, and married the local secretary of the Athletic, Aquatic and Water-Walking Association, and had six children, whom she did not even allow to paddle during the summer holidays and, except for that privation, they all lived happily ever after.

1930

The Voice of God

ONCE upon a time an inventor made an instrument by which he could listen in to the past.

Being a shy man, he kept himself to himself and told nobody of his invention; but he found his new instrument more entertaining than his wireless set, and would sit for hours when his day's work was over listening in to Queen Victoria scolding Prince Albert on a wet Sunday at Balmoral, or to Mr Gladstone saying whatever he did say in 1868.

One evening it happened that a young reporter, hurrying home from the offices of the *Daily Standard*, was knocked off his motor-cycle just outside the inventor's window. Though shy, the inventor was a kind man, and without waiting to switch off his instrument, he ran down, invited the young man in, bound his cut hands and offered him a brandy and soda.

'And how do you feel now?' he asked.

The reporter listened to the instrument, which was just then recording an interview between King Charles II and a lady friend, and he said, 'Thank you very much. I feel all right, but I think I must have had a bang on the head. I keep on hearing things.'

'What sort of things?' asked the inventor.

'Well, the sort of things you don't generally hear over the wireless,' said the reporter, and he blushed.

'But that isn't exactly the wireless,' said the inventor, and he explained exactly what it was.

'But that's impossible!' cried the reporter. 'It's more than impossible. It's a scoop.' And he ran straight off and telephoned to his newspaper.

The news editor was a cautious man, but he did not want to miss anything, so he sent down a senior reporter who arrived in time to hear Mrs Disraeli telling Mr Disraeli what she really thought about Queen Victoria. Then he rang up the editor, who sent down the dramatic critic, the chief sporting correspondent, three photographers, and the editor of the financial page. The inventor let them listen in to Nelson bombarding the neutral fleets at Copenhagen, but they said that this was not really British, and could not be genuine. So the inventor then tuned in to the last directors' meeting of the *Daily Standard*, and they heard the proprietor telling the editor just what he thought about the advertising figures; and after that they were convinced. They acquired the exclusive news rights on the instrument.

The invention as news was an immense success.

The proprietor of the *Daily Standard* himself wrote a column explaining that the instrument was a striking example of British enterprise, revealing to the world the whole story of our empire's greatness. The Federation of British Industries issued a statement that it would be good for trade and help to restore confidence in our empire market. The scientists said that it would enlarge the field of human knowledge, and the editor of the *Daily Standard* ordered a symposium on 'If I could listen into the past, which scene would I choose, and why?' commissioning contributions from a movie star, a tennis champion, an Atlantic flyer, an ex-Secretary of State for India, and a Dean.

The Dean sat down to write his contribution explaining that of all past scenes he would prefer to hear that in which John Knox denounced Mary Queen of Scots. But when he came to say why he preferred this, he found no good reason except the true one, which was that he disliked all women and thought well of their detractors, but this, he felt, was not good journalism.

So he sat biting his pen and contemplating a row of his own published works on Plotinus, Origen, the British

Empire and other sacred subjects; and as he looked at them, he had a great idea.

It was a really great idea. The longer he thought of it the more he was impressed, as a priest by its solemnity, as a patriot by its power, and as a journalist by its superb news value.

He tore up his tribute to John Knox, and scribbled along a sheet of foolscap half a dozen headlines: 'When Christ Returns to London,' 'The Scientist's Miracle,' 'The Voice of God.'

Then he began to write his greatest article.

Three mornings later, the readers of the *Daily Standard* left their breakfast bacon while they repeated to each other, 'Can it be true? Surely it can't be true.'

For the Dean had written that the invention was an instrument chosen by God Himself to enable man to hear the Voice of Christ. For two thousand years the world had tried to reconstruct from the inspired fragments of the Gospels the full record of His tremendous doctrine. The time had come to confess that Man had failed. Much was incomprehensible; much uncertain. Scholars had argued, armies fought and martyrs died because of Man's imperfect understanding. But now Science, the handmaid, not the enemy of religion, had wrought the miracle, and men might listen again, not only to the true Sermon on the Mount, not only to the evidence of the Resurrection, but to all those lessons which had never been recorded, to the full story of that Perfect Life. Everything would at last be known beyond all doubt. To the housewife in Clapham, to the savage in an African forest, to the Chinese mandarin and the professional footballer, the Voice of God Himself at last would speak.

The first time, wrote the Dean, that the Voice of God was heard an earth, the world was unprepared for it. Society was ignorant, the listeners few, the words went unrecorded. The Jews, a servile and uncultured people, proved quite unworthy of their splendid privilege, and responded only by the Crucifixion. But when God spoke a second time, the world would be awaiting Him. He would speak, not to a group of Jewish fishermen, but to a Great Imperial People. The whole resources of science and learning would lie at His disposal. Now would be no indifference, no misunderstanding. Suddenly, as in the twinkling of an eye, society would be changed. Worldliness and materialism, selfishness and sloth would flee away for ever, and we should be summoned to a new crusade for righteousness and true religion.

The effect of the Dean's article was instantaneous. Letters poured in to the inventor. Questions were asked in the House of Commons. Special services were held in every church and chapel. A Baptist minister stripping off his clothes, girded himself in sackcloth and ran down Piccadilly crying, 'The Kingdom of Heaven is at hand. Repent ye in the name of the Lord.' He tried also to live on locusts and wild honey, but locusts he could not obtain, though Messrs. Fortnum and Mason offered to procure some if given reasonable notice. The Vatican held aloof, but a rich manufacturer of wireless instruments offered to finance the construction of a new, larger instrument capable of listening in to Palestine two thousand years ago, and wrote off the cost as Advertisement Expenses.

The offer was accepted, the instrument made, the public informed, and a date fixed for the first hearing.

But then the trouble began.

The *Daily Standard* having acquired exclusive news rights on the instrument, demanded that nothing should be published save through its columns or under its auspices. The Archbishop of Canterbury considered that the invention should be placed in a consecrated building, Westminster Abbey or St Paul's Cathedral. The Nonconformists all protested that the Established Church had no monopoly of the Word of God, and the Rationalist Press declared that, this being a matter for scientific evidence, the sooner it was secularised the better. *The Times* brought out a special supplement on 'Church, Empire and the Voice of God,' but took no line that could offend the Government.

At length a compromise was reached.

The instrument remained where it had been constructed, in the inventor's house, but the Archbishop was permitted to bless the freehold property, which had just been acquired by the *Daily Standard*. The instrument was connected by wireless with loud speakers placed in every public hall and church and chapel in the kingdom. The King and Queen consented to attend a First Reception Service at Westminster Abbey, and the *Daily Standard* organised a vast meeting in Wembley Stadium at which its readers could hear the first words spoken by the Voice.

The day arrived; the crowds collected; the massed bands of guards in the arena played the Hallelujah Chorus. Led by a world-famed contralto, the audience joined in the community singing of 'Abide with Me.' The massed bands played a great fanfare on their trumpets. The people rose and stood in breathless silence, broken only by sobs of emotion and scattered sighs as strong men fainted from the strain.

Then, out of the silence, amplified on the hundreds of loud speakers, the Voice spoke.

The people listened.

At first they listened with awe, then with bewilderment, then with increasing agitation.

For the Voice spoke in a completely unknown language. They could not understand a word of it.

The editor of the *Daily Standard*, listening in at his private office, flung off his earphones in a rage. 'Something's gone wrong. The instrument's out of order. Ring through to the inventor at once and tell him that if he lets us down, I'll have him hounded out of England. It's a farce. It's a flop. With the King listening too, it's an insult to His Majesty. Why, a hitch here will send our circulation down by thirty-five per cent.'

But the inventor declared that nothing was wrong with his instrument. The voices that they heard were indeed voices, speaking in Galilee two thousand years ago, and speaking, as might be expected, in Aramaic dialect. 'Did you expect,' asked the inventor with surprise, 'that they would speak in English?'

As that was, indeed, just what the editor had expected, there really was nothing to say. Being a man of initiative, however, he had a microphone connected with the loud speakers at the stadium, and informed the waiting public that they had heard at last the authentic Voice of God. This fact alone should be sufficient to transform the whole course of their lives; but in order to make the Voice not only heard but comprehensible, English translations would be published henceforward serially in the *Daily Standard*, until the great sacred record was complete.

Having done that, the editor sent immediately to all the known scholars of oriental languages, offering immense salaries to those who could translate archaic Aramaic. Contrary to his expectation, the response was not immediate. In spite of its circulation of three million, very few scholars read the *Daily Standard*, and when approached personally, one declared that he was correcting examination papers for the Final Honours School of Oriental Languages at Oxford and did not wish to be disturbed. Another was excavating remains in Mesopotamia, a third was due to sail for a summer school in San Francisco, a fourth stated that he had never read the *Daily Standard*, never wished to read the *Daily Standard*, and refused to co-operate in any enterprise organised by the *Daily Standard*, even if it were the Second Coming itself. The Catholic theologians were forbidden to handle the matter unless the instrument was transferred to the control of His Holiness at Rome. A learned Unitarian quarrelled with an Anglo-Catholic about the translation of the first sentence that he heard, and the inventor himself, worn out by wrangling and discussion, succumbed to influenza and died after three days' distressing illness.

His death was followed by extraordinary demonstrations. The *Daily Standard*, relying upon the work of quite inferior scholars, published each morning a translated extract which it declared to be an authentic interpretation of the Voice. The scholars, bound to secrecy, shut up in their office, listened day and night to sounds recorded by the instrument. But as in Palestine two thousand years before, the Voice did not immediately reveal itself to listeners as the Voice of God, so now in Fleet Street it was difficult to distinguish the speaker of the words received. Sometimes the sentences recorded seemed quite trivial, sometimes incomprehensible, and sometimes it was quite impossible to translate their unfamiliar dialect. Yet each day the scholars had to be ready with their copy in order that the *Daily Standard* might not disappoint its readers. On one occasion, after the publication of a profoundly eloquent address on righteousness, the scholars discovered that it had been spoken by a Pharisee who was later condemned by the Voice for his hypocrisy. The scholars immediately informed the editor, asking him to publish an acknowledgment of error, but he replied by his usual formula, 'The *Daily Standard* never makes mistakes,' and told them to get on with their own business.

For the sales of the *Daily Standard* were now quite unprecedented. No scoop in the whole history of journalism equalled this. From every country in the world came orders from millions of excited readers, longing for the new revelation which should change their lives.

It is true that not every one was happy. The *Evening Express*, the *Daily Standard's* rival, published allegations that the scholars were tampering with the instrument. Students of oriental languages disagreed about the translations and filled the correspondence columns with amendments. Spain and Italy, as the leading Catholic countries, complained that England, being heretical, had no right to the instrument. The Soviet Government, bitterly distressed, declared that all the misery of Tsarist Russia, the lice, poverty, ignorance of infant hygiene, primitive sanitation and illiterate peasantry, had been due to this perverse and degrading interest in God, and that the attempt to revive it must be checked at once. The American House of Representatives, as a precautionary measure, rushed through a new tariff law, a bigger navy programme, and an amendment to the constitution. The International Federation of Trades Unions summoned a special conference at Amsterdam to discuss the bearing upon trade union regulations of the command that those who have been bidden to walk one mile should walk two, and the Stock Exchange suffered an unheard-of slump under the threat of the command to sell all that one had and give it to the poor. The National Savings Association made a plea for suppression of those passages relating to 'take no thought for the morrow,' and the World League for Sexual Reform temporarily suspended its activities. The Zionists petitioned the League of Nations for special police protection, and the British Israelites, after a meeting in the Albert Hall, led a demonstration against the Jews, Freemasons, Theosophists and revolutionaries that ended in a free fight outside the offices of the *Daily Standard*.

The editor of the *Daily Standard* responded heroically. He summoned his readers to a new crusade for the Protection of the Holy Voice, adopting the slogan, 'Keep it Pure and Keep it British.' The churches, restive and uncertain, failed to check the rising excitement of the people. A bishop was assassinated. An Oxford professor, who dared to question the authenticity of one published message, ate powdered glass in his boiled celery, and died in dreadful pain, while an attempt was made by armed and desperate robbers to kidnap the instrument from the inventor's house.

Finally, martial law was proclaimed in London. Day after day fresh bloodshed was reported. The Council of the League of Nations held three special sessions, and two British cabinet ministers died of apoplexy.

None watched these events with greater concern and foreboding than the Dean. He felt himself responsible. Had he been content to praise the admirable Knox, had his journalistic acumen not overcome his original impulse, bloodshed and misery, violence and scandal would have been avoided. Men would still have ignored the Gospels, or each would have continued to interpret them according to his own immediate interest. Economic advantage would have counter-balanced ethical law, and all would have been as well as ever.

The Dean repented his vainglorious action.

He witnessed the increase of mob violence. He read of the order to the New Crusaders to shoot at sight any one seen to tamper with the instrument. He made up his mind what he must do.

One night he went by himself to the inventor's house. As the most distinguished ecclesiastical journalist on the *Daily Standard*, he was at once admitted, the guards believing that he had come to write up a new descriptive article on 'The Instrument in Action.' He went into the room where the invention stood, and knelt before its complex mechanism.

'O God,' he prayed. 'Your Voice has spoken to us through the centuries, and always those who had ears to hear have heard, as You once warned us. We heard according each to our capacity. Two thousand years ago we were unprepared for Your high doctrine; to-day, O Lord, we are no more prepared. It is too much for us. Whenever You speak we fall into strange madness. In Your name we have slain, tortured, burned and persecuted; we have waged wars; we have thrust men into prison. We have heard You call us to whatever work our own desire indicated. When left alone we can, through patience, learn a little kindliness, a little wisdom. The churches have, through years of long endeavour, adapted Your teaching to the needs of men, remembering their difficulties and limitations. But when You speak, Your council of protection destroys our humble work of compromise. It is too high for us. We cannot stand it. Depart from us, for we are sinful men, O Lord.'

Then, raising the hatchet which he had brought with him for this purpose, he smashed the instrument, crushing its fragile valves, and tearing its slender wires till it was quite destroyed.

Hearing the noise, the guards rushed in and found him

hurling the screws and nuts around the room. They fired, and he fell with a dozen bullets in his body.

The destruction of the instrument was final, for since the death of the inventor nobody knew how to make another. The excitement aroused by the possibility of obtaining full records of the Voice died down; indeed, many began to doubt whether it had been ever heard.

The sales of the *Daily Standard* suffered a temporary decline, but this was received by the editor with the philosophic resignation of the really great. 'Ah, well,' he said. 'If the Dean hadn't gone gaga I should have to have put a stop to it all myself some time, for though a stunt like that is excellent for circulation, the uncertainty and excitement is bad for trade and puts a check on advertising. After all, taking it by and large, advertisements matter more than circulation. What about starting a new crusade for really womanly women and pleasing the big drapers? I think that, on the whole, that should pay better.'

1930

Ah, My Friends!

ONCE upon a time, in an otherwise commonplace community, there lived a Politician who was always noble.

The phenomenon obviously was unprecedented, but circumstances combined to make it possible.

The world into which the Politician was born lacked discipline. Children were spoilt, infants indulged, young mothers attended extravagant lectures upon child-psychology. Pleasure dictated habits even in the nursery.

Far otherwise was the experience of the Politician. In later years, when suggestions were made of extending free transport for school children, he recalled the ten (or was it twenty?) mile tramp that he had taken daily across his native hills. At educational conferences he referred whimsically to his old teacher, a hard man, but just, an advocate of Latin, scripture, and the birch-rod. When dealing with indirect taxation, social services and the wage level, he dwelt upon the nutritive value of his early diet. Porridge, potatoes and pease-pudding had sufficed as nourishment for patriots, and each morning he had broken the ice upon his water-pitcher. 'Ah, my friends,' he would say. 'And was our youth less happy?'

To-day, unfortunately, young people had been ruined. Girls painted their faces and drank cocktails. Boys went to cinemas on the Dole. The poor did not know the meaning of a good day's work. The rich frequented night-clubs and foreign lidos.

The Politician had earned his own living. While yet an infant he had corded flax beside his mother's wheel (or was it that he had cleared locks below her loom?) He had hoed potatoes, forked hay, and stuck labels upon blacking bottles. The sound of his clogs still echoed on the pavements of industrial cities; his bare feet padded among the stubble of the fields.

'Ah, my friends,' he would say, 'Science has lightened the labour of our hands, but let us not tempt providence by our idleness.'

The careless and self-indulgent evaded their responsibilities. Not so the Politician. He worked early and late, supporting his aged mother, before Old Age and Widows' Pensions indulged less devoted sons. 'Ah, my friends,' said the Politician. 'We who have known the cherished care of a beloved Parent . . .'

Later the path of the scholar was made easy. Bursaries, exhibitions and free places awarded natural intelligence. The Politician had bought his learning dearly. Far into the night he studied by a guttering candle, denying himself food that he might purchase books.

Yet he was not unmanly. Opening public playgrounds, kicking off at football matches, he would recapitulate old triumphs. 'Ah, my friends, in those days we were not content to be spectators . . .'

While still quite young, he became a Politician. His reading opened to him the wide fields of philosophy: his observation acquainted him with hardship. He saw ignorance, wastage and injustice, indifference in high places and misery in low ones. He rebelled. 'Ah, my friends, it is better to be a martyr than a slave.'

In those days persecution awarded protest. Malcontents staked lives and freedom for their causes. The Politician endured gibes and calumny. His motives were misunderstood, his aims derided. Herrings and rotten eggs were thrown at him. He went to prison. He abjured sleep and suffered tortures from dyspepsia, snatching irregular meals between meetings and journeys. 'Ah, my friends, we who have worked and suffered for the Right . . .'

He won increasing fame. He did not seek it. But if older men were passed over, and he elected as delegate, was that his fault? If he was made chairman of conferences, member of committees, spokesman on deputations, who appointed him? His celebrity was not self-sought; but he could not avoid awareness that the announcement of his name on posters filled halls, swelled collections, and doubled the police force along local beats.

Other men might have taken advantage of distinction to claim for themselves some greater comfort. The Politician still preferred to share the shepherd's humble pie, the miner's hot-pot. 'Ah, my friends; we are all workers in one service.'

Time passed. From one end of the country to the other, the Politician travelled, making his speech.

'Ah, my friends, we must make a united effort. The blood of our forefathers stirs in our veins. We must be worthy of them. We must have faith. We must cultivate confidence with caution. We must make haste slowly. We must take the broad view and the wide vision.'

There were twenty-four sentences in the speech, and since, as every mathematician knows, the number of possible combinations of two dozen units is considerable, the Politician was able to speak twice daily all the year round without repeating himself. The passion of his eloquence aroused multitudes.

But, in spite of all his efforts, the affairs of the nation did not prosper. Corn rotted in granaries; trade languished; foreigners dumped cheap products, and captured the treasured trophies of golf, bridge and racing.

In Parliament, cabinet ministers slept upon their benches; private members drank beer in bars; committees squandered thousands.

'Ah, my friends!' protested the Politician with such earnestness that in the next general election they made him Premier.

Then indeed began the reign of virtue. Those who had once abused, now idolised him. He filled his Cabinet with fellow-workers. He laboured, and he expected them to follow his example.

Never had the State been more assiduously governed.

Fresh laws were made at the rate of five hundred a session. Licences were suspended, aliens deported, reports circulated, commissions appointed, at the rate of two an hour. No sooner was a tax imposed than it came off again. Amendments flourished like weeds. Parliament sat without recess and civil servants worked a seven-day week.

Daily the Politician made his speech. 'Ah, my friends, we must be worthy of them. We must cultivate the broad view and the wide vision. We must make haste slowly.'

Success did not corrupt him. His home life retained its modesty. He spent his holidays among his native hills, the temporary inconvenience to secretaries, ministers and engineers installing special telephonic communications, abundantly outweighed by the spiritual refreshment of simplicity. Ambassadors, breakfasting with him, were offered porridge. Without sugar.

But still the affairs of the nation did not prosper. Idlers still grumbled; malcontents agitated. An undesirable alien circulated seditious pamphlets.

The King, disturbed, sent for the Politician and explained that the trouble arose from trying to change things too quickly. A virtuous Premier – that, of course, was excellent. But a whole government of Saints? There was a precedent, but its desirability was doubtful.

'Ah, my friends, it is hard to sacrifice my friends,' said the Politician. But he sacrificed them, and selected some new colleagues who understood the right glass from which to drink champagne and in what language to address the Bolivian Minister.

The Politician explained the nobility of his motives. 'Ah, my friends,' he said, 'we must make haste slowly.'

But still the affairs of the nation did not prosper. Foreigners still dumped; agitators agitated; trade dwindled and unemployment rose.

The Politician redoubled his great efforts. He read nothing but Blue Books, White Papers, and the Yellow Press. He kicked off at football matches until he acquired a hammer toe. He installed more portable telephones on all his native hills. His colleagues, conferring with him in speed-boats, aeroplanes and trout streams, sucked lozenges by the ton to soothe their aching throats, took peppermint tablets to relieve the indigestion caused by precarious meals, and entertained the ambassadors privately to make up for porridge breakfasts.

They found virtue expensive and uncomfortable and still the affairs of the nation did not prosper.

Besides, they knew their Premier's speech by heart.

So one day the King again summoned the Politician to his Palace, and gave him advice. The trouble, he said, was due to wicked foreigners. Virtue now reigned at home; but abroad?

The Politician knew what occurred abroad; repudiated debts, race-meetings on Sunday, cheap labour to undersell Home Industries.

'And how,' asked the King, 'can this be changed? Who, rather, can change it?'

The Politician knew that there could be but one answer. His colleagues knew he would know.

'Ah, my friends,' he said. 'We must take the broad view and the wide vision.'

He took it.

He went abroad. No lesser man could do what he must do and persuade foreigners of the advantages of virtue.

His aeroplane roared above the clouds; his special trains tunnelled below the mountains; his liner cleft the ocean waves.

The thunder of his eloquence reverberated along the gilded ceilings of international conference halls. His fountain pen hung poised above protocols and treaties. He rose; flash-lights exploded, cameras whirred, microphones offered mute invitation. He spoke; plenipotentiaries perspired, premiers paused, and pressmen panted into telephones telegrams longer than the Odyssey.

'Ah, my friends,' cried the Politician, and all over the world admirers listened-in to him. 'The blood of our forefathers still stirs in our veins. We must make haste slowly.

We must cultivate confidence with caution.' Esquimaux in their ice-built huts applauded. Negroes in ochred blankets clapped their hands. Red Indians grunted approval.

Nobody had the least idea, of course, what he meant; but it sounded splendid. The lilt and roar of his eloquence convinced them. They knew that this was a good man who had loved his mother, who ate porridge for breakfast and walked twenty miles to school. And virtue, even when misunderstood, is virtue. Truth, even handicapped by defective linguistic knowledge, shall prevail.

'Ah, my friends,' cried the Politician to the Eastern hemisphere, and when a danger arose that his speech might lose effect through familiarity, propellers span, motors throbbed, engines puffed, and away, by air, road or rail, he fled to other climes.

'Ah, my friends!' he cried to the Western hemisphere, and safe at home the dukes and the lords and all the cabinet ministers resumed their whiskys and sodas and golf on Sundays. Members of Parliament passed laws without amendment. Budgets remained almost identical three years together. Civil servants exchanged Blue Books for Thrillers, and foreigners, respecting virtue, presented the Politician with bouquets, fountain pens and treaties, which were good for trade.

The affairs of the nation prospered so far as any affairs in this vale of tears do prosper. The Politician accepted an invitation to an international conference on pharmaceutical measurements in Nicaragua. 'Ah, my friends,' he said. 'We must be worthy of them. We must have faith. We must cultivate confidence. We must make a united effort.'

And every one lived happily or miserably (chiefly miserably), according to his own nature ever after.

1933

Little Man Lost

HE congratulated himself that he had managed the Paris episode rather well. Not that this surprised him. He was the last man on earth to bungle his affairs, even though Paris was not quite his cup of tea and he distrusted foreigners; even though a little woman like Adah Parkinson was not the easiest creature in the world to handle. Temperamental. Nervous. Ah, well; he liked them sensitive.

He leaned back in the corner of his wagon-lit and watched his overcoat swaying gently on its holder to the motion of the train. It reminded him of something, some fragmentary echo from his vanished youth.

> To see a man swing
> At the end of a string,
> With his neck in a noose,
> Would be quite a new thing.

The unworn satin of the handsome lining gleamed in the electric light. There was nothing like good cloth and good silk. They wore for ever. The heavy monogrammed pigskin of expensive masculine luggage gratified him. Even when he travelled, he still moved in an environment of ease, solidity and dignified wealth.

'His neck in a noose.' Funny remembering that just now. As a schoolboy he had enjoyed the *Ingoldsby Legends*. Poetry – but not high-falutin'. Public executions and windows hired as for a royal wedding were barbarous. Mr Robert Berkenshaw peeled soft wash-leather travelling gloves from his well-kept fingers. Ah, well, we know better nowadays. Progress. Civilisation.

He smiled, fidgeting with a sliver of loose cuticle round his left thumbnail, and seeing, in his lively pictorial memory, Adah Parkinson sitting on the side of the hotel bed in the chill January morning, the rose-shaded lamp cheating the room into a false appearance of warmth. (Mr Berkenshaw disliked central heating; he thought it unhealthy.) Her faintly hennaed hair – so deftly and charmingly arranged by day – was tousled. During the night fatigue and emotion had crumpled the delicate skin of her still childish face. She swung her bare pretty feet forlornly, and the tears poured silently down her cheeks and dripped unchecked on to her flimsy nightgown. She looked paradoxically then, for the first time, both her forty-three years, and yet a child.

'I can't bear it, Robert. It you cast me off, I shall kill myself. I can't go back to Charley.'

He had never been averse from drying a pretty woman's tears; but it was tactless of Adah to talk about her husband at six o'clock in the morning.

'If you'd only been honest; if you'd never pretended that you loved me . . .'

Always love, love, love. He prided himself upon his patient tolerance.

'Come, come, little woman. Now you must have known all along that it would never do.'

The little fool. Had she really thought that he was going to break up his comfortable life, his home, his local influence (he was Justice of the Peace, Alderman, chairman of the Hospital Committee, chairman and manager of his firm – why, he should be Lord Mayor in another two years) for a whim, for a week-end in Paris with the wife of a minor official, a woman over forty whose fragile prettiness in another five years would have turned into skinny, querulous, and possibly neurotic middle age? Good lord, the fools – the egotistic, hysterical, romantic fools that middle-aged women were!

It appeared that she had actually taken this incidental amusement seriously, had thought the week-end in Paris a prelude to a prolonged continental honeymoon before the necessary double divorce. She had abandoned a lifelong discretion and spent her quarter's housekeeping advance upon an elaborate trousseau with which to charm her lover, recognising, perhaps half-consciously, that at her age women were definitely more attractive dressed than undressed. And now, because he was doing the only sensible thing and sending her back to her quite decent husband, with a perfectly watertight story already concocted for her, she must wake him at six o'clock in the morning, sobbing like an abandoned, frightened child, swinging her pale, slim feet till they were blue with cold (there was a corn, too, on her little toe; she wore ridiculous, high-heeled shoes) and telling him that he had given her her death-sentence.

'At the end of a string, with his neck in a noose' – no, no, my dear. Death sentences are grimmer affairs than that.

Nevertheless she had cried shamelessly off and on all the morning until he saw her safely into the Golden Arrow. He had tipped the attendant and said that Madame was unwell. He had piled the table before her with glossy expensive papers – the *Tatler, Vogue* and *Harper's Bazaar*. He had bought for her a basket of peaches, perfect, fragrant, decorative, and costing eighty francs. Yet all the time she had choked and hiccoughed from crying, and he had to admit that there was something faintly flattering, in spite of the expense and inconvenience, in being loved so desperately and so hopelessly even by a silly little woman like Adah Parkinson. She would not give him away. Her husband would think her an extravagant goose over that outfit, but at her time of life . . . middle-aged women often had their eccentricities. Parkinson might give her a bit of a time for the first month or two, then it would all settle down and Adah would adjust herself to the business of being a sober, middle-class provincial matron.

Mr Berkenshaw pressed the bell and asked for a double whisky. He had a series of short nights to make up for, and on the train he never slept really well. He had to take care of himself. He wanted to keep his brain clear for dealing with this Hungarian aristocrat with the unpronounceable name.

He spoke to the waiter loudly and commandingly in English. He did not know the man's nationality, but it was his experience that if a fellow knows what he wants and is able to pay for it, he gets it as quickly in English as in any language. Wherever he is.

Mr Berkenshaw did not know where he was. Somewhere in Austria, presumably. Until that evening he had travelled with two Lancashire men and an American, on their way to a textile conference in Vienna. They had played contract and Berkenshaw had held quite decent hands.

Adah had no card sense. Not like Florence. Damned nuisance women were, out of their proper place.

The whisky was weak. He rang again peremptorily and told the waiter what he thought of a so-called first-class continental wagon-lit service that could not produce his own particular brand of spirit. He felt his own precision and importance in the man's servile bow. Foreigners? Faugh!

With his second double he swallowed two tablets prescribed by the doctor, one to help him to sleep, the other to ward off indigestion. A man with important work to do had to be careful.

He opened a heavy pigskin wallet and turned over again with satisfaction his passport, visas, letters of credit, introductions for Hungary and Rumania, the draft of his scheme for Count Thingambob. There, too, was the receipt for the diamond spray he had given Adah – her ostensible reason for visiting Paris – a legacy from her recently deceased Aunt Mathilda, to be fetched in person. Well, well. He was a just man and never grudged payment for pleasure at its proper price.

The sight of his papers deepened his satisfaction. He was a Person, he, Robert Berkenshaw, a man of substance and significance. Doors opened to him; frontiers dissolved; barriers of morality, custom, language and difficulty disappeared. He, solid, compact, commanding, experienced, carried his credentials of success and civilisation in his appearance. His papers merely confirmed his personality.

Slowly and methodically he began to undress, folding his clothes, and balancing with caution in the carriage, now rocking with rhythmical regularity across Europe. When he pulled aside the blind, he could see the soft snow piling up against the ink-dark windows. But inside the compartment it was warm and snug. The rich, satisfying fragrance of his after-dinner cigar hung in the air. His personality had impressed itself upon the little lighted cell of security and comfort, hurtling at his will over snow-covered continent. He had never been to Rumania before, but that fact did not disturb him. Luxury hotels were luxury hotels all the world over. Business was business. Ability was ability. Power was power. His only qualm concerned the effect of prolonged travel upon a delicate digestive apparatus. At fifty-seven a man had to be careful.

Care, fortunately, came like second nature to him. In building up the family business till its profits trebled those gained in his father's lifetime, in avoiding the smash which sent poor Markham through five years' penal servitude into a clerkship at a wholesale grocer's in King Street, in choosing as his wife, Florence, the competent mother, brilliant bridge-player and excellent hostess, in managing Adah, Judy and other little affairs – he had been careful.

The tablets were beginning to work. He touched the electric switch and lay in darkness, submitting his relaxed body to the swinging of the train, his bemused mind to its mumbling harmony.

Marvellous thing, civilisation, carrying you across continents, warm and secure and confident. A word spoken, a signature on a scrap of paper, and time and space themselves were subjugated. Time, space, love, chance – men were their masters. Strong men. Men like himself. Solid men. With dreamy approval he let his dozing mind rest upon the future of International Merchandise Limited and his own immediate business, on the revival of the steel industry to which his transactions would contribute, on the City Council where he could get his way as well as any man, on his new greenhouses where he would grow peaches as good as those preposterous fruits that he had bought in Paris.

He thought of his sons, Geoffrey, young dog! at Cambridge; Dick at Wellington. The army was still, thank God, a career for gentlemen. He thought of his country place, the well-kept lawns, the brilliant borders of begonias. He thought of his country, England, solid, secure, in spite of the bleating of long-haired fanatics; of his passport, a guarantee of sanity in a distracted, ridiculous foreign world. Even sleep and digestion bought and paid for from the correct, expensive chemist.

Once the train paused at a frontier and officials came to inspect his papers, hardly rousing the gentleman sleeping snugly in his first-class compartment. At the moment of their visit Mr Berkenshaw felt a slight sensation of nausea, as though the whisky and tablets had not yet fulfilled their duty; but as the train rolled forward again he slept in confidence, benignly rocked by the rhythm of civilised travel.

He awoke at some hour, acutely aware that all was by no means well with him. His pyjamas were wet with perspiration; a weight loaded his chest; his stomach heaved. Clicking on the light, he reached for his overcoat, fumbled for his slippers, thought he was going to faint, recovered, and plunged into the corridor. He knew these gastric attacks of old. Damn the doctor. Damn the food on the train. Damn Adah and her exotic pilgrimage through expensive and indigestible restaurant menus. Damn the tablet that had not worked.

At one end of the red-carpeted corridor the attendant lay prone and motionless, fast asleep. Mr Berkenshaw made for the other end, swaying, retching, and praying that he might reach the lavatory in time. In the dimly-lit alcove a confusion of doors and white enamelled notices swam before his vision; he fumbled desperately and was hurled by the motion of the train as it rounded a curve so that his head struck a panel; he wrenched at a handle, felt the familiar swoop of cold darkness up towards him as his senses dissolved in the chill rush of vertigo; then he fell forward, down, down, down into an icy flurry of unconsciousness. His last recollection was of a trail of sparks curling away off into the distance.

How long he lay before he realised what had happened, he did not know. First, he was aware that in the ferocious pain of the cold his sickness had vanished. Groping for the door handle by which to pull himself up, he did not find it. His arms slid along icy powder, gripping nothing. He raised his head, and saw a hard blue clarity above him spangled with stars. He turned over and lay on his back, facing a small patch of clear sky.

Minutes, hours or years passed before he understood that he had fallen from the train and was now lying, barefooted, in pyjamas and overcoat (for he had lost his slippers) on a snow-covered embankment in an unknown country.

Above him rose the great rampart of the embankment, curving superbly off into the darkness. The train must have slowed down there, and the softly drifted snow broken his fall. When he rose dizzily, groaning from the anguish of cold, he knew that no bones were broken and that, except for a possibly sprained wrist and ankle, and the shock of the fall and the cold, he was undamaged.

But the train had gone. Though for the moment no snow fell and the one clear patch of sky had been uncovered, the wind assaulted him. He drew his overcoat about him and felt anxiously in its pockets, but found neither gloves nor muffler, purse nor handkerchief. So careful was he of his clothes that he never slept with possessions stretching his pockets out of shape.

The train had gone, and he stood up uncertainly, resting his aching ankle and staring at the sloping bank and the inky blackness at his feet. Even as he looked, the light above him, the clear vivid indigo of uncovered sky, began slowly to diminish. The ragged woollen clouds rolled silently together. An icy touch, soft as a fallen petal, kissed his upturned face and then another.

The snow was returning.

I must keep my head. I must do something, Mr Berkenshaw told himself.

There was the railway. Of course. There was the railway. Railways led to stations. Trains came along them. All he had to do was to climb up the embankment and follow the line forward to civilisation. With luck a station, even if only a rural halting-place or signal-box, should not be, after all, so far away, or, if a train passed before he reached a dwelling, he could signal to it.

He needed no light to guide him upwards, though the climb was painful. He slid, he fumbled on the steep embankment, and excruciating pains shot through his ankle. Perhaps, after all, there was a fracture. All the more reason then to get on quickly, to stumble somehow towards some habitation, to find some shelter before he froze to death.

His groping arm reached level ground. His knee reached it. He hit his injured foot against a bar of metal. He cursed with agony. Five inches of snow covered both track and sleepers, but he could feel one line and then another. He crawled angrily, feeling for the second track, groped into space, knelt perilously on air, and found himself plunging on his face head downward into another steep wall of snow. He learned thus, painfully, that it was a single track line on a high raised embankment.

Why? Lying there, breathless, for a moment beaten, he tried to face his situation reasonably. What lay below him? Forests? Rivers? Ravines? He could not see. His ragged pool of sky was now completely obliterated. Snow powdered softly on to his head and shoulders. The country was wild, alien, the darkness hostile. Only the railway line spoke of civilisation. He must get back to that. He must cling to that. Steel rods were laid by men; sleepers were bought and paid for. Trains rocked and swayed down permanent ways to cities. The lines were his hope, his safety, his contact with a known and friendly world.

Up again he toiled, and now he was on the level track. Now he was limping wildly along the sleepers. He did not know whether he was going back or forward. Though the darkness was complete, the whirling snow added to his confusion. The air, it seemed, was vibrant with distant roaring. A watercourse below the bridge? A rushing torrent flinging itself down the wild mountain precipice? Was there indeed a sound growing louder and louder, or did the thunder of nausea deafen his ears? Was there really a light pouring towards him? A monster swooping down on him from the darkness? Or was this an image of delirium?

Keep to the track. Keep to the track. Walk between the lines, he told himself. Sign along the dotted line, he giggled feebly, and, just in time, flung himself out of the way as a goods train roared and rocketed along the track which he had trodden. Clink-clink, clink-clink, went the great hooded vans and the open wagons in the darkness. Steel rods, bales of cotton, blankets, ammonia – the wealth and power of Europe thundered past him. Clink-clink, as they piled themselves against the withholding engine round the long downward curve.

Sprawled against the embankment then for the first time Mr Berkenshaw knew that he was lost. The track, which had been his hope of safety, had betrayed him. That road to civilisation spelled death. He must escape from it. The glaring menace of that fiery eye of the oncoming monster drove him in blind terror down the inimical slope. He was lost; he had nothing, and he was nothing. The real Mr Berkenshaw went swinging eastward, with his pigskin bags and passport and wallet and warm expensive clothes in the wagon-lit. He had thought that these were mere adjuncts of his personality. But he knew now that they were his personality. Without his possessions he was nothing, nothing, nothing. Not even a man. Not even a user of railways. He was as lost as an animal let loose in an alien country. More lost. Less self-sufficient. He was nothing.

Yet the will to be something drove him forward. Now he was in smothering drift to his knees; now he had struck a tree; now he was entangled in thorns. He must go forward, for if he stopped, if he surrendered to fatigue and cold, to the drowsy ease of unconsciousness, that would mean death to him. He did not know if he was moving now towards or away from the railway. He hardly knew if he was moving at all.

He cursed the wagon-lit attendant, sprawled in happy sleep along the stuffy corridor. He cursed his fellow directors who had sent him on this wild-goose chase to their slimy Count, their Hungarian expatriate – a crook, a renegade, living under an assumed name in Rumania, trading illicitly, corrupt, despicable. He cursed Adah, whose faded charm had led him to submit to the suggestion, making a week-end in Paris convenient and explicable. They would all be the death of him, the death of him. It was not tolerable that a mistaken door should inflict all this suffering upon a man who had deserved better of life.

> To see a man swing
> At the end of a string,
> With his neck in a noose.

Damn the verse! Damn the verse! He could not forget it. His overcoat swinging in the compartment. Adah's bluish-tinted ankles swinging from the rose-quilted bed. The blown snow swinging softly against the darkness. Was that another illusion, the light before him? It glowed steadily, a signal of hope? Or of menace? He trusted nothing.

He could no longer feel his hands and feet. If they were cut by thin ice on the stagnant water, and torn by thorns on a briar fence, he no longer knew it. He saw the faint speck of light growing into the square of a cottage window; he could look inside now and see in a whitewashed room, a young, plump, pretty woman, likely soon to become again a mother, in a faded gown of coarse pink cotton, bending over a baby in a cradle. A candle set on the table flickered in a faint draught so that the room quivered with palpitating welcome; the stove, the rough pottery dishes and mugs upon the dresser, the spoon and basin from which the woman was feeding the child in the cradle.

It was home. It was peace. It was security and warmth and comfort. It was life and safety for ever.

It was the most beautiful thing that Mr Berkenshaw had ever seen.

With his failing strength augmented by passionate hope, he stumbled forward, fell against the square of glass and knocked at it.

He saw the young woman start and stare at the window. He saw her face frozen to sudden horror. He saw her catch the child instinctively to her breast and stand there, glancing from right to left, as though seeking for allies in this hideous danger.

'It's all right. It's all right,' gasped Mr Berkenshaw through stiffened lips. 'Open the door.'

He stumbled round the black square of the cottage, falling against a tub, cutting his forehead.

Now a dog barked. Now the child screamed. Now he fumbled for the second time in that nightmare against a door, and this time it opened easily.

It swung forward and he stood rocking on the threshold – hardly seeing the fierce hostility of the woman, upright, rigid, against the table, her terrified child clutched to her left side, in her right hand something gleaming.

'It's all right,' cried Mr Berkenshaw, 'it's all right. I fell off the train. Look. I'm an Englishman. English. I have money, papers, no – not here – on the train. I need food, warmth . . .'

But she would not hear him. Alone at bay in the cottage, she clasped her husband's knife and faced, resolute to defend her honour, this hideous maniac.

'English,' yelled Mr Berkenshaw, but she heard only macabre, fantastic gibberish.

'Money,' he screamed, but he had now none with him.

'Passport. British. Letters of introduction,' he pleaded, calling upon his gods to save him. But these were whirling away eastward from him in the indifferent train.

He lunged blindly towards her, but she, formidable in her passion to protect her born and unborn children, calling aloud the name of her husband in his signal-box half a mile away, struck out with all her might.

Her knife caught only the roll of flesh above his collar, but it was enough. He turned and fled.

Trembling with terror and relief, she barred the door and crouched on guard, waiting for dawn and her husband's return.

But the man whom civilisation had betrayed and humanity repudiated, stumbled out, bleeding and sobbing, into the dark snow-smothered forest, lost, lost, completely, irreparably lost for ever.

1935

Reformers in Hell

ONCE upon a time a great Reformer who had spent his life in the service of humanity died and went to Hell.

He knew that this was Hell because the place was clamorous with controversy, and lit with smouldering fires.

Burning with the flame of his own indignation, the Reformer hurried down the street until he came to a tall fellow stoking one of the furnaces.

Recalling how he had once organised a stokers' union, the Reformer spoke to him with condescension. 'Well, my good man, and what are you burning here?' For he hoped to be thought an inspecting visitor, collecting evidence on the conditions of labour among devils.

The stoker turned to him a gaunt hawk-like face that was somehow familiar to the Reformer. 'Vanities,' he said. 'I still burn vanities.' And he neatly pierced a couple of soiled white robes with his fork, and pushed them into the flame. The Reformer then saw at his feet a pile of golden crowns, all bent or rusted, harps without strings, and torn white garments.

'Vanities?' asked the Reformer. 'And do you find many vanities in Hell?'

'Oh, no,' the stoker answered. 'My colleagues, Calvin and Knox, arrange for consignments to be sent from Heaven.'

'Calvin and Knox,' cried the Reformer, scandalised. 'Do you mean to tell me that those great and worthy reformers are in Hell? Then who, sir, may I ask, are you?'

'My name is Girolamo Savonarola, at your service,' replied the stoker. 'I came from Ferrara. But it was at

Florence that I lit the world by my great bonfire of vanities.'

'It would do no harm if you added this gentleman's clothes to that rubbish,' interrupted an old lady whose head was swathed in lacy shawls, and whose somewhat tart manner contrasted oddly with her gentle face. 'Shall I never teach any of you to observe the rules of hygiene?'

'Great heavens! Miss Nightingale,' cried the Reformer. 'There must be some mistake about this. Am I in Hell?'

'Certainly,' said the lady.

'But this is monstrous. Are you among the sinners? Then I was right. There is no justice anywhere. Savonarola, Calvin, Knox and you in Hell! If the saints are here, where are the sinners?'

'We are all the same now,' the lady replied. 'There are no saints or sinners.'

'Then there is no justice in life or after death,' the Reformer cried. 'I made no protest on my own account. It was never my way to defend my personal rights. Even my enemies spoke of me as a selfless idealist. But somebody must speak. This state of things is monstrous. I am the least of all this company, yet look at my case! Does it argue justice? I laboured all my life to make the world a better place. Even as a child, my courage and my vision were remarkable. At the age of twelve I organised my first procession against blood sports. At thirteen I fought the school bully. At fourteen I became a vegetarian. At fifteen I was a pacifist, at sixteen a socialist, at seventeen I wrote my first letter to the press on Sex Reform. I have sat on committees; I have walked in processions; I have drafted memoranda; I have led deputations; I have interviewed cabinet ministers; I have lobbied back benchers; I have written unpaid articles for the organs of societies; I have spoken at mass meetings; I have been imprisoned for sedition; I have amended resolutions; I have signed minority reports; I have resigned eight times in protest against injustice. No outrage has escaped my vigilance, no oppressor remained unpunished by my pen. I never sought my own advantage.

I lived in poverty. I took no fees for all my lectures; the expenses I was offered barely covered my railway fares. I slept little and ate less, avoiding the common forms of pleasure. And having fought the good fight without reward and without respite, I surely am entitled to a little recompense after death. Yet, if this is my case, what about you? You, Savonarola, for instance, who not only led an ascetic's life, but were hanged in the end for your beliefs? Oh, Death, this is thy sting! Oh, Grave, this is thy victory! The final virtue to be destroyed is justice.'

'You are mistaken,' said Savonarola, throwing another forkful of crowns on the fire. 'It is true that I was hanged, but hardly for my beliefs. I lived like a warrior, and died like a politician; but I cannot say that my life, though strenuous, was without recompense on earth. Any more than yours, or Florence Nightingale's. We all had our fair share of payment.'

'Payment?' the Reformer cried. 'Indeed, you are mistaken. I never took payment for any of my good deeds. Hunger and cold, discomfort and fatigue, criticism and misunderstanding were my payment on earth. I certainly anticipated something a little more adequate after death.'

'Oh, no,' Miss Nightingale declared. 'You are quite wrong. You do not understand yet. I will tell you how you were rewarded. You had the sense all your life of being engaged on work of great importance. You, who have never lived like a young lady of leisure in the early nineteenth century, can hardly estimate how splendid a reward that is.'

'You had the luxury of righteous indignation,' added Savonarola. 'Do you imagine that if you and I had lived as comfortable citizens, our conduct could have been justified for a moment? Look how we carried on, and lost our tempers, and denounced our enemies, and cherished holy malice! Look how we were able to indulge our rages, all in the cause of Righteousness on earth.'

'Do you think,' Miss Nightingale continued, 'that if I had lived like my poor sisters, prisoners of domestic convention, I could have matched my wits against cabinet ministers, fought with generals, and enjoyed the magnificent sport of beating my equals at their own game? Did you never enjoy intrigues and compromises, getting resolutions carried, defeating undesirable amendments?'

'If you had lived as an ordinary citizen,' said Savonarola, 'could you have known the glorious joy of oratory? Was there no pleasure in the sense of winning over your audience, holding it, playing with its emotions?'

'And though it may have come late,' murmured Miss Nightingale, fingering with her fine worn hand the order on her bosom, 'was there no satisfaction in public recognition?'

'Admit that you enjoyed the chairman's introductory remarks before you rose to speak,' Savonarola pressed him. 'Though you protested your embarrassment, had not even embarrassment its pleasures, especially when you knew you had deserved praise?'

'Of course, if you want to go to Heaven, there's nothing to stop you,' added the lady unexpectedly.

'What! I can go to Heaven if I like?' asked the amazed Reformer.

'Why not?' Miss Nightingale answered. 'No one could ever stop me from going where I wanted to. They did not want me to go to the Crimea, but I went. As for the War Office, it was easier when I was young for a Pope to become Lord Mayor than for a lady to get her way there. But I did it.'

'But how do I get to Heaven?' asked the Reformer.

'You'd better ask Dr Livingstone to take you with him. He sometimes goes there to visit his wife. Poor thing, after confinements in the jungle and organising a nursery in the primitive swamps, she finds the peace and quiet pleasant. I understand that at first she even regarded the doctor's visits with apprehension, but having been reassured that in Heaven there is neither marrying nor giving in marriage, she is happy, and he goes there quite frequently. His experience on the upper reaches of the Nile enables him to negotiate the gulf without difficulty, and he is accustomed to climatic changes.'

'But where shall I find him?'

'Probably arguing somewhere with William Wilberforce

and Booker Washington about the mental capacity of Africans. They all belong to some committee for the organisation of racial controversy, and never stop quarrelling.'

'But I cannot understand it,' sighed the bewildered Reformer. 'If you can go to Heaven, why do you all remain in Hell?'

'And do you think,' Savonarola answered, 'that after the life we lived on earth we could endure the tedium of perpetual peace? No challenging of authority, no joy of contest, no sense of being in a gallant but undefeated minority, no abuses to reform, no campaigns to organise?'

'Do you imagine,' continued Miss Nightingale, 'that having escaped from a Victorian drawing-room, I wish to resume a life of endless leisure? Who would exchange the stimulating discomforts of Hell for the eternal bliss of Heaven? I had known pleasure; I had known luxury; I had known refinement and art and music; everything that Heaven could offer me had been mine, and I had never known a minute's happiness till I forsook them all and chose instead disease, fatigue and hardship. Of course if you prefer Heaven' – she shrugged her delicate shoulders – 'you will find plenty of my contemporaries there. Poor creatures, they never learned to appreciate anything else. But I must leave you now. I have an interview with Elizabeth Fry and Josephine Butler. Admirable women in many ways though they may be, they still have a tendency to regard hygiene and discipline as matters of secondary importance.' And Florence Nightingale swept away, her crinoline swaying through the streets of Hell.

'If you do go to Heaven,' said Savonarola, 'you might tell the angels that the standard of robes and crowns that they send down to me is hardly what it was. I must have proper fuel for my fire.'

And he returned to his destruction of vanities.

The Reformer, chastened but convinced, quietly took his way along the streets of Hell, seeking a convenient corner for a protest meeting.

1931

Truth Is Not Sober

ONCE upon a time there lived a Realist who had no nonsense in him. He came from Bradford or Halifax or some place like that, and he was proud of it. He made a very good income by writing novels about the British Middle Classes, in which nobody was very rich nor very poor, very happy nor very miserable, very noble nor very wicked; dreams faded and youth vanished, and passion – mostly counterfeit – was quickly spent. He knew that to-morrow is another day, that every man has his price, that miracles never happen, and that it will be all the same in a hundred years.

His novels sold splendidly. People said, 'It's such a relief to have a writer who draws life as we know it. Wasn't his last book just like Uncle Arthur and Aunt Muriel? Other novelists give us day-dreams and fairy stories. He gives us the sober truth.'

They said this so often that at last Truth grew tired of it.

One day the Realist was sitting at his desk writing a novel about a middle-class matron of forty-five, living in a north country manufacturing town. He had reached the chapter where the matron saw from her window the corn dealer of fifty-seven with whom she had nearly eloped twenty-one years ago, and when she saw that he had grown fat and mean and greedy, and when she reflected that her husband stood a very good chance of being mayor next year, she rejoiced that she had been sensible, and had run away from the Station Hotel three minutes before she should have met her lover.

The Realist's novels were all like that. In them wisdom was justified of all her children.

But just as he was describing the way in which the matron sat down before her mirror and began to pat cold-cream into her wrinkles (for he never spared his readers any detail of physical infirmity), Truth entered the room and stood beside his desk.

'Good heavens!' cried the Realist, startled. 'And who are you, pray?' For he thought Truth might be the man who cleaned the windows.

'My name's Tr – er – truther – Truth,' hiccupped Truth truthfully.

'I beg your pardon?'

'Truth. I'm telling you. Er – hic – Truth.'

'Indeed,' remarked the Realist severely. 'And I'm telling you something else, my man. You are intoxicated.'

'Quite right,' agreed Truth, sitting down with a bump in a large leather-covered arm-chair beside the desk; for the Realist, as a sensible man, believed in creature comforts. 'Of course I am. S'habit of mine. Use your eyes.'

'I – er – really . . . I beg your pardon?'

'Use your eyes, man. Try to see life as 'tis.'

'I do,' replied the Realist.

'*You?* You think you look at Life as 'tis? Uh, huh!' laughed Truth rudely.

'That happens to be my one virtue,' said the Realist. 'As a writer, I may lack certain qualities of poetry and exuberance. But I have just this merit – that I tell the truth about life. "A poor thing, but mine own." Er – Shakespeare,' he added; for he always verified his references.

'Oh. And wha'd'you think o' Shakespeare?' asked Truth sociably.

'A great poet. A prince of entertainers,' said the Realist, who had lectured in America on 'What's Wrong with Shakespeare?' 'But of course, a wild romanticist. Deplorably hysterical and high-toned. King Lear. Macbeth. Othello. Absurd – and rather dangerously misleading. Fortunately or unfortunately, Life is not like the Elizabethan drama.'

'Oh, isn't it? Whas't like then?' Truth inquired.

The Realist coughed. 'Far be it from me to mention my own small interpretations . . .' said he.

'I see. 'Scuse me laughing. D'you never read the newspapers? Don't you know what's going on in the world at all?' asked Truth, who was not only drunk but vulgar.

'Even my worst enemy,' smiled the Realist, 'would hardly accuse me of looking for real life in the current press. Fortunately, human conduct is not exactly as it is depicted in – say – the *News of the World*.'

'Isn't it? Jolly old paper, *News of th' World!* I like it. Shakespeare w'd've liked it,' said Truth. 'Come on, m'boy. Put your 'at an' coat on. Come and see life.'

Truth rose unsteadily, taking the Realist by the arm, and led him out into the world. Moved by an inexplicable compulsion, the Realist went with him.

Truth took the Realist to Germany, and showed him a sculptor gazing at two thousand five hundred busts of a hero that he had modelled at the order of his followers; but before the order was completed the hero had shrunk to a failure, and no one would buy the busts except for door-weights.

'Within a fortnight,' said Truth, pointing to a heap of busts pitched on to the rubbish dump, 'that fellow will be dictator of Germany, the most-talked-of celebrity in Europe, and every one will be clamouring to buy these toys. Come on, then.'

He took the Realist to India and showed him an insignificant little man of mediocre intelligence and crude personality singing like a hero in his cell as he faced four years' imprisonment because he believed, erroneously, that thus he could undermine the power of a tyrannous King-Emperor. He showed him also, in a neighbouring village, a white servant of the King-Emperor crawling from a hut little more luxurious than the prisoner's cell, shaking with fever and dizzy with weakness, to resume his task of inspecting cattle for possible disease, because he thought that thus he would strengthen the power of the just and noble King-Emperor. He showed the Realist a saint asleep in gaol, whose presence there disturbed the rest of a thousand armed and authoritative administrators, a purdah-bred lady picketing a liquor shop, and a mystic enduring ecstasy while stretched upon a nail-studded board.

'This is Life,' said Truth, and led the Realist on to China.

There he showed him a spectacled General who had been educated at Harvard praying to his ancestors before stepping into an aeroplane manufactured in Yorkshire, from which he could inspect the damage done by bombs, imported from France, dropped by his followers upon the stronghold of his old room-mate, a Japanese biologist now leading a small band of irregular brigands. He showed him a couple of peasants selling their daughter into prostitution because regulations made by humanitarians had robbed them of their livelihood gained by the growth of opium poppies. He saw a band of five hundred villagers marooned on an island in flooded country and dying of starvation, while the rice which might have saved them was being burned by its producers to keep up prices.

'This too, is Life,' said Truth.

He took the Realist to Abyssinia and showed him a feudal landlord proving to his Emperor, from arguments invented six hundred years previously by English feudal landlords, that the sovereign had no right to enforce the abolition of slavery demanded by the League of Nations. He showed him two bishops praying to the Blessed Virgin for the success of a slave raid in which six unarmed villagers were to be annihilated.

In Nairobi he showed him a scrupulously honourable Irish gentleman trying to satisfy his conscience that breaches of faith were not dishonest if they concerned only square acres instead of square miles. In Egypt he showed him five students, educated in Manchester, Bristol and an international college at Elsinore, feverishly awaiting arrest because they had endeavoured to act upon principles learned from Milton, Hampden, Cromwell's Letters (edited by Carlyle) and John Stuart Mill.

In New York he showed him a theatre so immense that no member of the audience could obtain a clear view of the actors, erected at expense adequate to run a second-rate power's annual budget, on an island overbuilt with dismantled offices where nobody wanted to go to the theatre, anyway. In Buenos Ayres he showed him a rector's daughter from Gloucestershire submitting with rapture to the caresses of a Mexican-Indian, who had bought her from a Polish nobleman who was an agent of the White Slave Trade in Cardiff.

'Well,' said Truth. 'This is Life. What do you think about it?'

'I am grateful for the trouble that you have taken,' said the Realist. 'But fortunately Buenos Ayres is not Bradford, and Asia and Africa are, after all, only remote and semi-civilised continents. I have never expected foreigners to behave quite normally, and even the British, when they go abroad, must be prepared sometimes to meet with strange adventures. All that you have shown me is most instructive, but you can hardly expect me to believe that life is like that.'

'I see,' said Truth, whose intoxication had worn off in his travels. 'You don't really admit that Life exists then outside Bradford?'

'Or Leeds, or Halifax, or even Hull,' conceded the Realist. 'And, of course, people must sometimes go to London. The greatest thinkers, however, including Socrates, have maintained that one does not need to travel to learn wisdom. Indeed, the farther a man goes, the less he may see of reality.'

'It depends on the man,' said Truth. 'However. Have it your own way. Come on.' And he took the Realist back to Bradford, and showed him, across the road, the chemist's young wife in her lover's arms, her face transfigured by the radiance of reconciliation. 'Oh, George,' she cried. 'Never let me be angry with you. When I don't love you, I can't bear my life.'

'"... And when I love thee not Chaos is come again,"'

quoted Truth softly. 'Shakespeare understood chemists' wives. Now, look here.'

He showed him the half-conscious body of an over-worked curate, who had writhed all night on the cold stone of a Chancel, wrestling with the demons of apostasy because he could no longer believe that the Pope is not infallible.

He showed him a servant girl of seventeen in a basement scullery baptizing her new-born bastard with water from the tap before she strangled it with a picture cord, and threw the body into the area dust-bin.

He showed him an unemployed weaver tramping beside a canal into which he had three times thrown himself, and each time emerged because the instinct to live was stronger than the will to die.

He showed him a diseased and mentally defective mill-girl sitting in a cheap seat at the cinema intoxicated by dreams so ecstatic, that her vision of a coarse-grained Californian film star brought her the fresh wonder known to Dante, the Vita Nuova of Spiritual Love.

Truth showed the Realist a pimp bargaining for the price of innocence in a low tavern; he showed him an aristocrat choosing ruin and death rather than subservience to his inferiors in a mill-owner's office; he showed him young love, thwarted and desperate, in a high-school garden; and jealousy forging its own fetters, in a labour-saving semi-detached residence. He showed him outrage and hero-ism, villainy and honour, self-sacrifice and royal pride, all within five hundred yards of his own writing-desk.

Then he took him home and told him to write another novel, setting down the truth about life as he now knew it.

The Realist wrote his masterpiece of realism, and sent it to his publisher.

Three weeks later the publisher telegraphed asking for a personal interview, and inviting him to lunch in an exclusive London restaurant.

Over oysters, chicken à l'Americaine, and excellent

Burgundy, the publisher said to him, 'You know, my dear fellow, I never influence my writers. Other firms may try it. I always say "Choose the Right Men and Give Them Their Head." Well, I chose you. I gave you a free hand, didn't I? Your line was Truth. I let you be as True, as dull, as drab, as ever you pleased. Your readers look to you for the authentic flavour of life as it is. And what have you done? Written a hundred thousand words of battles, murders, betrayals, heroisms – and dared to add the sub-title, "A Realistic Novel!"'

'But,' said the Realist, 'real life is like that.'

'Oh, come now. I'll take a joke with any man,' said the publisher. 'But when you ask me to accept melodrama as sober truth—'

'But that's just it,' cried the Realist. 'I never said that. Truth isn't sober. That's just where I was wrong. Do you think if Truth were sober he could have invented Beauty Contests and the American Debt question and Manchukuo, and the Dolly Sisters and Radio City, and Hitler and Relativity, and the things that go on every day in basement kitchens? Don't you see that the real truth about Truth is that he is not sober, but drunk – drunk as a lord? Wild, crazy, splendid, heroic, shameful, spectacular? Nothing more hideous, noble, lovely and absurd has ever been invented by the craziest lunatic than the things that are truly happening in this world at this moment? Have we not always said, "In Vino Veritas"?'

'Well,' said the publisher. 'You may be right. But it would not do to say so, anyway. You'd better let me destroy this novel for you.'

And he did.

1932–3

Women's Lives

Winifred Holtby once wrote that she wished feminism did not have to exist because there were so many other social needs requiring her time and energy. But while inequality between the sexes remained, she would be a feminist. This group of stories, sketches of ironic, heroic or sometimes pathetic events in women's lives, illustrates a number of her feminist beliefs, particularly her strong conviction that women should share responsibility with men for social justice and not waste their lives in ignorance and safety, as does the heroine of 'The Creditors'.

Such a Wonderful Evening!

It was going to be such a wonderful evening. Jessie, laying the supper things, could hardly keep her hands steady. Yet it would be ungrateful to Mrs Crofts to set forks and spoons awry. For Mrs Crofts, an impulsive generous woman, had paid for the hired car which was to take Jessie and Eileen with their two young men to see the Military Tattoo at York.

'You've been such good girls,' she had said. 'All through Mr Crofts' operation and the children's measles. You've deserved a treat.'

She really meant that. She felt too that there was something about the York Tattoo which these young men and women ought to see. Mrs Crofts, who had been to the second night, had felt it herself, a tingling of the nerves, a catch of the throat, an excitement, a stir, as though a physical inoculation of patriotism were flowing into her veins from the massed bands, the searchlights, the singing crowds and the marching soldiers.

'Now, hurry up and get off at half-past seven,' she said. 'Cut plenty of sandwiches. And be sure you take your mackintoshes.'

And there they were, dressed in their outdoor costumes, the sandwiches wrapped in grease-proof paper, Herbert and Larry waiting at the back door.

It was almost too marvellous.

'We'll be late. Oh, do hurry,' fussed Jessie. But Eileen must change into her old hat, because it was sure to rain.

Bob Fletcher was waiting beside his car. He was taking his young lady too – a stuck-up piece, Eileen called her. She wore her hair in an Eton crop, and said she

193

was a farmer's daughter because her father ran a small holding.

'It'll never be dark by half-past nine,' she fretted.

'Dark enough for what we want,' chuckled Larry, squeezing Eileen closer to him on the back seat. Jessie and Herbert thought Larry rather low.

The York road was thick with traffic. There were charabancs and double-decked buses, and lorries packed with school children and boy scouts, and the Church Lads' Brigade. There were baby cars and great saloons nosing their way superciliously, and motor-cycles back-firing like pistol shots.

'It might be Derby day,' said Herbert, not that he had ever seen the Epsom Road, but to show that he was a man of the world.

'I'm sure we'll be late. We'll never find our seats. What if we have a puncture?' Jessie worried.

But they were not late, and they found their seats, and sat there eating sandwiches and joining in the community singing which was lovely, and brought tears to Jessie's eyes, making it difficult to swallow the meat patties Eileen had baked on purpose. And then the eight massed bands burst out together into music that took your breath away, and she forgot all about food and Eileen, and Mrs Crofts and her Dad unemployed and everything. In all the world only she and Herbert sat together, one couple among thousands and thousands of people, watching the soldiers.

The soldiers. Jessie had never imagined anything like that marching. Why, they weren't separate people. All those arms and legs moving together. Like a machine. No, like a huge animal. One animal. She felt her own slim, silk-clad ankle, so quick and neat to run up and down stairs. But it would never behave like that, never, not as if it belonged to eight hundred other people.

'How would you like me to be a soldier?' whispered Herbert.

She pressed his hand. 'I like you as you are,' she replied,

but, watching the rhythmical swinging of those arms and legs, she wondered.

Then came the horses. Oh, the horses were wonderful. The cavalry charged, head to head, across the great arena. Jessie shut her eyes. They must collide. They must. But there were no accidents that night. Horses waltzed to music. Artillery wagons swept in, swirling incredibly. A man did funny tricks with a donkey. He stood it right on a horse. Oh, they did laugh! And all the time the bands made a gallant and splendid tumult, filling the air with courage rendered audible. Jessie's heart swelled to its brave challenge. She wanted to do something, anything, something splendid and heroic and impossible. What a wonderful thing life was. What heroes men were. How glorious it was to be an Englishwoman.

The lights swung in long fingers across the darkness. The trumpets blared; the hoofs thundered. Closer and closer Jessie drew to Herbert, entranced in silent rapture.

The act of the toy soldiers came next. They were to take the soldiers out of a box and make them march. Mrs Crofts had described that. For all the world like the tin soldiers the children had played with during measles. They would cut off the head of one. Now, now, now. Off with his head!

'Ah, ah, ah, ahhhhh!'

The little man in the shabby raincoat, sitting just in front of Jessie, sprang to his feet, shrieking. It was not a loud shriek – a sickening, choking anguish.

Jessie screamed too, then clung to Herbert.

'It's all right.' 'Take him away.' 'It's a fit.' 'What is it?' From all the neighbouring seats came an uneasy stir of questioning.

The middle-aged man in the raincoat stood rigid, his mouth wide open. A fat woman beside him began to repeat soothingly, 'It's all right, Jack. It's only their fun. It's only a game. It's all right. Pull yourself together, lad.'

'He's had shell shock, you know,' she explained comfortably to the world at large. 'In and out of hospital.'

But Jack would not pull himself together, though the

crowd roared with laughter at the antics of the mock combat. Instead, he collapsed suddenly, a limp, horrible weight against Jessie's knees.

'Where's the blood? There's no blood!' he was asking.

'Now, Jack. None of that, lad,' said the fat woman. 'The ladies can hear you.' She had paid five shillings for her seat, and had so few treats in her drab anxious life.

'Jab him in the belly. Rip his guts out. Twist it. Jab it,' cried the shell-shocked man in a sad, monotonous voice, completely devoid of all ferocity.

'Oh, Herbert! Make him stop. I can't bear it!' sobbed Jessie.

'He's only cracked,' said Herbert uncomfortably; but others were interfering now, and the fat woman, whose pleasure the war still had power to frustrate, disconsolately led her charge away. He went quite quietly, only repeating dully, 'Where's the blood? What have they done with the blood?'

'Oughtn't to let such people loose,' said Herbert, annoyed because Jessie, instead of enjoying herself, was weeping helplessly.

But with the tableaux at the end they forgot all that, and stood up to shout 'God Save the King' with all the more fervour, because their nerves had been shaken.

When next day Mrs Crofts asked, 'Did you enjoy it, Jessie?' she cried enthusiastically, 'I've never had such a wonderful evening. Never.'

But when she asked, 'And did you want Herbert to be a soldier?' the image of the madman suddenly confronted Jessie, and she stood, the duster in her hand, silently troubled.

1933

The Resurrection Morning

WHEN Mr Barrow died, none of us knew quite what to say to Mrs Barrow. 'Deepest sympathy in your loss' perhaps was best, because you can sympathise with fortune as well as with misfortune, and loss may be good riddance of bad rubbish.

Not that Mr Barrow was exactly bad rubbish. The obituary notices called him a 'prominent citizen of Kingsport,' and he had been a town councillor and a sidesman at St Agatha's Church, and left a tidy sum invested in War Loan and corporation stock. A pious man, the vicar of St Agatha's called him, and sent a cross two feet by one, particularly handsome. Mrs Barrow, however, was not pious. After ten years of married life she had abandoned her belief in God. Her husband could insist upon her attending church, but he could not prevent her from sitting down whenever the rest of the congregation stood up, even during the Creeds. What he said to her after the services we never knew; but Mrs Barrow told me that if the Almighty was such that He could appreciate her husband, Mr Barrow was welcome to Him.

I watched her at the funeral. She was over seventy, a worn-out little woman in her new black. But she held her chin up and her hymn book in both hands, and sang with the perfect confidence of stalwart incredulity:

> 'On the resurrection morning
> Soul and body meet again . . .'

Of course there was no Resurrection Morning, and there was no God, and Mr Barrow was safely hammered down into his grand mahogany coffin with brass handles.

I remembered what cause she had had for triumph. Night after night she had told me that she used to lie awake sweating beneath her woollen nightgown for fear lest she should die before him and never know her freedom. 'And five hundred pounds was mine too,' she would repeat.

He had married her for her little bit of money, taking her away from Anderby where she had lived on her father's farm, and shutting her up in three little rooms over the shop in Grattan Street, Kingsport. He would not even allow her a window-box.

Her five hundred pounds went to start his business, a pork butcher's, and although it was a sound investment, she detested it. She was one of those people who are by nature vegetarians, and had had a weak digestion since childhood; yet she was compelled to mess about all day among trotters and chitterlings and blood puddings, hating the sight and smell of them. And after the shop was closed her husband would expect enormous suppers of sausages or spare-rib. If they were not cooked to a turn, he used to point across the table with a greasy finger, scolding her, just as he scolded her for her skinny figure, for the death of her three children in infancy, and for her indigestion.

He had nearly beaten her at the end too. She was seventy-two before he went to bed with the internal complaint which killed him after six months of strenuous nursing. She used to sit by his bed clasping her hands tight and willing herself not to break down before she could spend her five hundred pounds, and the little fortune that he had made from it.

> 'On that happy Easter morning
>   All the graves their dead restore,
> Father, sister, child and mother
>   Meet once more.'

She opened her mouth and sang, her high, quavering soprano carolling her atheist's triumph. Death was swallowed up in victory.

She went back to Anderby. Because most of the cottages were tied, she built her own bungalow, with half an acre of garden and hot and cold water laid on. She had a wireless, four valves, installed with a birds' nest aerial, and kept two cats and a parrot, and a little maid called Nellie.

We used to go to her tea-parties, to sit in front of her huge unnecessary fire and eat cheese cakes flavoured with rum. Our hostess wore no mourning after the funeral, but blossomed out into purple silk and brown velvet. Like a small, malicious witch, she would lean forward in her chair telling us scandalous tales of the sort which she hoped would have shocked her husband had he been alive to hear. She did not go to church, and she took pleasure in being rude to the rector. He was a kind man and could forgive her, but he was much perturbed about her soul.

We never knew when things began to go less well with her. Her garden was a failure. Her roses would not flower and the parrot turned out to be the kind that does not talk. She could not walk out so far as the wood where the primroses used to grow, and the buses down the village street disturbed her.

She used to lie, after long sleepless nights, cold in her neat narrow bed, fretting because Nellie had not brought the tea. Though it was only half-past six and the girl was not supposed to bring it till seven, she resented those last twenty minutes bitterly. Her dressing troubled her. She never could see well without her glasses, and she was too proud to call Nellie. Her husband had shouted at her roughly, 'Your placket-hole's undone again,' or 'Can't you see your blouse is out at the belt?' But no one scolded her now.

Time crawled.

She found herself listening for a heavy tread in the passage, and the creak of a chair as a heavy bulk was lowered into it. Sometimes when the Morse from the North Sea interfered with her wireless, she would shut it off and sit listening eagerly, her short-sighted eyes peering into the gloom of the November evening.

One night she could bear it no longer. It was about seven o'clock, but damp or no damp, she must go out. She put on her hat with the two crimson roses, and her tartan scarf and the brown fur coat. The village street gleamed pale and muddy out of the misty darkness, and the lamplit windows glowed like orange flowers. Through open doors she caught glimpses of home-comings and greetings, and pleasant gossips.

Nobody spoke to her.

At the street corner near the bridge stood a group of Salvationists from Hardrascliffe, shuffling their feet on the muddy road and coughing into their cornets. Two or three lads and a girl stared at them apathetically. They began to sing:

'There is no death for you and me, you and me,
Our loved ones once again we'll see, we shall
                                                    see.
   By the river we shall meet
   At our blessed Saviour's feet,
On the Resurrection morning, you and me.'

Mrs Barrow, who had come up alone out of the street, listened silently through three verses, then gave a little choke and slipped down on to the ground.

The doctor told us that it was a stroke, and we all felt sorry for the poor old thing who had enjoyed her liberty for so short a time. She was helpless, and could only make inarticulate sounds instead of words, but we knew that she was worrying.

'It's the resurrection morning, you know,' we told the rector. 'The Salvationists were singing about it when she fell. It's on her mind. She's terrified of waking up in Heaven and meeting the old man again.'

The rector was accustomed to most human situations, and even the dying doubts of a freethinker did not much perplex him. He assured her that in the Kingdom of Heaven was neither marrying nor giving in marriage. Further, of course, he could not go. But neither his tolerance nor the sympathy of her neighbours seemed to reassure her.

It was Nellie who spoke the last word. Nellie's mother is cleaner at the Primitives' chapel, and Nellie had been much distressed by the rector's perfidious compromise. Left alone with Mrs Barrow one afternoon, she decided that no soul ought to be allowed to face its Maker with a lie upon it. The agnosticism of her mistress had shocked her, but our condonation filled her with righteous anger.

'I don't care what you say to me,' she told us afterwards. 'You can call me a murderer if you like or anything else. But when the old lady began picking and grunting again like she does, you know . . .'

We knew.

'I just up an' said, "If you think to wriggle out of the Lord's power by denying it, ma'am, you're mistaken. If you was one of the elect you'd have been saved long ago, or even at the last moment by grace. But I'm thinking that the Lord's mercy would have its work cut out to save you now, and I'm afraid that you've not been saved. Nor has your husband from what you tell me, either, for that matter. So I'm afraid that it's to Hell you'll both go, unless you get busy repenting now. So you'd better make up your mind to it and stop worriting." And believe me or believe me not, she says to me as plain as anything, "William?" And I says, "Yes, William too, if he was the sinner you says he was. He's probably waiting for you." And she just gives one sort of smile, as you might say, for all the world as if she was saying "How do you do?" to some one, and goes right off, with a little sigh. And being as they were both sinners, I dare say that she's with him again by this time.'

So right to the end we never quite understood Mrs Barrow. But we have Nellie's word for it that she died happily.

1927

The Creditors

WHEN she was fifteen, Lucy Purdon's father retired from farming with something over fifteen thousand pounds, and bought house property in Mortock.

'Houses are summat,' he used to say. 'You can keep your eye on your securities in bricks and mortar.'

Lucy, sitting wide-eyed in the new drawing-room at Harrogate, heard him with respect. He had always been wonderful to her, driving in his polished gig from market, or stamping stiffly into the hall after a day's hunting. In the new villa, which had electric light and two bathrooms, he was even more wonderful; and when five years after his retirement the Knabside mine was opened two miles from Mortock, and Lord Mountleven refused to let further building sites on the moor, and Mr Purdon's property hence began to flourish exceedingly, Lucy thought him more wonderful than ever.

She had never been to Mortock. She knew no more of business than the two maxims which her father had revealed to her as the secret of all wisdom:

'Buy house property in a growing town, lass,' and 'Never let any man-jack on earth call himself your creditor.'

Lucy learned her lesson carefully. She never bought a dress nor a hat without paying for it immediately, and once when, returning from her school in the South of England, she lost her purse and had to borrow money for her fare, she was haunted by her sense of debt.

She was a good girl, cheerful and modest and quite conscientious. She loved her father and her mother, and her school, and tennis parties, and her singing lessons and dances at the Royal Hotel. She was not very clever, but her mother said that this did not matter because no really nice men liked clever women.

When she was twenty-three she met Bobby Haines. He came to Harrogate to do something in somebody's office, but Lucy's mother said she had heard that he did not do it. He had a slim, strong young body, and a voice that quivered easily into deep laughter. Old ladies liked him, and men at the club stood him another drink, and Mrs Purdon said, 'A dear boy, but I'm afraid he's a bit wild.' He was reputed to be of quite good family.

Lucy listened to all this, and thought that she knew better. She would catch herself smiling suddenly at the thought of his gay, keen face and the lift of his chin.

When she went to the Hunt Ball with her mother she wore a new dress of rose-pink satin veiled with chiffon, and she knew that she was pretty. After the fourth dance Bobby Haines claimed her and led her through the palms and azaleas of the lounge into a darkened corridor.

'I must talk to you,' he said.

Lucy shivered. She tried to pretend that she did not know what was going to happen, but oh, how glad she was that she had refused to marry Mr Matthews last year, although he had been so kind and very eligible.

Bobby began to talk, and Lucy sat holding tight to the little lace and ivory fan that was trimmed with rose-pink ribbon.

Bobby told her that he was a cad and a beast. He was in debt, heavily. Those swine of Jews were squeezing him. He was going away, out of this hole, but before he went he wanted to tell her something. He had known that she was rich, and he had meant to ask her to marry him. That was before he really knew her. And now he couldn't do it. He couldn't do it, because now it was the thing that he wanted to do more than anything in the world. He loved her, you see. He loved her. He loved the little curve of her head and the way that her hair curled like little soft feathers into her neck, and her quiet voice, and her dear little stammer when she was shy, and, oh, God, he loved her. He was a swine and a beast, but if only she'd say that she believed in him, that she would forgive him for all that he had ever done that was foolish, he would go right off to the colonies and work to be worthy of her. He wouldn't ask her to wait for him, only to say that she cared for him a little and that . . .

Lucy cried very softly, holding tight to the lace fan with the long ribbons; but she only said, in her prim gentle voice, that it was a terrible thing to get into debt, and that she really did not think that Mr Haines ought to come to her about things like that, and though of course she would always wish him well, yet she did not quite see what he could expect her to do about it.

All that night she lay, crying into her pillow, because she did not want to be good and sensible. She wanted to have Bobby Haines and she would have been so glad to go with him to the colonies to help him in his quest for a new life. And more and more it came to her that debt was a wicked thing, a thing in itself evil and powerful. It could wreck love and poison happiness, and take Bobby from her.

After Bobby had gone she cried a great deal, and did not enjoy dancing, nor arranging the flowers, nor going to tennis parties. Her mother took her to Torquay for a long stay, but that did not do any good, and when she heard that Bobby Haines had died of fever in West Africa she crept up to her room and sat for hours, waiting to die too.

She lost her prettiness somehow after this time, and people began to forget her when they arranged parties, and when, ten years later, her mother died, she found that she had suddenly become a middle-aged woman, who kept house for her father and was very careful with the money. Not that she had much chance to be extravagant, for Mr Purdon only gave her a very small allowance, and talked to her often about what he called sound business principles.

Then, when Lucy was fifty-one, her father died too.

The lawyers came and told her that she was a rich woman, but the money was all carefully tied up so that

Lucy could only handle the interest. They explained to her about the house property in Mortock.

'Yes,' said Lucy. 'I know about that. Father said that one ought always to buy house property in a growing town.'

Mr Lowe, the lawyer, laughed.

'Sound enough, Miss Purdon, but not all men are as lucky as your father was in finding a town that did grow.'

It was after this that he suggested that she should go herself to have a look at her property. Lucy, who took her position as a rich woman seriously, decided that she would go.

She went one day with Mr Lowe, motoring along the moor road from Harrogate.

It was a dull day. The bleak, dark moor alarmed her, and the wheels and cranks at the pit-heads, breaking stark and black into an ashen sky. She saw Mortock like a pool of grey lead poured into the mould of the valley.

The car dived into a slit of street. Flat-chested and blank-eyed, the houses stared down at her.

Mr Lowe asked her if she would like to see some of her tenants. They went into a thin house squeezed between others in the long street. She saw a kitchen, unbelievably crowded. On the table a half-opened tin of sweetened milk had been over-turned, and two children of about three and five years old, with sore eyes and matted hair, were licking the sweet stickiness from their fingers. On a bed in the corner a woman lay.

'It's my back,' she said. 'Ah can't get up no-how.' She was apparently going to have another child. One by the table coughed persistently. In a perambulator a baby of eighteen months was crying.

'Dick's under the doctor now. He's been in sanatorium, but they sent him back last month. Miss Mason, she's the health visitor, says as what they oughta sleep in different rooms, but my sister's got her three in the top room, so what can ah do?'

Mr Lowe was sorry that he had brought Miss Purdon

to this house. He wanted to take her back to the car. But she persisted gently. She went from door to door, and saw for the first time Johnny Peters, whose back was humped with rickets, and Maudie Grier, who was queer in her head because of what her mother's lodger, Jim Dale, had done to her. She saw Mrs Buckle in her upstairs room, where at night the rats ran across the baby's cradle.

Her tenants were polite to her, but not very talkative. Lucy said little; but when she was back in the street again she asked the lawyer, 'Does my money all come from these people?' And when he had answered her, she said, 'Why didn't father build more houses?'

He spent a long time trying to explain to her about economic rent, and returns on capital, and the difficulty of securing further sites. But Lucy had never been very clever about that sort of thing. His voice only drifted past her like smoke, as she thought of her school in the South of England, and her dances and tennis parties, and the house at Harrogate with two bathrooms.

'Can't I use my money to build more houses?' she asked. But he explained again, very patiently, how the capital was tied up so that she could not touch it, and the whole concern was in the hands of her trustees.

She thought of Maudie Grier, leering and chattering, of Mrs Buckle's haunted eyes, and the tin of sweetened milk on the cottage table. Then suddenly, out of her puzzled misery, the thought of Bobby Haines came to her. She saw again his lithe young body, and heard his deep laugh, and the gay tenderness of his voice. And she remembered how her mother had said to Mrs White that if he had had a good wife he would never have drunk himself to death in West Africa. She saw that she had run away from poverty with him to fall into this ruin. For she was faced at last by many creditors, and she was bankrupt.

'You are tired, Miss Purdon,' said the lawyer. 'I have made you come too far.'

'No, not too far,' said Lucy, and she began to laugh

and sob at the same time, very strangely. 'I've only come too late.'

date unknown
circa 1923–1935

A Windy Day

I HAD never known so unfriendly a sea, nor an esplanade with such bleak-faced, cynical houses. The wind screamed, whipping the grey water to angry foam, and tearing at the sign-board outside the tea-shop as though it wanted to hurl it at my head.

Suddenly frightened, I opened the door and took refuge in the parlour behind the shop. There were other fugitives here, it seemed, a rosewood piano with faded green silk behind its fretwork panels, a rickety table, with a tarnished silver vase to hold imitation chrysanthemums and dyed grasses, a dreary seascape in a chipped gilt frame. Here, with the wind shut out by the torn lace curtains, we were safe.

I had just ordered tea when a little woman entered, blown in by the wind like a drifting leaf.

She looked at me nervously, smiled, and then began to fumble in her purple reticule, making small gentle sounds of irritation. With her blown grey curls beneath a ridiculous flower-trimmed hat, her incongruous leopard-skin coat and her wild brown eyes, she seemed like a lost Bacchante, timidly rakish.

Directly our tea was brought she sat down close beside me, but instead of pouring out, she suddenly began to cry with quiet persistence.

'It's such a wind,' she said by way of explanation. Then, 'I haven't a hanky, please.'

I produced my own handkerchief and said, 'Perhaps you'll feel better after you've had some tea.'

She brightened immediately, like a confiding child.

'Yes. Of course. It may be the tea I want. Though for

years, ever since I was ill, I've never been able to bear letters. They always upset me like this. There's first the sound of the postman's footstep along the path, and you lie in bed and pray and pray that it may be *the* letter, only somehow you feel that if he does stop at your house, you can't bear it. Then the knocker goes, crack! crack! And then there's the soft flutter of the letter falling on to the mat. And after that you're so much afraid it mayn't be *the* letter, that you lie in bed with the clothes round your ears and try to pretend you haven't heard anything.'

'All day?' I asked.

She nodded, with her half-knowing air of wisdom.

'All day. If you came down, you see, you'd have to find it. And then you'd have to open it. And then you might know that everything you'd been waiting for for fifteen years had happened.' She shivered. 'The days aren't so bad. It's the nights, when you lie and think and think, remembering, and listening to the wind. And when there's a moon, you see all your clothes lying out on the chairs and tables, as though they grew there.'

'Are you quite alone?' I asked, beginning to pour out the tea for us both.

She pushed the wisps of hair back from her eyes, and smiled at me. 'I wish I'd washed my face,' she observed irrelevantly. 'I didn't know there'd be company.'

'I'm not company, and your face is charming.'

'Do you really think so? Oh, but not now. My hair's all grey. It was pretty once, I believe. People used to say so, but that was when my husband was alive. You didn't know him, did you? Yes, thank you, I will have a little bread and butter.' She stopped and began to eat with quick greedy snatches, as though she had been starving. 'I used to have such pretty clothes,' she said when she had finished two slices. 'This coat now. Of course, they do get crumpled. It's fifteen years, you see, and I've never thought it worth while to unpack properly. You see, sometimes you want a silk petticoat, or a pair of gloves, or a new dress, and you just go to the boxes and get it out, and when you've done with it, you can't bear to say, 'Good-bye, I shan't want you again.' So there they lie, just on the chairs and the floor. I don't know how many. But it doesn't matter, as no one ever comes. I'm always saying I'll get them put away, but then the letter might come any day.'

She waited. There seemed to be no adequate comment. She drank her tea, and then began again, in her pretty, hesitating voice. There was a charm about her more strangely touching than anything I had ever known.

'You see, we were Quakers,' she continued. 'Poor papa kept a store in York, and he did very well, people say, and I was the only girl and brought up so carefully, only he wasn't very careful with his money, always so good to every one, and after he died there was nothing left, only I was married then, so that didn't seem to matter, and my husband kissed me and was so kind, and I never thought about the money. You didn't know my husband, did you?'

I shook my head. 'I'm quite a stranger here, just waiting between two trains.'

'Of course. How silly I am. I forgot there was no one left. I almost forget how to talk. It's funny, isn't it? When my husband and I used to be such talkers. Like children, they said we were, although he was a mining engineer and so very clever. We lived in that big stone house on the right as you come in to the station. It's a lovely house. He built it for me. It's queer to think of that now, isn't it? Double windows it has, to keep out the wind. I hated the wind so and the noise it makes coming up over the sea. When he was with me it didn't matter so much, because I'd just lie tight in his arms, and when the wind made a noise he'd kiss me, and promise to take care of me. He was a dark man, my husband, very fine and upstanding and not afraid of anything.'

She rose and walked drearily to the window. The wind flung storms of spray across the esplanade; the sky was dark and malign.

'This is a common place now,' she said. 'In summer it's

full of trippers, like Blackpool. I think Blackpool's very common, don't you? And when I married, I lived like such a lady. When people called who weren't very nice, my husband used to say, "Now, Daisy, never you mind them. We don't want any one but ourselves . . ." So by and by they left us alone, because there aren't really any nice people about here.

'We used to dress for dinner every night. I'd come and sit all dressed at eight o'clock, waiting for the gong to ring. But he was so often late. He would go down those horrid mines, although he was an engineer and a gentleman. But he wasn't afraid of anything. I'd have the soup brought in in the silver tureen and sit in my low dress, waiting. Father hadn't liked me to wear low dresses, because we were Quakers, but my husband didn't go to church at all, although he was a very good man, and he said he liked to see my shoulders. He said there weren't any so pretty in the county. And sometimes he'd come in quietly and kiss the back of my neck, right in front of the servants, and I'd say, "Oh, for shame," but he'd only laugh. Weren't we silly? Like two children.

'But sometimes I'd wait and wait. One night he didn't come and didn't come, and I sat all night with the lights full on, though the maids did try to make me go to bed. He didn't even send a wire.

'Well, that time he did come back. I saw him walking up from the morning train, and then I couldn't stop crying. Not for hours. But there was one time.' She shivered. 'I was all ready. I had a new frock, I remember, very pretty, all pale blue and little roses. It's lying in my box now. And he didn't come and didn't come, and I sent the maids to bed. There was such a wind. Oh, you can't think what the wind was like that night, laughing at me. And in the morning I was still in my evening dress, and the lights on. And I ran to watch him come up from the morning train. And he didn't come. It wasn't till tea time in the evening that they came to tell me he'd had an accident and he was quite dead.

'I'd never known before how big the house was. He had seemed to fill it, but then I got ill, and there were no friends, though the maids were kind. And it was all so strange. And when I got a little better they told me he had been like poor papa, and hadn't any money, and there only was the house that he had built me because that was mine. And I was to move into this little cottage and let the house or try to sell it. But I'd never known anything about money, because my husband had done everything like that for me. It was all so strange, like one of those bad dreams that go on and on.

'They sent away the maids, and Mr Smallwood, the lawyer, took a cottage for me. A nice old gentleman he was, but busy, and there were no friends. And he told me that as soon as he had an offer for the house he'd write to me, and then I should have some money and could go and live in the South or somewhere where there were people.

'It isn't a nice cottage. Not at all nice. It's in a row and the neighbours are horrid people, fishermen, and miners and the like. Oh, not at all the sort of people I'd ever known. But it wasn't to be long, Mr Smallwood said. We had such a big, fine house. Some one would be sure to give me a lot of money for it.'

'And can't you let it?'

'It's the wind,' she said. 'People come to look at it and then go away because of the wind. But Mr Smallwood came to see me two months ago and said he really thought things were going to happen. For a school or something. But it's been fifteen years. And even the grocer's dog doesn't come to play with me now. It's getting old, I suppose, and I'm getting old . . . And if I were to move, where am I to go to? They say here I'm a bit queer in my head. But if I could get away . . . Somewhere where there isn't any wind.'

'Do you think your letter is from the lawyer?'

She glanced up at me fearfully, as though I were trying to trap her.

'It might be. It's in his writing. I always bring my letters here because I can't bear to open them alone in the cottage.'

'Would you like me to open it for you?' I asked. 'Perhaps that would be easier for you.'

'No, no. Not yet. You see, it means such a lot to me. To get away from this loneliness. After fifteen years.'

With trembling fingers she drew the letter from her reticule, and began to handle it, turning the yellow envelope over and over.

'Of course, if they buy the house, I shall have to move, and then there's the packing. I've never had to make decisions. My husband always did that kind of thing for me.'

Then, quite suddenly, with the quick nervousness of a child who knows that it is being naughty, she jumped up and tore the unopened letter into tiny pieces, and let them drip from her hand into the empty grate.

'I can't bear these letters,' she said. 'If only it weren't so windy.'

With a little sigh, half laugh, half sob, she left the room.

One piece of the envelope blew out of the grate and fluttered along the floor. I stooped and picked it up. It was that part which holds the stamp, and the postmark bore a date of seven years ago.

As I battled with the wind on my way to the station, the dead leaves danced in front of me along the esplanade. Yet I saw no trees.

1923

The Apostate

'BUT, of course,' I said, 'you still have Miss Julia.'

Maltby, the sexton, removed a worm cautiously from his spade and regarded its corpse with a professional eye.

'Her!' he ejaculated with concentrated bitterness.

Though only turning up the potato patch, his spade had an air. It made me a little nervous, even though I had sought out Maltby on purpose to gossip reminiscently.

'Yes,' I said. 'You know, all the ten years that I have been away, I've never forgotten her. In her quiet way, she was a sort of inspiration to me; her devotion, and the way in which she would go day after day from the church to her poor sister's bedside, then back to the church. And her Sunday school work, and those wonderful altar cloths that she embroidered. One does not meet with that simple piety every day.'

'Piety? Ho!' barked the sexton darkly.

'I suppose that her sister . . .'

'Miss Jane's the same as she always was, poor thing.'

'And Miss Julia's the same?'

'Not what you'd notice it.'

'Oh, dear; not ill, I hope? Not . . . good heavens, not married?'

'Worse, ma'am.'

'My dear Mr Maltby, what . . .'

'Damned,' said Mr Maltby.

'I don't understand.'

'No, ma'am, you wouldn't. You never was one o' these new clever ones. It was all these 'ere politics.'

'Not with Miss Julia, surely?'

'I was once on a jury myself,' reflected the sexton. 'A

214

nasty case it was. Not at all for ladies. Bigamy. Of course it takes men different like. Not but what I have seen some on 'em lose their heads over it. There was that poor chap Brierly, o' Foxton, decent God-fearing man if there ever was, let alone singin' in the choir a rare bass, if shaky on changes of key. An' what 'appens? 'E goes to York, serves on a jury where Lady Shuttleworth Ashton puts in a case against a trainer about a race'orse, an' Brierly knowing no more tail fra' head-end on a horse than a babe unborn. An' before the case were finished there 'e is. Done for, poor chap. Done for. Cycles in to Hardrascliffe every night for 'is late edition and the Major's wire.'

'But Miss Julia?'

'There's politics and politics, of course. I'm not saying anything against the Government, poor chaps. As I said to the vicar, I said, "Somebody's got to do the dirty work, though I'd sooner dig graves for corpses than for promises," I says, "an' chance the Resurrection. Sexton's haven't a Day o' Judgment every five years, anyway."'

'But Miss Julia?'

'It's women, though. Politics goes to their head something shocking. Take Miss Julia. Wasn't a church worker in t' East Riding to beat 'er for piosity. An' now, look at 'er.'

'Yes, but what has she done?'

'Only a week ago, I says to 'er, "Miss Julia, aren't you as good a woman as you once was?" "I hope so," says she. "I hope so. I hope I may have been of some little use to my country," says she, "though, of course, it's a great responsibility. God moves in a mysterious way, you know." "Well, 'E may do," says I. "But the devil goes straight at it in broad daylight." There's too much sin knocking round in a law court to be 'ealthy for women.'

'Yes, but what law court?'

'Two years ago back end o' Martinmas it'll be, she comes to me an' says, "Mr Maltby, I'm afraid that I shan't be able to do the church flowers on Saturday. I have to go to York, and I shall be staying over the week-end very likely. Mrs

Stevenson will do them if you give her the key," says she, a bit flustered like, but dogged.

' "Nothing wrong, miss, I 'ope," says I.

' "Well," says she, "not exactly. I have to sit on the jury."

' "I don't mind telling you, miss," I says, "I don't 'old wi' such. If it's juries this year it'll be Socialism next."

' "Well," says she, "I suppose that we must have progress. Though I will say that it seems a little queer."

' "Progress," I tells 'er. "Progress. There's a good deal too much o' this progress about nowadays, an', what's more, it'll have to stop."

' "Well, I dare say it will," she says. "We are in the Lord's hands." But what I say, ma'am, is that it wasn't the Lord that put Miss Julia on a jury. First it was jury, then it was the vestry meeting, then that there Woman's Institute, and now it's the Board of Guardians. I'll tell you what I think does it, ma'am. It's the swearing.'

'The what?'

'The swearing. That "truth-the-whole-truth-and-nothing-but-the-truth. So help me God." It kind o' gets hold o' women. Especially the pious ones. I suppose it's the novelty. But after oaths, it's committees. And elections. She's all over elections now, is Miss Julia. I once knew another woman a bit like that, over sales, though. Couldn't pass a shop without thinking of eleven three farthings. With Miss Julia it's canvassing. An' when I think what a fine district visitor's wasted!'

'But it hasn't affected her religion, has it?'

'Hasn't it? A lot you know, ma'am, if you think that the devil when 'e's got to work doesn't make a strong job of it. Thorough. I will say that for 'im, thorough. An' all wasted when you come to think of it.' He meditated sadly. ' "I haven't got time to be a Poor Law guardian, an' a sideswoman, an' secretary to the village readingroom, besides looking after my dear sister, and my own soul," says she. "So I asked the Lord if He'd look after my soul if I looked after the outdoor relief. An' I can't say as I feel a worse woman for it," she says. "Ah, it's not what we feel," says I. "My Uncle Joseph, poor chap, he had an annuity of the heart, and never felt anything of it until the day when he fell dead eating liver an' bacon. You'd better be careful. All you people nowadays, you think that the Lord keeps a kind o' crêche like these 'ere you make for babies, to look after your souls when you're doing work that you ought to leave to the men. It won't do," I tells 'er. "Give it up," I says. But next week, when I came past the Coach and Cushion, there was 'er photograph, for all the world like a play-actress, stuck up on the wall o' the pub, wi' "Vote for Julia Smith to be your Guardian." And she such a temperance body, too.'

I left him angry and sorrowful, mourning for the fall of his old friend. I thought of how sad a thing it was that friendships must be broken and ideals shattered to feed the new vitality of the awakened countryside. I pictured poor Maltby, sore and silent, meeting without a smile in the narrow street his former idol. I thought of Miss Julia, regretful as I knew she must be, the gentle spirit, suffering disapproval heroically for the cause.

That evening I met Maltby. He was creeping furtively down the village street in the gathering dusk, and pausing for a minute at each cottage door to drop a leaflet into the letter-box. The wind caught one and bore it timidly towards me. I peered through the gloom and read:

'Vote for Julia Smith, and let a Woman watch your Woman's Interests.'

1925

The Right Side of Thirty

WE have recently been invited by a publisher to welcome a certain volume of memoirs because the writer is 'still on the right side of thirty.' When I read the phrase I examined it with pleasure. A good phrase, it seemed to be, for to be on the right side of anything is pleasant. Moreover, I reflected, I myself am on the right side of thirty and am likely to remain so until I die. I was thirty-two last June.

But when I read further the publisher's announcement I discovered that the advertised memoir writer is still in her twenties. Her misguided publishers have fallen into an all too common error. They appear to think that the right side of thirty is the callow side, the side of immaturity, of ignorance, of helplessness, the side in which one experiences what Tessa in *The Constant Nymph* truly called 'the undignified state of being a child.' They think of life as a splendid progression up to the pinnacle of thirty, and a mournful slither down the other side. They share the illusion that youth is the season made for joy, that every one past forty lives in hourly peril of going gaga, that with the coming of the first grey hair all pleasure perishes, that innocence lies in ignorance, and that ignorance is bliss.

It is a grim illusion. It is grim for those under thirty, who realise that their time is passing and that soon they will face nothing but decrepitude. It is grimmer for those who have passed thirty and who feel that the best of life must lie behind them. Unfortunately, it is a common error. Most of us hug deception, cherishing a sort of snobbery of youth which is really very dangerous. For the sad thing is that those who believe age to be synonymous with senility, ultimately become senile. It is their own fault. They would not look facts in the face.

For consider youth. There is first of all this business of infancy. Is it really much fun to lie all day wrapped in bundles of shawls, to be dependent upon the precarious wisdom of mothers, nurses and elder sisters for movement, nourishment, warmth and cleanliness, to have a monotonous diet, to suffer constantly from small indigestions, fears, discomforts, hungers; to be, in other words, an infant wailing for the light, with no language but a cry? I had almost rather play golf than be a baby, though one occupation is not much more amusing than the other.

Then there is childhood. Think of it. A constant routine of getting up, being washed behind the ears (or not washed behind the ears, which is ultimately even more uncomfortable), of being told not to do all the things one wants to do, of simple meals, of playing in the garden, or in the street if one is unlucky enough not to have a garden, of being interrupted in the middle of a game to do something that one is told to do, of being constantly in danger of the ignominy of a scolding. How many of us who have reached riper years give adequate thanks to age for saving us from scolding? The shadow of reproof lies darkly over childhood. It is unavoidable. Discipline is unavoidable. The child who is never scolded and never disciplined is even more uncomfortable than the child who is often reprimanded.

For the trouble with children is that they have not learned how to live. Their wills have not yet been adjusted to the social good. They want to put their heads out of railway carriage windows, to throw broken bottles over garden walls, to laugh at hunchbacks, to make noises when silence is more seemly, to slide down banisters, to eat green apples, and to do a thousand other things which ignorance and maladjustment teach them. Discipline is a necessary evil, until the child has learned to mould its own will according to reason and experience. But because it is necessary, that does not mean it is no evil. It is uncomfortable, tedious, humiliating and a bore. Let those who doubt this just go and place themselves in the position of a child again for a day or two, and they will soon remember.

Youth suffers from discipline; youth suffers from ignorance. Contrary to popular superstition, ignorance is not bliss. Ignorance is impotence; it is fear; it is cruelty; it is all the things that make for unhappiness. It leads to hideous though unfounded fears of hell-fire, of horrible diseases, of public humiliation; of the dark, of ghosts, of tigers behind doors in English suburbs, of policemen who, for all their faults, are commonly well-meaning men, of creaking stairs, of dreams, of bogies. Ignorance and fear are both exceedingly unpleasant, and both are characteristics of the very young.

Then there is passion. Far be it from me to think that passion is confined to youth, but in youth it is apt to take a special shape. In the spring the old man's fancy sometimes lightly turns to thoughts of love. The young man's fancy is apt to turn thus heavily and all the year round. The adolescent falls in love with cricket captains, school teachers, companion adolescents, and other Olympian but unresponsive persons. Later he may find rapture in response, but the very intensity of his preoccupation in personal emotions inevitably leads to sorrow. Antony and Cleopatra, like Romeo and Juliet, came to grief; but for the middle-aged lovers, honour, power, politics, military failure and imperial pride alloyed their love. The matter was more complex. For the young, love must be all or nothing. The saving graces of humour, wisdom and experience have not yet been acquired through hard labour. Youth knows no remedy for grief but death.

For the young, ambition is unlimited, and though this is an admirable thing, it is accompanied by much suffering. For unlimited ambition leads to grievous disappointment. I do not to-day suffer immeasurable agony if an editor tells me to alter a leading article, but when at college my essays did not find full favour, I have wept into my cocoa. (A horrid beverage, anyway. I advise nobody to drown sorrow in cocoa. It is bad for the figure and does not alleviate the sorrow.) The young woman who wishes to out-rival Shakespeare flings curses to the sky when a local paper refuses her verses on the First Swallow. The future Florence Nightingale's humiliation is unmitigated when a ward-sister scolds her for leaving finger-marks on the brass steriliser. The ambitions of youth are one of its few merits. But let no one think that they are pleasant passions.

We are fools to mourn our passing youth. We should congratulate ourselves. It is time that some one called the bluff of youth and revealed it as the touching, comfortless, self-conscious, uneasy and preposterous period it really is. The sooner we are done with it, the better.

Of course there are disadvantages about growing older. This world is, we are told, a vale of tears, and it would be surprising and rather disconcerting if any period were quite perfect. A few discomforts make death tolerable, and since we suffer a small death with every passing moment, we need the compensation of misfortune. The greatest mercy, I have often thought, of the Mediterranean coast lies in its mosquitoes. Did we not suffer from their unwelcome attention, we could not bear our holidays to end. The small sorrow which I endured upon my thirtieth birthday prevented that unalloyed congratulation which is one of the greatest misfortunes of a mortal life, as Faust discovered.

It happened like this. I had been working for Equal Franchise with the Equal Political Rights Campaign Committee. I had sat on hard, hard seats through long, long meetings. I had stood on a collapsible (all too collapsible) platform in Hyde Park haranguing members of the public. I had lobbied in the House of Commons, bandied words with policemen, walked in poster parades, and taken those other curious actions which are supposed to have an effect upon our legislature. Oddly enough, they do have an effect. Such is democracy that the law is changed. To-day women do vote upon equal terms with men. But I, who thus sat, stood, walked and lobbied for my rights, was enfranchised by nature, not by His Majesty the King. Ten days before the Royal Assent made the Equal Franchise Bill law, I had my thirtieth birthday.

That was sad. One has these little troubles. But even sadder was a previous experience which temporarily clouded my pleasure in increasing years. It was through excessive age that I failed in friendship with a burglar. I was travelling third-class on an ocean liner, and so was a nice young man called Jock. He had looks; he wore a silk scarf twisted round his neck instead of collar or tie; he had a dark romantic forelock, an engaging squint, and an agreeable voice. He was being deported from Australia for illicit attentions to a safe.

I had never met a burglar before, and I desired to know one. I thought it might be useful to me professionally. But of his own accord, Jock took no notice of me. I therefore decided to take notice of him. At a ship's concert I sat myself next him and proceeded to make conversation. 'It's very hot,' said I. 'Uhuh,' said the burglar. 'The second mate sings rather well,' said I. 'Uhuh,' said the burglar. I felt that the dialogue was becoming too one-sided for social ease, but at that moment Jock's friend, Bill, dropped down into the empty chair on his other side. 'Hallo, Jock,' quoth Bill in a hoarse whisper. 'Who's your bit of skirt?' 'Dunno,' said Jock. 'She's none o' mine. Too long in the tooth for me.'

Since then I have avoided burglars.

This unfortunate experience happened, however, while I was still on what the publishers call the 'right side of thirty.' I will give youth all due credit. Had I been seventeen, Jock might have found me charming. On the other hand, he might not. At seventeen I was far more priggish, highbrow, bustling and impatient than I am to-day, and that is saying a good deal. I will say this for youth, that when one is seventeen one falls in love more easily, minds tepid bath-water less, and has a better figure. Having said this, I think I have said everything.

To turn to a more cheering subject, let us consider the advantages of maturity. Of course, I know that the vast majority of people never grow up at all. Those pink-faced volcanic gentlemen one finds in clubs, saloon bars, private hotels and the like, who go off like rockets at the mention of the dole, Mr Gandhi, short skirts, and outsiders who shoot foxes; those silly fluttering ladies who spend their time fearing that their grandchildren do not love them as they might, that maids are not as respectful as they were, and that there is a draught in the bedroom; all aged and deplorable bores who can think of nothing but themselves are not adult at all. They are victims, not of age, but of protracted infancy. They have never learned how to interest themselves in adult occupations. They have grown decrepit before they have grown mature. They are trying to play the games of children with the bodies of septuagenarians, and they fail miserably. The grasshopper has become a burden because they are totally uninterested in the laws controlling its life and movement. Desire has failed because they still only desire childish things. And they themselves go about the streets mourning the physical ebullience which was youth's one gift to them. They are the most tragic people in the world.

We cannot help their troubles. It takes us all our time to live so that when we are seventy we may feel ourselves at last on the right side of sixty-nine. For civilised living is an art for which some are born with more natural talent than others, but which cannot for any be matured without long patience. The acquisition of philosophy, decision, self-confidence, social ease and intellectual purity requires no short apprenticeship. Youth invariably wastes time in regrets, false starts, and egotistic hesitations. But middle-age should bring some technical mastery which is a pleasure in itself. The excitements of apprenticeship are as nothing compared with the ecstacies of achievement.

The achievement need not be spectacular. We make a grave mistake if we think that the art of life has been mastered only by philosophers, surgeons, explorers, sculptors, statesmen and the like. We simply happen to know of conspicuous figures – Nansen, Lord Balfour, Jane Harrison of Cambridge, Bernard Shaw, Edison, Dame Millicent

Fawcett. We know that these acquired spiritual wealth with added years. But I have seen the same grace of accomplishment in a shepherd on my father's farm, a tall, soldierly, shrewd, efficient man, with a blue frosty eye and a love for horses, whose life seemed to adjust itself perfectly to his environment. I have seen it in the natural ease of a fat old labourer cleaning turnips in the sheep-fold, bending to thrust his fork into the turnip, striking it with his short knife three clean blows for the root, one for the head, then swinging up to throw it on to the pile, striking knife against fork to knock it off, and turning, all in one movement, to pull up the next. This unity, this ease, this perfect identification with one's work, comes only from long, long familiarity. I have seen it in an old foreman's wife moving between table and oven on a big baking day in the long kitchen of the Hind's House in Yorkshire, surrounded by the evidence of her craft, pies browned to a nicety, cheese-cakes, saucer custards, bread exquisitely fragrant, and all accomplished with unhurried ease. Nor, as my intellectual friends too frequently suppose, is this natural ease and mastery of life confined to simple people performing the primitive tasks of husbandry and cooking. I know a woman county councillor of over seventy who is one of the gayest and most vital people in the world. She conducts discreet flirtations with aldermen; she lobbies, she cajoles, she negotiates little intrigues on committees, she counsels councillors, she advises technical advisers, she snubs secretaries, she carries resolutions. There are middle-aged and elderly reformers whose life is one progressive and intoxicating adventure. Nobody might think it just to look at them. It is sad that too often when they grow in years they cannot also grow in gracefulness. Bad taste, poverty and rheumatism are partially to blame. A distressing lack of frivolity is even more responsible. Every member of a committee who is over sixty ought to preserve at least one flirtation as a social tonic. But that is by the way. The really important thing is that public work brings a vicarious but assured sense of immortality. We may be poor, weak, timid, in debt to our landlady, bullied by our nieces, stiff in the joints, shortsighted and distressed; we shall perish, but the cause endures; the cause is great. Our corruptible has put on a species of incorruptibility; we have chastised chancellors, altered laws, built habitations in the desolate city. The wilderness and the solitary place shall be glad for us; the desert shall rejoice and blossom as the rose. Even if all that the world can see is a new clause in the constitution of the Mothers' Union, that at least is something. We have slipped for a moment out of the tangle of purely personal things. We have become arbiters of destiny.

Nor need maturity mean an end to physical adventure. Not long ago I read in the paper of a small yacht which crossed the Atlantic captained by a man of eighty-eight, the youngest member of the crew being sixty-four. Nansen was contemplating a new expedition to the Pole just before he died. One of our most famous British mountaineers is a general well past middle-age.

Indeed, youth should not be the time for rash endeavour. The young man or woman has frequently far more family responsibilities than the man or woman whose children are grown up, whose parents are dead, who is at last really independent. The young also have all their lives before them. They should not be cut off on the wrong side of thirty. Young men killed in war, young women dying in child-bed, are the real victims of death. The security of age lies in its knowledge of life. Whatever happens to us when we are over seventy, at least we have seen life. One of the youngest men I ever knew was travelling by himself to Madagascar. He had been given up by all his doctors. His grandchildren wished to settle him down in chairs, put cushions behind his back, protect him from draughts and tyrannise over him gently in the mistaken belief that they were thus demonstrating their disinterested attitude towards him and that money which they might one day inherit. So he shook the dust of their protection off his heels, accepted a business commission in Madagascar, and when I met him was sports president of his ship. He was eighty-five then. I understand that he is still travelling, still popular, and still enjoying life.

I would not suggest that after thirty life is a continuous progression of felicity till death cuts us short on the threshold of perfection. Until we have learned far more about our physical relation to the universe our joints will stiffen, our arteries harden, our sight grow dim. Even Bernard Shaw confessed in the preface to *Back to Methuselah*, 'I am doing the best I can at my age. My powers are waning; but so much the better for those who found me unbearably brilliant when I was in our prime.' We all can only do the best possible to our age. Our powers wane. But there are compensations. The words which Virgil gave to Dido were splendid enough for that deserted heroine, but they were even more appropriate for Virgil's self.

> Vixi et quem dederat cursum fortuna peregi
> Et nunc magna mei sub terras ibit imago.

> I have lived and accomplished the task that
>   destiny gave me,
> And now I shall pass beneath the earth no
>   common shade.

That is the phrase of an old and not a young man. In its dignity, its courage and its acceptance it reveals why the right side of thirty is the later side.

1930

Nurse to the Archbishop

ONCE upon a time a Nurse was sent off duty to hear an Archbishop preach. The Archbishop was visiting the parish to bless a new reredos, to preach at morning service, and to shake hands with the Rector, Curate and all members of the Church Council.

The Nurse's patient, a religious woman, was bedridden with phlebitis, so could not go to hear the sermon and shake hands in the parish room. She was deeply disappointed, for such an opportunity might not recur; but she made the best of a bad bargain, and said to her nurse, 'Well, you must go instead. Never mind about a blanket-bath this morning. Give me a lick and a promise, and run off early so as to get a good seat, and then come back and tell me all about it.'

The Nurse sympathised with her disappointment and said she would do her best. She did not explain that this Archbishop was no stranger to her, since once she had nursed him through appendicitis. That was a long time ago; he had not been an Archbishop then, nor had his case been in any way remarkable, and the only thing she remembered clearly about it was that he had an in-growing toe-nail on the left foot. But she did not feel that this was a proper subject for discussion.

So she said nothing to her patient and hurried off to church, panting, for she was not as young as she had once been, and was seized by strange pains if she ran.

The church was very full, for every one wanted to see the Archbishop. The organist had practised his music daily for weeks; the choir boys wore clean surplices; the altar vases were filled with lilies costing at least two shillings each.

The Nurse had not been to church for several years, for though the rules of her association laid down that its members must go off duty for two hours every day, and on Sundays at such times as made it possible to attend Divine Worship, she preferred to call upon her married sister, or to go for a tram-ride, or to sit in the gardens on sunny mornings with her crochet. For there was something about church services which she did not like, though she did not know clearly what it was.

'Perhaps I shall know to-day,' she thought, looking round about her.

The Archbishop entered behind a long procession that passed up the aisle singing 'The Church's One Foundation,' and all the people peered at him over their shoulders as though he were a bride. He was a fine figure of a man, tall and stately, in snowy lawn with a bright scarlet hood; a gold cross hung on his breast, and he walked with a great staff that shone like silver.

The Nurse wondered whether he still had trouble with his toe-nails, and whether he took his liquid paraffin regularly.

She saw the Rector, who suffered from high blood-pressure, and the Curate, whose wife lost her fifth baby, and Mr Barnes, the verger, who had a weak heart. She knew that two of the choir boys had adenoids, and she saw in front of her Nancy Grainger who should have been in Switzerland for her lung trouble – but her father was silly and would not let her go. He would probably kill her. She was coughing now.

'Rend your hearts and not your garments,' intoned the Curate, 'and turn unto the Lord your God.'

The Nurse remembered how the Curate's wife had wept when they cut her nightdress to avoid moving her, rending her heart with her garments, because her last child had died.

'Dearly beloved brethren.' The Curate's voice was a rich baritone. No doubt, thought the Nurse, he was hoping that the Archbishop would take notice of him, and who could wonder? For with that family to keep he needed promotion.

They all had to kneel for the General Confession. The Nurse no longer found kneeling very easy. She was sixty-two and stiff with rheumatism, and had once strained herself lifting a patient who had dropsy. Her back was tired, and there was no hassock for her.

She sat on the hard seat, leaning forward, and listened to the congregation confessing that men were like lost sheep.

She raised her eyes, and looked at the lofty pillars, the long stretch of the chancel, the carven choir stalls; and she compared the dignity of this building with the ugliness of the infirmary ward, and the squalor of the rooms she visited when working on the district. In church men worshipped among colour and space and scarlet and fine linen; there upon broken floors, between walls of sodden peeling plaster, women gave birth to children, laid out bodies, served food and patched old garments, that life might endure.

'Wherefore let us beseech Him to grant us true repentance, and His Holy Spirit,' sang the Curate, 'that those things may please him which we do at this present; and that the rest of our life hereafter may be pure and holy; so that at the last we may come to his eternal joy.'

And now the Nurse knew why she disliked church services, for as she raised her head, she observed that the Curate, and the Rector and the Archbishop were all men. The vergers were men; the organist was a man; the choir boys, the sidesmen and soloist and church wardens, all were men. The architects who had built the church, the composers of the music, the translators of the psalms, the compilers of the liturgy, all these too, the Nurse pondered, had been men.

And she thought to herself, 'I could have preached a sermon. I could have stood in scarlet and fine linen, wearing a golden cross. Why has no woman been an archbishop? Why has no woman built a great cathedral?'

Then she remembered how she had held that Archbishop's

body, when the man was witless from the anaesthetic. She had washed him and soothed him, and dressed his wound and ministered to his humblest physical needs. She had scolded him for neglecting his in-growing toe-nail.

And then she thought of women as she knew them; women groaning and retching in labour of child-birth; women bending over the sweaty bodies of the sick; women airing blankets and cooking meals, and washing dishes and cleaning rooms. Their movements were not controlled by ordered ceremony. They could not ordain now to stand up and sing, now to move forward, now to kneel, now to bow to the altar. For their movements were controlled by such necessities as could not wait on any ceremony. Death would not wait; birth would not wait; the burning anguish of fever would not wait; the restless bodies of children would not wait, for women to set themselves in grave procession, or honour each other in tremendous hierarchy.

'Is there no place for women in religion?' asked the Nurse. 'Are we to have no part then in this beauty? Shall we not come to that eternal joy?' She was standing now for the canticle and psalms.

'Praise the Lord, O my soul,' sang the congregation, 'and all that is within me praise His Holy Name. Praise the Lord, O my soul, and forget not all His benefits; who forgiveth all thy sin; and healeth all thine infirmities; who saveth thy life from destruction; and crowneth thee with mercy and lovingkindness; who satisfieth thy mouth with good things; making thee young and lusty as the eagle.'

And yet, thought the Nurse, whom does the Lord employ for these His mercies? Who most often forgive the sins of men, their cruelty and indifference, their irresponsibility to the children they have begotten, their recklessness with each other's lives? Whom, she thought, does the Lord employ to heal the infirmities of men? Who save their lives from destruction, when as foolish children they would run across roads, or fall into fires, or eat unwholesome food? Who crown them with lovingkindness? Who satisfy their mouths with good things, making them young and lusty as the eagles? And the nurse knew that women did these things.

The Nurse saw women acting as vicars of the Lord on earth, that men might be released to play their splendid games, to build their churches, to robe themselves as archbishops.

'Yea, as a father pitieth his own children,' sang the congregation, 'even so is the Lord merciful unto them that fear Him.'

The Nurse bowed her head over her prayer-book, smiling. For what was a father's passing pity, to the day-long solicitude of the working mother? The father might stoop in the evening to touch the cheek of his sleeping child, but it was the mother who through the day had tended it.

Oh, she thought proudly, then let men play their games; for it is fitting that some one should erect a palace of honour and dignity and ritual on the foundation of necessity. It is good that for a little while some one should speak and move and act as though all men were celestial beings, as though disease were nothing but a dream, helplessness a shadow, and the needs of imperfect bodies the matter of a moment. It is good that women should make this possible, setting men free for comely and untroubled movements.

She did not hear the Rector read the lesson. She was rapt in her dream of the power and generosity of women, who made this service possible, and of the day when they should reap their due reward.

But she knew that this was not the end of the whole matter. This proud stateliness was but a part of life, a flight from the realities which women had to face, a flight upward, perhaps, but still a flight. And she thought, 'Are we to bless the Lord only for those matters in which we cannot partake, seeing that we, being busy as His deputies serving the bodies of men, can spare no time for ceremonial exercises? Surely it cannot be so. Surely, if life is good, it is good throughout its substance; we cannot separate men's activities from women's and say, these are worthy of praise and these unworthy; we cannot separate those who minister to the body from those who minister to the soul. We, who spread the tables are at one with those who spread the altar, and I, who nursed a young curate in his sickness, am a partaker in the honour of the Archbishop.'

The congregation stood for the canticle, 'Benedicite, Omnia Opera,' and the Nurse stood with them.

'O all ye works of the Lord, bless ye the Lord: praise Him and magnify Him for ever.'

'All ye works of the Lord,' the Nurse considered. 'Not just selected works, but all activities, all manifestations of life, in youth and age, in sickness and in disease.'

'O ye sun and moon, bless ye the Lord: O ye stars of Heaven, bless ye the Lord: O ye showers and dew, bless ye the Lord: praise Him and magnify Him for ever.'

'This is splendid,' thought the Nurse, swept in spite of herself into the song of praise. And her heart took up the canticle, translating it into the terms of life as she had known it.

'O all ye fevers and tumours, bless ye the Lord: O ye child-birth and anguish, bless ye the Lord: O ye sickness and squalor, bless ye the Lord, praise Him and magnify Him for ever.'

'O ye light and darkness,' sang the congregation, 'bless ye the Lord: O ye lightnings and clouds, bless ye the Lord; O let the Earth bless the Lord; yea, let it praise Him and magnify Him for ever.'

The Nurse thought of light and darkness as she knew them through the long watches by the sick; she thought of lightnings and clouds as she had known them, soothing the fears of children at their fury; she thought of Earth as she had seen it, waiting to receive the dead who rested there at last.

'O let Death bless the Lord,' sang the Nurse, for she was very tired. 'Yea, let it praise Him and magnify Him for ever.'

And the organ, and the choir and the congregation shouted the mighty tumult of her blessing, until it seemed as though Heaven and Earth and Life and Death had answered her.

The congregation, however, did not understand this. For the Nurse at that moment fell sideways from the pew and was carried down the aisle by two church wardens. The people peered over their shoulders as though she were a bride, for they did not like to feel that they had missed any new excitement.

They learned later that she had died from heart failure brought on by excitement, which seemed a handsome tribute to the occasion. And as she was not as young as she had been, and failing a little, it was not really sad; and the hand-shaking in the parish room went off very well; and quite twenty people called on the Nurse's patient and told her all about it, so she did not miss anything. Indeed, the patient became quite a heroine, since it was from her house that the Nurse had gone to die in church in honour of the Archbishop.

1931

Remember, Remember!

BEFORE he spoke, they all knew what father was going to say. As a prelude to every family expedition, he thrust out his lips, frowned magisterially, and repeated his unchanging formula: 'The point is, somebody must look after Grandma.'

The point was also that the somebody could not be himself. That went without saying. They all knew that he had to tell them how to light the bonfire; he had to warn Gladys not to stand right over an exploding rocket. He had to tease Miss Lester, and make pretty Flora Cheniston feel at home, and keep his eye on the garden gate, and everything. Besides, when he had been at the office all day earning the money which kept Grandma sitting so snugly in front of her bedroom fire, you could not expect him to stay in too. After all, she had only been his stepmother.

They stood in the hall, solemnly, like a jury considering its verdict. Betty jogged up and down, peering into the delightful box, full of little coloured cubes and sticks and coils, with twisted blue paper tips and mysterious cardboard packets labelled 'Japanese Fountain,' 'Silver Storm,' or, most exhilarating of all, 'Stand Clear after the Fuse is lit.'

'Gladys stayed in last time,' murmured Mrs Barclay. 'No, Flora, certainly not, dear, as if we should let you! Your first night here too. Miss Lester . . .' But Miss Lester really ought to have been having her night out, and Betty was too small, and one simply cannot ask these things of Cook. She turned to Barbara. 'Run upstairs, dear, and tell Grandma that we are just going to let the fireworks off in the garden, and that you'll run up every ten minutes or so to see that she's all right.'

Thus disposing of a collective responsibility, without any immediate inconvenience to themselves, the family set off down the moonlit path, carrying matches and waste paper, and potatoes to roast in their jackets, and squibs and rockets; and Barbara leapt light-foot up the stairs to Grandma's room.

The old lady sat over the fire, wrapped in a tartan rug, reading the *Church Times*.

'We're going to let off the fireworks!' shouted Barbara, very clear and helpful.

'Well, I don't want you to do your needlework again up here,' snapped Grandma. Her deafness made conversation a matter of continual cross-purposes. 'The last time that governess sewed here she left bits of silk all over the floor. Hand me the peppermints off the mantlepiece. I can't reach them.'

'I'm going *down to the fireworks*!' persevered Barbara. 'You know. Remember, remember the Fifth of November!'

'It's about time you did remember. Please tell your mother that if it's boiled fish again for supper, I don't want any. And draw the curtains over the window. There's a draught.'

'In the garden,' pointed Barbara. 'It's not fish to-night. Veal!' And turned to the window. But even then she heard the first low detonation, and from the black gulf below the window rose a golden meteor. It blossomed surprisingly into three crimson stars, that dipped in the gentle loveliness of a perfect curve, sinking until the inky darkness erased them, as though they had been wiped from a child's slate. The fireworks had begun.

'I'll be back in a few minutes,' shouted Barbara, and was gone, her long legs leaping down the stair, racing the robber Time which stole from her such brief, ephemeral beauties.

She was gone; and Grandma, left alone without her

peppermints and with the draught, sat mumbling over her grievance as though it were a kind of sweet. It all began with those lawyers who had messed up her investments and left her dependent upon her stepson. Eddie had been a nasty little boy. She had never liked him. Pale-faced and pimply, and too fond of food. He had twice been sick in his bedroom, and she had had to clear up after him, because you could not ask the maids to do things like that. And now he had grown into a pompous, stupid man, and there she was, stranded in the middle of his commonplace, selfish family. And even Barbara ran off and left her with the draught prowling round her shoulders. 'I oughtn't to be alive,' she muttered. 'I oughtn't to be alive.'

But alive she was, and while she lived she would never knuckle under to them. Eddie's banked-up coals of fire could not burn her head. She'd show them. She had not walked by herself to the window for quite three months; but Barbara was a naughty girl. It would serve her right to show in what straits she had left her grandmother. She wasn't done yet. Not she.

Cautiously, grimly, feeling her way along by the bed and the back of the chair, Grandma moved to the window. Her knees quivered. Her ankles felt as though they did not belong to her, but at last she stood, holding with both hands on to the crimson curtains – dyed curtains from Mrs Barclay's room, another grievance.

Below her lay the lawn, milk-white in moonshine. The dark, leafless trees dripped heavy shadow on to the garden path. Against the moon floated a filmy cloud, a puff of smoke, feather-light. Suddenly from the deep blackness of the shrubbery shot a single flame. No sound came to the watcher, but from velvet silence leapt another and another, and another, slender tongues, waving fronds, blossoming into vivid life. Dark figures moved against the dancing flame. A red spark glowed, twinkled, and suddenly broke into a fountain of gold and silver spray. A spinning wheel of light whirled from the leafless elm-tree, a flaring wick trailing its fiery hair. All over the garden the bonfire had curved an arc of tawny light. The apple trees twisted their branches under a sky no longer inky blue. Pale amber flowed into the crowning darkness. A rocket flew up, silent as a bird, split into radiant stars, hovered and sank, a bird, seeking its nest in the soft darkness. The trees were alive. They budded with dancing flames; they bloomed with brilliant flowers, circles and wheels and points, and sprays of light. Up soared a Roman candle; white star, red star, blue. It was gone. Bravely the great flames of the bonfire shone; their torches lit the secret shadows of the garden. There lay an overturned plant pot; there a derelict turnip. There lay a doll with a broken torso, brought by Betty as an offering to the lordly flame.

Lovely, lovely garden! Exquisite mirage of the apple boughs weaving fine lace against the livid sky! Lovely ephemeral lights that leapt into stars and died. Grandma, standing upright between the curtains, her lips parted, her eyes aglow, no longer only saw the lights; she heard. For here again were youth and pride and gaiety. Here came snatches of songs, ballads which she had sung, holding a tarlatan scarf about her drooping shoulders; she heard the applause of elegant young men; she heard the sound of laughter and the frosty ringing of skates on the sunlit ice; she heard the horses clattering down the hard road, and Richard in gallant scarlet waving to her again; she heard the crackle and hiss and roar of the bonfire; the rockets whizzed and whined in the frosty air. It was in the dark shrubbery, left in shadow by the flames, that Harold had kissed her on her wedding eve. But it was Richard whom she had married. She tasted again power and strength and the sweet wine of flattery and success. She saw; she heard; she knew.

'Remember, remember, the Fifth of November!' Ah, she remembered now. No neglect now could quench her memories. The flame had never died. It had been hidden. What did this silly family know of the hot aching perilous joy of life, the flame that soared so high, blossomed so bravely?

The fire flickered down. The last sparklet tossed its fiery circle. The last squib jumped and spluttered. The family returned across the garden, their hands and faces blackened, their pockets full of potatoes roasted success-fully in the smouldering ashes. Into the hall they came, laughing and teasing. And suddenly they remembered.

'Grandma! Oh, Barbara, I told you to go up!'

It was no use. Barbara had forgotten too. They looked at each other with amused commiseration.

'We shall catch it,' laughed father. 'Up with you, Babs. A clean breast. Let's take her a potato.'

They all went, giggling, penitent, carrying their offer-ings.

They found her sitting, a trifle flushed and breath-less, beside the fire, nibbling peppermints and reading the *Church Times*. Her curtains were tightly drawn.

'Hallo, Grandma. We wish you could have been with us.'

'Such fun! It's a perfect night.'

'Marvellous. We brought you a potato.'

She regarded them, indomitably disagreeable.

'You see, I had to draw the curtains and get the pepper-mints myself, Barbara. Fortunately, I could just manage to draw them. I'm very glad I could not see your fireworks,' she triumphed. 'Nasty, dangerous, noisy things. Just think what a mess there'll be on the lawn in the morning.'

1927

Abroad

Winifred Holtby and Vera Brittain travelled together to Europe frequently, on League of Nations business and also on holiday. The year after Vera's marriage in 1925, Winifred visited South Africa for six months, to lecture for the League of Nations Union, to see her wartime friend Jean McWilliam, now a headmistress in Pretoria, and also to recover from what she believed, wrongly as it turned out, to be the loss through marriage of Vera's close companionship. Appalled by what she saw of the working conditions of black South Africans, she returned home determined to improve these through effective unionisation. To send to South Africa and finance an experienced trade union worker became the cause that preoccupied her for the remainder of her life. These stories, as well as the novel Mandoa, Mandoa!, are by-products of that last great voyage of commitment of Winifred's life.

The Travelling Companions

I MET them travelling together on a third-class steamer from Australia via the Cape. It was the fourth evening, and after six o'clock tea the passengers were dancing. I sat on the hatches alone, listening to the music, watching the gay cotton frocks of the young girls, the darkening water and the little tropical sun floating on its golden brim like a straw hat thrown into the water.

'Haven't you got a partner?'

I looked up startled, and saw an enormous creature grinning down at me. His vast shoulders strained the seams of a shiny blue serge suit; his thumbs were thrust into the top of his trousers; his round head was covered with tight black curls. I hardly saw behind him the picturesque little man whom I had noticed once or twice before, who wandered, encircled by a cloud of tyrannous children, rescuing seasick parents, or fingering the volume stuck into the belt below his silk shirt. For this was my first sight of Bullocky, and Bullocky was not a person to be seen without surprise.

I shook my head in answer to his question, and when he bellowed, for his tenderest whisper was a roar, 'Can ye waltz?' I said 'Yes,' more from astonishment than from desire. His companion's delicate eyebrows lifted, but the Doc made no comment as Bullocky seized me as though I had been a refractory steer, and swung me into a wild, whirling career. His huge, hobnailed boots stamped on the deck. We spun to the right; we whirled to the left. We hurled ourselves into the scuppers and out again, avoiding collisions by most hazardous miracles. But we did avoid them. Bullocky had a curious dexterity behind his clumsiness, and a wild sort of elephantine splendour in his dancing. When the music stopped he almost flung me on to the hatches and stood above me, grinning and wiping his forehead with a grimy, immense handkerchief.

'Where's Doc gone?' he asked.

I did not know. He looked round for a minute discomforted, then hooked his arm into mine. 'Gee!' he gasped; his gasp was a tempest. 'That was a dance. You're Atalanta, you are.' He bent down, calmly unlaced his boot, straightened his blue woollen sock, and said, 'Come for a walk.'

I waited while he replaced his boot, then let him lead me to the stern of the ship. As though we had known each other for years he began to talk about his farm in Griqualand, his sisters, and the reason for his nickname. He was very proud of this. Once at Bloemfontein market he had been challenged to eat a whole leg of mutton at a sitting, and had won for accomplishing this feat a live bullock. He knew a vast store of tales about horses and cattle and fairs and rides at night through the veldt and fords across flooded rivers, and these he told with a flowery eloquence oddly interspersed with classical references.

It became quite dark. The wake of the ship led straight into the silver pathway of the moon. Huge stars of jade and crystal formed and shivered in the phosphorescent water. Bullocky's tone changed.

'Gee!' he exclaimed suddenly. 'Gee! Can't you see something walking on that water? It's Christ, I tell you. Christ. Those green stars under His feet. He's come again. He won't let me alone. I'm done for, I am. The years of my youth are withered away like last year's leaves. I met Christ when I was riding from Durban. I saw Him as clearly as I see you now. "You crucify me who crucify love," He said. All because I took a bottle of Cape wine on an empty stomach, and she wouldn't believe it wasn't whisky. Broke it off, then and there, she did. An' she was my Soul Mate. Broke my heart, she did. And hers. And hers. My Soul Mate. Hands same shape as mine too. Wild days. Wild days.' He looked down into the swirling water with a thundrous sigh. 'Not psychic, are you?'

'No,' I said. 'I'm afraid not. Or perhaps I'm glad.'

I was relieved when the little doctor appeared, looking for his companion. Bullocky introduced us. The doctor bowed. I never saw him when he was not overwhelmingly polite. I noticed then that he was wearing Turkish slippers of emerald-coloured leather and that the book tucked into his belt was Anatole France's *La Vie en Fleur*.

'I do not dance,' he said. 'But if I might suggest it, could we not all go up and have a small vermouth?'

We went. After that I saw the two friends continually. The Doc and I exchanged books. His library on board consisted of that one volume of Anatole France, *The Odes of Horace*, and Dante's *Divina Commedia* in Italian. Bullocky did not read. He told me that he was no scholar; but we soon discovered that at the bridge table he was a brilliant and indefatigable player.

We used to play morning after morning in the hot bar, with Jock, a sulky Lowlander with a broken nose, as a fourth. Throughout the day Bullocky would drink more and more heavily. Towards evening, hanging on to the arm of the little man, or, if he were absent on one of his errands of charity, on mine, he would stagger down to the dining-saloon, seize a bottle of Worcester sauce, toss off the contents, and appear again, ready for battle.

The doctor never wearied of talking to me about his friend. Did I know that he was going to enlist in the army? Did I think that he was any happier? He deplored his intemperate habits for aesthetic rather than moral reasons; but one night, when I returned very late to my cabin after gossiping with another girl, I found him crouched on a camp stool under the light outside the door of the men's bathroom, reading Dante.

'Is somebody sick?' I asked.

'Yes,' he said, and for the first and only time his charming voice was grim. 'Bullocky. In my bunk.'

I said no more, but next day my loquacious cabin

companion told me that the Doc had been seen in the men's bathroom, washing Bullocky's only shirt for him. 'How you can go about with them I don't know. One's a great drunken cow and the other's been in prison.'

The prison may not have been genuine, but the shirt was. Punctual to the minute at our hour for bridge the doctor appeared, a little heavy-eyed after his night's vigil, followed by a sober and chastened Bullocky in a clean shirt.

The last glimpse I had of them was at Liverpool Street station. The Doc wore a neat tweed suit, his small figure more dapper, ingratiating and urbane than ever. Bullocky, enormous, ungainly, with a pair of racing glasses swung across his shoulder and his arm round the neck of his friend, was roaringly, gloriously drunk.

'I suppose that there weren't any really interesting people on board a third-class boat?' asked my friends.

1927

The Third-Class Concert

THE liner crossed the Equator. Day after day she drawled
lazily through motionless blue seas, encircled by the brave
sweeping flight of the albatrosses. It was very hot, and
on the third-class deck the passengers gathered in listless
groups, playing cards, sewing and endeavouring idly to
amuse the ubiquitous children.

During the first week of the voyage they had sorted
themselves with almost uncanny certitude into clear-cut
sections. The smart young wives, all affirming that this
was the first time that they had travelled third-class, and
that it was quite good fun, and that in these days of
the new poor it was no use pretending to be opulent;
the young men adventuring to make their fortunes in
the new platinum mines or on citrus farms; the older
couples, uprooting themselves too late in life for comfort
from a country which had no longer room for them;
the convivial commercial travellers, the troupe of Guitar
Girls, bound for South African Theatres, Limited, the
amorphous Irish families, the prim schoolmaster, there
they were, all keeping themselves to themselves with a
spontaneous social adjustment peculiar to passengers on
a long voyage. And there, also, was the isolated, dark,
despised, curious company of sixty Jews from Eastern
Europe, travelling under the protection of their small,
dapper, voluble interpreter.

Some said that they were bound for Portuguese East
Africa. Others, that they were coming to replace the Indians
expatriated from Natal. Others declared that they had no
valid papers and that they would be turned back at Cape
Town. Yet others said that it was a shame that the country

should grow overrun with pestilential Jews who had hardly two tickies to rub together, and reminded each other of the celebrated cartoon which showed South Africa as a cow, with a Dutchman pulling her tail, an Englishman pulling her horns, and a Jew milking her.

The Jews said nothing. They kept very close together on the hot, congested deck. The women, with shawls over their heads, watched their docile, precocious children, calling them away from the more boistrous Anglo-Saxons. The men in shirt-sleeves, with scarlet handkerchiefs round their necks, smoked, spat and played cards with a queer sombre vivacity.

They slept, a steward said, right down near the hold, below the rabbit warren of the third-class cabins, and the bathrooms which stank of Condy's Fluid, and the bare white dining-saloon, which looked, said one of the young wives, for all the world like a public lavatory. They wore the same clothes day after day, and read no books, attempted no sports, but only waited, as though their minds were heavy with memories of pogroms in Poland and famine in Latvia. Like the Dutch Voortrekkers, they sought a Promised Land, terrifying and desirable, and with the courage of patient humility they set forth into the unknown.

Among them all, a chartered libertine, authoritative, indefatigable and amused, went Captain Christopher Langley. He had been elected as Sports President by the third-class passengers, and he flung himself into the labour of organising potato races, quoits tournaments, fancy-dress balls and sing-songs, with that disinterested devotion to administrative detail which characterises the British colonial civil or military servant. He said that he had been 'axed' from the Indian Army, and was joining his brother in a motor business in Durban. It was only at the end of the voyage that most people realised that the delicate, dark-haired little woman with the three naughty children was his wife. He himself appeared always unruffled, confident and neat, treating with good-humoured superiority even the unaccommodating Jews. To the other passengers he spoke of them as the 'Squgs.' The name spread.

Captain Langley was arranging a concert. After much coaxing he had discovered a lady who could sing only a trifle out of tune, 'A Perfect Day,' and 'Yearning,' and 'God Send You Back to Me.' Mr O'Malley, prompted by his fat, jolly wife, could recite 'The Crockery Cart,' and 'Pat O'Flannigan's Ball.' Two 'comics,' a dancer of Irish jigs, the Guitar Girls, a young farmer with a decent baritone who knew no songs, but was quite willing to learn, and a little girl who played the violin, made up his company. He took them down to the hot, beer-scented lounge, and rehearsed with them conscientiously, thumping on the tuneless piano, repeating choruses, chaffing, praising, questioning.

The hot evenings died into the windless nights. Captain Langley's preparations went forward slowly. The Jews' interpreter came to him one evening and asked whether his men might borrow for an hour a guitar belonging to one of the Guitar Girls. The Captain hesitated, but the girl, with giggling sportsmanship, surrendered her instrument. The interpreter withdrew and the rehearsal continued.

Upstairs a few first-class passengers, who found it too hot for dancing and were tired of playing Bridge, lay on the boat deck watching the stars sway backwards and forwards behind the long mast of the ship. Suddenly out of the darkness a tenor voice, pure, melancholy and exquisite, rose into the quiet air.

The song was in a foreign tongue, but the short, lilting verses ended in a refrain which cried with an anguish of beauty and of pain, 'Sonia! Sonia!' then three lines of reiterated melody, then the swinging rhythm of the climax and a final call, 'Ohee!' After eight of such verses the chorus was at last caught up by a deep-voiced choir singing in harmony. It was repeated; it rose in wild protest, drooped and died again on one long-drawn, sighing note which swung out across the water and melted into the encircling night. 'O-hee!'

247

'Jove, what was that?' they asked. But only one rose from his chair and ran unostentatiously down the companion, along a labyrinth of passages, through an unlocked door, up more steps, and out on to the third-class deck. It was an exploit not encouraged by the ship's authorities, but the young man was a journalist and skilled in finding access to forbidden places.

Standing in the shadow he saw the packed ranks of the third-class passengers gathered about an open space on the deck. On the edge of the circle of lamp-light crouched a small, uncouth man playing a guitar. His head with its straggling grey beard dipped over the instrument, as he plucked with clever, careless fingers stray incoherent notes and dropped them into the silence. Beside him stood a slight boy in shirt sleeves who had just been singing. His head was thrown back, his cheeks flushed bright pink, his lips parted. He began another song.

This had a racier tune. It seemed to be of a humorous quality, for the dark-faced Lithuanians and Poles and Latvians broke into spasmodic bursts of shaking laughter, and stamped on the floor and clapped their hands, until the infection of the song spread to the outer ring of the Gentiles, and they too, began to rock their heads and beat on the deck, and clap voraciously for more.

More followed. The man with the guitar fumbled easily until he seemed to find a little monotonous tune, a repetition of two notes, then three, then two again, fiercely accented. 'Tá-ra, tá-ra, la-la-la, la-la-la, tá-ra!' The music wove a rippling circle of magic over the listening crowd.

Then two dark, solid-looking youths separated themselves from the others and stepped forward into the ring of lamplight. With arms locked they swayed to the music, throwing their legs from side to side, and humming 'Tá-ra, tá-ra, la-la-la, la-la-la, tá-ra!' Their eyes were heavy with brooding contentment; they breathed deeply; the sweat ran down their flushed faces; they swung their legs in clumsy, rhythmical abandon.

The music quickened. Two girls moved forward, one

shyly, one boldly, yet with an assured, pre-destined gravity. They thrust their arms through those of the young men and together the four swayed in a solemn line. There was no gaiety in the dance; their movements might have been part of a religious ritual, the song an incantation. Closer and closer together swung the two girls at the end of the line. With a shout from the onlookers, they caught hold of each other's arms and suddenly locked the line into a circle. The magic ring was completed. Round and round it span, as wilder and wilder the music rose, and louder and louder sang the Jewish chorus.

Isolated, incomprehensible, withdrawn, bound together in this invulnerable circle, the young men and maidens danced under the swinging lamp. As David might have danced before the Ark of the Covenant, with the triumphant solemnity of a Chosen People, interlocked in a mysterious union, they stamped their coarsely-shod feet, they tossed their dark heads backwards and forwards, they danced before the wondering Gentiles, on their way to the Promised Land.

Poor, ill-treated, despised, fugitive, with that close interlocked circle of their blood, their history, their religion, they made a kinship of suffering, and an exultation of defeat. It was the outer ring of Christians which appeared then to be isolated and desultory. For all their confident voices, the pink jumpers of their pretty wives, the sophisticated boasting of the young men, they were a haphazard, estranged, heterogeneous gathering of wanderers at best. They had no secret communion which suddenly drew them into a tight, whirling circle, no corporate power of song like this that rose and fell over the listening sea. They were shut out. They were scattered.

The young journalist felt a strange, secret triumph. His forefathers, also, long ago, had been Jews. He felt in his veins some thin savour of the vintage which ran so warmly through the interlocked bodies of the dancers. Here was something worth seeing. Here was something real and vivid and glowing.

'I'll tell the world. I'll tell the world,' he muttered under his breath.

Captain Christopher Langley, emerging hot but cheerful from his arduous performance in the lounge, saw the last wild gyrations of the spinning circle before it broke, scattering the dancers into the outstretched arms of their applauding friends. He recognised the journalist, and smiled at him.

'Come to see the animals perform for a bit?'

The younger man turned on him in great excitement. 'Say, you run this entertainments committee right here, don't you?'

'I do.'

'Then why in the Lord's name don't you give a show and invite us poor benighted creatures from the first-class to come and see? We're fed up to the back teeth with our own stuff. You can give us something worth seeing.'

Fresh from his labours, amused and gratified, Captain Langley sucked meditatively through his fine teeth, smiled, and said he'd see what he could do.

On the boat deck, in the library, in the bar, the music room, and the dining saloon, the first-class passengers listened to the tales spread by the young journalist with the American accent, who promised such rare sport at the Third-Class Concert.

'I tell you, it's the genuine article. No faked ballet stuff imported via Paris. No watered-down Diaghilaff nonsense. Real peasant ritual dancing, hot from the villages in Poland and Esthonia, and Latvia and God alone knows where.'

The intellectuals thronged round him. They spoke of the Chauve Souris and Gogol, and Russian-Jews as they appear upon the platform of the Coliseum. The young journalist scored a triumph. It was not only that he could provide a new sensation for their jaded appetites. He felt the power and beauty of the Jewish chorus to be in some way a vindication of his inmost self, of the fears which he had stifled as a boy, of innumerable humiliations when his black hair and long nose had called to the memory of acquaintances the resemblance of his profile to that of a race which was not 100 per cent. American. He wanted to see the Jews impress these lordly English.

The night of the Third-Class Concert arrived. The iron gates in the railing which separated first-class sheep from third-class goats swung open. The stewards carried across chairs and chairs and more chairs, and the first-class passengers streamed through. They brought with them a whiff of perfume, the satisfying scent of good cigars, a glimmer of jewels and a flutter of tulle veils. They took their places in the front rows of the great semi-circle before the cleared space of deck. The single light hung above the piano, and tarpaulins covered the hatches upon which the singers were to stand.

The pretty girls in the pink and blue and white jumpers handed round neat printed programmes. By the piano, smiling, unflustered, indefatigable, stood Captain Christopher Langley, much gratified that his labours were about to be rewarded.

On the programme the journalist read:

Piano Solo   'Selections from Il Trovatore'   MR SPICER
Song   'The Perfect Day'   MRS LANGESTAFF
Recitation   'The Crockery Cart'   MR O'MALLEY
Selections on Guitars   THE FOUR GUITAR GIRLS

And so on, till 'God Save the King.'

The Squgs had not even been invited.

1927

The Voorloper Group

To reach the camp we motored for three hours from Pretoria, striking northward through a wilderness of brown, crouching hills. Twice we passed through native villages, our track furrowing their scorched and close-cropped commons, between the raw huts with black, gaping doors from which came a hot foetid scent to vex our nostrils. Once our wheels revolved impotently on the clinging sand, until eight young men extricated us, their faces alight with the amusement of the unembarrassed. But near the camp the brown changed abruptly to vivid green; willows like golden fountains drooped above the water of a dam. The two tall Zulus, silent as shadows on their bare feet, spread for us under the canvas awning a meal of young buck and river fish, stewed guavas and pineapple.

We ate at leisure, soothed by tranquility and perfect service. We drank sweet Cape wine, and watched the swift dusk drain the colour from the sky to enrich the dancing flame of our camp-fire.

There were in our company Higson, the mine owner, Malden, Rosalind Daintree, Marie Kritzinger, who has published two volumes of verse in Afrikaans, Hendrik, her husband, a considerable artist, and myself. Malden was planning the publication of a new monthly review, to be devoted to the art and literature of South Africa. Higson, always eager for new and interesting ways of diminishing his immense fortune, was to finance this undertaking, and we had been invited out to Malden's camp to offer our advice. Even while enjoying his hospitality our gratitude was tempered by our appreciation of his judgment. We knew ourselves to be people of distinction, the pioneers, however unrecognised, of a young civilisation. What we thought to-day, South Africa would think tomorrow. He was fortunate in our counsel; and when we had supped admirably, and tasted exquisite leisure, our enjoyment was flavoured by the pleasant acidity of intellectual conceit.

'I have decided,' announced Malden, as with cigarettes, coffee and Van de Hum, we withdrew to the seats around the fire, 'that it shall be called the Voorloper.'

'And we shall be known in future history as the Voorloper Group,' cried Rosalind.

We raised our glasses.

'Aha!' Marie Kritzinger, like a small bright bird, pounced upon her triumph, 'good Afrikaans, of course. I told you, Miss Daintree, that though you may scorn our simplified syntax and phonetic spelling, yet you could not deny that we have splendid words. Your "Forerunner" is not a tenth as good.'

'Voorloper will make a good cover,' murmured Kritzinger. 'A great ox-wagon, slow, cumbrous South Africa trekking forward, and the figures running ahead. A wood-cut, I think.'

'I never scorned Afrikaans,' exclaimed Rosalind. She was tall and articulate and Irish, and taught philology in a Transvaal college. 'I only said that it was a bastard dialect, without character or flexibility. I only tell the truth which the Anglo-Saxon is afraid to do. The English go about the world being tactful to the people whom they have destroyed.'

'At last! Now we have the truth, Malden,' crowed Kritzinger.

'I don't quite get this Voorloper business Higson relit his cigar laboriously.

Malden turned to him with elaborate patience, murmuring half-audibly, 'Pecuniae obediun omnia, in order to impress Rosalind. He wished her to see him as the weary scholar stooping to propitiate Mammon. 'We call it the Voorloper because we run ahead. I take it that we may consider that we see just a trifle farther than our contemporaries. We believe South Africa already to be the only young extra-European nation with an individual literary tradition . . .'

'Is that so?'

'. . . A tradition arising, perhaps, partly from the mixture of race; partly from the accident by which the Huguenots brought over with them ideas for furniture and architecture learned in the court of Louis Quinze; partly, also, I hold, from a social organisation singularly favourable to the artist. One recommended by Aristotle for the provision of creative leisure.'

'The slave basis,' interposed Rosalind, but the poetess was aflame.

'Mixture of races! Ach nee, nee! It is the mixture which has checked us. If, indeed, our Afrikaans culture is immature, that is due to the snobbery of the English, exactly as in the fourteenth century your English was immature owing to the snobbery of a court which would speak French, follow French fashions, introduce French ideas. You laugh at us now for our verses, but listen:

> Mooi meisies, fraai bloeme
> Al die meisies, wil ik soene
> Sit die nonnas op'n ry
> Ky hoe mooi lyk hul vir my . . .

It is our early singing. You wouldn't compare that with Keats or Wordsworth, but with

> Bytwene Mershe and Averil
> When spray biginneth to springe . . .

'Our paper shall be bilingual to express the two streams of culture,' Malden soothed her. 'At the moment our most urgent problem is not whether our literature will be Afrikaans or English, but whether there shall be a literature at all. Can a young country afford to expend its vitality upon the creation of an aesthetic standard? I believe it. I believe it. But can we make South Africa believe it? Our school teachers aim at Matriculation and a safe job in the civil service. Our farmers are wrestling with drought and cattle disease. We are so much absorbed by the problem of how to live that we forget the enrichment of life. Yet I maintain that from the beginning there should be a few who run before, who, having visualised a need, set about to fulfil it. It is for us . . .'

'For us who see, beyond our differences, the value of European civilisation,' interjected Rosalind. 'Of humanism.'

'We can at least make a few good pictures,' said Kritzinger.

'Well, I told our Rotary in Jo'burg that what this dorp needed was a bit more culture.'

Marie ignored aspiring Capitalism, so lamentably deficient in intellectual subtlety, so lamentably necessary to the forerunners of aesthetic appreciation.

'It is rather wonderful,' she said, 'to realise that it is we upon whom the future depends. Such an opportunity . . .'

'South Africa – Elizabethan England – Marlowe coming up from Cambridge to London, "a boy in years, a man in genius, and a god in ambition . . ."' breathed Rosalind.

'Our country,' returned Malden with dignity, 'will be . . . I mean, that the burden or responsibility . . .'

'Our opportunity . . .'

'We – we . . .'

From the shadow behind us we heard low voices, whose subdued monotony hardly penetrated the circle of our vehement talk.

'A CAT SAT on a MAT. KAN jy dit NIE ZIEN nie? Can you Not see IT?'

'The first phrases of all modern literatures,' murmured Malden.

We turned, and saw, crouching behind us as near to the fire as they deemed it decorous to approach, the two Zulu servants. They were using the flickering light, not hidden from them by our bodies, in order to teach each other to read out of a child's primer.

'What is it?' I asked.

Higson still contemplated his old problem.

'The Voorloper Group . . .' he said.

1927

Missionary Film

Mr Grant, cycling along the country road, felt too happy even to whistle. Security intoxicated him. He drank it from the green twilight that tasted of new-ploughed stubble, wet straw and smouldering wicks. He heard it in the soft clashing of dead leaves below his wheel, and in the hollow cropping sound of ewes among the turnips. He saw it in the vision of his wife as he had left her, reading aloud to cousin Lucy and Ellen Deane in the fire-lit cottage, the lines of fear soothed from her darling face. Sight, sound and scent flowed together in the pervading consciousness of safety. Not a voice spoke, not a bird twittered in the darkened trees, but they brought the reassurance of familiarity. He was at home. In every cottage of the valley lived men and women who had known his father. He passed his brother's farm, and the graveyard where his forefathers rested. Death brought nothing for sorrow, when it meant only closer communion with the familiar earth. This was his world; these were his friends. Never, never would he leave these things again.

The cottages crouched nearer to the road. Light suddenly gleamed on scattered pools. Mr Grant rode into the Street of Market Brindle. A jolly little street he thought it, where friends called greetings to him from the glowing doors of little shops. He told the pork butcher about Mrs Brown's old sow, and teased the grocer about his part in the new play run by the 'Lit. and Phil.' He bought corn for his hens from the dealer whose second cousin married his Aunt Jennie's niece. He talked to every one.

In the market place the cinema beckoned to him, flaring with joyous light, festooned with small electric bulbs like jewels, emerald green and ruby stars. Such stars, thought Mr Grant, set all the Sons of God shouting for joy.

He paid eightpence and went in.

The honest friendly darkness engulfed him, but against the flickering pallor of the screen he saw the clear outline of Mrs Fitton's Sunday hat. He liked Mrs Fitton; he liked the rural English audience; the scent of warm humanity and muddy boots reminded him of Sunday school treats in his childhood. The orchestra, a local pianist, and a girl playing the violin, broke out into Mendelssohn's 'Spring Song.' Bending to light his pipe, Mr Grant missed the first title of the film. He read only '. . . missionary propaganda, but rather education in its broadest sense.' He felt a twinge of disappointment, for he did not want to be educated. Above all, he did not want to be reminded of a man who had once been a missionary educationalist. He wanted to see Harold Lloyd or Tom Mix.

'The first sight of land which thrills the heart of the traveller,' he read with faint distaste. What trash about travellers. The best thing about travel was the last mile on the way home. He wanted to see Charlie Chaplin; but he saw instead a line of flat-topped hills, mottled about their base with little houses, and towering starkly over a placid sea.

He sat up rigidly, frowning.

'Adderley Street,' danced the caption. 'The gateway to a continent.' Tall buildings, faint against the sunlight; dark trees tossing in dusty wind; bearded farmers in knee breeches; Indian schoolgirls with prim plaits of hair hanging down muslin dresses; a market-gardener swinging baskets of melons and yams; pretty typists in sleeveless summer frocks; here they came. Then a couple swaggered down the road, the wind flapping in their ragged coats and wide trousers. They carried canes, and wore handkerchiefs in their breast pockets. Their black faces grinned, growing larger and larger until they filled the screen, blotting out towers and trams and all the paraphernalia of the European.

Click! They had gone. The orchestra began to play Liszt's Hungarian Rhapsody. A train started up from the veldt like a frightened snake and slid out of the picture. An ox-wagon lumbered between the scorching hills and twisted thorn bushes. A naked boy with a round, gleaming belly ran ahead of the beasts. Mr Grant could hear the creak of the leather and the grinding of heavy wheels on the dry red soil.

A group of women stooped beside the spruit washing sweet potatoes. Their white bead anklets clanked as they moved. Water dripped from black wrists and flat pink palms. One carried on her head a blanket in which two fowls roosted cackling.

Mr Grant's pipe had gone out. He sat clutching the plush arm rest of his eightpenny chair. The sweat round his lips tasted salt and cold.

He saw raw mud huts thatched with reeds. From their gaping doors came a hot, acrid smell, a hateful savage smell. Chickens prinked themselves on a pile of mealie cobs, and two curs fought over a piece of goat-flesh. In the white shimmering light a man was dancing. His flat, hard feet struck the burnt soil; his black body glistened with sweat; brass ear-rings swung like little censers as he leapt forward, free, free, free, dancing in the sunlight, glorying in his black naked body, in the dry crumbling earth, in the hot valley.

The valley disappeared. Mr Grant saw a row of tin and concrete huts leaning against the wall of the mine compound. A kaffir in rags sat laboriously pedalling a sewing machine. The steel jaws of the engines chewed shrieking stone; the orchestra played 'Valencia,' but Mr Grant could hear nothing but the huge inhuman din of the machines. The caption explained that the mine compounds of the Transvaal were very hygienic and that the men had Every Comfort. A black policeman with bare feet below his puttees walked through the location.

The orchestra played, 'Jesus shall reign where'er the sun,' and the picture shifted to the Missionary Settlement at Lovedale. Below a dim arcade of oak trees, the black school children were singing hymns. Half a mile away a girl leaned her back against the hut; her baby lay between her pendulous breasts; she pushed mealie-meal porridge into its reluctant mouth. Mr Grant knew all about her. Three of her children had already died. Her husband was away at the mines. The goats had eaten all the grass on the common land. 'Each year,' said her mother, 'the common grows smaller, the goats are fewer, and the mouths to fill grow more. How can we pay taxes?'

'The House of Assembly, Cape Town,' ran the caption. But Mr Grant did not see the film before him. He saw the table of the committee room covered with papers about his own case. He heard the voice of Authority telling him, 'Of course we shall be sorry to lose your services, Grant, but if you feel you must take this line of action . . .' He saw his wife entering the low house near Pretoria. She folded her parasol, and stood fingering a little spray of plumbago. 'I can't bear it,' she said. 'They called you a race-traitor. I'm never going to a tea-party again.' Mr Grant remembered the Bishop's worried gentleness. 'Of course I honour your motives, Mr Grant. The Church has fought long and loyally on this very ground. But experience teaches us that we must proceed with caution. We have the weaker brethren to consider.' And all that he had done was to protest against the slamming of a door in the face of educated natives, boys and girls whom he had taught in his own mission school. He had protested until his name was the signal for laughter or abuse, until he himself was subjected to quiet, relentless pressure. Until his wife had said that she could bear no more. It was all very well to be a martyr; but has one the right to offer up one's family as a sacrifice?

'End of Part I. Five minutes interval.'

The lights sprang up, Mrs Fitton turned round. 'Well, I thought I should see you here. And how's your wife? Very interesting, very, isn't it? Especially to you, with your knowledge of South Africa. Do you ever want to go back?'

Mr Grant mumbled a reply and made for the door. He found his bicycle entangled in a jungle of steel in the stableyard. The night closed in upon him down the country road, but he no longer tasted its sweet autumnal scents. His nostrils burned with a harsh acrid smell. He fled between the elm trees. Dead leaves like small birds floated round his shoulders. How could he take his wife again from this sweet safety? How could he snatch her from the chicken farm, where people were kind and friendly, and where the only problems lay in the market for eggs? He passed his brother's farm again, but only saw the men and women crouched on sodden bundles waiting for the midnight train. It was, as usual, two hours late. The platform became strewn with nut-shells and mealie cobs. A woman on a pile of blankets suckled her child. A man played a mouth organ. Mr Grant heard again the clicking guttural speech. His head ached with the attempt to understand.

The Administrator said, 'But, my dear fellow, don't be quixotic. You can do nothing against economic forces and race prejudice.'

'You can do nothing,' Mr Grant repeated menacingly. 'You have tried before and failed. It will kill Laura. You can't go back again.'

Irrelevantly, he remembered that his brother and sister-in-law were coming to Sunday night's supper. He could not tell them. He could not leave his family again. And yet. And yet. In his vision, the train crawled into the dark station. The men and women shouldered their bundles and rose from the ruins of their orange skins and mealie cobs, and in rising looked at him with dumb reproach for his desertion, then one by one sat down again. What was the use of their attempt to move forward if their friends deserted them? Yet how could he sacrifice his family, or how desert them in order to return to these black men and women who were nothing to him?

'. . . And he looked round on those which sat round about him and said, "Behold my mother and my brethren."'

Mr Grant rode home to tell his wife that he was going back to his mission work in South Africa.

1927

Uncollected and Unpublished Stories

Twenty years of Winifred Holtby's writing life are repre-
sented here, from the very early, unpublished 'The Picket',
written when she was sixteen or seventeen, the manuscript
inscribed at the top in Mrs Holtby's handwriting, 'A true
story – on E. Coast Yorkshire', to the posthumously pub-
lished 'They Call Them the Duchesses', prefaced in the
Woman's Journal *for October 1937 with the comment*
that 'This story was discovered recently among the author's
papers by her friend, the famous novelist Vera Brittain'.
'Brenda Came Home' (unpublished) was chapter eleven
from the 'The Forest Unit', the story sequence Winifred
wrote while serving in the WAACS in France in 1918. The
strange 'Unto the Hills' (unpublished) was probably writ-
ten in the mid 1920s; it uses a passage from an unsuccessful
work on Wyclif, 'The Runners', which Winifred worked
on obsessively during these years, and it has links with
her third novel, The Land of Green Ginger, *published in*
1927. Like 'Brenda Came Home', it has autobiographical
elements, particularly relating to Winifred's relationship
with Harry Pearson, her 'young man who is not quite
my young man', as she described him. In 'Brenda Came
Home', the war-wracked Harry figure unites with Brenda
but in 'Unto the Hills' the love affair becomes no more
than a memory and its energy is sublimated into work.

The Picket

The clock of the distant village church struck ten, and the soldier shifted his rifle and stamped his feet on the hard path. It was bitterly cold and very dark, save where the lantern on the gate stretched a delta of light across the country road. On each side were dark masses of shadow, where the trees closed down on the high hedges. Behind one of these, three of his comrades were sleeping after their long day's work in straw-filled carts that a kindly farmer had provided.

Somewhere down the road came the warning 'toot toot' of a motor car. The soldier stifled a yawn and came forward. The next moment the occupants on coming round the curve observed a light swung across the road, and heard 'Halt' ring out from the darkness. They pulled up sharply, and the soldier coming forward to examine the car noticed the startled face of a pretty girl peering anxiously through the window.

'It's all right,' he assured her, 'I only want your name and address please.'

In another minute the car was humming swiftly up the hill, and the soldier found the place still more cold and dreary. There was a humped shadow about twenty yards up the road that worried him. He knew that it was nothing but a mile-stone by the bushes, but every time he turned that way his eye caught on it with a little start of surprise.

He wished another car would come to relieve the monotony of his vigil. He wished it wasn't so blooming cold, and that the moon would come out from behind the bank of clouds instead of looking so like a bally . . . Oh!

What rot he was thinking, it would never do to think. He tried to imagine what it would be like indoors now, before a jolly fire with a good cup of steaming tea, but that made him remember the cold six hours between him and his next meal, so he checked his imagination and took a turn down the path.

From the brow of the hill a motor-cycle buzzed like an angry mosquito, and the soldier again shouted his challenge. This time it was the despatch-rider from another picket four miles away, with a bad attack of the jumps, and perfectly certain he had seen a Zeppelin flying from the coast. The sentry pacified him by telling him not to be a 'darned fool' and other soothing counsel, and sent him on his way not a little comforted.

Again silence, and darkness, and another hour before he would be relieved. The cold nipped his ears, and made his feet feel as though they belonged to somebody else. More sounds – this time from the direction of the village. What a night of it he was having! Jove! Whatever could it be? A surprise inspection? The sentry straightened himself and peered into the darkness.

'Halt!' The footsteps came to a standstill.

'Who goes there?'

'Supper!' rang out a merry voice from the shadows.

'Welcome supper!' cried the sentry with a chuckle. 'All's well.'

And there stepped into the circle of light the farmer's wife, who had passed earlier in the evening, and her three daughters carrying covered baskets and a can of steaming tea.

'If you'll excuse me, I'll call my mates. They're off duty and sleeping behind the hedge.'

'All right', said the farmer's wife. 'How many of you are there?'

'Five and an officer m'am.'

Then scrambling up the bank he called lustily. Smothered groans were heard and 'Wasthematter?' issuing out of the shadows. At the magic word 'Supper', the camp on the other side of the hedge showed signs of activity. The farmer's wife was seated by the side of the road pouring out tea by the light of one small lamp.

'It's quite a picnic,' she exclaimed, handing a hard-boiled egg to the sleepy corporal. Just then the sentry who still patrolled the path with fixed bayonet passed and she held up the basket to him.

'I'm awfully sorry,' he explained, 'but I'm on duty you see; I can wait, I'm not very hungry.' But his eyes were wistful as he looked into the basket.

'At least you can drink this,' she said, coming forward with a mug of tea, and was about to hand it to him when the sound of footsteps sent him down the path to challenge the wayfarer.

This time there was no reply as the newcomer shuffled awkwardly into the light.

The farmer's wife glanced up with understanding eyes. 'Is that you Billy?' she called gently, then turning to the officer she whispered: 'It's all right, he's the half-witted boy who works for the Squire.' Then aloud: 'What do you want Billy?'

'Coffee and sandwiches for the soldiers' was the reply in an almost inaudible voice. Billy was clearly overawed by the war-like scene before him. There was a smothered snigger among the men while the corporal groaned to himself: 'Good Lord! What rotten luck, and on any other night not a blessed soul will come near us. I call it blooming irony of fate.' And he took a long drink.

The farmer's wife laughed. 'It's more than a picnic, it's a feast;' she said. 'We'll go now.'

The officer came forward. 'It's been awfully good of you to come,' he said. 'I'm afraid you'll have a long dark walk; I can't tell you how it's cheered us up.'

'Oh, we're glad to do it,' said the farmer's wife, and the lantern light on her face showed it very tender and wistful. 'You see I've got a boy in the trenches, and somehow it seems that if we do this little bit for other people's boys, somebody may do it for ours.' She rose to her feet and was off down the dark country road before they could stammer their thanks.

The corporal lay back on a pile of straw by the roadside and gazed dreamily up at the clouds driven across the moon. Then he started up: there were more footsteps and the challenge rang out again. He leaned forward, listening for the answer.

'I've brought some supper from the Vicarage for the soldiers. It's a cold night isn't it? I won't wait for the basket, leave it beside the gate when you've finished. Goodnight.'

'Oh Mary Ann!' moaned the corporal, as he ran to the side of the road where under a bush two baskets were carefully hidden. 'And after the Captain had hired a car and taken all the trouble to bring out a surprise supper for us. Lord, won't he be mad.' And chuckling comfortably he turned over on the bank and slept.

1915

When Brenda Came Home

Phoebe: 'If this be so – why blame you me to
love you?'

'Have you heard about Brenda Munford?'

'No – at least – that is, I'm always hearing about Brenda
Munford these days. What is it this time – has she got the
military medal, or broken her arm in a motor accident, or
married a Frenchman, or what?'

'She's come home.' Mrs Dawes allowed her voice to
sink to a whisper like one who makes a statement of
overwhelming importance.

Her companion gasped. 'Not after—?'

Mrs Dawes nodded, her thin lips pressed together significantly.

'Really. You don't mean it? Well, I expect that Mrs
Munford will be glad to know that she is away from it all.
Poor woman, I really am sorry for her, but she never did
know how to manage her household, and lately troubles
seem to have come pressing upon her like – like—'

'Like locusts on a fair green field!' suggested Mrs Dawes.

'Well, something like that. You always are so poetical,
my dear Jane. But then, of course, we all know how talented
you are in the literary world, – your charming letters to the
Church Magazine—'

'A mere trifle, I assure you – but we were saying—'

'Oh yes – Mrs Munford – of course. What with Jack
being killed in 1915 – or was it '16? – I forget dates so
– '16, I think, because I put the china down in the cellar
that year in case of air raids and I remember hearing the
sad news when we were busy packing it up – and then

losing that nice maid of hers – Mary, wasn't her name? –
and the baby getting scarlet fever and Brenda joining the
W.A.A.C.s'.

'Ah—'

'Ah—'

'But then, I never did think that Brenda Munford was
really somehow a very *nice* girl. Do you remember that
time she spoke at the Drifton Literary Society on Infant and
Maternal Mortality? Such a subject for a young girl—And
she said that if we allowed places like Higg's Court to exist
in our own town we could not expect to produce a healthy
generation – and about the expectant mothers working in
the cake factory.'

'She was most indelicate. I always knew she would do
something very unwise. I, for one, was not at all surprised
when they told me she had joined the W.A.A.C.s – and
when one reads in the papers about their goings on. Well,
all I can say is, no nice girl would ever have gone. If she
wanted to go to France, at least she ought to have gone as a
V.A.D. Such a nice uniform too—But to be mixed up with
all sorts of girls – why, it's no better than – I'm afraid that
Mrs Munford will have had a great deal of anxiety. I hardly
know whether we ought to mention Brenda's name—'

'Why, there she is—'

'Who?'

'Mrs Munford – coming out of Louis's Stores.'

'Good-morning, Mrs Dawes – good-morning, Miss
Ashton! How are you both?' Mrs Munford's cheerless
voice fell wailfully on the ears of the two agitated ladies,
who stood fingering their morning's purchases, and endeavouring to look unconcerned.

'Er – good-morning, Mrs Munford – quite well, thank
you. Fine morning, isn't it? What do you think of the price
of butter now—Isn't it scandalous?' Mrs Dawes remarked
valiantly.

'Yes – oh yes—' assented Mrs Munford indifferently.
She was a pale, flimsy, little woman, who always seemed
as though she was ready to cry if only she could anchor

her mind sufficiently on to one subject, but it was always drifting off again before she had gathered enough tears to her eyes to shed them.

'Have you seen the notice about the church bazaar?' contributed Miss Ashton.

'Er – no – that is, yes—'

Mrs Dawes's curiosity could be restrained no longer.

'Have you had any news of dear Brenda lately?' she asked. Mrs Munford's face brightened a little.

'Oh, haven't you heard? She came home last night. We were so surprised. She never gave us any notice. Just arrived with no more luggage than a handbag and an Australian saddle. Such awkward things to have about the house – and now that we have lost Margaret, our last housemaid—'

'An Australian saddle? How interesting and how original! She always was an unusual, interesting girl, wasn't she? A souvenir perhaps?'

'I don't know, she says it is. Perhaps you'll come over and see us one day. I'm in rather a hurry now. These coupons and things make such a lot of worry over shopping, don't they? Now, where did I put that parcel from Bradley's? Ah – here it is – some stockings, you know, but such poor material. Goodbye!' – and she drifted off again, with her numerous parcels, her umbrella, and her handbag, in great peril of falling from her indefinite clutch at every step.

'An Australian saddle,' remarked Mrs Dawes meaningly. 'Did you notice that?'

'My dear, I hope that she has not added to her mother's other troubles by becoming entangled with one of those wild colonials. I've heard awful tales about things that they have done on Salisbury plains. It is Salisbury, not Dewsbury, isn't it? – and out of France, one knows—'

'I should not be surprised at anything, Barbara. Why look—'

'Where?'

'There—' Round the corner of the narrow street came the tall, khaki-clad figure of an Australian soldier. The free stride of his spurred boots, the breadth of his splendid shoulders, the clear sunburnt brown of his complexion marked his as an alien in the cramped little street of the country town. He looked from one side of the road to the other as he passed along by the shops, wholly unconscious of the impression that he was creating in the minds of the two ladies watching him.

Even as they watched a girl came out of the drapers on their right. She was tall and slim, and her well-cut tweed skirt revealed a pair of neat slender ankles. Her face was slightly sunburnt, but this added to, rather than detoriorated the magnificent healthiness of her fair complexion, her honest blue eyes, and the radiant vitality of her whole appearance. She recognised the ladies with a smile and came forward. 'Good-morning, Mrs Dawes – Good-morning Miss Ashton – How are you? Have you seen mother anywhere about?'

Mrs Dawes pulled herself together sufficiently to say – 'Good morning, Brenda. I expect that you are glad to be home again. You certainly look very well, if you are sunburnt. Your mother has just gone down the road.'

'Thanks awfully. Goodbye,' and Brenda Munford swung off gaily down the road, nearly running into the tall Australian, who stopped with a quick smile and held out his hand.

'Why – Joe, I didn't expect to see you today. How simply splendid!' She took his large brown hand in both her daintily gloved ones and shook it warmly.

He smiled slowly. 'You see they let me sail a day earlier than I thought, and I came straight on. I hope it isn't inconvenient?'

'Not a scrap. It's perfectly splendid!' Brenda kept her hand on his arm as they walked off down the road.

'You see—' said Mrs Dawes.

'Fancy bringing him here – The amazing impertinence—' And the two ladies were left wondering.

Brenda Munford's return from France was discussed from one end of the town to the other. Mrs Sharp, the Vicar's wife who had worked in the G.F.S. and said she

knew a lot about the W.A.A.C., could not imagine how
the girl had obtained her discharge. 'I know they are
being very particular just now,' she confided in a great
friend. 'They aren't discharging anyone now, except for
very urgent reasons. I can't see any urgent reasons myself –
unless—Have you seen her since she came home? To speak
to, I mean? No – I thought not. She is usually out with that
Australian. Well – I only hope, for Mrs Munford's sake,
that he'll marry her at once.'

'You don't mean—?'

'I never talk scandal. Dear Herbert does not approve of
it. But as the wife of the vicar of this parish, I think it will
be my duty to refrain from calling on Mrs Munford until
I hear the announcement of their wedding.'

'Really—This is very sad. Very. But, of course, we know
what the temptations in France must be. It behoves us all to
be charitable. Poor Mr Cartwright – Captain Cartwright,
I mean. I never shall get used to the idea of calling a
grammar-schoolmaster, Captain.'

'Captain Cartwright? What has he to do with this unfortunate affair?'

'Well, you know, before Brenda went to France, they
used to be very friendly. We all thought it was a certain
thing – very suitable, too, for Brenda. When he came back
so badly wounded from the front, she even went to London
to see him in hospital – a thing no nice girl would do if
she were not engaged, or nearly so, to a man – and then,
after he had been discharged and came to be instructor to
the O.T.C. at the grammar school, he used to go about a
lot with her. But I suppose that with his lungs and that
dreadful scar across his face, she didn't find him good
enough. At any rate – there we are, and all I can say is,
I'm sorry for him.'

'Oh, he'll get over it. A girl that would – well – behave
as Brenda has done – is not worth troubling over.'

And so it went on. And Digby Cartwright, limping down
the High Street on his stick, saw Brenda walking down
the road by the side of the tall Australian. They seemed

an ideally matched couple. Both the man and girl were physically magnificent. There was a wonderful air of health and broad spaces and sunlight about them both – the sun of the south and the tall, gold-haired English girl. Cartwright saw her turn and smile suddenly at her companion – that vivid, spontaneous smile that had made him feel that the world was all sunshine in the old days when—He caught his breath suddenly. He had come away from a tea party in which he had faced and fought Mrs Dawes's half-veiled innuendoes with all the chivalry of his loyal nature, but the conflict had left him sore and full of bitter heartache. He was too sensitive to fight a woman of her coarse calibre – and now this sudden encounter made him realise his own position more intensely than ever. He caught sight of his reflection in the long glasses of a shop window that he passed. His lean figure, stooping a little over the strong stick, the scar on his pale face. He was uncomfortably conscious of his wounded leg that day.

You ugly beggar, he thought, what the devil do you mean by daring to think in this way. Look at that fellow and then at yourself. Which is the most fitting mate for her? As for that old cat up there—But in his heart, in spite of his loyalty and love for Brenda, Mrs Dawes's scandal rankled. He had never spoken to Brenda since she came home.

They met a few days later at the church bazaar. Brenda was helping her mother at the flower stall. From the other end of the decorated hall, Digby Cartwright saw the pose of her graceful figure as she raised her arms to fasten a trail of creeper to the awning covering the stall, or bent to pick a buttonhole from the basket at her feet. In her white summer frock, with a bunch of pink roses on her breast, she looked indescribably young and fair and desirable.

'Ah, there you are, Mr Cartwright – Captain Cartwright – I should say. One so easily forgets – Why only yesterday when I was calling on Colonel Townsley's charming wife, I—'

'It's quite all right, Mrs Dawes. My soldiering days are over, and it signifies very little what you call me.'

'A rose by any other name—' suggested Miss Ashton, simpering. She was helping Mrs Dawes at the jumble stall, when she was not ogling the curate. Now she abandoned him to engage her attention exclusively with this rather interesting, war-worn young man. Unfortunately for her intentions, he appeared to be distracted by a businesslike flapper selling little silk flags. 'They'll be awfully nice for you to give away as wedding presents,' she giggled.

He moved away restless and miserable. He did not see the tall Australian anywhere, but he could not bring himself to go and speak to the beautiful girl at the flower stall; of course, he did not believe the disgusting scandal that those old cats were talking. It did not seem to worry her either, he thought, as he saw her turn to a new customer, laughing, her arms full of flowers. Of course, their poisoned shafts were powerless against the armour of her splendid purity – and yet – anyway, he was out of the running. He only hoped the other chap was worthy. He had been staying at the little inn opposite the Munfords' house for over a fortnight now, and had been with Brenda all the time. Ah well—

Two people were talking the other side of a curtain hung across an alcove, behind which the preparations for tea were taking place. Cartwright had not noticed them until he happened to catch his own name.

'Captain Cartwright too – poor fellow. Well, she's come a cropper this time. He left by the eight-forty this morning – saw them go – my maid's sister at the station – yes, isn't it? how can she appear here in this position – face the music – get her away before it happens – poor Mrs Munford – Oh yes, certain – best authority – Another of those W.A.A.C. scandals – "One of the tragedies of the war" the dear bishop called the corps – well rid of her—'

The words burnt into his brain. Without waiting to think, in a burst of impetuous fury he tore aside the curtain and faced Mrs Sharp and her companion. They turned round, amazed to see his white face, quivering with rage and his blazing eyes.

'I could not help hearing – you took no trouble to lower

your voices. How dare you manufacture scandal like this
to damage the reputation of a girl who has been giving
up everything to help her country! To help cats like you
to live in peace and have your tea parties and jumble
sales without interruption? How dare you sit there in
judgment on someone whose boots you aren't worthy to
black? Why shouldn't a girl have friends? I can't tell you
what a wonderful help those girls have been in France to
men who haven't had the chance of speaking to a decent
woman for months. I tell you they've often saved the very
souls of some men who are simply hungering for the sight
of a little that reminds one of home. And if, on the impulse
of the moment they should err as you call it – if they should
sacrifice everything to give happiness to a man who may
be killed next day . . . I tell you that it is you who love to
think filthy things and whisper them in corners who ought
to be ostracised by society – you and you and all like you
– snug and respectable, who hint here and whisper there
and imagine unthinkable, beastly things. It is you who are
unclean. And as for Miss Munford – how dare you speak of
her like this – how dare you? Can't she make her friends as
she pleases? What business is it of yours whether she cares
to favour an Englishman like myself, or a fine Australian
fellow who has come thousands of miles to save you and
your kind from the misery of defeat? Kindly mind your own
business in future, and keep your filthy tongues quiet.'

And he stumped away on his stick.

Nevertheless, as time passed, and he saw nothing of
Brenda, but only caught glimpses of her from time to
time, his heart sank. He thought she was looking paler
than usual. Her gaiety seemed forced. She seemed to be
keeping up appearances in spite of some hidden anxiety.
He caught himself avoiding her, and thought she avoided
him. After their old intimacy it hurt him, but something
within him prevented him from breaking down the barrier
between them.

One day about a month after his outburst at the bazaar
he was wandering idly through the crowds outside Drifton

after afternoon school. He thought he heard the sound of sobbing. Turning round he saw Brenda Munford kneeling on the ground, her arms clasped round the trunk of a slender young beech tree, her face pressed against its bark. Her back was towards him, but from the heaving of her shoulders, he could see it was she who cried. Obviously she had not heard him approach. He felt wretchedly embarrassed. If he went away now, she would see him, and realise he had seen her – if he stayed – anyway, what was she crying there for? All sorts of thoughts flashed through his brain. Hating himself for doing so, he wondered whether Mrs Sharp had perhaps spoken the truth after all. That the Australian had loved and left her – that—He remembered his own fierce defence of the girls who had sinned socially in France. But Brenda – it was impossible. He made a sudden movement, and she flashed round. It was impossible to avoid an encounter. He raised his hat, and she controlled herself with a tremendous effort, and smiled, 'Good-afternoon, Captain Cartwright. I don't think I have seen you to speak to since I came home? How's the leg? Aren't the woods lovely tonight?'

He admired her self-possession and endeavoured to play up to her lead. 'Glorious, aren't they? How do you like being home again? Your mother is looking well, I think.'

'Yes – Mother's all right. Your boys are playing cricket against St Stephen's this week, aren't they?'

'Yes, are you coming?'

'Oh, I think Mother may be there – I may go.' She said indifferently, 'Well, au revoir,' and turned to go.

He muttered, 'Good-evening,' and watched her turn and pass down the green path. The evening sunlight filtered through the leaves on her retreating figure. With a passionate yearning he longed to follow her – to take her in his arms – to kiss away the tears from her proud, fearless eyes. But the realisation that she was not his – another's – held him back. With a muttered curse of impotent fury, forgetting his lame leg, he flung off into the bushes.

The bank leading down from the path into the thick

underwood was steep and slippery with recent rain. Missing his foothold he slipped, and wrenching his wounded leg, he fell heavily to the bottom, striking his head against a stone.

Brenda heard the crash of breaking twigs and rushed back. She saw him lying stunned and insensible at the foot of the bank.

Cartwright was only unconscious a moment. He awoke to find her binding the narrow cut on his head with her delicately scented handkerchief. What was it she was saying – 'Digby – my darling – my darling?' Her wonderful face was deathly white, and her breast rose and fell quickly in her distress. He could have lain like this for ever with her blue, startled eyes on his face, and her soft voice breathing his name. Then he gave a whimsical smile and began to stagger to his feet. 'I'm awfully sorry I gave you a fright, Miss Munford. I tried to volplane down the bank, and it didn't come off, somehow.' He caught his breath with a quick little gasp of pain. The damage to his wounded leg was worse than he had thought, and he sank again on to the bank. 'I'll be all right in a minute,' he said. She was once more perfectly calm and self-controlled and he wondered whether it had all been a delusion that she had said, 'My darling.'

There was an embarrassed silence for a minute, while Cartwright endeavoured to collect his scattered wits. Then Brenda said – 'If it's all right for me to leave you for a minute, I'll go and get someone from the farm to help you out of the wood. I think you've wrenched your leg badly, and you oughtn't to walk like this.'

'If I sit here a minute it will be quite all right,' he said. 'I would not think of bothering you to fetch anyone. It was entirely my own stupidity.'

Brenda looked round hopelessly. She had no desire evidently to stay with him, yet it would not be sporting to go and leave him. Cartwright felt this and stiffened immediately.

'I won't think of detaining you, Miss Munford', he said.

'Thank you for your help. I will return the handkerchief.'

She turned at once, accepting her dismissal and began to mount the bank. A smothered curse drew her back. 'Oh, you're really hurt!' She gave a little cry of dismay. 'Do let me help.'

He had risen to his feet, and faced her, white-lipped, but smiling, leaning on his stick. 'There's no reason why we should not be friends, is there, Miss Munford?' he said.

She flushed slightly. Brenda was adorable when she blushed. 'I was not aware that we were anything but friends, Captain Cartwright,' she said, rather haughtily.

'Well' – he seemed far more boyish than she had ever dreamt him to be, and there was an unsuspected twinkle in his eye – 'You can't say that we have been actually intimate since you returned from France.'

'Don't you think that was your fault?' asked Brenda. 'You always seemed to avoid me, and knowing that I have been almost in disgrace since I came home, I did not intend to force my society on any old acquaintance who might wish to discontinue their friendship.'

'But Brenda—'

'Don't you think I know what they have been saying about Joe Forrest and me? Do you imagine I have felt comfortable the last few weeks, knowing what people have been thinking about me? Not that I care twopence for their narrow-minded gossip, but it was not exactly easy to see poor little Mother so upset and uphappy about it all. How do you think I enjoyed going about with Joe, knowing that at every corner there was an old cat whispering? I wanted to give him a jolly leave—He didn't know anyone in England, and he was awfully good to us in France. He used to take us rides in his car, and was really ripping and it seemed such a little thing to try and return some of the generous hospitality that he and other Australians had showed us – and then this—' she paused, and looked at him with mingled scorn and shame for her own outburst.

He stood silenced by her vehement youth, admiring the

pose of her splendid figure, the light in her frank, blue eyes, aflame with indignation. Then he spoke slowly. 'And you thought that all your old friends would listen to those scandal-mongers?'

'It looked like it, didn't it? You never came near me.' He was secretly delighted that she should reduce the impersonal plural of 'friends' to the singular, to himself.

'But I thought—'

'Exactly. You heard the old cats gossiping and you thought and probably think, that I was Joe Forrest's mistress – or something of that kind. I'm surprised you ask why we aren't friends now.'

'But—'

'Oh yes – but it is all very well now – I have suffered quite enough from chivalry of the kind people of Drifton. Please stand aside and let me pass.'

He faced her still. 'You have misunderstood me, Brenda,' he said quickly. 'I am not even going to bother to deny that I believed those liars who have agitated themselves about you; but I did think that your affections were so much engaged by that good-looking friend of yours – and he certainly seems rather a fine fellow – that I supposed you would not have time to spend with a cripple like myself—'

She winced at the word 'cripple' and her face softened involuntarily. 'Joe Forrest is engaged to a perfectly charming girl in Australia. I was simply his friend *pour passer le temps* – because he was lonely and England is very far from Queensland. I never cared—'

He came forward and dropping his stick, clasped her in his arms. She pulled herself away. 'Aren't you going to ask me if this story is true or whether the old gossips were right before you go any further?'

'I am going to ask you one thing,' he said. 'Brenda, will you marry me?'

1918

Unto the Hills

'It's ten o'clock,' said Lydia. 'She's been away six hours.'

'It's no use,' I repeated.' We can't do anything. If we tried to find her we should only be lost too.'

Lydia shivered, and I saw that she was crying quietly. 'Oh, I'm so miserably anxious. The poor child. Why is it that one can never really help people?'

Outside the wind howled, hurling itself from the immeasurable spaces of the ice-bound north, from the chill altitudes between the stars.

'Hush!' I cried, for its note seemed to change, crooning now low with grim ecstacy, then rising shrill and fierce to wilder fury.

I thought that the latch rattled, and went to the door, letting in for a moment the black tumult of the storm. Moor and sky clashed together in a dark embrace, but no living creature stepped within the tattered circle of our lamplight. Yet the wind seemed to be charged with human passions. Strange meetings and partings, wild loves and fierce denials, moved out there in the clamorous night.

'No one is there,' said Lydia drearily.

We shut the door and listened, waiting and waiting and counting the minutes as they fell away, ticked out by the round-faced clock on the cottage wall. Time seemed to stop, waiting with us for the sound of a lifting latch.

'We are behaving ridiculously,' I said, 'because Miss Naylor chooses to go out on a stormy evening. She must be sheltering somewhere. This place is so completely out of the way, she couldn't let us know.'

I tried to think of her just as a big unpleasant girl with a north-country accent, who had first snubbed me across the

279

table of the teachers' hostel, and then insisted upon coming with us up to the week-end cottage on the moors, when I had only this week-end with Lydia after five years teaching in Cape Colony.

'It's no use,' said Lydia at last. 'I can't pretend any more. We're both thinking that she probably went off like that to kill herself. What's the use of trying to sound unconcerned?'

'But why should she? People don't do that sort of thing.'

'No. No. And yet, I think that there's a special sort of Hell reserved for those who hate their work. I don't mean just dislike it, or are bored with it. I mean those who actively hate and loathe it, as a woman of the streets might loathe her trade.'

'Why should she so hate teaching? She's quite efficient,' I said.

'She didn't always hate it. It was her free choice, an adventure to her . . . Oh, what's the use of talking, if she's dead? I keep on hearing her at the door.'

'Lydia, you must explain to me.'

'Well, she was a grocer's daughter. Her family lived at Leeds, terrible people, but she spent most of her time with an aunt on the moors near here. She was my pupil at the high school, a big sullen girl even then, with a splendid physical development. I remember how she used to run in the school sports, with her hair streaming in the wind. She *was* the wind . . .'

'Clever?'

'No not exactly clever, though she had her gift, the gift of tongues. It comes, you know, sometimes to the most unaccountable people. There's a trick, I suppose, a sense of sound, of rhythm, an agility of the tongue. Gabriel was like that. You've heard her speak English. It's appalling. Leeds at its worst. She reproduces what she hears most, you see. But her French is perfect. Fortunately we had a very good mademoiselle when Gabriel first came to school. Gabriel liked her, and she became our star pupil. It was this that won for her her Board of Education scholarship at the university. You know the sort of thing. You have to sign a promise that you will teach for so many years or refund the money. She wanted to teach. Curiously enough, the abstract idea of education appealed to her then, and the sense of community of interests between nations learnt through their language. She filled herself with romantic idealism.'

'She doesn't look like it,' I observed.

'No. That was all before she went to Paris. I've never seen anyone as excited as she was when she came to tell me that she was to be sent for a year to Paris to polish up her French before she trained as a teacher. She came to see me at the school, in her terrible new coat, and her hair newly pinned up. Raw, shy, gauche, she seemed. I trembled for her, thinking of her alone in Paris, and the loneliness, the possible isolation, the strangeness.

'Well, she went. I can quite believe that she was miserable, living in a small pension, where the other students found her awkward and difficult, working with a sort of blind ferocity, seeing nobody but the students who secretly terrified her and to whom she would be atrociously rude, and homesick. Homesick every minute.'

'For Leeds?' I asked. I could feel the sneer, hating myself for it.

'Not Leeds. The moors. The moors above Wharfedale where her aunt lived. She wanted the moors. She hungered for them. She has told me that when she had read for eight or nine hours she would sit on the side of her bed and shut her eyes and see the sweep of hills black against the sunset on a windy evening, and feel the race of the wind through her hair. "I've picked bilberries," she said. "Bilberries and young bell heather. I've crushed between my finger the little red balls of mountain ash berries. You can imagine places until your body sweats and aches for them."'

She stopped, watching the door and listening. The moors which Gabriel loved kept the secret of her wandering. Lydia went on.

'It was in that wild mood that she went out one night to a lantern lecture at the international students' club. It was one of those American Save the Children Fund efforts, where they show slides of Greek Refugees and views of the Balkans. She wouldn't have gone but the loneliness had become unendurable and this thing was free. She had not been watching very carefully, she told me, when suddenly she found herself staring at a sweep of upland west of Rikashu that just tore her heart out because of its likeness to her own moor. She says that she sat staring at it as a drowning man might stare at his last glimpse of sky.

'Then George, sitting beside her, cried out aloud.

'She says that she turned without thinking and saw him there, absorbed, ardent, his profile darkly outlined against the pale glow from the screen. And he too was devouring the picture with his eyes.

'The slide changed. He, turning to apologise perhaps for his exclamation, saw the light die from her face. By way of explanation or of friendship, he said, ' "That was my home." '

' "Yours?" she said. They spoke of course in French. "But those are my hills, mine." She repeated herself stupidly, she told me, for fear lest he should contest her claim.

' "You are Romanian?" He asked her in his own tongue, overjoyed.

' "No, English. Those hills are like the Yorkshire moors."

'That was of course the beginning of it all, their love for high altitudes, their sense of exile, their hatred of Paris. But where Gabriel was shy, George poured himself forth in a stream of ardent confession. He was a Romanian, a patriot, and by a stroke of incredible misfortune, a passionate devotee of the Roman Catholic Church and thus member of a suspected minority in a Greek Orthodox country. Was ever such perversity? It wasn't enough for him to be of a different race, tradition, and social position from Gabriel. He must needs be a heretic in all these things, a fanatical educationalist, and a deacon in Holy Orders. Yet they fell in love.

'Believe me, it was no little thing that touched them. He found in her the strength and silence as of the hills for which he craved. She found in him—Oh, what does a girl of twenty-one find in the man whom she for the first time passionately and blindly loves?

'But he was bound. In spite of his young vitality, he had suffered much. His home had been broken up in the Romanian retreat during the war, and later his father's estates were confiscated during the anti-Catholic land reform. He had even been a fugitive among his beloved Carpathians; he had slept in their valleys, hidden among their remoter uplands, and under their influence found his vocation.

'He was to be a priest and a teacher. He had a vision of Romania wedded to the West by her culture and by the Catholic Church. He saw her wise through experience, purged of schism and ignorance, her forests towering straight and tall to heaven, her willows spirit-haunted, her beauty sanctified. And in this high exaltation he met Gabriel.

'Well, they fought it out. Fought is, I think, the word. She has told me of long tempestuous walks, driving themselves, poor children, till bodies rebelled and drooped and were forced on again, till the fever died from their veins through very weariness and they dragged home to their separate lodgings. She told me of the arguments, their fierce quarrels, their fiercer reconciliations. Then she could bear it no longer.

'She was tormented by pride. I told you that she was proud, didn't I? Proud and rubbed raw by constant friction, by fighting at times his vocation, at times his desire for her. She saw herself suddenly in the sitting room above the grocer's store in Leeds, with her family. She saw herself as she thought that he would see her, if he knew. Well, she could easily end it.

'In a sort of bitter, reckless anger, she invited him to come home with her when the term was over, knowing that he would come.

'He came, of course.

'She has told me since of that first evening, when she led him into the sitting room. There was her mother and father, and Ted, the commercial traveller, and Lizzie who worked in the shop, and Maud and Gladys. They had tinned salmon and Worcester Sauce for tea, and her sister Gladys upset the milk-jug. And Gabriel watched him. Can't you see how she'd watch him? With every nerve straining to catch the least hint of his amusement or disdain. She did not help him at all. She says, and I quite believe it, that she was horrible to him for those first few days; having determined to make herself hateful to him she would leave no loophole for his affection.

'After a week I met her in the town, by herself, outside a big provision merchant's store. I believe that she had been spending all her pocket money buying delicacies for him – which her family ate. She looked ghastly. That week must have been sheer torture to her. I induced her somehow to come in to my rooms to rest a minute, and she, who never cried, flung her pitiful parcel of chicken galantine, I think it was, which she had bought for his tea, down on the table, and clung to me sobbing uncontrollably.

'"He doesn't see", she cried. "He doesn't see anything queer about us. He just takes it all for granted as being English. He's known such poverty and discomfort that he thinks it's all just grand. And when they all make their silly foolish jokes, he doesn't understand. And he likes Ted. He's out with him now, playing billiards. Ted was in Salonika, you know, and George knew it all, and—' She just broke down completely. 'Oh I've been such a beast, and he's so sweet, so grateful to me – grateful—What shall I do, Lydia?'

'It was after that outburst that I invited them both up to this cottage for part of the holidays. I loved George at once, for his simplicity, his idealism, his disarming youth. For all his experience, she was years older than he in spirit. She saw through his enthusiasms and longed to protect him from disillusionment.

' "There's no place in the world for people like him who see no evil" she once told me.'

Lydia stopped. We both turned our heads to the door and waited. The storm was dying.

'It's not so rough outside,' I said.

'She won't come now. I always knew that one day this would happen.' Lydia pressed her forehead down on to her clasped hands. She continued quietly; 'I thought that I could help them. There's not one girl in a million that I would have advised to marry a Romanian and live perhaps for the rest of her life in poverty and discomfort. But with Gabriel, it all seemed to be quite different. For what else had she been given her splendid strength, her incongruous gift of tongues? And she was right in that George needed her. I still think that

'I brought them here together, that the hills might woo for her. Down in the town she might be clumsy and reticent, but here she was herself. Here was no difference of national convention, or creed or social tradition. Here they had only the wind and the rain and the fire of wood by night and the strength of the hills.

'I was right. They were her strength. She grew calm and sure. She even looked quite different. She began to brush her long bright hair, caring for her body as only a woman cares who knows it to be deeply loved. And he did love her.

'On the last night, they went out together. It was a wild evening, such as this, and I begged them not to be too long. She only turned and laughed at me, and I knew that she had won him.

'We had been very clever, clever enough to forget nothing but this, that it was in the hills that he had made his vow to God of service and celibacy. He too looked unto the hills that night and they gave him courage to resist her. He went straight back to the town and away, out of her life. I waited for them both to come in. The supper was prepared, the kettle boiling. When the door opened, I turned to greet them from my friendly fire.

'Then I saw that she was alone, and I saw her face.

'I was due back at school next day, but I dared not leave her, and for the first time I sent a message to say that I was ill, and for a week I stayed up here with her. She was, I suppose, a little mad. Certainly if blasphemy, if anger and bitterness beyond control are madness, then these possessed her.

'After a week we went back to the town together, and next term she began her training at the college. But sometimes still I dream at night that I am up here with her during those first awful days, and lie trembling in an agony of fear lest the dream should be true.

'She endured her training, largely I think because every weekend I let her come here, and afterwards, when I became second mistress, I persuaded the head to take her to teach French. She teaches, hating it. But every week she comes back to the hills and walks like a mad creature, seeking him. She told me once that she would bear it as long as she could, but "one day" she said, "he will come for me, and I shall go to him. You must not try to stop me, Lydia . . ." And I, oh, I am a wicked woman, I promised her.'

'That was why?' I said.

'That was why I let her go off without a word this afternoon.'

'You suspected?'

'It was three years ago today,' she whispered.

There was silence in the cottage. Only the fire rustled, and somewhere outside a flooded pipe dripped monotonously.

Then the latch clicked and the door swung open.

On the fringe of lamplight, her back to the wild darkness of wind and rain, stood Gabriel. The light made a flaming glory of her wind-tossed hair, and shone in her triumphant eyes.

We rose, but she came straight forward to Lydia and took both of her hands. She did not even seem to see me.

'It is all right,' she said quite simply with a queer, serene dignity that had no trace of self-consciousness. 'He came to me. It was as I thought. We understand each other now. We were wrong about the hills, Lydia. They do not give to you your heart's desire. It is strength that they give you for your soul's purpose. If he had come to me then, I should have lost him. Always I should have stood in his mind for treachery.'

'But, what are you now?' asked Lydia softly.

'I am the memory of all fair things that he forewent to win a fairer thing. And because we never can lose the things we give, I am his always.'

'But you? What will you do?'

'I must learn to win him', she said, very humbly, yet with her new strange confidence. 'I also can keep faith. There is work for us to do, Lydia. One work for both of us, one door to open, that the stunted may reach full stature, that the blind may see and the deaf hear. Because he loved no woman but these things better than he loved me, he is mine for ever, and I can become one with him, through faith in this.'

She swayed forward suddenly, and Lydia caught her arm.

Then we watched her wake slowly as from a dream, drawing her hand across her eyes, and staring at us, as though she just now saw us for the first time.

She said at last, 'I declare, the light quite dazzled me. I was fairly done up. Nearly lost, must have been wandering for hours. Then I saw the lamp in the window. Oh, I'm tired.'

She allowed us to take from her her wet clothes, and smooth her tangled hair, and to feed her as one feeds a tired child.

Then she slept.

Eight years afterwards I met Gabriel again. I was attending a teachers' conference in London and amongst the delegates I saw a tall red-headed girl, curiously familiar. For a little while her identity puzzled me. But when she rose to speak her deep voice with its north-country accent recalled to me a firelit cottage room and Lydia's strained face. Gabriel was speaking of the coordination of geography and language teaching. Into a conscientious and uninspired debate her ardent vitality suddenly burnt like flame.

A woman beside me said, 'That's Miss Naylor of Mortley. She's a splendid girl. One day you'll hear great things of her, I shouldn't wonder.'

After the session I went to her with several others to congratulate her upon her speech. She looked at me with a shade of her old sullen shyness, but it was obvious that she thought me quite unknown go her.

I said, 'You teach at Mortley. I used to know the moors near there, and loved them. Surely there are no others quite like them.'

'The moors?' she said. 'Yes, they are beautiful. But there are hills in Romania not unlike our Mortley moors, and quite as beautiful.'

'Romania? You've been to Romania?' I asked, genuinely startled.

A look, half wistfulness, half peace, transfigured her face.

'Not yet,' she said. 'I have my work to do. Perhaps some day . . .'

And she passed on.

mid 1920s

The Capital of the Canaries

THE international steamers from London to Cape Town have a pleasantly discursive habit of calling, sometimes at Madeira, sometimes at Teneriffe, sometimes at any other of the Canary Isles, before wandering on to Ascension Island and St Helena. The islands have noted this, and consequently the traveller is plentifully provided with literature for the voyage in the way of little handbooks, proclaiming the merits, hotels, shops, tariffs, histories and populations of the various ports of call.

It happened that upon one voyage I did not go ashore at Teneriffe, but left Miss Mackenzie to do my sightseeing for me. As her furthest adventure abroad before had been to Cheltenham, I was eager to learn of her experiences, and it was with unfeigned pleasure that I watched her, five hours later, tuck down her skirt and step from the dancing, pitching tender on to the ladder up the ship's side. She carried a green umbrella, five parcels, and the triumphant air of one with perils overpast.

She braced her feet stoutly against the deck, as though it were still tossing like the blue waters of Teneriffe Harbour, then sank into the deck-chair which I pulled forward for her.

'Terra firma again,' she observed cheerfully. 'Though the terrors were no laughin' matter and the firm is not so firm as it might be. But I thank ye for the chair, lassie. It's no bad to meet wi' a bit Christian charity after yon heathen place.'

'Heathen? But the island, surely, is most devout Roman Catholic,' said I.

'Lassie, they're an awfu' grovelling set o' folk yonder.

289

I was no' referring to their theology, but to their habits. Roman they may be; Catholic I'll hae ma doots. But Christian they are not. Nae land could be Christian wi' sic a system of sanitation. Cleanliness may no' be godliness, but it mak's a bonny preparation for it. An they puir bodies ken neither one nor other. Not that I've been one for keeping a duster behind the picture myself, like my Aunt Maggie who lived at Inverness; I'd rather drop the blind a wee if called upon without warning, which is not deception but only decency, ilka wifie's dust being an affair between herself and her God, and not for the scorn o' neighbours.'

'But surely you found the island very beautiful?'

'Beautiful?' she sniffed. 'Ane man's meat is another's poison, an' I'll thank Providence not to be taking me there a second time. We hae some bonny hills in Scotland, an' nane could love them more than I. But a land that's naething but hill is overdoin' it. 'Tis not as if the Creator were short o' space with all that water lying around, to go on pilin' yon island ane hill on top of another till even the kirk stands at a tilt.'

'But what about the flowers?' I asked pacifically.

'Flowers? Och aye. Though I never was one for liking sic gaudy colours mysel. We were brought up genteel, and at the Art class in Dunfermline oor teacher wad no' let us pit red and purple in sic close proxeemity. But they folk even paint their houses. Painted houses indeed! About as respectable as painted women. 'Tis only the outside o' the cup too.' She sniffed significantly. 'I mind the smell that came fra' the interior.'

'I suppose that they clean them sometimes?'

'That is as it may be. But they're an awfu' idle lot. Their motto ye ken, is "Montana", which well it may be in sic a hilly spot. But it means Tomorrow, though I call it tempting providence to put your faith in the morrow in a land where they drive the motor-cars so fast.'

'But you didn't drive in a car, surely?' I asked, knowing her habits.

'Weel, lassie,' she began, almost apologetically. 'Ye ken,

it was this way. There was Mrs Maconochie, an' James Edward, an' Mr and Mrs Fraser and the wee bairn an' mysel. An' I was wishful to tak' some photographs to mak' into slides for the lecture I'll be giving at the Women's Institute when I get hame, if ever I do, which seems doubtful. Well, we had read in one o' they books they give you in the cabins that ye can ride all roond the island and see the best views o' the capital of the Canaries in Madeira for thirty shillings.'

'But . . . this is Teneriffe . . .' I was beginning.

'I'll thank ye not to interrupt me,' said she with dignity. 'It was Madeira in the book, and the price was thirty shillings which wi' the six of us mak's five apiece. So Mr Fraser goes up to a wee laddie minding a car an' asks him if he wad tak' us roond the Capital of the Canaries for thirty shillings. But they're puir daft bodies and cud'na understand the plain English until Mrs Maconochie comes up and speaks to them i' the French.'

'I thought that they spoke Spanish?' I suggested feebly.

'Ane foreign tongue is good enough for any man,' she said scathingly, 'and the French is the mair genteel. Be that as it may, we got inside, though it was mair providence than screws that held yon car together. An' off we went . . . An' I was ready wi' my camera, though there was little enough for edifeecation until we met the camels.'

'Camels?' I had really not expected camels.

'Camels. A string o' them wi' little shawls on their heads for all the world like bonny old ladies. Though what they were doing in yon heathen spot, I cudna say, being sae closely associated wi' the Scriptures. An' wishfu' I was to tak' a photo o' them for my lecture. "Stop," says I to the driver, but he quirket yon wee thing by the wheel, and we twirled up the toon, like Tam o' Shanter w' the bogles after him. "Stop, ye daft loon," says I, an' gives him a wee clap ower the head wi' Mr Fraser's umbrella. "I paid five shillings, nae less, to tak' some photographs for my lecture at the Women's Institute, an' I canna get my distance richt at sic a pace." But stop he wouldna, and only the Almighty is to be praised that we had nae worse than Mrs Maconochie losing her hat and the wee bairn being sick frae the motion o' the car. Though may be there is meaning in all things, and the place was no' edifying for the congregation of our kirk. The meenister's unco strict, ye ken,' she added with illogical wistfulness.

'Still,' I said. 'You had a fine ride for your five shillings.'

'Fine ride?' said she. 'And for five shillings? Na, na, lassie. When we got safely back yon heathen body was for charging us twa pound nae less, till Mrs Maconochie, though sair put about through losing her hat, went and fetched yon interpretter mannie frae the hotel. "We've ordered yon body tae drive us round Madeira," says I, "an the wee guide-book tells us that we can see the Capital of the Canaries for thirty shillings. Though what wi' its dirty ways and unchristian look, I wadna mysel say that it was worth half a sovereign. But let it pass." "But, madam" says he, and you could tell frae the nasty look in his eye he was in collusion wi' the driver. "'Tis Teneriffe, and not Madeira that you've been visiting." "Is it?" said I. "Then yon fellow's been deceiving us. T'was for the capital of the Canaries that we engaged him. And Madeira is the capital, is it no'? an' if he took us elsewhere, 'tis a breach of contract. Come along, Mrs Maconochie," says I. "They low fellows is not worth an argument," and we steppit off down frae the quay into the boat and left the heathen fellows squallin' and yelping like a pack o' starlin's.'

'Then – you didn't pay?' I gasped.

'Pay? An' for what should I be paying?' she asked complacently. 'Pay, indeed. It was luck that I didna prosecute. He hadna taken us round Madeira at all. An' I can show ye the price market in black and white in the ship's wee bookie, just to save sic as me frae being cheated.'

And she did.

1927

They Called Them the Duchesses

I'm not saying that Mrs Scott was stupid. She was clever enough. We always thought that her courage and energy would have run an empire or directed a big business, if she had chosen that way of life.

But, of course, she didn't.

'I'm a mother first and foremost,' she said once. 'But I've no patience with those old-fashioned women who treat their children as if they were their property. My daughters didn't ask to be born. But I'm going to do my best to see they're glad of it. No sacrifices to "poor dear mother in her old age" for them, thank you.'

It was all very well for her. Mr Scott was a wholesale miller, and whatever happened to the rest of us in Binster he had money to burn.

And it was all very well for her, being as strong as an ox, so we thought, and with vitality enough for twenty women. Did she imagine that I liked being half-crippled with arthritis, and having to depend upon my Jean even to get me downstairs?

Of course, she could give her girls every advantage. She sent them to Coulson House, one of those big schools in old country houses where they teach you to walk across polished floors without slipping, and to mention titles as though you'd been brought up with them. And in the holidays, the Scotts had a tennis pro to stay and show the girls the proper grip for their backhand strokes, and old Barney the groom took them out riding on their ponies. And when school in England was over, off they went to Paris to be 'finished'.

Oh, yes, Fanny Scott did her best for them. She knew

what she wanted. She was going to make her girls happy, to give them every opportunity, to marry them off soon, and to marry them well.

I must say it did not look as if she would have much difficulty. I'm not one of those women who think that every other mother's swans are geese, and the Scotts were as fine a couple of girls as you could wish to meet. I always said so.

The year they came home from Paris and Mrs Scott opened her great matrimonial campaign, I even told Marion Bristowe that there wasn't a girl in Binster to touch them – no, not though my Jean was less than ten yards away in the kitchen washing up the tea things. Della was nineteen, one of the blonde, plump, gentle kind, with fluffy fair hair in a knot at the back of her neck, and Clare was a year younger, dark, like her mother, lean and fine, like a greyhound. They said that she was the clever one; but Della was sweet.

I'm not a bit surprised that the Scotts were proud of them. Mr Scott certainly didn't *do* much. He gave the girls a hunter each, and a car between them, and strings of pearls for their coming-out ball, and Sally Rogers says that he doubled his wife's housekeeping and left the rest to her.

He well may have. Fanny Scott just spread herself. She attacked the enemy along the entire front.

She gave a big dance in Kingsport and a little dance in Binster, and almost every week there was an informal 'hop' up at the Grange to the gramophone. They asked Jean once or twice, and, though it was difficult for me to spare her, I let her go. When she came back she said that the carpet had been pulled up in the drawing-room, and the floor polished, and there was a regular sit-down supper with cold chicken and jellies and claret cup, and cocktails on the terrace, and a lot of young naval men from the 'Aphrodite' that was in Kingsport docks just then. Chris Thorold was there, too.

The Scotts went out to dances as well, and then in the hunting season Fanny sent them both out together. But Della never cared for riding, so Clare took over the horse, and hunted three times a week. The men said she was a wonderful horsewoman, one of the lean, nervous kind that sticks at nothing. It was a splendid idea from her mother's point of view, because you really can meet what's left of the County in the hunting field, and what with death duties and so on, I think Fanny hoped to get Clare off with one of the young Hernes or Willoughbys. Either family could do with the Scott money.

Once during that spring, when they'd come in for a quiet game of bridge with me, I remember Sally Rogers saying: 'Aren't you afraid, Mrs Scott, to let your daughter ride like that?'

'Afraid?' asked Fanny, with her great, hearty laugh. 'Mrs Rogers, I'm terrified! Sometimes at night I dream of her being carried home on a stretcher. But what's the good? She lives for her hunting, and I believe in letting young people have a good time.'

You couldn't help liking her in a way. At least, I couldn't. Though Sally Rogers and Marion Bristowe had plenty to say when she was gone about cocktails on the lawn, and latchkeys for the girls, and that car dashing through the village at two and three in the morning bringing Della and Clare back from dances.

'She'll be sorry one day,' said Marion. 'A good time's all very well. But if she thinks plucked eyebrows and painted lips are pretty, *I* don't. When Della came to help with the church decorations at Christmas, my husband nearly told her to go and wash that stuff off her face before coming into the House of God.'

But of course he didn't quite. None of us ever really said what we thought of the Scotts to their faces. You can't, in a place like Binster, when Fanny did so much good and spent so much money, and would take complete responsibility for the fancy stall at the Church Bazaar, or lend her car twenty times if anyone was ill. And as for grapes and vegetables – why, she'd turn a sick room into a Harvest Festival out of sheer generosity.

Still, there was no getting away from it, the girls were not popular. It wasn't that they appeared conceited or anything. I'm sure there were times when I've wished Jean would learn a few manners from them, and they certainly were always nice enough to me. But they were too grand for us. Their clothes from Paris made us feel dowdy, and their fine airs made us feel provincial, and even when they were doing you a kindness you felt as though they were really living in another world and just putting in an appearance at Binster as a sort of social duty.

So they called the girls 'The Duchesses' and left it at that.

I must say that the girls didn't seem to mind. They had a wonderful time. All day the gravel drive up to the Grange was churned by horses and cars and motor-cycles, with young men coming to ride with Clare or play tennis with Della. Directly Mrs Scott found that Della was not going to be much use in the hunting field, she put down a hard court so that tennis could go on all the year round.

During the second summer, the village was betting five to one that Della would be got off before the shooting season.

I remember one occasion at the American Tea for the Cottage Hospital. Jean had taken me there in my wheeled chair, and we were all laughing about Della's tennis court.

'And Clare?' I asked.

'Oh, Clare,' said the vicar's wife – who was very thick with the Scotts just then because she was hoping that Mr Scott would pay off the debts on the new organ. 'Oh, Clare's going to marry Chris Thorold, of course. Didn't you know?'

I felt Jean give the chair such a jerk that I was terrified they'd notice and I wasn't going to have them laughing at my girl. So I said, 'Oh, it's all settled, is it? The Scotts are to pay old Thorold's debts so that Chris won't have to sell up, and he and Clare can hunt four days a week till they can't sit in the saddle, is that it? And now tell me, *who* is Della to marry?'

They took up the tale and had got about ten weddings planned and over before I felt that Jean was fit to speak for herself again. Not that she ever had been a great talker.

But she never said a word to me on the way home.

Of course, I knew that she'd been in love with Chris since they were both in the nursery. And certainly he had shown her more attention than was fair from a man who meant nothing. He was the elder son of William Thorold of Langton Howe, and a farmer like his father. The Thorolds had always lived in a big way, hunting and shooting and keeping open house. Too big by half. But they were down now. Gossip said that unless a miracle happened and wheat prices rose they'd have to sell up after harvest, with only the outgoing crops between them and the bankruptcy court.

But if Chris married Clare, that might save them.

Still, the summer passed, and Della's engagement was not announced, though tennis, and riding, and bathing trips to Olmouth, and a yacht at Hardrascliffe should have done the trick. And the cubbing season began, and there was no word of Chris and Clare.

But one morning in November, lying awake waiting for Maud to bring the tea, I heard the clot clotter-clot of trotting hoofs along the road, and I knew that horsemen were tracking to the meet. Then Chris Thorold's voice – I'd have known it in a hundred – said, very earnest and deep, 'But, my dear, don't you see—' And in a minute came Clare Scott's pretty, ladylike laugh.

Then they were gone.

So I knew that it was all over for Jean. And I should have been thankful, for Chris hadn't a penny, and people said it was only the credit he got from his courtship of Clare that kept the dealers from foreclosing on his father. Yet I'd seen Jean's face in the hall mirror when she'd helped me in from the Hospital Tea where we'd heard that Chris was to marry Clare, and, wise or foolish, I should have been less than human not to wish that she should have the boy. For Chris was a nice lad, and I had always liked him, and always hoped that he might turn to Jean in the end.

Lying there, in the grey half light, and Maud late as

usual with the tea, I certainly cursed Fanny Scott and all her money. For it wasn't fair. I knew that Clare had more style and more go and better looks than my Jean; but money had bought them. Money gave her the good time that must fascinate any sportsman like Chris. Money had given her a good seat on a horse, and her fine manners, and even the pretty laugh that floated up from the morning mist. And it wasn't fair. If envy, hatred, malice and all uncharitableness could have murdered Fanny Scott, she'd have died that morning. And I wasn't the only mother in Binster to feel like that about her. She set the standard too high for other girls. We couldn't keep the pace.

Yet it was Freda Bristowe who married young Redvers Willoughby that winter. After that, the village began for the first time to wonder if Fanny hadn't made a mistake somewhere.

'The truth is,' Tom Bristowe told his wife, 'Fanny's put too much energy into marrying those girls. It's like harnessing a thirty-six-cylinder engine to a sewing machine. It's overpowerful, and she's backfiring.'

'The young men are scared,' Sally Rogers said, when Marion repeated her husband's remark. 'That's what they are. Scared. They see the yacht, and the horses, and the cocktails and the pearl necklaces, and they know they can't live up to it. They'll never be able to support the Duchesses in the way they're accustomed to, and if you ask me, they aren't going to try.'

Perhaps Fanny heard something of the kind herself. She was no fool. Soon after the Willoughby wedding, she developed blood pressure, or a heart or something, and took Della off for a Mediterranean cruise. But Clare stayed with her father to finish the hunting season.

'She *would*,' was all Jean said when we heard, and I made no comment. But how would you like to see your own girl growing whiter and more haggard, to say nothing of short tempered, day after day, and Miss Clare riding off on her chestnut mare with the lad, and dancing his shoe leathers through at night, when he ought to have been working on the farm? Not that *she* looked much better. I will say that for her. What with days in the saddle and nights in the ballroom, she looked about as fat as an anchovy and as tranquil as a dynamo. All nerves and nonsense, I said.

There wasn't much to choose between them.

Yet nothing happened. It was passing a joke.

The hunting season moved into the tennis season again. Mrs Scott brought Della back unmarried, though she dropped hints like brickbats over the tea-tables about all the proposals she'd had while cruising. Cruising! And, the summer being wet, she took both girls to Gleneagles for golf.

Summer didn't do it; but the spring did. They went again after Christmas, just Fanny and Della, and, at the cost of about two pounds a second, picked up a real baronet and came back in triumph.

It was in *The Times*, of course, and the local papers, and if Fanny Scott had had her way, it would have been written across the heavens, too. Della was engaged to Sir Henry Harnover, Bart., and was to be a June bride, and Fanny would be able to manage a wedding at last.

Of course, you can't hide baronets under a bushel, and Dr Lane, who has a *Who's Who*, soon showed us that Sir Henry was a widower with two children, and he didn't give his age, which is always suspicious. Still, it was an oldish title, four generations, and he had a place in Worcester, Mapplingham Hall, which sounded well. And if Della didn't look radiant, she looked relieved.

So we all got new frocks for the wedding in anticipation, for we knew that Fanny could be relied upon to do it well.

She did, indeed.

There was a marquee on the lawn; there were eight bridesmaids, and an orchestra from London, and champagne flowing like water, and the church decorated from top to bottom with arum lilies and palms from Dean's of Kingsport. So there was hardly time to notice that the bridegroom was a plump, podgy little fellow, with heavy eyelids and a bald patch. A gentleman, of course, and wore his clothes well enough. But it would have taken a lot of champagne to get me to face that figure in a bridegroom.

Della took it. Quiet and sweet as she generally was, a bit of a dreamer, we said, she was lively enough that afternoon, standing in the marquee under the shower basket of roses, her veil thrown back from her flushed, pretty face, drinking toast after toast, and talking nineteen to the dozen, while Clare stood by, drinking nothing and saying less, and looking thunder at her sister under her black eyebrows. White as a ghost she was, for all her paint, until the minute when I saw her catch Chris Thorold's eye. Chris was carrying champagne to one of the tables, and he just smiled at Clare as he passed. She only nodded, as though there were some agreement between them; but I saw her face change, and I knew then that not only was Chris hard after the Scott money to save his father's farm, but that he would get it.

Clare was in love all right.

That was why she hated so terribly the mockery of her sister's wedding.

Still, Della was Lady Harnover, and her son, if she had one, would inherit the title, and Fanny Scott that day was a happy woman. It would have been a pity to waste all that expensive education on anything less than a baronet.

As Jean pushed my chair home after the reception, I puzzled at the meaning of that look Clare had given Chris Thorold, and light suddenly dawned on me.

Now that Della had carried off her title, perhaps the Scotts would allow their younger daughter to marry a penniless farmer if she wished. True love, I decided, was a luxury that the rich who are parents-in-law to a baronet could afford. I would have given my elder daughter, if I had one, to a plump, perspiring widower, if I could have bought that look for Jean which had passed between Chris and Clare.

Three weeks later Jean went into Kingsport one afternoon. When she came back she didn't, as she usually did, hurry straight to tell me who she'd seen and what she'd been doing, but I heard her go upstairs to her bedroom, heavily, you know, as though she were very tired.

She didn't come down for supper, and I told Robert she wasn't very well. But my heart was as heavy as her feet, for I guessed she'd heard that Clare was engaged to Chris, and I couldn't bear it for her, though I knew she had to go through with it, for beggars can't be choosers.

I got Robert to help me upstairs, and all the time I was wondering how we could afford to send Jean away for the holiday she needed. She was lying face downwards across her bed and sobbing.

I shut the door and moved to the chair and sat down and said nothing, until Jean had controlled herself enough to cry, 'Oh, please go away, Mother. I'm all right.'

I said then, 'I can't go away, my dear, until you help me. But I know all about it. It's Chris, isn't it?'

She sat up then, her poor eyes all red in her white face, and asked, 'How did you know?'

'I've seen it coming,' I said, for one has to be cruel to be kind. 'And you've seen it coming, too, Jean, if only you're honest enough to admit it.'

'Oh, I'd heard the gossip,' she said. 'I knew all about Clare. But not this – this insult!' And she flung herself down and started to cry all over again.

'Insult?' I asked. 'Pull yourself together, dear. You're getting quite hysterical.'

But she only gasped out, 'I won't take her leavings! Not if he was to beg me on his knees, I won't. I told him so. Oh, Mother, Mother. And I love him so terribly!'

I saw then that we were talking at cross purposes, and told her to sit up sensibly and explain just what had happened.

'He asked me to marry him,' she said. 'I met him on the way back from Kingsport – in the little lane behind the church. Just as I'd once dreamed he might. But it was all different. He had the *beastliness* to say he knew it wasn't what it might have been, but if I'd take the – the remnants of what he might have offered me – oh, how could he? How could he? Just to spite Clare, because she's turned him down!'

I could have killed Chris then. I could indeed. I could have killed Fanny Scott, too. But what good could that do? It was my fault, in a way. For if I had not been a cripple, and such a drag on Jean – still, it's no use tormenting ourselves with these things.

I saw Jean's point of view. If she is gentle, she's proud. And with the Scotts always so conspicuous in the district, it would have been impossible. Besides, they said it depended entirely on Mr Scott whether the Thorolds could keep on at Langton.

So there was no help for it but to tell Jean that she should go to stay with her cousins in Buxton for a change, and that I'd manage somehow with Lizzie Watts from the village.

We fixed it up, and Robert gave Jean a five-pound note for a new dress and her return ticket, and she was away one afternoon buying the things in Kingsport, poor child, when I heard the bell ring, and in walked, of all people in the world, Clare Scott.

'Good afternoon, Mrs Turner,' she said, and there was none of the trained-to-be-a-lady graciousness in her manner that time. 'Where's Jean? I really came to see her!'

'She's out,' I said, pleased. For if it was to be a fight, I was in better trim than Jean. 'As a matter of fact,' I said, 'she's going away tomorrow, on holiday.'

'Is she?' asked Clare, and began to walk about the room. 'That's a pity, because—' Then she seemed to change her mind.

'No, it's not. I believe you're really the person I want to see. I believe you'd tell me the truth.' She turned and stood looking down at me with those dark. burning eyes of hers. 'Look here, Mrs Turner. Please will you tell me something. Does Jean *really* not love Chris Thorold at all?'

You could have knocked me down with a feather, but I said, 'I'm not going to answer that question, Clare. It's a question you've got no right to ask me. Why—' Then I'm afraid I lost my temper. 'It's time you girls had a straight talking to,' I said, forgetting there was only one of them left. 'You think you own the world because your father has made a pile of money and can buy you almost anything you like. But you don't, and he can't, and it's time you knew it. If you think you can cover up your heartless behaviour to Chris Thorold by marrying him off to my girl, you're mistaken, for she wouldn't touch your cast-offs with a barge pole. So you can go and ask your father to buy you another baronet, for you'll get no change out of Binster.'

I admit my conduct wasn't that of a lady, but I was beyond feeling ladylike, and small wonder.

But I was not beyond noticing that Clare didn't take it at all as I had expected. She didn't fly into a rage, or play the high duchess. She just stood very white and still against the window, turning over her gloves, and waiting for me to finish.

She was silent for quite a few minutes. Then she said, 'You know, Mrs Turner, I think we've got to come to an understanding. You see, if Jean's refused Chris because she thinks he wants me, it's got to be stopped, because it isn't true.'

'Unfortunately, it's too late. What I've seen with my own eyes, you can't deny,' I said.

'I don't know what you've seen,' she replied, and her voice was as sad and grave as an old woman's. 'But if you think Chris ever wanted me, you're wrong. You see, I asked him to marry me just after Della's wedding, and he turned me down, because he said that he loved Jean.'

'You – *what*!' I cried.

'Oh, I admit it was the wrong way round,' she said, 'But how could I have known? You see, I—' Her voice trembled, but she pressed her hand against the sharp corner of the reading stand and steadied herself again. 'You see, I've always cared for Chris more than for anyone else in the world, and meant to marry him. You said, just now, that I was brought up to think that money could buy everything. Perhaps you are right. Perhaps I did think that. I loved

Chris, and I wanted him, and I saw a lot of him. Probably you know that Daddy paid him to ride with me and look after my horses, and he did it because he's trying to save his father's farm, and a great deal depends on Daddy because he holds the mortgage on Langton. I knew it was no use Chris and me being engaged till Della married, because Mother had other ideas for me. But when she was so pleased with Harry Harnover, I thought it would be all right – and so it would have been.'

She stopped then, and I think she wanted me to say something to help her to go on, but for the life of me, I couldn't think of anything to say, so she had to manage by herself.

'I – I've had a good deal of admiration, you know, Mrs Turner. And I knew Chris was fond of me. We've always seen a lot of each other, and have tastes in common, and all that, so when after Della's wedding he still said nothing. I thought it was because he was poor and I was rich and he had silly ideas about such things. So – so I took my chance, and asked him, and he said he couldn't, because he loved Jean too much and always had done, though he couldn't ask her to marry him, with his father's affairs in the state they were, and so much depending on my father and whether he'd go on accepting the wheat instead of the interest on the Langton mortgage, and taking the risk of the crops as before. So – so, I went to Dad – and – well, it's all right anyhow. He'll stand by Langton, because he's always liked Chris, and he's so mighty relieved that I'm not going to marry him – and now – now, when it's all settled so splendidly, Jean says she won't have him.'

She did break down then. She sat with her face in her hands, and cried quite silently, not in great sobs, like Jean, but without a sound, only the tears trickling between her fingers.

I was sorry for her at that moment. She had been humiliated, as only a proud girl can be, but she could still soothe her pride by playing providence and buying

Chris the bride he really wanted, with her father's money. And now even that had failed her.

I blamed Chris for having led her on. No nice man ought to let a girl do what Clare had done, and I suppose I said as much. For she suddenly dropped her hands and faced me, all tear-stained and quivering as she was.

'Oh no, Mrs Turner. You mustn't say that. It was wonderful. It was the loveliest thing that ever happened to me, or ever could happen. You see,' – and she was giving her mother away left and right, without knowing it – 'he was nice about it. He did it beautifully. He hadn't the least notion what was coming. He'd always thought – he'd always been made to think in our house – as though he were a sort of dependent – a cross between a poor relation and a groom. He couldn't have expected anything like that. At least, he didn't. It took him entirely by surprise, and he was splendid. You know a man, after you've given yourself away completely to him. He didn't make it horrible. He made it fine. He gave me back to myself – not humiliated, but enriched. As if I'd paid both him and myself a compliment. I'd met so many men before, and they'd been all venal, all insincere. But Chris – oh, don't you see, Mrs Turner, he *must* marry Jean – because he loves her! Because he's made love a lovely thing. Because – because I know now that there *are* splendid people in the world – people you can't buy, can't tame, can't flatter.'

She was standing up then, and her face was radiant.

'There are some things that life can never take away,' she cried joyously.

And then Jean came home from Kingsport, tired and sad after her listless shopping—

Well, I must say it's all turned out very well, and Chris *is* a dear, and though times are bad for farmers I think we shall get through.

Clare Scott took to motor racing, and her mother encouraged her. She drove in an international rally to Monte Carlo, and the car overturned on the way. But it was Fanny who died of shock, when she heard of the accident, before they got the news that Clare wasn't even dangerously hurt. Only slight concussion and a broken collar bone. It turned out that Fanny always had had a heart, or high blood pressure, or whatever it was, and the energy she put into marrying those girls had been too much for her.

She really had given her life to make them happy, as Marion Bristowe remarked.

But Sally Rogers said no. She gave her life to satisfy her own idea of what *ought* to make them happy. And I believe she was right.

For once, when Clare came over to spend the afternoon at Langton's (she's living with her father, and helping him in the office at Kingsport now, so they say), she said quite suddenly, 'You know, the one consolation about Mother's death is that I needn't race or hunt any more, and I needn't marry. She'd have been so terribly disappointed, poor darling, if I'd settled down into a dull working spinster, and never got into the *Tatler* again. But now I needn't bother. Daddy doesn't mind, and I love working in the business. And when I think of Della—'

We both stopped there, for Lady Harnover's story has not been exactly a fairy tale.

But I couldn't help being glad, though of course it's puzzling for mothers. Chris fell in love with Jean's unselfishness, he told me, and the pleasant way she did things for people, and pushed me about in my wheelchair. And I always felt that I was sacrificing Jean – yet I didn't know how else to manage. That's the real reason why I hated Fanny Scott, I think, because she could give her daughters exactly what they wanted, and devoted her whole health and wealth and life to the job.

Yet, when you come to think about it, what are mothers to do?

1937